# IRON
# NIGHT

## A Generation V Novel

## M. L. BRENNAN

A ROC BOOK

ROC
Published by the Penguin Group
Penguin Group (USA) LLC, 375 Hudson Street,
New York, New York 10014

USA | Canada | UK | Ireland | Australia | New Zealand | India | South Africa | China
penguin.com
A Penguin Random House Company

First published by Roc, an imprint of New American Library,
a division of Penguin Group (USA) LLC

First Printing, January 2014

**ROC** REGISTERED TRADEMARK — MARCA REGISTRADA

ISBN 978-0-451-41841-8

Printed in the United States of America
10  9  8  7  6  5  4  3  2  1

When I was young, my family had a newspaper subscription. Every morning my brother and I would turn it to the comics page, and we would read our two favorite comics—*Calvin and Hobbes* and *The Far Side*. On most mornings, this would then result in a twenty-minute period where my mother explained what various words meant, and (in the case of more than a few *Far Side* comics) why something was funny. One I remember in particular (I must've been six or seven at the time) had the punch line: "How entomologists pass away." This led to a discussion on how a bug curls up its legs when it dies, what an entomologist is, and how those concepts were glued together in a funny way.

Recently this came full circle when I sent my brother a T-shirt that featured a number of sentient cartoon marshmallows roasting one of their unlucky comrades over a bonfire while other marshmallows fiendishly readied the chocolate and graham crackers. The first day that my brother wore the shirt, he got to explain to his young children why cannibalism was (in this instance) funny.

# ACKNOWLEDGMENTS

I am extremely grateful to the entire team of people at Roc who made this book possible: the marvelous Anne Sowards with her insightful and wonderful editing, Brad Brownson for his work in publicity, and Robin Catalano for copyediting. Heartfelt thanks as well to my agent, Colleen Mohyde.

Sarah Riley and Karen Peláez once again went above and beyond the calls of friendship by reading through my first draft of the book and telling me where things were going off the rails. I am deeply grateful to my family for their continued love and support, from my ninety-one-year-old grandmother for reading what must've seemed like a rather weird book, to my mother's decision to take on the task of selling my debut novel as if the second coming of Girl Scout cookies had just arrived. Writing a sequel was very hard work, and my brother was kind enough to pitch in and give me regular phone calls asking whether I'd hit my target word count for the day. It was appreciated. I'm also grateful to my husband for hobbling my Internet access (at my request) during the last big push on the manuscript.

I also owe a heavy debt to all of the lovely, supportive, and extremely funny people who I have met through Twitter, Facebook, blogs, and at conventions. Thank you for the support you showed to a debut novel about a slacker vampire. I am so much richer for having met all of you.

*Spirits, Fairies, Leprechauns, and Goblins: An Encyclopedia* by Carol Rose and *Demon Fish: Travels Through the Hidden World of Sharks* by Juliet Eilperin were invaluable in the planning stages of this book.

# Chapter 1

There are a lot of things wrong with being awake at four in the morning. I once spent two months working in a bakery, so I'd thought I knew them all.

I'd been so wrong.

"Stop dawdling, Fortitude! We have much to accomplish today!" My brother, Chivalry's, voice blasted in my ear, unnaturally chipper for someone who hadn't even had coffee. I blinked at him through bleary eyes, unwilling to move from my current position of being huddled in the passenger's seat of his Bentley. That part wasn't entirely due to the time—Chivalry's Bentley, with the best springs, ergonomics, built-in ass warmers, and buttery leather seats that money could buy, was actually more comfortable than my bed at home.

Beside me, Chivalry did not look like a guy up and about before the crack of dawn. He was impeccably and expensively dressed as always, with his chestnut hair achieving the level of coif that most men experience only when the subject of a *GQ* photo shoot. His face, with chiseled good looks that made Brad Pitt look homely, was freshly shaven, and he had even splashed on some aftershave. He looked like a guy in his early thirties with that most desirable trifecta of traits: money, looks, and taste.

Some people would've assumed that as a vampire, Chivalry's ability to look perfectly turned out on third-shift hours was some kind of inborn trait. However, my very existence put that particular theory to rest.

I'm very aware that the genes that make Chivalry look

like he should be posing for magazine covers completely passed me by, but even by my own significantly relaxed sartorial standards, this was a rough morning for me. Because I'd skipped shaving yesterday, I was now sporting a level of stubble that, combined with the rather ragged jeans and sweatshirt that I'd scored at Ocean State Job Lot (where people shopped who couldn't afford Walmart) three years ago, made me look like I made a living Dumpster diving for recyclable bottles. My hair is a few shades darker than Chivalry's, and anyone who glanced at it would clearly be able to discern that last night I'd slept on my left side. I had managed to brush my teeth, though, and I was feeling somewhat proud about that.

No, I definitely wasn't anyone's vision of a vampire. That did make a little sense, of course—I wasn't entirely a vampire.

Yet.

I'm closer than I used to be, though. Four months ago I'd started the transition into vampire adulthood, but instead of a cake or some bar mitzvah bonds, I'd gotten an increased role in the family business of keeping a solid chunk of the Eastern seaboard thoroughly under the control of our mother, Madeline Scott. This had resulted in the kind of ride-alongs with my brother that, like this morning, led us to weird and unsavory places to deal with the kinds of creatures that most people are happy to convince themselves are nothing more than fairy tales.

Today, that also involved livestock and the Claiborne Pell Bridge, just a few miles from my mother's mansion in the charming coastal town of Newport, in the mighty state of Rhode Island, best known for our feature of being completely drivable in any direction in less than two hours.

After hauling myself reluctantly out of the comfort of Chivalry's car and into the chill of the early-October predawn morning, which was exacerbated by the icy wind currently whipping in our faces from over Narragansett Bay, I devoted some attention to what I'd been too sleepy to look at when Chivalry had first pushed me into the car. A little animal trailer stuffed with fifteen goats had been attached to the back of Chivalry's immaculate Bentley. It should've looked weirder than it did, but somehow Chivalry had located an animal trailer of such sleek chrome construction that it actually managed to work with his charcoal gray, twice-weekly waxed car.

"Fort, stop petting the goats."

Chivalry was born just around the time that the Civil War was heating up, and sometimes I think he spent all that time honing his ability to be a bossy big brother. He had a lot of time to do that, since I wasn't born until hair bands were topping music charts. So he has some well-crafted skills of bossiness, which he'd been deploying regularly on my every move all summer.

"Why can't I pet them? They like it." I gave the little black goat I was currently rubbing an extra scratch around its horns, and it closed its little goaty eyes in bliss. "I think I'm going to name this one Titus," I said. "Doesn't he look like a Titus Andgoaticus?" At this point I was just yanking Chivalry's chain, but the look on his face as he stood there in a black suit that probably would've cost me six months' worth of rent was too perfect.

"Fort . . ." Chivalry shook his head helplessly. "Don't name the goats."

I'd let my petting hand go slack, and Titus nudged it impatiently. I was standing on the tailgate of the trailer, and a few more of the goats were getting curious and nudging closer. I could feel a few bumping their heads against my stomach. Clearly I was handing out some grade-A head rubs.

"Did you buy these guys from a petting zoo or something?" I asked.

There was a huge sigh, and I glanced over to see Chivalry rubbing his face with his hands. I could almost hear him mentally counting to ten.

"Fort," he said, clearly reaching hard for patience. "Please get down from there."

"Why?"

"Well, for one, the goats are eating your sweatshirt."

I glanced down at my stomach, and, sure enough, all of Titus's friends who I had thought were going for nuzzles had actually been getting mouthfuls of fabric. I pulled back fast and jumped down, then looked at the damage more closely. In a surprisingly fast amount of time, the goats had managed to make me a belly shirt. I looked up at Chivalry, whose thinned mouth and twitching left jaw muscle were hinting at some displeasure.

"So . . . are we meeting up with anyone particularly important today?" I asked, somewhat belatedly.

Chivalry made a very disgusted sound, then whooshed out a deep breath and visibly collected himself. "I'll get you my spare coat," he muttered, stalking back to the Bentley.

There was a sad little bleating sound from the trailer, and I looked back to see Titus hanging his head over the side.

"Don't try that with me," I warned. "I see your plan now. You were just distracting me with your soft fur while your buddies got some piranha action on my clothes. Well, I'm not going to fall for it again."

Titus bleated again, even sadder this time.

I probably would've fallen for it again if Chivalry hadn't come back and shoved a knee-length brown suede coat at me. Only my brother would not just carry a spare coat in the car, but have his spare be something like this. Not that I could really picture him toting around a wadded-up Windbreaker, but it was the principle of the thing.

I slid the coat on. It had probably been made to be put on over silk shirts, but it did cover up my goat-gnawed sweatshirt and at least the upper half of my jeans—which had definitely seen better days. Chivalry and I are the same height, both clocking in at six feet, but the coat probably wouldn't have fit as well a few months ago, when I was significantly scrawnier than my brother. Four months of weight lifting, working out, and protein shakes had made it clear that I'd always be built a bit leaner than Chivalry, who, when he went to the beach, actually had men come up to ask him what gym he used. But my body had finally filled out and lost the half-finished look that I'd had since puberty.

Feeling warmer now, I muttered a thank-you, then asked, "So, who are we meeting?"

Chivalry gave me a very deadpan look. "Look at where we are."

I did. At four in the morning with no moon in autumn,

with a lot of fog on the bay, it should've all been a big black blur to me, but my night vision had significantly improved lately. I wasn't as good as Chivalry, who used his car headlights more out of courtesy for fellow drivers than actual need, but I was better than the average human.

We were parked near the base of the Claiborne Pell Newport Bridge, the suspension bridge that spanned Narragansett Bay and carried in the majority of the mainland traffic. There are two bridges on the north side of the island, above Portsmouth, but neither of them is as beautiful as this one, the longest suspension bridge in the entirety of New England. It used to be the Newport Bridge, and a lot of the natives still call it that, but it was renamed in 1992 when some of the guys at the state house realized that there was a schmoozing opportunity to be had. We were standing in a dirt turnoff from a side street that gave us a nice view of some of the metal underside and, farther out, the white lights installed along the sides that, against the black of the night and the lapping dark water beneath, gave the bridge itself a glow.

I scuffed my shoe against the dirt. "I think we're in the local make-out spot." It didn't take much effort to dislodge a few condom wrappers from where they'd been ground in. Chivalry glared at me, silent, until I gave in. "Fine. At the Pell. So what?"

"Look at what we brought."

I looked back at the trailer. "Sweatshirt-eating goats," I said.

"Put this one together." Chivalry sounded like a teacher coaxing the paste-eating kid in the back of the room.

I looked from Titus and his buddies over to the massive metal structure that loomed above us. Unwillingly, my brain stopped thinking the way I preferred, which was like a regular human guy, and the pieces fell together. "Holy shit. You're going to feed Titus to a troll?" I felt appalled.

"This is why we don't name or pet the goats." Chivalry said blandly.

We ended up walking a small path that zigzagged down the hill until we were standing on the rocky shore right under the bridge. This close to the bay, with nothing as a wind-break, I was deeply grateful that I was wearing Chivalry's jacket. Icy winds and exposed bellies weren't a good combination.

We stood in the dark for a few long minutes, listening to the sounds of lapping water and the occasional early car driving over the bridge. Once something flapped over my head and I thought that I caught sight of a bat, but that was it.

"Chivalry," I finally whispered.

"What?" His voice was so low that I almost couldn't hear it.

"Shouldn't you, you know, call the trolls?" I'd never seen a troll before, and I wasn't sure that I wanted to now, but I also didn't really want to keep standing around indefinitely on slippery rocks in the dark. My balance had improved somewhat, but I just knew that every additional minute increased the odds that I would somehow end up in the bay.

"They already know we're here," he said softly. "They've known since we pulled into the parking lot."

"Really?" I asked. I glanced around us nervously.

"Oh yes," he continued, his brown eyes boring into the darkness. "In fact, they're already here."

I glanced around, still not seeing anything. A low but sharp sound suddenly echoed around us, one that reminded me of being back in Cub Scouts and watching a few of the adults attempt to start a fire using two rocks to strike a spark. Then I finally caught some movement to my left, and I watched as a huge shape, easily nine feet tall and built like a fifties refrigerator, seemed to detach itself from the bridge tower itself and move closer to us. The sharp sound continued as it moved toward us, and I struggled to keep standing right where I was and not look terrified, though I couldn't help glancing over to Chivalry a few times, who managed to look completely nonchalant as it came over.

It took me a minute to realize what I was seeing, but then I realized what my eyes were actually telling me. Whenever the shape moved a step, I'd lose track of it again until it took another, because in the moment when it was still, it blended perfectly into its background. It was like in *Predator*, which was not a comforting thought to have.

Eventually it moved until it was just about two feet from us, then came to a halt, disappearing again. I could smell it now that it was close—strong, very salty; not necessarily a bad smell but not a good one either. It was like getting close to the seal exhibit at the aquarium.

There was more movement and then something seemed to shift in the upper part of it, and suddenly, as if some kind of hood had been pushed back, two glowing green eyes came into view, each as big as a golf ball. They were set in a long, inhuman gray slab of a face that looked like it had been chipped out of granite, and a mouth suddenly gaped open below that, huge and black, but with big, long teeth that gleamed like pearls.

Beside me, Chivalry nodded once. "Good morning, Brynja."

The glowing eyes focused on my brother, and, in a voice that was so low and grinding I could feel it rumble in my feet, like a Leonard Cohen CD with the bass turned way up, it said, "*Velkommen*, son of Scott."

"Has everything gone well this month?" Chivalry was as polite as last week, when the seventy-five-year-old head of the historical society, Mrs. Forbes, had stopped by for a lunch-and-gossip date with my mother.

"*Ja, ja.* My family and I have been very comfortable this month." Brynja's big eyes almost closed, leaving two long, glowing slits watching us out of the darkness.

"And have those humans who live and travel around you also been comfortable?" Under the extreme politeness in Chivalry's tone was something very sharp, and the troll dropped its mouth open very wide and made that rough rock sound again, which I was starting to guess was its version of laughter. Its eyes rounded out again, the glow as brilliant as what was coming from the bridge.

"You have so little trust in my family, Chivalry," the troll said, sounding amused. "*Nei*, we have not been naughty, as you fear. The little goats keep us quite full, and we are content to watch the birds and the waves and the boats that pass us by."

"I am glad to hear that. I have brought this month's goats."

"*Ja*, we smelled them as you arrived." The troll's voice

dropped even further, becoming hungry and possessive. "We smelled their hot blood, their fat little bodies; felt their tame, content little minds. *Ja*, we are always pleased when you visit our home, vampire." Those big eyes shifted then and focused on me. The troll's voice changed again, becoming almost curious. "But not alone this time. *Kva er dette*? Not in half a century have you brought someone down to us." Ten feet from us, closer to the shore, another pair of glowing green eyes suddenly appeared. Then another, huddled among the rocks.

"This is my brother, Fortitude," Chivalry said, dropping a hand on my shoulder. I was glad he did it, because I'd just glanced at the underside of the bridge and seen a sea of those glowing eyes staring down from the metal trusses. It was not a comforting sight.

"Ahhhh . . ." The troll's sigh was grinding on my eardrum. "Another son of Madeline Scott. But very young, *very* young. He does not smell as you do, Chivalry." The green eyes drifted closer, and that large mouth was working, and I could hear a low sound like bellows being pumped at an old-fashioned forge. I realized that it was tasting my scent, bringing the air to sample in that massive maw. "He smells more human, this one. Smells like fear."

"Your fealty to him is equal to what you owe me," Chivalry said, and now his voice was complete steel. His hand still gripping my shoulder, he took a step forward, toward Brynja, and dragged me along for the ride. Immediately the troll backed up, and around us those other glowing eyes disappeared, leaving only Brynja. Chivalry continued pulling me forward, advancing on the troll, who kept moving backward. "My brother will be delivering next month's goats without me, and the next." That was certainly news to me, but I didn't let it show on my face. "But"—and Chivalry's voice became silky here—"if my brother is not treated with the same respect I receive, I would become quite angry. As would my sister. Perhaps Prudence would feel the need to express her displeasure in person."

"*Nei, nei*," the troll said immediately, ducking down and lowering himself almost to the ground, judging by those glowing eyes. "*Unnskyld*. My apologies. There will be no insults to your brother. No need for your sister to trouble herself with us."

"I'm glad to hear that," Chivalry said coldly. "My brother will see you next month, and we will both be keeping an eye on your activities. Enjoy the goats, Brynja."

All the eyes opened again, and there was a chorus of whispering, grinding voices all around us in the darkness. "*Takk for maten*, Chivalry. *Takk for maten*, Fortitude, brother of Chivalry, son of Madeline Scott. *Takk for maten*."

Chivalry's arm propelled me as we turned around and headed back up the path. It was extremely creepy to turn my back on all those eyes, knowing what huge bodies and shiny teeth they were attached to, but I did my best not to hurry away. Clearly the monthly feeding was combined with a monthly intimidation routine, and I didn't want to mess up all of Chivalry's work. Particularly since I had suddenly been volunteered for two months of goat delivery.

Given their reaction to the thought of getting a visit from Prudence, though, I probably didn't have too much to worry about. Not that I blamed them. Chivalry can be pretty scary when he wants to be, but Prudence is a century older than he is and has a violent streak. Like the trolls, I avoided her as much as possible.

Back where we'd parked the car, which I now recognized as the worst make-out spot ever chosen, Chivalry leaned down and silently unhitched the trailer. He motioned me to the car, and I hesitated.

"You're just going to leave everything?" I asked.

"I'll send James down in a few hours to pick up the trailer." James was one of my mother's household staff. Like the rest of the staff, who were all human, he made great money and benefits from never asking any questions or showing any curiosity about any tasks he was asked to perform.

I tried not to look at Titus as we drove off. As a vegetarian, I usually don't have to deal with this kind of guilt.

"So . . ." I said as we drove through the streets of Newport. The sky had lightened to a very pale gray when we reached the car, but it was still too early for many other cars to be around. "Trolls, huh?"

Chivalry nodded. "Norwegian imports. They like rocky shorelines, and bridges give them extra coverage. They're big, and their skin folds work even better than a chameleon's for blending in. Stealth hunters for the most part, but they can be about as fast as a running crocodile when they really need to move. They're not very active, but at your age it wouldn't be a good idea to get in a fight with them on your own, since they are almost always in a group."

"And the goat deal?" I'd spent almost all my life trying to pretend that I was a regular human guy, and that included not learning anything about trolls or other critters that crept around in the dark. There were a few things I hadn't been able to completely ignore, like my need to feed off of my mother's blood every few months, but I'd tried to treat those instances as flukes in my otherwise normal life of post–college graduation underemployment. But I'd had to give up my state of willful ignorance, and now I spent a lot of my time with Chivalry, trying to catch up on the things I should've been learning for years.

"Their low activity level and something kind of reptilian about their metabolism means that they don't have to eat much. Most of the time they like to grab stray dogs and that kind of thing, but they won't turn up their noses at the occasional wandering toddler or solitary boater. A lot of times humans are even easier to catch than animals, so when the troll colony first moved in there were a bunch of disappearances. All you need is one person to see a troll grab a kid and you get the kind of publicity that no one around here wants, so Mother sent Prudence down here to teach them some manners." A lifted eyebrow was enough for Chivalry to convey the level of destruction Prudence probably delivered. "After she'd made an impression, I sorted out an agreement. We provide small farm animals every month, enough to keep them fed and content, and in return they control their predations and occasionally do a service for the family."

"That sounded a little Mafia there," I pointed out.

Chivalry shrugged as he turned the Bentley off of Ocean Drive and down the long white gravel driveway that led to the mansion. With almost thirty acres of land, all of it immaculately landscaped by Madeline's team of full-time gardeners, it's a long driveway. "They are very good at hiding, not unintelligent, and are good at disposing of bodies without leaving much evidence behind. It's a fact of the world that those qualities can be very useful." We pulled into Chivalry's parking space, which was between Madeline's gleaming silver Rolls-Royce and my decaying yet faithful Ford Fiesta. The sun was just starting to peek over the horizon, shading the sky with little orange and pink layers. My mother's mansion is a huge two-story white marble structure with an unimpeded view of the ocean, and it was considered an exceptionally beautiful house even in the heyday of the Gilded Age, when Madeline's neighbors were having entire rooms from French châteaus or Italian villas stripped down, boxed up, and shipped across the Atlantic to be recreated in their second drawing rooms. It's the kind of house that you can never really get used to, and Chivalry and I both paused to give it a moment of appreciation as the sunrise hit it.

After a second, Chivalry checked the car clock and said, "Okay, five a.m. We have time to eat breakfast, then fit in a quick three-hour training session."

There is nothing good about being awake at five in the morning. Especially when it's in the company of my brother.

# Chapter 2

At some point in the past century my mother had the old carriage house on her property converted into a fully outfitted gym for Chivalry. In the past, I'd avoided the gym just as I'd avoided anything that hinted of exertion or some kind of sporting event, but the events of several months ago, plus my new responsibilities within Madeline's power structure, had forced me to admit that I needed to be less easy to beat up. So, not without a few reservations, I'd gone to Chivalry and asked him to help.

What had followed was the most physically grueling summer I'd ever experienced. Every day I'd driven down to the estate and spent hours working with various cardio and weight-training devices of torture until I was nothing more than a limp rag on the floor, at which point I then got the pleasure of getting in my car and driving forty-five minutes back to my own apartment in Providence to head off to work.

Realistically, it hadn't made much sense to keep living in my apartment, working at whatever abysmal minimum-wage job I could find to eke out a living where I barely made my bills, and even then had to have a roommate. There was a large and luxurious room for me at the mansion, and I was well aware that my mother would've started paying my bills and providing me with a more-than-generous allowance the moment that I moved in.

But I'd spent nine years living in the mansion, from the day my foster parents had been killed until the day I left for college, and I had no intention of going back. I never felt like I could really breathe there—not in the beautifully appointed rooms, not walking around the gorgeous grounds and looking out over the wide expanse of ocean, not even when I was just in the surrounding town of Newport. Everything was wonderful, and every part of it was a reminder that I wasn't really human. I was turning into something else, my body transitioning, and I hated all reminders of that.

After all, a vampire had killed my foster parents. It was my own older sister, Prudence, who'd sprayed their blood on the walls of their little house in Cranston, with the same emotional involvement that most people engage when swatting a fly. From what I'd recently seen of other vampires, she was the typical example of our species. There were a lot of reasons why I'd spent years pretending as hard as I could to be human.

I'd had to give in a lot lately, though. In the old days I'd avoided Newport, coming down only when my biological needs couldn't be put off any longer. At my age, I didn't feed off of human blood; I drank my mother's. I'd pushed it off for four or five months when I could, but once I'd started training with Chivalry I'd started feeding every other week. I hadn't wanted to, but the results had been hard to argue with; fed by my mother, I healed far faster than any human could. I'd had a fractured arm at the beginning of Chivalry's brutal training regimen, but the cast had come off in two weeks rather than six. Bruises went away faster; sore muscles recovered practically overnight.

I benefitted from all of it, but I didn't have to like it. All of it worried me, no matter how essential it was. I'd spent seventeen years waking up from nightmares about my foster parents' deaths, dreams where I'd had to relive every horrible moment in Technicolor. Lately those dreams had changed. Now, Jill and Brian still died, but now I watched it happen and felt nothing. I woke up sweating and afraid after those dreams, worse than ever before.

I tried to avoid the dreams by wearing myself out physically, hoping that if I could just get tired enough, I would drop into a sleep so deep that my brain wouldn't start up the REM cycle. That motivation had helped me continue walking into the gym each day.

Chivalry had a more purist approach to working out than I did, but he'd given in and had a TV installed in the gym after it became abundantly clear early in training that I was incapable of working out with nothing to distract my brain except counting my sweat droplets. With a degree in film theory, my previous favorite activity in the world had been lying on my couch and watching movies. Working out while watching movies wasn't quite as fun, but it was an acceptable compromise. Since Chivalry always made sure that he was in the gym every minute I was, the better to monitor my every heartbeat, I'd taken the opportunity to expand his appreciation of movies. I liked a lot of Chivalry's favorite movies, but his enjoyment of cinema started stagnating when color was introduced, and lately the only movies he showed any interest in seeing were foreign art-house flicks. What was any self-respecting younger brother to do except forcibly expose him to *Hannah Montana: The Movie*? It had been fun for a while, but I'd finally had to tone things back after Chivalry completely lost it and threw a seventy-pound kettlebell through the screen halfway through the Justin Bieber movie. He'd replaced the TV, and I'd agreed to moderate my movie selections.

My film geekery was a freshman conversion in college, but the rest of my interests had deeper roots, harking back to eighth grade and my conversion into the lifestyle. Before then I'd spent a lot of years afraid to make close human friends after what had happened to my foster parents. But eventually I'd drifted into the orbit of a few other outcast boys, and in the hobbies and fandoms that I shared with them I had found a sense of community—and, better, a sense of escape. Playing video games or raiding an imaginary dungeon in a friend's rec room had helped make me feel human. My mother had encouraged human friendships when I was younger—superficial ones, preferably, and with children who would bring good connections with them. She'd envisioned me forming social ties to the sons and daughters of the politicians and preeminent city lights who graced her dinner table. Her disappointment in my preferred companions had been palpable on the many afternoons that I'd headed to my friend John's house for a day filled with Nintendo, *Star Wars*, and tabletop role-playing games rather than sailing, tennis, or any of the other activities that she and my siblings wished I'd embraced.

After my television détente with Chivalry, I'd taken the chance to expose him to all five seasons of *Babylon 5*—a small piece of vengeance, perhaps, for the hours of lectures on preferred socialization that I'd endured from him over the years.

Today there had been an hour of workout, and then Chivalry had shifted us into his regulation boxing ring. He'd taken up boxing back in the late 1880s, when it had enjoyed a surge of popularity among the younger upper-class gentlemen that he was friends with, and had continued practicing on his own even when other fads eventually replaced it. Even with all of the new working out, I still lacked the strength and speed of a full vampire, so my brother had decreed that some self-defense work was in order. Accordingly, he had proceeded to instruct me in the correct Marquis of Queensberry rules of boxing.

"You're showing good improvement, Fort," he said brightly to me. He was bouncing around in front of me, arms up in perfect form, having spent the last two hours doing nothing but blocking punches and giving me reminder taps with his fists whenever I dropped my guard. He looked crisp and fresh, practically a deodorant ad.

I, on the other hand, had plopped on the floor like an exhausted toddler and was barely able to lift my arms anymore. I was sweating so badly that I looked like a miniature rain cloud must be directly above me, and I could actually track my recent movements by looking down at the damp trail on the canvas of the ring.

"Stop trying to encourage me," I panted.

"No, I really mean it," he said. "You have the strength and speed of an exceptional human."

"Which still leaves me well below the level of an asthmatic vampire." I tried to wipe my face with my shirt, but since it was completely saturated with sweat, it was like using a warm washcloth. I gave up and just let it run down my face.

"Well, yes," Chivalry conceded. "But that's still an improvement."

It was true. Four months ago I'd been a mugger's dream come true. Of course, I'd still managed to kill a vampire older than Chivalry. I'd almost died in the process, but it had happened.

There was a long moment where the only sounds were the ceiling fan and my panting breaths.

"Come on," Chivalry said, breaking the silence. "One more round, then showers, then second breakfast." I'd also made him watch all three of the *Lord of the Rings* movies— extended editions. It had had an impact.

Every muscle in my body shrieked as I pulled myself upright and into the stance that my brother had drilled into my bones: gloves up, ready to block or throw a punch. Feet moving at all times, even if it was just a little shuffle. I'd asked Chivalry to help me get into shape, I reminded myself.

Chivalry gave me an approving smile, then put up his own gloves. "All right," he said. "Now hit me."

I didn't, of course. My trying to land a punch on my brother was like a kitten trying to attack a cougar. I reflected on that as I stood in the gym shower, letting the cool water drench me. Compared to the opulence of my mother's mansion, Chivalry's gym was extremely austere, something that had required a few compromises. One of those was the bathroom. The gym was all gray slab cement and plain walls, but the bathroom was my mother's creation. The tiling was mosaic style, with individual tiles smaller than a quarter, all in dusty orange or black and used to recreate scenes from Greek mythology—in the case of the shower, Hercules cleaning out the Aegean stables. My mother's decorating often reflects her highly questionable sense of humor.

Feeling halfway human again, I dried off quickly and changed into the clothes from my gym bag, jeans and an old *Farscape* T-shirt. There was a huge selection of hair-care products, as well as three different brands of cologne, laid out beside the sink. All of them were unopened. My brother came of age in a time when men had grooming expectations that would boggle most modern metrosexuals, and he never gave up attempts, both subtle and overt, to bring me up to snuff. I ran a comb quickly through my wet hair and, not bothering to shave, called it a morning. I could do that later, after the sight of my stubble had caused my brother to despair. After all, what were little brothers for?

I walked slowly across Madeline's lawn, which would put most golf courses to shame in terms of regimented grooming, and waved to the gardeners already hard at work. Chivalry's promised second breakfast was waiting on the back terrace. I'd been fairly lanky before I'd started working out, and Chivalry had fully embraced the caloric challenge I faced. There are, after all, a wide range of fit body types—take a look at an Olympic long-distance runner sometime, then compare that to the guy playing water polo. One is built like a beanpole and the other is built like a tank. We were going for something in between those two, though my body seemed to naturally gravitate toward beanpole. Thus the completely bizarre situation of working out for three hours, then having my brother try to fatten me up.

My first breakfast of the morning had been light out of necessity—eating heavily before working out was a quick recipe for vomiting. Now there was a buffet selection of eggs, sausage, bacon, and silver-dollar pancakes, along with the makings of either fruit smoothies or mimosas, all set up with white linen tablecloths and fine china. Casual dining was a foreign concept to my family.

I stared at the buffet and sighed a little. My vegetarianism was something else that Chivalry was determined to reform. I went for toast, pancakes, and a hefty shovel of perfectly scrambled eggs, resolutely avoiding the siren smell of sausage and bacon. One strawberry and banana smoothie, and I was set. Once I got all the plates over to the table, I started doing my best to inhale breakfast.

I was almost done when I heard the soft noise of a wheelchair being pushed across Persian rugs coming from the morning room that accessed the terrace. I controlled a wince as I turned to see what I'd been trying to avoid. Chivalry appeared, recoiffed (not that he had gotten all that messy to begin with) and dressed in ironed khakis and a blue polo shirt, looking ready to head off to the country club. His wife, Bhumika, sat in the wheelchair that he was pushing. She didn't always join us in the mornings—her health had been deteriorating steadily for the past year, and there were some days that she didn't leave their bedroom at all. Today was a good day, though, since she wasn't using a full oxygen mask, just subtle tubes in her nose to make her more comfortable. She was dressed in a beautifully embroidered set of turquoise shalwar kameez—traditional Indian loose cotton trousers and a matching shirt. We'd had a long summer this year, and even now the early-October morning held a breath of heat, but a cashmere blanket was still carefully wrapped around Bhumika's shoulders.

Her smile was as brilliant as ever as Chivalry carefully pushed her wheelchair down the small ramp that, like all the ramps in the house, had appeared overnight when she'd first started needing assistance to walk. They were all fully integrated into the house, and not a single one of them had the slightest feel of impermanence. They were beautiful, all lovingly crafted out of hardwood and designed to fit the look of whatever room they were for. A few were made out of stone.

None of them were new, of course. Madeline's staff had simply removed them from where they'd been stored after Chivalry's last wife, Linda, had died. And before that, I'd seen them set up for his earlier wife, Carmela. We'd all known from the first day that we'd been introduced to Bhumika, the day of her wedding to Chivalry, that she would end up like this. So had she, of course. A few short years of health, then a long decline that ended only one way.

I leaned down and kissed her cheek carefully. Her long black hair was starting to thin a little, a few strands clinging to the back of the wheelchair. Chivalry transferred her to one of the terrace chairs, making sure it was the one with the best padding, in her favorite sunny spot. Then, while Bhumika and I talked (mostly she talked and I listened—I never felt completely comfortable with her, even though she'd always shown me nothing but loving interest), Chivalry carefully filled a plate with her favorite foods, approaching the task with complete absorption, sorting through the entire bowl of strawberries to make sure he'd chosen only the best pieces.

When all three of us were settled around the table we spent a few more minutes like that. Bhumika was telling me some anecdote about her rose garden, and I was nodding mechanically. Chivalry was eating the omelet that had been prepared for him in advance, periodically nibbling at a sausage. Vampires continue to eat food for centuries after our transitions, but the selection starts narrowing the older we get. For Chivalry, the morning sausages that he'd enjoyed for two hundred years were becoming harder to handle, even though he still loved them. Had my mother been at the table with us, all she would've been able to sample were the mimosas.

Of course, breakfast with Madeline always had to be held in rooms that had no windows.

I forked the last of my pancakes into my mouth and had just started my good-byes when Bhumika abruptly said, "Honey, I'd love it if we could find the time for one last sail with Fort this year."

I couldn't help the expression of surprise that I knew had appeared on my face, and I looked carefully over at Chivalry, who had gone completely poker-faced at the comment. Chivalry was a huge fan of yachting and owned a fifty-two-foot cruiser-racer boat that was completely sail driven and whose deck I had spent many grumpy hours swabbing as a teenager. Early in his marriage, he and Bhumika had done a lot of sailing in all weather, once even participating in the annual Newport-to-Bermuda yacht race, but they had cut back considerably in recent years. In the entire summer, I actually thought that they'd been out on the water only twice. "I don't know, Bhumika," I said cautiously. "I have been pretty busy. Training with Chivalry, plus all our outings, plus my work schedule . . ." I let my voice trail off.

Chivalry smoothly added his. "It's hard to say how much longer this weather will last. And even with these temperatures, I don't know if I'd want to take the *Gay Belle* out for anything other than an afternoon sail." Chivalry had named his yacht back in the 1880s, and even though he'd had it completely dry-docked and rebuilt multiple times down at the Newport Shipyard, he'd always kept the name, even as the connotations of the words changed very fundamentally and various other yacht owners periodically gave him side-long looks, or, depending on their feelings on the topic, enthusiastic toots of their horns. As a teenager, I had repeatedly begged him to change the name to something slightly less mortifying, but Chivalry flatly refused. Of course, no one understood the art of outlasting a fad like a vampire, and he remained convinced that eventually the word would swing back to the old meaning. Of course, he'd also held on to his entire collection of top hats, cravats, and VHS tapes.

"I thought it would be nice to do, though," Bhumika said. Her tone was pleasant, but I got the impression that she was digging in. "After all, I'd hate to wait all winter before we all went out together again."

I glanced frantically over to Chivalry, waiting for him to say something. Everyone at this table knew that even if Bhumika lived through the winter, she'd never be going out on the water again.

My brother reached out and ran his fingertips gently across the back of Bhumika's hand. "We'll see if the schedules work out," he said, very quietly.

For a man who killed all of his wives, it was always stunning how very much Chivalry loved them.

A chill ran down my spine, and I wondered if someday that would be me, caressing the hand of the woman who I was slowly killing. Abruptly, it was all too much for me, and I made a quick escape from the table. I dropped a kiss on Bhumika's cheek and waved to my brother with a promise to see him again tomorrow. Then I was off to my car at a lope that was as close to a run as I could get without being rudely obvious.

Cutting through the house, I did my best to avoid getting in the way of two maids who were giving the front entrance hall its thrice-weekly mopping, and only barely avoided knocking over a bucket of sudsy water. Out the front door, I walked across the white crushed-gravel driveway, giving in to the urge to kick a few times and listen to the pattering sound of dispersed stones falling back to the ground.

My car came into sight, tucked in like a mutt among show dogs, and I froze. Chivalry was leaning against the side of my dilapidated Ford Fiesta, watching me patiently. He must've run around the outside of the house to beat me, but he was looking cool and casual, as if he'd just strolled over.

There was no escaping him, so I trudged over.

"Is this about the trolls?" I asked, hoping to distract him. "Or maybe we're going to go feed sardines to mermaids on tomorrow's field trip?"

He stared at me for a second, then slowly raised one eyebrow. The rest of his face stayed completely bland.

I've never been able to withstand Chivalry's bland expression. "I don't want to go sailing," I said mutinously. "I'm working forty hours a week and taking the Chivalry Atlas program for bodybuilding. My afternoons off are rarer than bald eagles, and I'm not going to spend one of them with a sweater tied around my shoulders while you nag me about moving sails around or hoisting the spinner."

"That's not why you don't want to go," Chivalry said, his voice cool.

I glared at him. "It's one of the reasons. Isn't it enough?"

"Bhumika has asked for this," he said. He met my glare and simply looked back at me. We have the same hazel eyes, but as I watched, his pupils slowly began expanding until the hazel was completely covered. Besides the occasional fang flash, the eyes are where vampire tempers are most apparent. I looked away—lately I'd spent a lot of time nervously checking mirrors to make sure that my eyes weren't pulling that trick.

I glanced back, and Chivalry's eyes had returned to normal, and now he looked thoughtful. "She isn't asking for much, Fortitude," he said. He always used my full name like most parents use middle names: when I was in trouble.

"Yeah, fine. Put something together," I said, looking away again and leaning down to ostensibly brush at the side of the Fiesta. Chivalry had surprised me with a professional paint job for my elderly car, but a few weeks ago I'd come out of a grocery store to discover that some asshole with faulty spatial relations had practically sideswiped my car. There hadn't been any serious damage, but now my blue Fiesta had a streak of transferred orange paint completely up one side that I had been utterly unable to remove. "You have my work schedule," I muttered, wiping ineffectually at the streak with the hem of my T-shirt. "Call me with a time."

Chivalry didn't say anything, but he stopped leaning against the car and strolled a few steps away, toward his own Bentley. My brother was as bossy as they came, but at least he never rubbed it in whenever he won on something.

I'd unlocked the Fiesta and slid into the driver's seat when Chivalry spoke again, sounding almost tentative. "You know, I read a good review the other day of Peláez. Perhaps if Bhumika is feeling well tonight she and I could—"

"Oh, don't even think about it," I said, shooting a dark look at him. "I told you when I got that job—if you go there, you do it when I'm *not* working."

Chivalry frowned and made an expression that on any other guy I actually would've called a pout. "I don't understand this attitude, Fort. I've been to many of the establishments that you've worked at. I'm simply being supportive of your career choices."

"Being a waiter is not a career choice; it is a job-hunt default," I said. "Plus, you are not fooling me. You've been desperate to eat there ever since you found out that the staff is in black tie, and I refuse to feed into this formal-wear fetish that you have."

"In more civilized times, all gentlemen wore formal clothing in the evenings," he sniffed, grumpy because I'd seen his motive so clearly.

"Yeah, those gentlemen also died of dysentery because they didn't wash their hands after they took a crap." I slammed the Fiesta's door shut. While it suited my mood at the moment, that actually wasn't the reason I'd done it. Lately the driver's door was having trouble latching, and had popped open a few times at stoplights. Since I had about five issues more immediately concerning about the car to bring to the attention of a mechanic whenever I finally saved up the money, I was trying to figure out how to live with this one.

It was all part of the Fiesta's charm.

The drive from Newport to my apartment in Providence was between forty minutes and an hour, depending on the traffic. Today there hadn't been any elderly drivers or sight-seeing tourists on the two-lane road that always made or broke my time, and I pulled into the small parking lot behind my building just after ten a.m.

I lived in an old three-story Victorian that had been broken into apartments sometime in the 1950s. The first floor was an upscale women's lingerie shop, which actually sounded more exciting than it was, since usually the women going into it were the ones who could *afford* expensive undergarments—mostly middle-aged to elderly women. Each of the upper floors was a single two-bedroom apartment in a state of highly questionable repair, and the owner had a policy of ignoring necessary fixes until we tenants either gave in and fixed it ourselves or just moved out in disgust. Since moving in four years ago, I'd learned a lot about emergency plumbing.

Climbing up three flights of stairs always felt like the last-rep set after a morning of working out with Chivalry. During the first few weeks, I'd actually started giving serious consideration to the thought of moving somewhere that had an elevator, but had given up the idea after I remembered that I'd then have to move all of my stuff out—down all those stairs.

My sofa had originally belonged to a couple in the second-floor apartment. During their move out, they'd abandoned it halfway down the staircase. After climbing over it for three days, I'd finally decided it was good and abandoned and hauled it up to my own living room. Those thoughts kept me company as I made my way to my apartment in a zombielike fugue. In my door, through the dual kitchen and living room, and then I was tumbling into my bed, asleep almost before I hit the sheets.

It felt like barely ten minutes had passed before I woke up to a hand shaking my shoulder none too gently. I came into consciousness in slow stages, registering first the hand, then the loud beeping of my alarm, and finally registering that I hadn't even bothered to take off my shoes.

"C'mon, Sleeping Beauty," my roommate said. "You have to get up."

"Don't want to," I muttered, pulling my pillow over my head. It was immediately pulled away from me.

"Either get up or turn the alarm off. I can hear the damn thing out into the hallway."

"What time is it?" I asked muzzily.

"It's a quarter after twelve, dude," Gage said, jostling my shoulder one last time.

I was suddenly, horribly awake. "Oh, fuck me." I pulled my head up and stared at my roommate in horror. "I overslept by half an hour?"

"Apparently. I just got home and heard the alarm going off."

I'd had a lot of horrible roommates in the past, all of whom would've heard my alarm going off, known I'd overslept, and probably just laughed about it while they dropped a wet towel on the hardwood floor. Whether I'd just finally run through Providence's available jackass male roommate population or whether I'd cashed in some karmic bennies, the result was that I'd put out my usual Craigslist ad and had found Gage, who was not only a nonasshole (as specified in my ad), but was actually a decent guy.

Gage watched as I half rolled, half fell out of bed, and gave a wholly exasperated sigh. This was unfortunately not the first time this scenario had played out. "Dude, I can run you over if you don't think you'd make it on time with the bus."

I was already halfway across my room to pull my work clothes out of the closet, and I stopped and said, "That would completely save my ass. But are you sure?"

Gage shrugged. He was even taller than I was, and a former college wrestler built like he was ready to audition for *300*. His dark blond hair tended toward the sheepdog look, and a recent set of Celtic tattoo bands at his wrists and upper arms had just healed enough to remove the bandages and serve as catnip for every girl he passed in the street. At first glance he looked like the kind of brain-dead douche who needed an operating manual to toast bread, but he was actually completing a master's degree down at Brown University.

Burned too many times before, I'd been a little reticent

when he'd first moved in. But he'd done his share of cleaning, kept his stuff from encroaching on the common areas,
and always paid his half of the rent on time. Admittedly he
made a huge lasagna every Wednesday that incorporated
about two pounds of Italian sausage and ground beef and
forced me to undergo a test of willpower every time I
opened the fridge and saw the delectable leftovers sitting in
conveniently-portioned plastic containers, but no living situation was perfect.

"I just got back from class," Gage said. "It's not like I'm
in the middle of anything. Besides, it's not exactly in my
best interests for you to get fired."

Given that he'd signed a yearlong lease, that was certainly true, but beneath Gage's grumbling I knew that he
would've ferried my oversleeping ass to my job regardless.
I routinely caught him helping our elderly downstairs
neighbor, Mrs. Bandyopadyay, carry in her groceries. Each
time he claimed he was just keeping his kept boy-toy options open.

"You're saving my bacon, Gage," I called as he left the
room.

"Yeah, your tofu bacon," he grumbled loudly from the
living room.

I changed as quickly as I could in the bathroom. My
stubble was reaching wolfman proportions, and in my hurry
to shave it off I nicked myself three times, once badly
enough that I had to stick on one of those little round Band-
Aids. My hair was a predictable disaster, but the restaurant
I worked at had specific hair policies, so I shellacked it
down until I looked ready to head out to a Prohibition
speakeasy. Basic needs met, on went the tuxedo pants and
the white buttoned shirt. Technically we were supposed to
get them dry-cleaned between every two shifts, but since
the restaurant refused to reimburse us for the costs and
paid only minimum wage, I got by with just Febrezing the
crap out of them each day and tossing them into the laundry at the end of each week, while keeping my fingers
crossed that the delicate cycle would be okay. Then I pulled
on my black dress shoes, which I'd purchased secondhand
and which had required only a few applications of glue and

a Sharpie to look (from a distance) acceptable. Then the black vest, and finally I put the finishing touches on my bow tie. There was a rule against clip-ons, so I'd had to learn how to actually tie it—after months of practice, I'd gotten to the point where the end result was only a little crooked.

A glance in the mirror confirmed that my appearance met and did not exceed the base minimum standards expected at my job. It would have to do, so I shrugged and grabbed my keys, ran out the door, and pounded down the stairs. In the parking lot, Gage was already waiting in his little green hybrid. I jumped into the passenger's seat, and he handed me a sandwich.

"I was making my own lunch anyway," he said, clearly heading off my thanks before I could even start. "And if you pass out from hunger during your shift, your boss would probably take the opportunity to fire you."

I took a huge bite and groaned. "I'll do your dishes for a week," I promised.

Gage glanced over at me from the road. "A straight guy just made you food. Try again."

I took another bite. "Two weeks?"

Now he shot me a grin. "Sounds a little closer."

"I know your game. You're just trying to guilt me into more dishes."

He shrugged. "Or, you know, doing a real grocery run when it's your turn."

"I'm a vegetarian, Gage. I have moral objections to standing at the deli counter." Mostly because of how good everything looked. I'd gone vegetarian in order to date a vegan, but I'd stayed one because it helped suppress some of my creepier vampire instincts. That didn't make being around a sizzling hamburger patty any easier, though.

"And I have moral objections to tofu hot dogs. Also, beer?"

"I got the beer! Keystone Light!"

Gage rolled his eyes. "Like I said. Beer?"

"You're a snob," I accused him. After all, the Keystone Light was drinkable. Kind of. Mostly it was just really cheap.

"I'm just saying, Fort. When it was my week I bought Sam Adams. After one of those bottles of piss that you're trying to call beer, I was giving serious consideration to going and siphoning off some of your Fiesta's antifreeze instead."

I finished the last bite of the sandwich, balled up the paper towel that he'd wrapped it in, and threw it at his head while we were stopped at a red light. Gage whipped it right back, but I ducked and it went out the open window, where it bounced against the Honda next to us. The girl driving was so involved in her texting that she didn't even react, and we both cracked up.

"That crazy fitness routine of yours is paying off," Gage said after a final snicker. "Your reflexes are getting fucking catlike here."

I managed an uncomfortable little chuckle. Working out was why a drag queen had wolf-whistled at me last week when I'd been bending down to pick up a quarter at the bus stop. The evolution of my reflexes from their previously arthritic state was part of the transition, and something I preferred to try not to think about.

"Oh, hey. Are you just working the lunch shift today?" Gage asked.

"No, dinner as well. Full nine hours. Why?"

"That speed-dating thing is tonight and I just wanted to check to see if you had changed your mind."

I snorted. "I appreciate the offer, but I still don't even know why you're so excited about it."

He shrugged. "Looks fun, and I'll be meeting twenty women in an hour and a half. Plus finger food. It's worth trying." He slanted a look at me. "Why, did something interesting happen to you during your ten free minutes last week?"

"Yeah, I figured out that the reason the shower is draining so slowly is because your boy-band hair sheds like a Wookiee." Gage laughed again and let it drop. We talked about other things for the rest of the drive, until he dropped me off at work with five minutes to spare.

Since breaking up with my last girlfriend, Beth, I hadn't gone out at all. Part of it had been sheer exhaustion from my new schedule, but a large part had also been reticence. Dating Beth had ended pretty badly, with her cheating on me blatantly and often. Gage had heard the whole story, and seemed to have made it his private mission to prove that there were plenty of nice women out there. I'd stopped bothering to count the number of times that we'd been picking up takeout or going to a movie and just happened to run into one of the women from his master's program, or that I'd come home to find that an old friend of Gage's had just stopped by for a drink, and just happened to be ador- able, single, and age appropriate. It hadn't worked, of course. It wasn't Gage's fault that I was less human than I used to be, and feeling a little conflicted about going out on a date with some nice nursing student whose blood I might sometime in the future want to drink.

Clocking in and getting to work was a relief because it got my mind off of both my existential moral headache and the thought of just how long it had been since I'd gotten laid. I'd worked in food service before (sometimes I thought I'd done just about every possible minimum-wage job be- fore), but mostly at diners or the occasional chain buffalo- wing joint. Working at Peláez had been a very new experience. For one thing, there was the joy of carrying huge trays of food while in black tie. For another, they ac- tually employed a guy whose entire job was to go over to the table and advise people on their wine selection. Then there was the food itself.

In most restaurants, bringing the food over was a maxi- mum of three trips. Once to bring over salads or appetizers, another for the entrée, and one last visit to bring over des- sert and coffee. Peláez, though, took itself pretty seriously. Part of that manifested in its no-clip-on-tie policy, but the bulk of it resulted in portions so tiny that a typical plate actually consisted of a single mushroom wrapped in bacon and sprinkled with caviar. Serving a single person their lunch involved ten trips with ten different plates, and I wasn't allowed to just stand there while he popped the bite into his mouth, and whip the plate away. Oh no. I had to busy myself by scampering over to another table and bring- ing over *their* minuscule bite of food. Then swinging back to pick up the now-empty plates from table one and bring those ones back.

It was probably a good thing I'd started working out, because all those trips from the dining room back to the kitchen racked up some serious miles.

The benefit to the job was that it left me with very little time to brood. On the downside ...

"Where's the fucking vegetarian?" boomed across the kitchen halfway through the main lunch crowd. Like a deer in the headlights, I froze in the act of taking a plate. All down the line, the sous-chefs and assistant cooks eyed me while keeping up the controlled chaos of chopping knives and boiling pots. Down the main aisle rolled my personal nemesis, Chef Jerome, and all around him people ducked down into instinctive head bobs of respect, doing everything possible to avoid attracting his gimlet eye.

I gave a deep sigh. "Here, Chef," I called.

He came toward me. Chef Jerome looked like old photos of Rasputin, only instead of weird robes he wore bright orange Crocs and an impeccable white chef's coat. His long wiry mass of black hair was always contained in a ponytail, but he'd had to rig an old hairnet into a beard net to prevent his strange, straggly, end-of-days-prophet, chest-length beard from contaminating the food. His eyes were always dialed to ten on the fanatic scale, but for Chef Jerome, the only true religion was Foodie, and I was a heretic in the eyes of his lord.

Coming up to me, he held a fork wedged into a single mouthful of food. Also known in this restaurant as a thirty-nine-dollar entrée.

"Open," he said balefully.

I did my best. "Chef, really, I—"

"OPEN." The vein on his forehead started to throb, a sure sign that he was nearing the breaking point. The last time he'd hit it had been last week, when Lorraine was on meat duty and had miscalibrated her micrometer, resulting in lamb cubes that were two centimeters larger than Chef Jerome had asked for. The ensuing fit had broken eight plates, violated two chicken carcasses, and required fourteen completely comped meals for the people in the dining room who'd overheard language that made Gordon Ramsay sound like a Mormon.

Heeding the throbbing vein, I shut up and opened my mouth. Like the parent of a toddler, he popped the little food niblet in.

Chef Jerome's feverish eyes documented every movement of my jaw as I chewed. "And?" he asked, his eyes going full Manson-lamp.

I swallowed reluctantly, my mouth already mourning the loss even as my stomach practically danced a jig. "Yes, it's amazing," I muttered.

"Filet mignon in an orange glaze with a dusting of jalapeño, motherfucker," Chef Jerome screamed in my face. Then he looked up and shook his fist at the ceiling, as if challenging the heavens. "There will be no goddamn vegetarians in this kitchen!" This Scarlett O'Hara moment of Chef Jerome's happened several times a week. And it was a small comfort that as bad as things were for me, they were far worse for Josh the vegan.

My day then got even worse as I walked back into the dining room and noticed the homicidally envious looks that my fellow waiters were shooting me. That only ever meant one thing, and I gulped as I went back to my tables.

Sitting in the middle of my section was Suzume Hollis, kitsune, sometime friend, and all-time tormenter. She caught my eye, raised her wineglass ever so slightly, and gave me the smallest curl of that smile that always hit me like an electric shock to my spine. Then, without missing a beat, she turned her attention back to the expensively suited middle-aged man who sat across from her.

I'd met Suzume when my mother hired her as my bodyguard, but after she'd risked her life to save me from a homicidal pedophile vampire we'd kind of become friends. Being friends with Suzume involved receiving a lot of forwarded e-mail humor and having to endure her love of pranks. In the first month alone of being friends, she'd TPed my car twice, sent a male stripper-gram to my door, and broken into my apartment to fill my closet with 237 cotton-candy Tribbles.

Those incidents had been various levels of amusing (particularly the Tribbles, which had been funnier *before* Gage and I had had to get down to the serious business of actually trying to eat 237 cotton-candy Tribbles), but then Suzume had decided that my work hours were fair game.

All of the kitsune in Providence were the daughters and granddaughters of the White Fox, who had been a geisha in Japan before emigrating to America. Upon arrival, she'd gone back to what she'd known best and had set up an escort business. While none of the kitsune actually did any of the escort jobs themselves, they did manage and run all of the other aspects of Green Willow Escorts, and lately Suzume had been put in charge of screening prospective clients.

The other waiters were insanely jealous because Suzume never sat in their sections. Instead she was always perched in mine, balancing perfectly on that edge where appropriate business attire starts meeting the opening act of a male sexual fantasy. Today she was in a dark blue silk blouse tucked into a black skirt that ended demurely just below her knee but was so formfitting that I wondered how the hell she maneuvered herself into her car. The string of black pearls around her neck made her skin look luminously pale, and her black hair was in a sleek yet complicated arrangement held together by two long red lacquered chopsticks. She had only a little makeup on around her eyes, drawing attention to the most obvious marker of her Japanese ancestry, and making them look even darker than usual. The man sitting across from her, who probably spent all of his time in boardrooms or wherever rich and powerful men hung out, was clearly already completely enraptured by the time I went over to tell them the day's specials.

I wasn't sure if it would make my fellow waiters more or less jealous to know the particular method that Suzume used to torment me during these meals. Somehow she arranged the conversation so that every time I arrived at the table it was just in time to hear the filthiest, most ear-searing and brain-fragmenting portion of a conversation focused on what particular sexual practices this potential client was interested in. And each time I had to try to keep a straight face after hearing a horrifyingly salacious fragment concerning people's front ends, hind ends, or other parts that I'd never even particularly considered, she'd look up at me with the most demure and ladylike expression, blandly asking for another roll or complimenting the most recent dish, and her eyes would be gleaming with foxy amusement. Meanwhile the rich and powerful men across from her would be putty in her hands, completely eager at the end of that dinner to pay the exorbitant fees that Green Willow Escorts charged.

After an hour of torture, I was finally able to bring over the bill. As always, Suzume reached for it just a hair too slowly, and the newest client insisted on paying it himself, puffing up with importance as Suzume murmured her appreciation in velvety tones.

The next time I swung around, her dinner partner was gone and Suzume was nursing a cup of coffee. She always stuck around—she couldn't stand not being able to gloat to someone.

"Did you like the bit about the hot wax?" she asked as soon as I came over. With her financial prey gone, she'd dropped her Mysterious and Demure Woman of the East routine and was grinning at me with her usual enthusiasm.

"I am going to have nightmares for a week thanks to you," I bitched as I started collecting the dessert plates. Usually I'd leave that for the busboys, but despite my front I could never resist the chance to spend a few minutes talking with her.

"I almost thought you were going to miss the spanking bit, but then you showed up with the reconstructed artichoke. It was awesome."

"The food or the other thing?" I asked. "I would've thought that you'd heard every weird sexual fetish on the planet by now."

"I have," she admitted frankly. "But watching your face makes it interesting all over again."

"Damn it, Suze, he stole the freaking napkin. You do this on purpose every time. Get them all riled and worked up, and then I've brought the coffee and they have to walk out of here, so they grab the napkin to provide a visual block."

She gave me a very smug look.

"Do not look that proud," I scolded. "That's not nice to do to any guy."

"Are you saying that on behalf of your gender, or"— she swept her gaze downward—"are you speaking from more personal experience?"

"I'm immune to you now," I said, picking up the pile of plates and stomping off to the kitchen.

Not fast enough, because I could hear her taunting, disbelieving laugh behind me.

She was right. I wasn't immune at all.

Suzume was gone when I went back to deliver more huge plates with tiny portions to the rest of my tables, and the rest of the night dragged on, noticeably duller after the excitement of her presence.

We stopped seating people at nine, which meant that the last stragglers didn't head out the door until quarter past ten, and the cleanup didn't finish for me until almost eleven. I pulled off my bow tie and wadded it into my pocket while I waited at the bus stop, keeping a leery eye on my surroundings. Peláez was in one of the nicer sections of Providence's downtown, near art galleries and the theater, but it was still dark and nearly deserted, so I stayed as alert as my poor, tired brain could manage. It had been a long week, and I felt deep relief when the bus finally pulled up and I climbed aboard. Tomorrow was Saturday, and it was not only my day off work, but the only day that I wouldn't have to get up at the crack of dawn and drive down to Newport and train with Chivalry. He and Bhumika always had a standing date on Saturdays—brunch at a charming local restaurant, then over to one of their favorite auctions.

Gage was still out when I got home. He was a night-owl kind of guy, and usually he and I would watch a few episodes of whatever was on Adult Swim that night while I ate a quick dinner. But his shoes weren't in their usual spot by the door, so he was apparently out somewhere, still having a great time. I grumbled a little to myself as I heated up my cup of ramen noodles and reflected on the sadness of our standard routine being one of the highlights of my current social life.

Tonight it was a rerun of *The Venture Brothers*, but my sleep-deprived eyes started getting bleary halfway through it. I tossed the ramen noodle cup in the trash and staggered off to bed, deciding that a shower could wait until tomorrow. My head hit the pillow just after midnight, and I was asleep almost instantly.

I woke up suddenly, in one of those complete awakenings that left me confused but alert, catching the end of a loud crashing sound that echoed through the apartment. It was followed immediately by a dull thud. I glanced at the clock and saw that I'd slept for only two hours.

My hearing had been intermittently flirting with achieving vampire levels lately. Most days I had regular human hearing; then suddenly the sound of Buttons, Mrs. Bandyopadyay's bichon frise, scampering across the linoleum sounded like he was right next to my ear. Five minutes later everything would be back to normal. Chivalry had told me that this was a normal part of transition, but had been his usual tight-lipped self with any other information, like how to make it stop or if this would eventually become my new normal.

I waited a moment but couldn't hear anything else, which meant that I was back to regular human levels and my auditory system had just gone haywire again. This wasn't the first time that Gage coming home had sounded like an approaching army, and I relaxed back into my pillow, listening for the rest of his usual routine. Gage swore by the properties of an antioxidant juice for warding off hangovers or the aftereffects of a late night—I'd tried it once on his urging, and had spent the next ten minutes running my mouth under the faucet to try to clean out the taste, which had been on par with raw sewage. I waited for the sound of the juicer to begin.

I waited, but there were no sounds in our apartment— not the juicer, and not even the usual sounds of Gage's feet across the floor.

I sat up in bed and called softly, "Gage?"

Just silence.

I got up completely and walked out of the bedroom. The living room was dark except for the small light above the main door, which I'd left on when I went to bed so that Gage wouldn't have to fumble around completely in the dark when he got home. I glanced down at the small mat beside the door, noting that Gage's sneakers were still missing. He hadn't come home yet.

That sent my mind back to the noise that had woken me up. It had sounded like it had come from the apartment, but if vampire hearing had been involved it might well have been feral cats knocking over the outside trash cans again.

Maybe. But I was less trusting than I used to be, and I padded quickly back to my room to retrieve the .45 Colt automatic that was hidden under my bed, disguised under an old pair of boxer shorts. My foster father had raised me with a strong respect for proper gun safety, meaning that I felt daily guilt over not keeping the Colt locked in a regulation gun safe, but the guilt wasn't enough to overpower my desire to be able to get at the Colt quickly if something not entirely human presented itself.

The ammo was separate from the gun, hidden in the toe of an old slipper that also stayed under the bed. I slid the clip into the Colt with the ease of long practice, then, feeling significantly braver, left the bedroom again.

The thing about having a roommate was that it made it a lot easier to go back to sleep after a weird sound, because there was always a built-in explanation available. With Gage still out, there was no way that I was going to be able to close my eyes again until I'd checked everywhere. I started with the bathroom, because that was on my side of the apartment, right across from my door. Then I went back to the main room, checking around the sofa, looking under the kitchen table.

I tapped lightly on Gage's door and called his name again. He was regular in his habits, and I was confident that he wasn't home, but I had no desire to run the risk that he'd gone straight to his room without taking off his shoes or drinking his antioxidant crap. Really, there would be no good outcome to that one—particularly since I hadn't exactly mentioned to him that I was a gun owner.

There was no response, and I held the Colt in my left hand, down at my side, while I reached for the doorknob with my right. For a moment I smelled something weird, and I paused, sniffing. It was almost familiar, but then it was gone again. Shit, now my nose was getting in on the transition business.

I opened the door and looked around. The dark room looked normal. A cool breeze came in from his open window, and the moonlight was bright enough to illuminate Gage's neatly made bed.

Nothing weird at all. It must've been feral cats. I started to turn, but then I suddenly smelled that weird thing again, and this time it was much stronger. I sniffed, trying to place it. For a moment I couldn't think of it, then it suddenly hit me what I was smelling. Blood. Not a lot of it, but enough that it was tickling at the part of me that was a vampire, like a chocoholic would feel walking past the open door of the Newport Fudge Company.

I walked farther into the room, raising the gun so that now I was holding it in a two-handed grip at chest level, no longer bothering to hide it. Closer now, I could see that the window I'd assumed was open was actually broken—someone had knocked a hole in it so that they could get to the lock, and there was glass on the floor that I tried not to step on.

I still couldn't see anyone, but I could definitely smell the blood, and the glass on the floor was probably from the sound that had first woken me up. I leaned back quickly and flipped the wall switch.

Cheery light filled the room, illuminating what had been hidden in the shadows at the base of the bed. Gage lay face-down on the floor of his room, completely naked, with both arms outstretched. There was something wrong with his arms, but at first my brain refused to register what it was.

I was moving toward him before I fully registered what I was seeing, and it wasn't until I reached down and actually touched his shoulder that I realized that he was already dead.

# Chapter 3

Gage's skin was icy under my hand, and I jerked backward instinctively. I'd been around dead bodies before, sometimes even ones that I'd been responsible for turning into corpses, but finding Gage like that was different. My brain felt foggy from the shock, and I sat down heavily on the floor, staring at what was in front of me.

Gage was lying on his chest with his face turned toward me. His eyes were open, empty and staring, and there were a bunch of cuts and dried blood around his mouth. His hands were gone, cut away with an almost disturbing neatness just below his freshly inked tattoo band. There'd been no hacking—his wrists looked like sliced salami at the deli counter.

Had I not already been a vegetarian, that image would've turned me off of salami for life.

For a second I had to battle nausea. I closed my eyes tightly, fighting the urge to vomit, but when I opened them up again Gage was still in front of me, still lying there. His surfer-blond hair was matted with dried blood. I'd just been making fun of his hair this afternoon, I remembered.

Somehow that thought broke through my shock, and I was scrambling out of the room, back to my bedside table and my cell phone. I'd dialed 911 and was talking to the dispatcher even as I stuffed the Colt under my mattress. That was definitely something that was not a good idea to have in hand when the cops showed up.

I hung up as soon as the dispatcher assured me that the police were on their way over. The next number was the one that I knew I should've called first, a fact that I consciously ignored as I punched it in. It wouldn't matter to Chivalry or my mother what had killed Gage, whether deranged human or something less natural. What mattered to them was keeping our profile low, making sure that the Scott name didn't come up any more than absolutely necessary. If my first call hadn't been to the police, I knew without a doubt that Chivalry would've hopped in his car with the intention of walking me through a body disposal. Then there would've been some false trails, maybe a forged e-mail, something that made certain that when Gage's family started looking for him, the trail led away from this apartment until going cold somewhere far, far away.

Gage had been my friend. He didn't deserve that.

Chivalry answered on the second ring.

"My roommate is dead," I said as soon as I heard his voice.

There was a brief pause. Then Chivalry asked, completely calmly, "Did you attack him?"

"What?" I yelped. "No! What are you— How could you think that?"

"You are getting older, Fortitude," came his icy voice. "It is a reasonable question."

"*No*, no, it is *not* reasonable. Something else killed—" Unbidden, the image of Gage's empty wrists flashed in front of my eyes and I gulped hard. "Something else killed Gage. I don't know what. There are cuts on his face, and his hands were cut off." I paused again, taking a deep breath. "The police are on their way over."

"Why?" Chivalry was no longer calm, and his voice lashed out sharply. "Did a neighbor see something? Hear something?"

"I called them."

"What?" He sounded truly stunned.

"I panicked," I lied. "I just . . . panicked and thought like a human."

"This is most inconvenient." There was a long pause, and I closed my eyes and slumped down onto my bed. "I am unable to come tonight, little brother. Bhumika's health has . . . we are in the hospital, and will need to remain overnight."

"I'm sorry," I muttered. "Is she okay?"

"Nothing to concern yourself over," he said, putting me sharply in my place. "I will call the lawyers; someone will be there soon to handle things. Don't say anything to the police. And you might want to call that fox friend of yours—she's annoying, but the kitsune know how to handle themselves discreetly. She can prevent you from any more of these problematic slips."

I swallowed hard. "What about Gage?"

"I'll call the mayor tomorrow morning," Chivalry said, misunderstanding my question. "This will all be cleaned up quickly. Don't worry." I heard my brother's concern for me in those last words.

"So, you'll come over after you make the call?" Bhumika must've been in very bad shape if he wasn't already in his car and on his way right now.

There was a pause on the other end, and when Chivalry spoke, he sounded confused. "Why? Is something wrong?"

I blinked. "Chivalry, *something* killed Gage."

"A human sociopath, no doubt," my brother said dismissively. "Or your roommate had unsavory ties."

I slapped my head in disbelief and had to bite down the urge to snap at him. Instead I just drenched my voice in sarcasm. "Really, you don't find it coincidental that out of all the guys in Providence, it's *my roommate* who is gruesomely murdered?"

Chivalry sighed. "And what dire enemies have *you* made lately?" I could tell across all the miles that he had that Humoring Baby Brother look on his face—the one that always made me want to punch him, or, barring that, force him to watch the Justin Bieber movie for three days in a row.

I tried reason. "Oh, you don't think Dominic doesn't hold a grudge over me killing Luca?" Frankly I deserved a goddamn medal, a parade, and a fist bump from Patrick Stewart for killing that Eurotrash pedophile, but his father might not agree.

Chivalry actually made a *pish* noise over the phone. "Dominic is in Italy and wouldn't dare risk such an act of aggression."

"What about—"

My brother cut me off before I could start listing everyone else who lived under my mother's rule and wasn't blissfully happy—namely, everyone. "Fortitude, there is no creature in our mother's territory that would be so foolish as to do this. Before you construct some martyr complex over this, remind yourself that, however distressing this has been, you merely rented a room to this human and this almost certainly has no more relevance than that you really need to conduct some kind of background check on your roommates."

My free hand curled into a fist, and I pressed it into my leg as hard as I could, pushing down what I wanted to say to my brother. He was in the hospital with his dying wife, I reminded myself. It wasn't entirely his fault at the moment that he was being an empathy-stunted prick.

Finally Chivalry gave another heaving sigh and said, "Fortitude, Providence is a big city. Big cities are riddled with crime and murder, and if you would just give up this childishness and *move home*, you would not find yourself in such unsavory situations—"

I cut him off before he could warm to one of his favorite topics. "I have to go. The police are here," I said through clenched teeth.

"I'll call you tomorrow," Chivalry promised.

I hung up and immediately dialed another number. I'd lied to Chivalry—the police weren't here yet, but I knew that I didn't have much more time. I also had no desire to sit through another of my brother's lectures about moving to Newport while Gage's body rested a mere two rooms away from me.

And despite Chivalry's confidence, his reasoning still felt wrong. What were the odds that Gage being murdered had absolutely nothing to do with him rooming with Providence's *one* vampire?

No one in my family had killed him. I would've known if any of them had been in the city tonight. But once Chivalry called in a cover-up, even if he was right and it had been some human psychopath who killed Gage, that person would never be caught. My mother's interests were in the political theaters, and there wasn't a politician in this state who didn't jump to attention when she made a phone call. My foster father had been a decorated policeman, but when Prudence murdered him and my foster mother, Madeline's influence had made certain individuals falsify or destroy evidence, then pin the crime on a homeless man who was then, very conveniently, found dead in his cell.

Calling the police meant that Gage would go back to his family, and they wouldn't wonder about him for years, but there wouldn't be justice for him.

The first police car had just pulled up in front of the building, siren wailing, as I hit the Send key on my phone.

Suzume's voice was raspy from sleep when she answered, but there was that usual layer of amusement that made me close my eyes and drink in that moment of normality. "Just to let you know, Fort," she said when she picked up, "etiquette dictates that the *woman* has to initiate a booty call relationship."

"What?" I asked, momentarily distracted.

"I know, it seems sexist to me, too"—her voice dripped reasonableness—"but Miss Manners is very clear on the subject."

For half a second I smiled; then it was wiped away by the pounding on my door as the police reminded me of everything that had happened tonight.

"Suze, it's nothing like that," I said, and quickly filled her in.

"I'll be right there." All playfulness was gone now. "Don't say a word to the cops. Let your mom's lawyers earn their money for once."

She hung up, and there was no avoiding it anymore. I went to the door to let the police inside.

I'd never known that so many people could fit in my apartment.

The first uniformed officers were joined by two plainclothes detectives, then a horde of even more officers. Beyond a few basic questions, people mostly left me alone. Apparently some big boss had already let it be known not to bother "the nice Scott boy." I accepted it, knowing that I'd done what I could.

Twenty minutes after the first officer arrived, there was a ruckus in the hallway and then, to my shock, Matt McMahon rushed through the door. He must've been on a stakeout, because although he was several kinds of rumpled, he was dressed in slacks and a button-down. His eyes swept over the scene until he picked me out; then he said, "Oh, thank Christ," loudly in that booze-weathered voice that I knew so well, and came straight over, completely ignoring the doorway officer's futile efforts to herd him back outside—about as effective as a teacup poodle against a Great Dane.

I opened my mouth to say something—what, I had no idea—but the words (and breath) were knocked out of me as Matt swept me up in a rib-bruising hug.

I'd known Matt most of my life. He'd been my foster father's partner, and he hadn't been able to turn the other way during the murder cover-up. It had cost him his career as a cop, and become the obsession that had shaped the past seventeen years of his life. He'd become a private detective, working on a lot of other cases but always trying to uncover Brian and Jill's real murderer. He'd also kept an eye on me, and we'd been close. That had all changed in the spring, when there had been vampire victims on the ground. He suspected that I'd been involved in the rescue of Amy Grann from her kidnapper, and seen the Scott cover-up machine swing into action again in a way all too reminiscent to be a coincidence. I'd lost his trust, and that had hurt. But even worse was that, I was all too aware that if my family realized that Matt was now a threat, none of them would hesitate to kill him.

The past four months were apparently forgotten as Matt broke off his hug and I began struggling for air.

"Matt," I wheezed, "You're here." It wasn't my most insightful commentary ever, but my brain was struggling after being cut off from its supply of sweet, sweet oxygen.

"Of *course* I'm here, Fort," Matt snapped. "One minute I'm photographing some pharmacist getting her extramarital freak on and the next I hear over my police radio that there's a body of a young male at *your* address?" He smacked me upside the head hard enough for me to yelp, then immediately dropped his hand to squeeze my shoulder tightly. "*Call me*, for Christ's sake. I think I lost five years off my life during the drive over here." His dark eyes were darting over me, cataloging my state of nondeadness, and there was a residual tightness to his jaw that sent a spark of shame through me.

I squeezed the hand that still rested on my shoulder, relieved despite everything that was going on at the proof that beneath his suspicions of me he still cared. I hadn't realized until now just how much that had been hurting over the summer. "I'm sorry," I said, meaning it on a lot of levels.

Matt cleared his throat, dropped his hand, and stepped back. Clearly we were back to being Men. Behind him the door cop, who had been shifting his weight awkwardly, gave up and headed back to his post, apparently deciding that we were clearly too well acquainted for him to toss Matt out. Or, more likely, ask the guy who outweighed him and clearly lifted a lot of weights to leave—politely. "So, what happened," Matt asked, glancing around the room with a professionally cool expression.

I told him what I'd told the police—waking up suddenly, investigating the sound, finding Gage. I could see Matt's eyes narrow as he listened, and I knew when the wheels started turning in his head. He shifted away from me, and I felt a pang as the reprieve and return to our old relationship ended. He'd been suspicious of me since Amy Grann had unintentionally implicated me to him, and now my roommate was dead. I could see him connecting some dots.

"I'll check this out," he said, and all I could do was nod as he slipped into Gage's bedroom, currently cluttered with police and crime-scene personnel. I didn't follow. I didn't want to see any of that again. I just sat on the sofa in a pair of worn flannel pajama bottoms and a T-shirt so old and ratty that I'd had to retire it from day use, and watched as people moved around the apartment.

One of Madeline's lawyers arrived soon after that, a no-nonsense looking woman in her late forties. I don't know if she lived in Providence or had just happened to be in town, but from the looks of it she had interrupted a pretty fancy date. I'm sure she didn't mind, of course. Billable hours and all that. The boss cop (either he or one of his superiors was apparently angling for some kind of bonus attention from Madeline) had already been doing a good job making sure no one went near my room, but the lawyer took over from there, fussing over me briefly, then stepping back to hover expensively at a distance, glaring at anyone in a uniform who even glanced in my direction.

Suzume slipped into all of this chaos with surprising unobtrusiveness for a woman whose preferred spot was the center of attention. Saying nothing, which was a shock in itself, she sat down next to me on the sofa and squeezed my leg once. I shot her a grateful look, and after that we just sat there, neither speaking, as everything swirled in motion around us.

After almost two hours, a long gurney with a black body bag was wheeled out the door. I glanced away, but there was no way to forget any of what I'd seen tonight.

Matt walked up to me. He'd never taken off his jacket, something I'd noticed with the rest of the people in my apartment. He fit in with these people, I realized. Not that I should've been surprised—after all, he'd been a cop for years. But I was so used to seeing him working on stuff alone, with only me for the occasional help with a stakeout, that it was weird seeing him in a crowd. That's where he was meant to be, I reflected. With his own kind.

He glanced over at Suzume, who for once took a hint and cleared out, muttering something about hitting the bathroom. She didn't go there, of course. Just walked over to stand in the kitchen and fuss with a cupboard. Far enough to give the illusion of privacy, but I was quite aware that her exceptional hearing was trained completely on our conversation.

Matt hunkered down a little, putting us on the same level. I gave a brief nod to the attorney, who had automatically started over to hurry him away from me, and she stopped, though there was an unhappy look on her face. Maybe she got a bonus for every person she blocked from talking with me.

"They've picked up everything they can from the scene,"

Matt said. His voice was soft, but his eyes were very alert, darting over me, taking in everything about me. It reminded me again that I was on a high wire, and one false step could get Matt killed. My family had a very low tolerance for humans poking too close to unsavory truths. "I'm going to head out as well. I have a few friends in the department; might be able to call in a few favors."

I nodded. "Do you think you'll be able to get any information?" I asked.

He smiled grimly, less of a smile than a baring of his teeth. "I'm planning on it. Copies of everything I can get a hold of. After all, evidence has a way of getting lost around your family."

I didn't bother to try to deny it—a few calls from my brother or mother and files had a way of ending up in a shredder. "Can you tell me what you find?" Nothing short of a straightjacket would stop Matt once he started poking around. Better if I kept tabs on him, I figured. Besides, it wasn't a vampire killing, I reminded myself. If Matt got involved, there was nothing here that should bring him in contact with my family. Madeline ran her territory with an iron fist—there wasn't anyone living here in the supernatural community who would risk her wrath or my sister's version of enforcement by doing something like this near me. Chivalry had been confident enough of that on the phone that he wasn't even going to come out tomorrow to check up on me—that had to count for more than my own suspicions.

His salt-and-pepper eyebrows went up sharply. I'd surprised him. He gave me another of those considering, uncomfortably astute looks, then gave a quick nod and leaned closer, dropping his voice so that I was the only one who could hear. "There's a lot that only the lab can tell," he said quietly, "but your friend was killed somewhere else. If he'd been killed here, that room would've looked like a slaughterhouse, and it didn't. The only blood they've been able to pick up looks like it had dried on the body, then got rubbed off onto the floor. He lost almost all of his blood wherever it was that they killed him, and he'd been dead for a while before they moved him, judging by the rigor. Between the broken window and a few smudges that a uniform found, the working theory is that he was carried up the fire escape. Your friend isn't small—it would've taken two people to carry him. They broke the window to open it, threw him inside, and left. There are people waking up all of the neighbors right now, but so far it looks like no one saw anything."

"Thank you," I said, and meant it.

Matt looked me over again. "This wasn't casual violence, Fort," he said, and I could hear the undercurrent in his voice. "There's a lot of damage here, and nothing that could've been accidental. Did your roommate have any enemies?"

I shook my head. "Gage was a good guy."

Matt waited, and I knew what he wanted to ask me about. Any enemies I might have who would've done this. I wished that I could've been honest with him, but the last time I'd told the truth about what I was, my sister had slaughtered my foster parents in front of me. I stayed quiet, and after a minute of intense staring Matt's lip gave a small curl that I'd seen a thousand times before when he was frustrated about something, and he walked out.

When he left I let out a deep breath that I'd barely been conscious of holding. I'd spent a lot of time in the past few months doing my best to ignore the situation I was in with Matt. Having him here, seeing his newfound suspicion of me, was hard.

A hand dropped on my shoulder, and I looked up to see Suzume back at my side. I waited for the onset of questions about Matt, but again she surprised me when all she said was "Pack an overnight bag, Fort. We're getting out of here."

In our odd little friendship, I'd never seen Suzume's place before. But after loading me into her slick little Audi Coupé, that was where she took me.

I wasn't certain what to expect, but I didn't feel like talking, so we drove in silence completely across the city, from my nice little apartment in the aptly named College Hill section of Providence to the Silver Lake neighborhood. Silver Lake had its good sections and its bad sections, and it actually bordered Cranston, where my foster parents had lived. Suzume turned into an area filled with tidy little one-story houses that looked like they had all been built in the fifties. One thing I noticed was the significant increase in the greenery. All of the houses had at least a small yard, and most had a few trees in addition. We pulled into the driveway next to a small duplex. Judging by the position of the fences, the property extended about two feet beyond the driveway and the house, but looking out across it I could see nothing but darkness—definitely an unusual experience even in the more residential areas of the city.

I glanced around, then asked, "Are we near the park?"

The interior light came on as Suzume turned off the motor, so I could see her nod. "Yeah. The house is right up against one of the forested areas of the Neutaconkanut."

It was a grim night, but I managed a small smile as we both got out of the car. The Neutaconkanut Hill park was eighty-eight acres of mostly undisturbed forest and a few walking trails. Deer ran freely, and every once in a while there would be rumors about black bears. "I bet no one thinks twice about seeing a fox run through the neighborhood, then."

Suzume had walked ahead of me to unlock the door, but she tossed me a grin over her shoulder. "Definitely one of the perks of the place. You wouldn't believe what I had to pay, but it was worth it. My neighbor is in her nineties, and my cousins keep leaving competing bids in her mailbox. They're terrified that she'll leave it to one of her kids when she dies and they won't be able to get their hands on it."

"Would you want to live next door to your cousins?" I asked.

Suzume shrugged. "It's good to have family around. Besides, I've already talked the old woman's son into agreeing to sell it to me when she goes. Then I can make my cousins get into a bidding war with me, and I know how high they'll be willing to go."

We walked inside, and I had to raise my eyebrows. As the outside had suggested, it was a small house. Someone had remodeled, opening things up, and my first impression was a long main room that combined the living room and kitchen. There were three doors on the left-hand side of the room that I could see led to two bedrooms and a bathroom between, but Suzume's style of decorating had a heavy hand of whimsy, and I paused for a moment to take it all in.

The walls were a pale green, and silver leaves the size of my palm had been painted on them with no discernable pattern. The ceiling was blue, with painted fluffy clouds, something I'd seen before in some Newport mansions. The kitchen was extremely modern, with granite countertops and all the stainless-steel appliances that someone could wish for, but the cabinets had been liberally strewn with little white Christmas lights. There was a pair of comfortable-looking sofas set up around the television, both upholstered in bright red corduroy. At least a dozen pet beds of varying bold colors were strewn about, and there were enough throw pillows to build a working fort. An actual carousel horse was standing in the corner, painted black with gold flowers in its mane. Framed pictures were hung everywhere, containing everything from a really beautiful inked anime-style picture of a girl changing into a swarm of butterflies to a poster of, of all things, the periodic table. It was busy and energetic, the kind of room that I imagined would be hard to spend a lazy day watching TV in.

"It's nice," I managed. "Do either of those couches fold out?"

"Not the reaction I usually get," Suzume said, giving me a thoughtful look. "I'd better give you some recovery time before I start making jokes about sleeping arrangements."

"I'd really appreciate that," I said honestly.

Suzume led me to one of the bedrooms and waved me in. I looked around, a bit surprised. It was a big change from the main room. Decorated in restrained tones of white and chocolate brown, it looked like nothing so much as a moderately expensive hotel room. Even the bed looked like a hotel bed—a standard double covered in pristine white sheets and elegant decorative pillows with a neatly folded blanket at the bottom that perfectly matched the color of the walls and looked like no human had ever slept in it.

"I hadn't known you had a guest room," I said. "Thanks."

"Normally as a good hostess I would give you my room,

since my bed is queen-size, but I thought you'd like something with boring décor, rather than awesome."

I considered what the main room looked like and couldn't argue with her reasoning. As I put my duffel bag on a chair, Suzume pulled down the covers for me. I glanced over, and she patted the bed, giving me an encouraging smile.

I shook my head. I was beyond exhausted but ... "I don't think I can sleep right now," I said. The thought of lying in that inviting bed and having nothing to distract me from what had been done to Gage made me shudder.

"Give me one second," Suzume said, and was out the door before I could stop her. I could hear her banging around in the kitchen, opening and closing cabinets like she was looking for something. I shook my head a little and walked around the room. There were only two pictures in it, both framed black-and-whites. One was of a fox with two kits, and the other was clearly of Suzume as a young girl, maybe eight or nine, standing with another girl her own age who was too similar to be anything other than her twin sister, and an older woman who stood with a hand on each of their shoulders.

Suzume walked back in, holding a glass of pale green liquid that reminded me of Gage's energy drink. I gestured to the picture to distract myself. "Your family?" I asked.

She nodded. "Both pictures. Me, my sister, Keiko, and our mom."

I looked over at the fox photo. "Oh, so that's—"

"Yeah, that's us. I have a color version in another room, and you can see our fur. My mother's fur was dark red, almost cinnamon. Really pretty. Keiko's is the same." She handed me the glass. "Here, this will help you sleep."

"No, I'm fine." I tried to pass it back, but she pushed it into my hands insistently.

"Seriously, you're not going to do yourself any good by staying up and brooding. There's plenty of time for that after the sun rises. Drink it."

I looked down. The color had been a bit concerning at first, but up close it looked basically like the flavored water that my ex-girlfriend Beth had really liked. An exploratory sniff didn't reveal anything except a slightly sugary smell, so I took a cautious drink. The first sip didn't kill me—it tasted a little sweeter than I usually liked, but not bad—and Suze gave me an expectant look, so I shrugged and put the rest of it back.

I handed her the empty glass. "That's kind of licorice-y," I said. "Was it some weird kind of lemonade or something?"

"Nope, just absinthe," Suzume said calmly.

My jaw dropped. "*What*?" I sputtered.

"It's medicinal."

"It makes people go insane!"

"Please," she scoffed. "You barely had any."

I sat down heavily on the bed and dropped my head into my hands. "I'm pretty sure it's illegal, Suze."

"Not since 2007," she said in that blithe tone. "Stop being such a baby."

"I'm never drinking anything you hand me again. And I cannot believe you didn't tell me!"

"You didn't ask." She tugged my shoulder until I was sitting in the middle of the bed. "Get comfortable. Absinthe will sneak up you."

"All I could taste was sugar and licorice. You don't seriously expect that I'm about to pass out, do you?"

"With the night you've had, plus a drink that is twenty-five percent alcohol?" Suzume asked. "Yeah, I do."

That was the last thing I remembered, except for the feeling of Suzume pulling off my sneakers and settling the sheet over me. I didn't dream at all.

I was woken up suddenly again, this time by the sounds of a woman shrieking less than a foot from my ear. The sun was streaming in the windows now, so I'd been asleep for hours, but I felt bleary and disoriented, and it took me a few seconds to remember where I was and what had happened.

Standing over the bed was a woman who looked a lot like Suzume, but with a shorter and sleeker haircut, and she looked pissed as hell. She had one of those tiny purses that women carry in the evening, and she was winding her arm back in a way that made it clear that she was about to start smacking me with it.

Suzume appeared in the doorway, dressed in a pair of flannel sleep pants and a tank top, her long hair still rumpled from bed. She looked completely calm, though I noticed that she had a rather sizable knife in her left hand. She noticed me looking at the knife, and a moment later her hand was empty. I blinked, but couldn't figure out how she'd managed it.

"You're yelling like a bear who just found Goldilocks, Keiko," she said to the woman. "Calm down."

Keiko lowered her arm and glared at her sister. "I'm out for one damn night and you sublet my freaking room?"

"Oh, this is your room?" I said. "I'm so sorry. I thought this was the guest room."

Neither of them even glanced at me. I started to get out of bed, then realized that at some point after taking off my shoes, which I remembered, Suzume had also relieved me of my pants, which I had no memory of at all. I tugged the sheet back up.

Suzume rolled her eyes. "Christ, Keiko. Take a breath and use your nose. That's Fortitude Scott."

Keiko looked surprised, and gave a genteel little sniff in my direction, still managing to avoid making any eye contact with me. She sniffed again, then raised her eyebrows. "He doesn't smell like a vampire. It's there, but not like the others."

"He's still on his vampire learning permit," Suzume said.

I was starting to feel really awkward as I sat in the bed and the two women talked as if I wasn't there. "Uh, hi?" I tried. Neither even glanced at me.

"Yeah, I definitely smell it now," Keiko said, and there was a definite sneer in her voice. "That's never coming out of the sheets. What the hell is wrong with you?"

Suzume didn't look any happier than her sister. "If you'd been here on four feet like you were supposed to be, we could've discussed it. But you were out running around on two, so I made an executive decision." This was starting to sound like a personal argument, so I looked around. My pants were on the other side of the bed, crumpled up on top of my shoes.

"It was Corrine's bachelorette party. What was I supposed to do?" Keiko sounded defensive. I leaned down and snagged my pants, pulling them under the sheet.

Suzume's voice was very cold as she spoke to her sister. "Say no. Make any excuse, but say no. Don't go, and definitely don't spend the night with all your former sorority sisters." I paused in the act of trying to pull my pants on under the covers. I'd never heard Suzume give a lecture before. I was used to hearing her coax, cajole, or just outright insist, but this was definitely new.

"Fine. It won't happen again," Keiko said shortly.

"So, you'll be around the house today?"

Putting pants on under covers involves a certain amount of contortion and rolling around, and the whole situation was feeling a bit like some bad French farce.

Suzume's question had apparently crossed some invisible line, because Keiko swung straight back to fully pissed off. "No, actually," she snapped, "I'll be at the office doing the payroll. Do you have a problem with that too?"

"Takara agreed to handle that while you were—" She paused suddenly, and looked straight at me for practically the first time in the conversation. Typically she'd caught me at the worst possible moment, as I was just trying to wiggle my jeans up my ass, which had involved the kind of maneuver usually only seen when someone was drunk enough at a party to attempt to do the worm. I froze and looked back at her. Surprisingly, her expression was slanted and thoughtful, and she seemed to rethink whatever she had been about to say, and turned it into a very delicate and pointed "indisposed."

Keiko also looked over at me, and it was not a friendly look at all. It was probably the same look she'd give a cockroach right before stepping on it. I was suddenly missing the good times when they'd just pretended I didn't exist.

"I want to check up on her," Keiko bit out, and there was a clear note of finality in the statement. "Now, if you can get the slumber party out of my room, I can change and head out."

That last part was actually directed at me. "Yeah, sure, sorry again. But if you can just give me a sec—"

"OUT."

"Right." And with no other option and still blathering apologies, I rolled out of the side of the bed farthest from Keiko, yanked and zipped in a way that not only set new records for time but also risked my own personal future happiness, grabbed my shoes, and hurried past Suzume and out the door, which Keiko slammed so closely behind me that I had to make a quick hop to avoid getting hit with it.

I stood in the main room, breathing heavily and holding my shoes. This was definitely making my top-ten list of crappy ways to start the morning.

Suzume was frowning at the closed door, but as I looked at her she seemed to shake something off. She turned to me, gave me a thorough up-and-down glance, and that sneaky little smile started spreading across her face.

"Smooth, Fort. Smooth."

"Cram it, Suze," I said, turning away.

Suzume's amused heckling continued through both breakfast and a quick phone call to my mother's lawyer, who told me that the police were completely done with the apartment and that I could go back whenever I wanted. She suggested sending over a cleaning service, but I said that I would be fine on my own.

As much as Suzume could drive me up the wall, I was actually grateful for her ongoing jokes about the level to which I had completely dropped the ball on a situation that could have easily been misconstrued as the opening act of a porno movie. It distracted me from what we were driving toward. I think she knew that too, because as much fun as she'd been having, she dropped it completely as we pulled into the parking lot of my building.

There was still some police tape on my front door, and we pulled it down. Inside, things looked eerily normal in my living room, other than enough dirty shoe prints to indicate that half the Providence police force had tramped around. I hesitated for a second, then went into Gage's bedroom. Suzume followed closely behind.

Someone had taped a garbage bag over the hole in the window before they'd left, but the glass was still in the carpet. In addition to the dirty shoe prints, I could see a few dull brown smudges on the floor where I'd found Gage. Again, though, I was struck at how little evidence there was of what had happened. The bed was still made, his laundry was still in the hamper in the corner, and his backpack was propped up against his desk, which overflowed with notes and textbooks. Everything was here, except Gage.

I took a deep breath and blinked a few times. I didn't have time to fall apart. Looking for a distraction, I glanced over at Suzume. She was looking up at one of Gage's posters, a very thoughtful expression on her face. I nudged her with my elbow and raised my eyebrows.

She gestured at the poster, which was a print of the painting *Ecstasy*. "You usually don't see these outside the dorm rooms of freshmen girls with literary pretensions."

"Maxfield Parrish was his specialty," I said. "He was getting his master's degree in art history." I looked up at the picture, which was of a woman standing on the edge of a mountain with her dress billowing in the wind. I'd asked Gage about it once, assuming that it was an artsy version of a pinup picture, but then he'd talked about light and composition for a solid hour.

"Yikes," Suzume said, sounding appalled. "What did he hope to do with a degree like that?"

"Auction houses, restoration, appraisal. That kind of thing." Depression sat like a rock in my stomach as I stared at the poster. "I told him that we could wait tables together. What a jackass thing to say."

For a second my vision blurred, and I had to close my eyes very tightly. I felt the weight and warmth of Suzume's hand as she touched and then squeezed my shoulder.

"He was your friend," she said, and now she was utterly serious. "He understood."

I opened my eyes and saw that she was very close, barely an inch away. Her hand curled tighter, and now her arm was pressed against mine, a contact that seemed to resonate down into the bone. We both paused, and the air was charged.

I swallowed, moistening my suddenly dry throat. Focus, I thought. I need to focus.

"Suze—"

"Yes?" Her dark eyes were unreadable.

"Can you find who did this?" I asked. I'd spent my entire shower this morning trying to convince myself that Chivalry was right and it was just a coincidence. And that lottery tickets were great investments. I couldn't help it—it still felt like what happened to Gage had been meant for me.

For a second she looked surprised, then blinked and absorbed my request. "Sure, Fort. You know I can." She lifted an eyebrow. "But your private-eye buddy is already on the trail. Aren't you worried about us bumping into him?"

"We'll find out what he gets from the police; then we'll handle it ourselves. The less he's involved, the better." I wondered what the odds were of cashing out my checking account and sending Matt to Bermuda. Then I thought of my current balance and readjusted that to a cheap bed-and-breakfast in New Hampshire.

"No arguments on that, but why you even stayed in touch with him in the first place is kind of beyond—" I glared at her, and she threw her hands up. "Fine, fine. Don't regret the past—that's my motto on this one." She took a step back, then took a deep sniff. She tilted her head, narrowed her eyes, and sniffed again, this time dropping her mouth open and almost seeming to taste the air. I watched, always fascinated by how she worked.

Then she sneezed twice and quirked her mouth up in bemusement. "This would've been easier before the room got stuffed with cops. All I can smell is cheap aftershave. This is going to take forever to pick out the humans who did it."

I felt a small tug of relief. "Yeah, it had to be humans, right?" It was small, venal, and stupid, but I desperately didn't want to be the reason that Gage was dead.

"No one else is dumb enough to mess with someone living with Madeline Scott's son," she agreed; then she shot me a cautious look. "If we find these dicks, you're not going to get all Superman on me, are you?"

"What?"

"You know, wanting to leave them tied up in front of the police station and ready to confess their crime."

I snorted derisively. "I'm not an idiot, Suze. We find them, we kill them. The people who did that to Gage don't deserve to be called human anymore." And human murderers would mean that renting with me hadn't killed Gage.

She shot me a bright smile. "Excellent. Vigilante justice the way it was meant to be. Now give me a second while I slip into something a bit more furry."

Suzume went into the bathroom; then a moment later a fox trotted into the room, black everywhere except the perfect white tip of her tail. Her winter coat was coming in, replacing her sleek summer form with something reminiscent of a plushy doll. Her tongue lolled out of her mouth as she dropped her jaw in a fox version of a grin; then she immediately got to work.

I'd seen Suzume hunt for scents before in fox form, but it still impressed me when she began methodically working her way across Gage's room in a grid pattern. It was a slow process, and I sat on Gage's desk chair to watch as she worked. Her nose was moving constantly as she walked around slowly, her body hunched down almost to the floor. When she got to the spot where Gage's body had been, she slowed down even more, sniffing every inch of it. I swallowed and looked away when she rubbed her face carefully against one of the dried streaks of blood, reminding myself sternly that this was what I'd asked for.

Suzume made a small whine, and I snapped my head back around to look. Her eyes were slitted almost shut in concentration now, but she made that whine in the back of her throat again, and began walking very deliberately toward the window.

"Did you find something?" I asked.

She gave a low growl and shot me a look that very plainly told me to stop bothering her. I grimaced but shut my mouth. It was hard to keep it shut, though, especially when she stood on her hind legs to get a closer sniff at the window ledge, and even licked one spot. There was a pause, and then her eyes popped open and her fur actually stood on edge. She dropped down onto all four feet and just sat there, looking as stunned as a fox can. She turned to me and yapped loudly.

"What?" I asked, assuming that the interdiction on questions had just been raised.

She yapped again, a shorter and somehow more irritated version, and bounced up and down twice.

"Seriously, Suzume, I don't speak fox. You're going to have to mime this one."

She huffed out a breath, then got back up on her delicate hind legs, rested her front feet on the window ledge, and started wedging her head against the window itself.

"The window? You want me to open the window?"

She dropped down into a sitting position again and nodded her head slowly, rolling her eyes.

"Don't be like that," I scolded as I walked over and unlocked the window. I raised it cautiously, trying to make sure that no more glass fell. Suzume waited impatiently as I did so, making little foxy grumbles at the delay, then jumped neatly out and onto the fire escape as soon as there was enough room.

I leaned out and watched her as she gave the fire escape a thorough sniffing. It took a long time, and I noticed that she visited a few spots more than once, almost as if she was checking something. At last she seemed finished, and walked back to the window. She looked up at me and wagged her tail a little.

"What?" I asked. "Come on in."

More wagging, and she made a little crooning sound.

"Oh, no way." I said. "You jumped out, now jump back in."

Now she bent down until her belly was on the metal of the fire escape landing and gave me full-on sad eyes.

"Damn it," I muttered, and leaned out the window to pick her up and haul her back in. "Lazy jerk," I said as she wriggled happily, her tail beating against my leg. "Just wait until you're human and can talk again."

As I set her on the floor she gave a rather dismissive tail flip and padded back to the bathroom. I followed her, waiting at the bathroom door. When I heard the sink turn on and knew that she had hands again (and presumably a human mouth), I asked loudly, "You found something, didn't you? You found the smells of the guys who did this?"

"Not exactly," she said through the door.

"What?"

The door opened so abruptly that I nearly stumbled into

her. Suzume lifted an eyebrow, and I stepped back enough for her to come out.

"Seriously, Suze. Talk."

"Whoever broke the window and was carrying Gage's body wasn't human."

"Oh . . ." I paused for a long minute, trying to move past my initial gut reaction of *Oh, shit*. "Well, what was it? A vampire?" I'd known, *known*, that stupid vampire etiquette rules wouldn't stop Dominic from trying to get payback, but did my damn superior family listen—

"I don't know."

I stared at her. "You. Don't. Know."

She nodded grimly. "Yeah. Definitely not a vampire, but whatever it was, I've never smelled anything like it before."

I was so used to Suzume being an expert on all the supernatural stuff that I'd ignored for so long that this pretty much officially blew my mind. Also . . . "A creature you've never encountered before killed my roommate? Tell me that can't be a coincidence." Maybe Dominic was outsourcing vengeance.

Suzume shrugged and wobbled her hand in a so-so gesture. "Hard to say. There are plenty of nasties that Madeline banned from the territory, and a lot of them leave body trails. If one slipped in, then it was probably just an accident."

"An accident?" I asked disbelievingly.

"An accident in the way that a shark attack is an accident. A surfer is in the wrong place at the wrong time." Now she made a little chomp-chomp gesture with her hand. I thought back to what I'd seen of Gage's body and shuddered.

If Suzume wasn't able to identify this, then I knew who could. "Let me call Chivalry," I said.

She nodded. "Good plan. I'll go take a whiff around the base of the fire escape and see if I can get a trail."

"Do you need to go fox again for that?" Foxes were definitely not something regularly seen in College Hill. The last thing I needed was to have my neighbors start calling animal control at the sight of Suzume in her furrier form checking out the scene of the crime.

From the twinkle in her eyes, Suzume could clearly follow my train of thought. "Nah." She tapped her nose and grinned. "I've got the scent now." Then she wrinkled up her nose and made a face. "And I'm not worried about mistaking it for anything else. Whatever this thing is, it has a hell of a funk."

Suzume strolled out the door as I dialed Chivalry's number. He picked up on the second ring, and it didn't take long to fill him in on everything.

"The kitsune is in all likelihood correct, Fortitude," he said once I'd filled him in. "While most things that our mother has closed our borders to will stay out from a sense of self-preservation, there are some that still wander in and leave a few bodies. I have never personally encountered anything that kills in this way, so it's probably something very rare. In my experience, creatures like that are always on the move. Even if you go looking for it, it will probably have already left the area."

"So, we're not going to do anything at all?" I asked.

I could hear Chivalry heave a rather deep sigh on the other end of the line. "Mother's contacts with the police department have already located a pair of locals with rather unsavory pasts who have been convinced to confess to your roommate's murder, so this is tied up. If you wish to spend the next few days chasing shadows, then I certainly cannot stop you. Bhumika's doctor has advised that we stay in the hospital for at least four days, so I will be quite occupied for a time and sadly unable to either continue our training regimen or chaperone you on this endeavor. At least take along your annoying friend—I would hate for you to be all alone as you circle aimlessly." He paused. "My earlier assumption of human origins might have been wrong, but a supernatural component does not change my underlying point: accidents happen. Your roommate ran afoul of something on his own and was killed. If you could accept that forming these kinds of guilt-ridden attachments to humans you come into tertiary contact with is futile and self-destructive, you could step back and realize that this death has *nothing* to do with you. Send a wreath to the funeral, hire a cleaning service, and move on."

I gritted my teeth. Chivalry certainly wasn't pulling punches today. Knowing that he was sitting in a hospital bed beside his dying wife kept me from snapping back, but barely. My good-bye was on the sharp side, but it was as courteous as I could manage. After hanging up, I headed out to see what Suzume was finding, but met her halfway down the stairs as she was coming back up. She was shaking her head before I could even ask her what she'd found.

"Trail's dead," she said. "Whatever killed Gage, it has a car. The smells begin and end in one of the parking spots behind your building. It's alone, too, so it must be pretty damn strong to be slinging your friend around up a fire escape. Was your brother able to tell you what we're looking for?"

I told her about the Chivalry situation as we walked back upstairs. Inside the apartment, we both dropped down onto the sofa, which let out the tortured wheeze of cheap furniture being asked to go above and beyond its basic design parameters.

"Well, now what?" I asked.

Suzume shrugged. "The scent trail is dead, and usually when I'm trying to hunt someone down I at least have a description or a name. Think that private-eye buddy of yours might have something?"

I immediately shook my head. "Getting Matt any more involved is too dangerous. And now that we know that we're trying to chase something supernatural, nothing he finds from the police would even help us. I don't think profilers consider monsters when they make their suspect lists. I'll call him in a week, and if he's still looking I'll try to derail him. But odds are that he'll be either as dead-ended as we are or he'll believe that the real killers were already caught." I knew that the last part was wishful thinking. Maybe in a normal case that might've fooled him, but not in this one. He'd seen my family at work before, and he would've been counting the hours until a false confession was obtained and the case was officially closed.

"Well, where does that leave us?" Suzume asked. "Chasing shadows, like your brother said?"

I looked over at her. "Gage was a good guy," I said seriously. "He deserves more than he's getting. I'll look until I hit a brick wall, but I won't ask you to help me if you think it's a waste of your time."

Suzume made a little *tsk*ing sound, then reached over and flicked my nose with her finger, hard enough to sting and make my eyes water. I immediately clapped a hand over my abused nose and said, "What the hell was that for?"

"For being an idiot," she said, in that tone of voice that made the word *idiot* sound like the most loving of pet names. "You're my friend, so I'll help you. It's that easy."

I stared at her. "It's not that easy," I said. "You know it isn't."

She just smiled at me, her dark eyes gleaming. "Idiot."

Unwillingly, I could feel myself starting to smile back. It made no real sense, as the situation was almost as grim as it had been a minute before.

"So, what's our first move going to be?" Suzume asked.

I had already thought of this one. "We follow Gage's movements on his last night and try to figure out where whatever killed him found him." Assuming, of course, that my brother was actually right and it was just a coincidence that my roommate was monster killed. But I couldn't think of any other starting place.

Suzume quirked an eyebrow. "Oh, good. Some old-fashioned police legwork. Just what my weekend was lacking. Where do we start?"

"He told me that he was going speed-dating, so we'll start with that and see if he ever got there."

Suzume gave me a long and very unamused look. "I just filled my nose with crappy cop aftershave and now you want me to go smell the dregs of cheap perfume and desperation? Besides, I've seen your roommate. What was that tall drink of water doing going speed-dating?"

"He saw a flier and thought it would be fun. Tried to get me to go along, but I had to work."

Suzume shook her head. "Oh, he was clever."

"What? Why?"

She gave me that superior look that she always reserved for when she was going to lay a particular kind of knowledge down on me. In a classic Pavlovian response, I was gritting my teeth even before she started talking. "Basic rule of the dating scene, Fort. Always bring along a wingman, and that wingman should always be less attractive than you are. Personally, I use my cousin Hoshi." She leaned closer and dropped her voice to a stage whisper. "She has a great personality."

I glared. "Check my computer for speed-dating listings. I'll look in Gage's room and see if he still has the flier."

"Hate the game, not the player." Suzume tilted her head and looked at me. "You're willingly letting me use your computer. Change your passwords?"

"Twice," I said.

She smiled. "I wonder how long it'll take me to guess all of them."

# Chapter 4

A large part of my bravado in inviting Suzume to check my computer was a solid understanding of how anal Gage had been about updating his weekly planner. Sure enough, a quick check of Gage's desk revealed the planner, and neatly penciled into the spot for Friday evening was the name, time, and street address of where the speed-dating was held. I hauled Suzume off of my computer, where she'd already been hard at work trying to guess my new e-mail password, and we loaded into my car and drove out.

We were well before the lunch rush, so I found a parking spot right in front of the restaurant.

"Indigo, you said," Suzume said.

"Yeah, exactly." I nodded and started unbuckling my seat belt.

"And you think your plan is going to work?"

"Why wouldn't it? I talk to the staff to see if Gage ever got here or if he left with someone; you sniff around and see if you can pick up a trail." I stared at her, and she glared back at me. I threw my hands up in frustration. "Ten minutes ago you were fine with this plan!"

"Ten minutes ago I hadn't seen the restaurant."

"What could possibly be wrong with it?" I looked over. It was small, brick, with big green awnings and a few outside tables available for anyone who didn't mind a late-autumn chill with their lunch.

"Fort, the name is IndiGo."

"So?"

"We're twenty feet from the front door and I can't smell anything other than curry."

I looked from her to the restaurant. Sure enough, the front window proudly announced its authentic Indian cuisine.

"*Oh*," I said. I paused, then asked, "Now, are you really *sure—*"

"Fort!" There was a very distinct expression of outrage on her face.

"Okay, okay." I sighed heavily. "I guess I'll talk to the staff and you'll . . . supervise."

"Hrmph." Now she was looking thoroughly pouty.

I opened the Fiesta's door to get out, and had to admit, there was a distinct whiff of curry in the air. My stomach growled loudly, reminding me that we were beating the lunch crowd, but not by too much. I glanced over again cautiously. "Unless . . . I'll talk to the staff . . . and you can buy lunch to go?"

"Don't push your luck."

Suzume did eventually relent and grab lunch while I was busy getting information out of the IndiGo manager. By posing as a fresh-faced cub reporter for the business section of the *Providence Journal*, I'd been treated to a long rendition on the ways that speed-dating sucked at drawing in business.

"I would've thought that it would've been a bonanza in liquor sales," Suzume commented around a bite of her roti wrap. We were sitting in the parked Fiesta, eating lunch, while I filled Suzume in on what I'd learned.

"Apparently just a few sales on appetizers. I guess people on five-minute dates don't want to spend a lot of time chewing."

"Exactly. That's why they should've been spending a lot of time drinking."

I rolled my eyes and took another big bite out of my aloo gobi curry. One of the best things about Indian food, in my opinion, was how well it catered to vegetarianism. "Yeah, the manager was disappointed too. Really took a chunk out of his bottom line. Twenty tables taken up from six to seven-thirty, plus all the disruption from the egg timers going off and people moving seats, and apparently they even had to make room for a table to sell tchotchkes and gifts. The manager said that he'd rather take a swim down the Blackstone River than do this again."

Suzume snorted. "He really said that?" The Blackstone River was one of Rhode Island's claims to fame, declared by the EPA in the nineties to be the most polluted river in the country. Providence had spent years dumping industrial sewage into one of its tidal extensions, but it was still a rather resonating event for most members of the Ocean State. After all, who would've thought that something was dirtier than the Hudson?

"Made sure I even wrote it down so that I could quote it correctly in the paper."

"Hm." Suzume shrugged, then nudged me with her elbow. "What was the thing about the tchotchke table?"

I pulled my notebook out of my pocket and checked it again. "Turns out that they didn't do this on their own. There's this New Age store called Dreamcatching," Suzume's massive and completely predictable eye roll made me laugh; then I got back to the notes. "They're the ones coordinating the speed-dating. They get the people, collect fees—the whole thing. Apparently they've been doing a whole bunch of them around the city over the past year. The restaurant is ensured business for the night, and the Dreamcatching people set up their table with candles and pretty rocks and the usual crap to try to get extra business."

"Does the guy remember seeing Gage?"

"Doesn't remember anyone other than one cougar who was the only one who ordered any drinks and ended up vomiting on the floor of the women's bathroom. None of the servers from last night are on shift now. But the IndiGo guy says that there were two people hosting the speed-dating, both from the other store."

"Ah, and I assume that you got names?"

I smiled. "Yup. Tomas Doubrant and Lilah Dwyer. If they were running it, one of them probably would remember Gage."

Suzume balled up her roti wrapper and tossed it into the

backseat of my car, which I would've been more irate about had it not joined half a dozen similar comrades of fast food. "Great. So the next station of the cross for my poor nose will be crappy incense. Onward."

"Don't grumble, Suze," I said. "If you're really good, I'll buy you a sparkly geode."

Suzume's retort was mercifully lost in the grinding sound of the Fiesta's engine struggling to turn over.

Dreamcatching was everything I expected it to be. Books on harnessing inner power or earth goddesses lined the walls, while the rest of the store was devoted to awkwardly placed displays filled with colorful (and, from the advertisements "powerful focuses for psychic energy") rocks, selections of incense, sparkly scarves, cheap pewter jewelry, and racks of CDs that boasted themselves to be entirely whale song or wolf howls. The walls were hung with more than enough dream catchers to justify the business name, and there was a pervasive aura of smug self-congratulation posing as spirituality that set my teeth on edge.

"I want to shove a handful of lit incense sticks up the owners' noses and see how they like it," Suzume muttered behind me. "Get information fast so that we can get out of here." Clearly she was also not a fan.

With Suze staying by the door and exhibiting no intention whatsoever of taking one step farther, I headed up alone to the main counter. The woman behind it looked around my own age, and gave me a friendly smile with only a hint of mercantile intention. Her hair was the color of a shiny new penny, a bright coppery gold, and was braided around her head like a crown, but strands seemed determined to escape, making it look like a somewhat fuzzy halo. Her complexion was a true redhead's, with freckles trailing over both cheeks and her forehead, light brown pinpoints that formed their own constellations on the map of her skin. Her eyes were large, and as I walked closer I saw that they were a bright, almost golden brown. She was dressed in a long, gauzy green skirt, the kind with layers and embroidery that my ex-girlfriend had been a fan of. She'd paired it with a rather plain cream blouse whose scooped neck revealed just the top of her collarbone (along with another universe of freckles) but that fit well enough to reveal a nice hourglass figure.

Apparently my perusal had been too much on the obvious side, and her smile widened in amusement, crinkling her nose. Caught, I could feel my face reddening, and I cleared my throat and pretended to closely examine the contents of the counter display case.

"Interested in tarot cards?" she asked. Her voice matched her hair—almost fluorescently chipper. I obediently examined them.

"No, not really. But I'm sure that they're really nice and, you know. Tarot-y." I kicked myself internally.

"How about jewelry? We have necklaces, rings, and bracelets in every shade of pewter."

I glanced up and saw a twist of irony in her smile and a refreshing twinkle of cynicism in her eyes. It was like bumping into an agnostic at a Bible revival, and I relaxed and grinned back at her. "I'm sure that pewter has all sorts of inherent earthy powers."

She laughed. "We're happy to say it does, at least." Then she tilted her head slightly and asked, "Did your girlfriend drag you in here? That happens a lot. I've suggested putting a pile of sports magazines by the door, like in a doctor's office, but my boss shot it down."

I glanced automatically back at Suzume, who had somehow acquired a pen and was writing something on one of the many fliers attached to the bulletin board. I shuddered at the thought of what she was composing, and forced myself to put it out of mind and look back at the counter girl. "Oh, Suze isn't my girlfriend," I assured her. She gave me a somewhat skeptical look, and I hurried to elaborate. "We've never even dated." The thought of dating Suzume, I reminded myself, should be enough to frighten years off of the life of any red-blooded American man. It should definitely not be remotely enticing.

Apparently I hadn't quite convinced the counter girl either, since she raised one feathery copper eyebrow and said, "Really?"

Clearly I wasn't going to win here, so I hurried to change

the subject. "Actually, I'm looking for someone. Are either Tomas Doubrant or Lilah Dwyer here? I have a few questions about the speed-dating they ran last night."

She dropped her Scully-like expression of skepticism and went back to smiling. "Then you're in luck, because I'm Lilah, the store manager."

There was the smallest hint of self-deprecation in the way she'd said her title, and I found myself fighting a smile. "Impressive."

Lilah made a face and shrugged off the compliment. "Four people work here. I wasn't exactly fighting my way to the top. Tomas owns the store, but he's not in today." She tilted her head again and gave me a more thorough once-over. I did my best to subtly flex. "I don't remember you from the speed-dating last night, but"—she grinned again— "of course, I was running the merchandise table, so you might've been running in the other direction."

"Candles and shiny rocks?" I guessed.

"We also had a sign-up sheet for classes about harnessing your personal bubble of living energy," she said seriously, then laughed at whatever expression crossed my face.

"What a thought," I said, striving for blandness in my tone. "No, actually my friend Gage was planning on going, and I'm just trying to find out if he ever arrived."

Lilah immediately dropped her smile and looked concerned. "Oh, I'm sorry. Did something happen?"

I cleared my throat, considered, and lied. "Yeah, he's . . . missing. I'm just trying to track him down." In this ridiculous store, talking to a girl who practically radiated wholesomeness, it felt wrong even saying the word *murdered*, as if that would make Gage's death real on a level that touching his body and having cops swarm my apartment hadn't.

"Can you describe him?" she asked, helpfulness radiating off of her.

"Tall, blond, kind of built, mid-twenties."

Recognition immediately bloomed across Lilah's face. "Oh, THAT guy. Yeah, he was definitely there."

"You remember him?"

"Sure. He made a big impression on the female participants. It was kind of like chumming shark-infested waters. I was sending out the e-mails this morning to the participants, and pretty much every woman asked to have her info sent to him." Lilah considered for a moment, then asked tentatively, "I'm sure you're really worried about him, but have you thought about whether he went home with someone? People aren't supposed to do it at the dating events, but I know that sometimes they slip phone numbers to each other." She shrugged, dropped her voice, then said almost apologetically, "It seemed like a really nice group, but sometimes when one person is so obviously popular a few of the daters try to . . . you know . . . make an impression. There have been a few incidents."

Lilah's expression suggested that those incidents were weird, probably sexual, and definitely good storytelling, and I was about to ask for details when Suzume walked up beside me, apparently done with whatever form of vandalism she'd come up with to occupy her attention. She opened her mouth to say something, then suddenly stopped, frowned slightly, and peered hard at Lilah. She leaned across the counter, well into Lilah's personal space, and gave a very obvious sniff. A wide, slightly malevolent smile spread across her face, reminding me of the cartoon Grinch, and she said, "Well, if it isn't one of Santa's little helpers."

Lilah went completely white at the statement, her freckles suddenly stark against the pallor of her skin, and her hands flew instinctively to her hair, patting frantically at the braid that circled her head. "I have no idea what you're talking about," she said thinly, even as the patting continued.

Suzume snorted. "Oh, give it a rest, halfsie." She rolled her eyes at me, as I continued to attempt to puzzle out what exactly was happening. "If it wasn't for the level of patchouli funk in this place, I would've smelled it earlier." At Lilah's persistent hair groping, Suze gave a rather mean smile and said, "Don't look so horrified. You didn't flash an ear. Let's get this thing rolling. I'm"—she pointed at her chest—"a kitsune, and he's"—now the finger went in my direction—"a vampire."

I choked. Apparently all secret identities were off.

It didn't seem possible, but Lilah got even paler and

shuffled backward. "Chivalry Scott?" she squeaked, like she'd just been introduced to the boogeyman.

Trying to recover myself, I hurried to correct her. "No, no, that's my older brother. I'm Fortitude Scott." I paused, then added lamely, "Everyone calls me Fort." The statement hung there in the air for a long minute.

It did have the positive effect of returning some of the color to Lilah's face, and she sounded surprised as she said, "Oh, I didn't know about you." Then she realized what she'd just said and scrambled to cover it up, talking quickly and in the tone that girls use when they've implied that a guy has a small penis. "But I don't know much about the vampires at all. I mean, Tomas is the one who handles the store tithes."

"Tithes?" I asked. Clearly my brother had left something out.

Suzume gave another eye roll. "Fifteen percent of earnings off the top go to Madeline Scott, Fort. Jeez, I thought Chivalry was filling you in on this shit." She leaned back across the counter and said to Lilah, in a very loud faux whisper, "Don't worry about him—he's still new."

In an almost normal tone of voice, Lilah said, "Huh. I never really thought of vampires as new."

I smiled reassuringly, hoping to reclaim our earlier rapport. "That's because the rest of my family qualifies as antique." She smiled back at me, amused.

Suzume looked from me to her, then gave a very blustery sigh. "Good grief." She shook her head, then pushed back to business. "Anyway, something killed Fort's buddy last night. We don't know what, but it wasn't human."

"God, that's awful," Lilah said, then looked over to me and said, with almost charming earnestness, "I'm so sorry," and actually sounded like she meant it.

"Thanks," I said. "I'm just trying to figure out what happened."

"Of course." Lilah nodded, then frowned, clearly thinking very hard. "The blond, I mean Gage, he was there for the whole event. The speed-dating ended at seven-thirty, and people left really quickly. I remember that Gage was at the merchandise table and looked things over, but he didn't

buy anything, and I'm pretty sure that he left on his own."
The frown deepened. "I didn't talk with him ... No, I just
don't remember." She looked back at me. "I'm so sorry.
There were just too many people."

"Was there anyone there who wasn't human?" I asked.

"Me, of course, and Tomas—he's like me." Here she
stumbled a bit, then blushed. Apparently this wasn't a usual
conversation topic for her.

"Yes, yes, halfsie," Suzume said impatiently, making a *Go
on* motion with her hand.

Lilah glared. "We prefer to be called the Neighbors," she
said stiffly. Then she gave a small shrug and her glare dis-
solved into a self-mocking expression. "Not that it really
matters to you. But, yeah, we're both half-bloods. Tomas is
a first-generation; I'm second."

"Second generation?" I was confused. I'd had one brief
encounter with a half-breed elf before, and both Suzume
and my brother had given me a sketchy background on the
species, but this was like trying to go from a Psych 101
course to a graduate seminar—I was lost on most of the
terminology.

"Both my parents are half-bloods," Lilah explained, then
shrugged again. "It doesn't really make a difference, but you
know how people are. When my parents were little, all of
the half-bloods had human mothers. But then there were
enough that they could marry each other, and now, with
people my age ... The Neighbors make a big deal about the
ones who had human mothers." She sighed. "It's all Gilded
Age snobbery, really. Like the millionaires whose parents
had made money looking down on the nouveau riche."

"And back on the topic of why we're here ..." Suzume
hinted loudly. I winced a little as Lilah blushed. I'd been
interested in what Lilah was saying, but at the same time,
Suzume was right. We were here about Gage, not for cul-
tural anthropology.

"Uh, yeah," Lilah smiled apologetically, then concentrated again. "As far as I know, the only people there who
weren't human were me and Tomas. But"—she spread her
hands helplessly—"it's not like I'd know if someone wasn't.
I don't have a fox's nose."

"You wouldn't know at all?" I asked.

"Just if it was another of the Neighbors, and only because I'd see their glamour."

"You all have one?" Okay, maybe there was a little time for my inner anthropologist.

"For some of us it's small," Lilah said. She glanced around almost reflexively, but the store was just as deserted as when we'd come in. Reassured, Lilah leaned across the counter toward me, then pushed her braid up slightly, exposing her right ear. I looked, curious, but it was a perfectly average ear. There was a short pause while Lilah closed her eyes and bit her lip, concentrating, then something changed. It was almost like the kind of heat shimmer I'd seen on pavement on record-hot days in the summer, but for just a moment that round, average ear became sharply pointed. It was thinner at the base than a human ear, and along the back of it there was the slightest hint of fur that matched her copper hair, reminding me of a cat's ear. Then I blinked and it was a regular human ear again, but there was something wrong with it now. Now it was as if that round ear was just a wispy front, and if I concentrated I could almost see that real ear again.

Lilah tugged the braid back into place, covering up most of her ear again. She smoothed it nervously with her hand, in the kind of reflexive motion I guessed she did hundreds of times a day. I looked back at her face, feeling oddly like she'd just accidentally flashed cleavage and we were both aware of it and now trying to ignore that it had happened. She patted her hair again. "For most of us, that's all we can do," she said, and met my eyes. I was struck again by how brilliant her eye color was, and I wondered what part of her ancestry had supplied it.

Suzume broke the moment when she asked, very slyly, "A few of you need something more, though, don't you? More than just a little ear muffling."

"What do you mean?" Lilah looked nervous. I reflected that she was probably not a great poker player.

"Don't play dumb," Suzume scoffed. "There are more than half-bloods running around."

Lilah nodded reluctantly. "It's not a secret; we just don't

talk about it much to outsiders." Suzume snorted loudly, apparently taking issue with Lilah's use of the term *much*.

"Lost? Really lost?" I complained, feeling irritated at being left out. Apparently spending a summer with Chivalry hadn't brought me nearly as much up to speed as I'd assumed.

"I thought the vampires knew," Lilah said, looking surprised.

"I only got involved in this kind of stuff a few months ago," I explained. "I'm picking some things up as I go."

"Oh, well—" Lilah paused at a small tinkling sound, and a moment later the beaded curtain behind the counter below the prominently displayed Employees Only sign rustled. A woman emerged—around the same age as Lilah, maybe a little younger, since she looked like she would be carded every time she ordered a drink. Her hair was very curly, cut just above her shoulders, and the kind of brilliantly glossy gold that should've been the result of coloring products but somehow seemed like it wasn't. It took me a second to look beyond her hair, just from the sheer visual impact of it, but glancing at her face made me recoil slightly. There was a severe sharpness to her features that a runway model would've envied, but it was more than just the angles themselves—there was something that made me think of big predatory lizards, and her thin lips were pressed together in a way that reminded me strongly of the way that my mother sometimes held her mouth to carefully conceal her fangs. The last thing I noticed was probably the first thing I would've on any other woman: her giant, heavily pregnant belly. I didn't spend much time around pregnant women, but it was clear even to me that she was ready to drop at any time.

Lilah looked over at her and asked, "Allegra, do you need something?" Her voice confirmed the age difference— the tone and familiarity made me wonder if she'd been Allegra's babysitter at some point in years past.

Allegra looked annoyed, but gestured vaguely at me and Suze. "You can finish with them. I just need something off of one of the upper shelves and"—she patted her gigantic belly—"probably not a great idea to climb for it."

"I'll be back in a second," Lilah promised. With a nod, Allegra turned and left, moving with a decided waddle, which only had the unfortunate effect of increasing her eerie resemblance to a komodo dragon. I looked over to Suzume, wondering what her reaction was, and noticed that her eyes were almost slits as she examined Allegra speculatively, and I was close enough that I could see the slight twitch of her nostrils as she sniffed.

When the tinkling sound came again, clearly the result of bells attached to some back door, Suzume spoke. "So, that's one of your three-quarter jobs. Definitely different. She's got glamour caked on her like a transvestite's makeup job, and she's still barely passing for human."

Lilah definitely didn't like that comment, and there was a warning edge as she said, "Allegra is a nice girl, and Tomas's daughter." Suzume raised a mocking eyebrow, and Lilah flushed but didn't back down, clearly protective of the younger woman. "I've got to get back to work." Her tone had a definite snap to it.

I nudged Suzume with my elbow, making her bite back whatever comment she'd been about to make, and inserted my own. "Okay, thanks for your time. If you think of something else, will you give me a call?"

She paused for a long second, assessing my level of culpability in Suze's comments, then relented and nodded. "Yeah, I can do that. I'm sorry your friend died, but I just don't know how much help I can be. Whatever killed him, it did it after he left the restaurant." She handed me a piece of paper and a pen, and I wrote down my name and cell phone number. Lilah took it, glanced quickly at it, then folded it and tucked it into a pocket in her skirt. "Good luck," she said, but it was clearly a dismissal.

I thanked her and we left.

Back at the car we both buckled in, but then just sat, lacking a direction. Our last lead on Gage had just gone up in smoke.

Something was clearly on Suzume's mind. She looked at me thoughtfully, then said, "So, that's your type, huh? Kinda granola and yogurty? Making sure that her deodorant is earth-friendly?"

I flushed. "I don't know what you're talking about."

Suze poked me playfully in the side. "Seriously. It was like I was in the middle of some meet-cute setup. But that's the type of girl you usually go for?"

Giving in, I considered her question. It was true that my ex-girlfriend Beth had been about as granola as possible, from her very militant veganism to her clothing choices to her enthusiastic support of cannabis laws. I wasn't sure where Lilah fell on the first or the last, but in terms of clothing she and Beth were probably shopping in the same places. "I guess." Certainly before Suzume had come over there had been a noticeable level of bantering going on.

"Hm." Suzume turned to look out the window.

Suddenly getting where the drift of this conversation was going, I immediately tried to cover my tracks. "I mean, not exclusively. Just kind of happens. I mean—"

Suzume gave a little shrug. "No, it's cool. Everyone has a type."

With a little desperation, and not actually kidding, I said, "Your hair is really pretty today, Suze."

That made her laugh, and just like that the weird tension was broken and things returned to normal. After a moment's silence I asked, "What was all that fuss about a three-quarter something?"

"Just curiosity. There are only a handful of the real elves left—like, think single-digit levels. They're frantic to breed themselves back up, but all the females are gone."

"Gone?"

Suzume nodded. "Gone. Don't know what happened, because they won't talk. So the elves get it on with human women to make a halfsie. Works okay, but the result is just like what your buddy back there is—pretty weak. She's a human with a pocket's worth of glamour and pointy ears. But breed a weak little halfsie to a full elf and you get . . ."

"A three-quarter," I finished, comprehension finally hitting.

"Yup. They're still rare. That one back there is the first I've ever seen close-up. I heard a rumor that the first crop of them just hit their twenties. Probably why this one is pregnant. Must be labor-intensive work to breed back a species."

She glanced over to me, a huge smile on her face. She wiggled her eyebrows broadly and nudged me. "Get it?"

I refused to acknowledge the pun, partially out of jealousy that I hadn't thought of it first, and resolutely turned the conversation back to the topic. "Why is it that every time we talk about elves, we start talking about breeding?"

She snorted. "Because halfsies are head cases and full elves are sociopaths, just like I've told you before. I'm not sure where the three-quarter jobs fall, but my bet is farther up the crazy scale."

I paused for a moment, considering this comment against the way that her normally taunting and borderline antagonistic behavior had taken on a newer, sharper edge against the completely innocuous Lilah. "You don't like the elves, do you?" I asked.

"I don't," she said without hesitation. "I have to deal with them sometimes, but it's not something I'd go out of my way to do." Suze eyed me, then said, "When that girl back there calls you for a date, just keep in mind what kind of in-laws you're dealing with."

"What? Suze, I just gave her my number because of Gage. I gave my number to the guy at IndiGo too, and I sure wasn't hitting on him." I paused, considered the situation, then asked carefully, "Why, did it look like I was hitting on her?"

"Like I said, Fort. Meet cute." Suzume checked her watch. "So, now that we're shit out of leads, how about we fumigate my nose? We passed a bakery down the street."

"Are you always hungry?" Hosting Suzume was already proving to be a drain on my wallet, and I winced.

"I'm a fox, Fort. We're opportunistic predators."

"Meaning that you're always hungry as long as I'm buying."

She smiled. "We can discuss that further when you get me a cannoli."

In a good film noir, running out of leads would've resulted in a cinematically significant rainstorm and maybe some ruminating at the bottom of a bottle of whisky, finally punctuated by the entrance of a femme fatale. For me, though, it resulted in finally having to do what I'd put off: I called Gage's parents to express my sympathy. It was a painful phone call, made more so because of just how very nice they both were to me. They were trying to find some comfort in the fact that Gage's "killers" had been caught. I didn't like the lie, but I hoped that it would at least give them a little closure. I knew they were dreading a trial, but at least they'd be spared that. Madeline never let any of her frame jobs go that far—there would be a tragic accident in the prison very soon, to tie up any potential loose ends.

Trying to appease some of my own guilt, I offered to box up all of Gage's stuff for them, which they accepted. His parents had moved from Rhode Island down to Key West about three years ago, after his dad retired, and this would at least save them a trip up here. They promised to make arrangements for a moving van to pick up the boxes and Gage's car in a few days, and after a few more painful minutes of conversation, I said good-bye and hung up.

Suzume was stretched out on the sofa, openly listening to the call, and lifted an eyebrow. "So," she said, "I guess you'll need some help."

I couldn't help being a little surprised. "I knew you said you'd help me look for Gage's killer, Suze," I said, "but if you don't want to do this, you don't have to."

She shrugged, stood up, gave a bone-defying stretch, then smiled crookedly at me. "I meant what I said before, Fort. I'll help you. Even if it's boring."

I stared at her for a long second, trying to read into her inky black eyes. Finally I shrugged helplessly and just said, "Thank you."

She nodded. "If you give me your keys I can go down to the grocery store and get some boxes. That way you can get a start on sorting things."

"Thanks," I said, tossing her the keys. Then I went into Gage's room and took a long look around, seeing all of his stuff just sitting there. For a moment I felt stuck, unable to take the first movement of breaking down his room and removing the last parts of my friend from my life.

There was a small scuff of a shoe, and I turned to see Suzume leaning in the doorway, watching me. There was so much sympathy and empathy in her eyes that I was almost viscerally reminded of how foolish it was to ever assume that I'd figured her out.

"While I'm out," she said, very gently, "you should probably take the chance to find and dump your friend's porn."

I gaped, and she gave that familiar slow smile. I couldn't help it—I laughed. At the sound of it, Suzume gave a little *my work is done here* gesture and sashayed out the front door.

I turned back to the task, feeling lighter. Gage would've laughed at that joke, I knew. And he also would've recognized, as I did, that there was a certain truth to the matter. So the first thing I did was check under the bed, then at the bottom of his closet, then in his bottom drawer, and when I found the box I was looking for, I immediately walked it out to the Dumpster.

We spent the rest of the day boxing things up. Knowing that his parents might take a long time to unpack on the other end, and wanting to spare them anything unexpected, Suzume and I took much more care with the packing than I think either of us had ever taken with ourselves. Everything was completely sorted into similar boxes—there would be none of my usual moving experience, where I'd just throw toiletries in the same box as winter sweaters. We also wrote out inventories of each box—both on the side in black Sharpie marker and on included sheets of paper.

"This must be how Martha Stewart packs," had been Suze's only comment when I'd told her the idea. Other than that, we hadn't talked much.

Other than one quick pizza run around eight, we worked without pause. By the time we'd finished it was almost one in the morning and we were both completely wiped out. Suze and I sat on the floor of the room, staring at the results of our work. The bed frame and mattress were the only items that had belonged in the apartment, but everything else had been stripped down and packed. We'd even taped cardboard around Gage's dresser to prevent it from getting scratched up during its trip down to Florida.

"This is why I bought a house," Suzume said after taking

a long swig of her beer, then failed to control her shudder. I felt a brief twinge, remembering that my last conversation with Gage had been about me buying shitty beer. "I got so sick of having to pack up all my stuff."

"Yeah, it does suck," I admitted. "Last year my landlord jacked up my rent. I got incredibly pissed off and started looking for a new apartment, but then I remembered what a pain in the ass moving is, and . . ."

"Knuckled under?"

"It was the three flights of stairs with no elevator that did it."

Suzume nodded sagely and took another drink. The silence between us was comfortable.

"So," Suze said after a long minute, "are we crashing here or heading back to my place?"

I thought about it. I'd swept up the broken glass basically on autopilot, and Suze had scrubbed the tiny blood stains while I'd packed Gage's clothing. Once those two signs had been gone the room had looked so deceptively normal that it was easy to imagine that Gage had just left without warning. Keeping busy had helped me ignore the thought of Gage's body lying on the floor just last night, but it all came flooding back at Suze's question. I looked over at the window, with its taped garbage bag. There was a small but noticeable breeze, and I wondered whether my landlord would actually have it fixed before winter.

"You don't have any of your stuff. I wouldn't want you to be uncomfortable," I offered.

"I threw an overnight bag in your trunk this morning while you were showering," Suze said calmly.

"Oh, good." I paused. "You'd be uncomfortable, though. I don't have any sheets that would fit this bed." Gage's room had a double, but I made do with a single mattress.

"Nah, I'm good with the couch." Suze continued looking at me.

I thought for a second. "Suze, do you want us to stay here?"

"That's not what's important. The real question is, do *you* want to stay here?"

I considered, then answered slowly. "This is more than

just tonight. You're asking if I'd be okay living here, even though I found Gage's body here."

She shrugged. "We packed up everything Gage owned in a day. I could go get some more boxes and we could have you out before Monday."

"Do you think I should want to go?"

She shook her head. "I'm not saying you should want one thing or another. I'm saying that if you don't want to stay here, we'll pack you up and move you out. If you do want to stay here, I'll go put my jammies on and crash on your couch. There's no right answer, Fort."

It took me a long time. While I thought, Suze just sat quietly, her eyes almost closed, taking small sips of her beer, looking completely relaxed.

Finally, I said, "Go get your jammies."

She nodded once. "Okay." She stood up and stretched, then looked down at me. "Probably the better choice anyway. Three flights of stairs would've made moving a real bitch."

I woke up once that night, one of those abrupt surges into wakefulness. I lay perfectly still for long minutes, straining my ears, but I heard nothing beyond the usual night sounds of the apartment. I retrieved the Colt from its hiding place under my bed and walked into the living room, intending to check Gage's room.

In the glow from the streetlight streaming in from the windows I could see the black fox on my sofa, completely dark except for the brilliant white tip of her tail. Her paws were tucked under her, and her head rested on the arm of the sofa as she watched the open door to Gage's room. I knew she heard me, because one of her long furry ears twitched sharply in my direction, swiveling like a radar dish. After a moment she turned to look at me, and I could see the gleam of her dark eyes. She wagged her tail twice, making a soft little thump against the nest of sheets and quilts I'd made for her, then turned back to continue her watch.

I felt a warm sense of comfort. I backed out of the room as quietly as I could. I thumbed the Colt's safety back on and slid it under the bed again. As I got under the covers, I called out, once, "Suze?" and heard her immediate yip of acknowledgment. When I closed my eyes again, I slid back into a dreamless sleep.

The next morning the night's interlude seemed like something I might've imagined, but when I went into the living room I saw the black fox sleeping peacefully in exactly the position I remembered her. She woke up while I started putting together breakfast, padded into the bathroom, and returned on two feet, dressed in a T-shirt and a set of red argyle lounge pants. Her hair had that kind of sleepily mussed yet sexy look that I'd secretly always considered a Hollywood trick, given that every woman I'd previously seen first thing in the morning had looked like they'd been caught in the middle of a windstorm. Beth had been particularly notable in that department, as the perfect Grecian curls of her hair had required a really frightening level of maintenance and preparation before they were ready to be seen by the world.

I'd made cheese omelets, and I slid one onto a plate and handed it to Suze. She nodded her thanks, and we spent a few minutes with no sounds filling the air other than those of mastication.

Eventually I glanced over at Suze, cleared my throat, and brought up the elephant in the room. "You were up all night watching Gage's room. Did you think that whatever killed him was going to come back?"

"Fort, if I'd thought that thing was coming back, there's no way I would've let you trot out off to bed. We would've been waiting for it with extensive firepower." Suze took a long swig of orange juice.

"Then why—"

She frowned. "Sometimes shit happens, Fort, and people get killed. Meteors fall out of the sky, texting teenagers plow SUVs into pedestrians, and roaming monsters get hungry and are too lazy to just order takeout. It's not personal; it's just bad luck. I still agree with your brother that it was a sucky coincidence that it happened to be *your* roommate. But it's been bugging me that whatever did this dumped Gage's body in his own bedroom."

I nodded. That particular thought had been very uncomfortably itching at the back of my own brain. "I was thinking that it might've looked in his wallet and found the address. We don't know if it robbed him as well."

"It's possible," Suze acknowledged. "Maybe even likely. Most things that prey on humans will mix a mugging with dinner. But to specifically return Gage's body to his own room is kind of excessive."

"It's almost like a sick sense of humor," I said. Suze nodded grimly, taking another mouthful of eggs. I considered what we knew again and asked, "You keep referring to food. Do you think that whatever killed Gage wanted to eat him? I mean"—and here I gulped a little, regretting that I'd made this a breakfast discussion—"most of him was still there."

"You told me that his hands were gone," Suze pointed out. "And your detective buddy told you that most of Gage's blood was gone. I called my grandmother after you passed out like a sorority girl after one drink." I protested the characterization indignantly, but she just continued talking over me and I had to give up. "Grandmother said that there are lots of things that would drink blood, even besides your family, but the hands have her a bit stumped as well."

I deliberately ignored the pun. "Gage's hand wasn't bitten or ripped off. It was sliced."

"Then I have less than no idea, Fort," Suzume said. "But it didn't seem like the worst idea in the world to keep an eye on you last night."

"I do appreciate that," I said, and I meant it.

"You could appreciate it even more by making me some bacon."

"I have a whole package of tofu in there. I can fry it up and you could pretend."

Perhaps it was a residual bitterness over my lack of real pork products, but Suzume suggested we try sparring after breakfast. Despite the unexpected holiday from Chivalry's fitness regimen, I agreed that it seemed like a good idea.

We pushed back all of the furniture in the living room to make an open space and centered the rug so that there would be a nice surface to both potentially fall onto and to also muffle the noise to avoid bothering Mrs. Bandyopa-dyay downstairs. Suzume hadn't bothered to change out of her pajamas, but I'd taken the opportunity to put on my usual workout clothing.

I'd seen Suze in action several times, and had a high level of respect for her ability to kick ass and take names. "Don't take it easy on me," I said as I finished stretching out.

Suzume's sole concession to the workout portion of our morning had been to pour herself a second cup of coffee, which she saluted me with before putting it on the counter behind her and pulling her hair into a messy ponytail on top of her head. "I would never dream of doing such a thing, Fort."

"No, I'm really serious," I said, pulling my fists up into the correct fighting position that Chivalry had drilled into me, as we started circling each other. "I've been working really hard this summer, and I'm definitely not where I was a few months ago."

"I have no doubts," Suzume said. She tossed a lazy right hook at me, which I blocked easily. "See? Last spring we'd be trying to get your nose to stop bleeding right now."

I dropped my guard just long enough to make an extremely rude gesture, which she laughed at. She then gave a little shrug to her shoulders and threw a quick set of three punches at me, all of which I blocked. She lifted an eyebrow at me, looking moderately impressed, and made another few hits, all of which I also blocked. We were still circling, and her smile was gone, replaced with a slight frown, as if she was working out a small, confounding puzzle. My self-confidence took a distinct step upward, and I felt good about myself, finally seeing some very real payout from my summer of physical misery.

I made a sharp left jab, but she quickly sidestepped the blow. Her frown was now much more pronounced.

"See?" I said, not fighting my own desire to smile.

"Yes," she agreed, "very instructive."

Five seconds later I was on my back with her arm pressed into my throat and her left knee digging into my kidney.

"What the hell has your brother been doing?" she demanded, looking profoundly irritated.

"Guh?" I choked out with the small amount of air I was somehow dragging into my lungs. Suze noticed my distress and took the weight off of my throat, at which point I gasped in air desperately.

"Seriously, what is wrong with Chivalry?" Suze continued, undeterred. "You've been blocking every punch I threw at you instead of trying to move out of the way, you are doing nothing with your legs except for shuffling, and you were completely unprepared for the most basic sweep I could come up with. What have the two of you been doing all these months?"

I scooted out from under that kidney-jabbing knee before I answered, wary about exactly what would happen if Suze put all of her weight onto it. "This is how Chivalry fights, Suze."

She gave a derisive snort. "Your brother has all the vampire bennies going on, Fort. Inhuman speed, strength, and accelerated healing. Remind me what you have again?"

I sighed. "A degree in film theory and a can-do attitude?"

Suzume's expression spoke volumes. "You've got at least a century before you catch up with Chivalry and can fight like a Victorian gentleman defending the honor of queen and country. Let's do our best to keep you alive until then."

As she gave me a hand up, I had a very sinking feeling in my stomach about the direction that this morning was going in.

"Right." Suze pulled her hands up again, and there was a distinct gleam in her eyes that boded poorly for me. "Now, this is the kind of gutter fighting that you'll actually be up against."

What followed was a forty-minute demonstration of all the things that Chivalry had decided didn't apply to the way real men fought. It was extremely illuminating and rather painful, given that Suze seemed to direct an inordinate amount of her strikes to my throat, kidneys, or knees.

"I'm leaving out most of the groin hits for today," she said cheerfully at one point, circling me at a safe distance. "But you need to start working on making your height work in your favor."

"What do you mean?" I asked. I'd finally managed to block her latest attack toward my legs and was feeling a bit better about myself. A second later I made nose-first contact into my rug as Suze slipped behind me, gave me an extremely painful kick in the back of my right knee, and rode me to the floor with one arm wrapped around my neck in the perfect position for a good throttling.

"Well," Suze said, as I gagged, "I'm shorter than almost anyone I get into a fight with, excluding my own family. This means that if I want to hit someone, I usually have to get inside their strike zone. I use a lot of what I learned from my mother and aunts, but I also took some Krav Maga classes because I like that the whole point of that style is to end a fight fast instead of being showy. So you'll notice"— she tightened her arm slightly for emphasis—"that most of what I aim for are the most vulnerable parts of the body. Your face, neck, groin, knee, eyes, and joints are all good spots for me. You"—and after one last, almost affectionate, choking she let go and let me wheeze—"have been aiming punches at the center of my body only."

"Point taken," I said as I pushed myself upright again. "Dirty fighting."

"Not dirty—effective," Suze corrected. She bounced lightly on the balls of her feet, looking obnoxiously fresh and pleased with herself, in a bizarre reflection of how Chivalry always looked at this point in our lessons. "Also, knock it off with your two-point contact system."

"Huh?"

"This," she made two quick jabs at me, each of which I blocked. "You're using just your fists. Have you heard about muay Thai?"

"Does it come with a little umbrella?"

She grinned. "Not quite. It's a fighting system that relies on eight points of contact—punches, kicks, elbows, and knee strikes. With your freakish height it actually might be a good fit."

"Let me put that on my to-do list."

"Good, and while we're on that—" And with another of those incredible bursts of speed, Suze had dropped to one knee in front of me and I felt a sharp prick just under my rib cage. I froze, then looked down very carefully. An open switchblade was in Suze's right hand, pressed against my skin with just enough pressure that a single drop of blood had welled up and was slowly staining the fabric of my T-shirt. The heel of her left hand was resting casually against the handle of her knife, innocently placed yet clearly prepared to add an extra boost of muscle to send the blade slicing into some fairly critical organs.

Suzume lifted one eyebrow slowly. "Questions?" she asked.

"One," I managed, being very careful not to move. "Exactly where did you get that from?"

She gave me a slow, feral smile. "I always try to keep one stashed. You can always try to pat me down and figure out where I had it."

"I'll take a rain check on that." I moved backward carefully, keeping an eye on her. "So I assume that your lesson here was that I should be prepared for anything?"

"It's pretty hard to be prepared for anything," she scoffed. "The lesson here is much simpler: always bring a knife to a fistfight."

"And in a knife fight?"

Suzume gave me that bright, brilliant smile that made me catch my breath for a second. I told myself sternly that it was just all of the injuries my body had suffered, possibly combined with some head trauma.

As easy as Suzume had made wiping the floor with me look, we'd both needed showers before being fit for the company of the outside world. While Suze was taking hers, I pressed a bag of frozen peas against my abused kidney region and called my brother. Chivalry hadn't called that morning, which was unusual—lately he'd made a daily check-in whenever I wasn't meeting up with him at some point in the day, apparently to make sure I was doing lots of push-ups on our off days. My call went straight to voice mail, so I hung up and tried the mansion. This time I was connected—but to my mother.

"I'm sorry, darling," Madeline explained, "but Chivalry is very occupied with his wife at the moment. It's horribly inconvenient." I winced. My mother was not known for her empathy.

"Is Bhumika okay?"

"She's doing exactly as we can expect, so do try to give your brother a bit of consideration. It's very thoughtless of him to forget to call you, but this part of the process has always been difficult for him." She paused, then scolded, "Oh, Fortitude, I can actually hear you biting your tongue." My mother was right, and I was barely withholding several comments about her blasé attitude toward Bhumika's failing health. "But he did tell me that you had your own bit of excitement with that renter of yours managing to get himself murdered. Bad luck, my turtledove, but, really, what do you expect when you rent in Providence? The city has been going downhill since the Irish arrived."

"*Mother!* You can't say that!"

"Really?" She sounded surprised. "Goodness, you should've heard the things we said just a century ago," she mused. "Things do change, don't they?"

I gritted my teeth. "I have to go now, Mother."

"Have a lovely day, my precious. I'll let your brother know that you called."

Sadly, that was a better-than-normal phone conversation with my mother.

It was just after lunch that Suze and I stood in a lane at my usual gun range. Given that it was Sunday, we were surrounded by off-duty cops, guys with their acne-ridden teenage sons who were more interested in texting than shooting, and one very badass-looking nun who was definitely adding some of the Holy Spirit to her paper target.

Suzume freely admitted that she far preferred knives to guns, so she stood next to me (looking unnaturally adorable in her oversized ear protectors and safety glasses) and watched with interest as I made my way through three clips in my Colt. I'd spent many Saturday mornings in a gun range with my foster father as a child, but he'd always specifically trained me to aim for only one spot on my paper targets: the midway point between the shoulder and the neck, where one shot would usually break the collarbone and cause an excruciating but completely non-life-threatening injury. Several months before I'd discovered at a very inopportune moment that this might've been a great stopping shot for the average home burglar, but it did not exactly have similar effectiveness on a nonhuman opponent. Since then I'd begun working on training my aim into kill shots: head and heart.

Once I'd finished the clips I'd brought with the Colt, I hit the retrieval button and examined my target. In the black silhouette of a man I could see the holes where my bullets had gone through. The majority were right in the areas where I'd intended them. Not bad for twenty-five yards.

Suzume leaned over my shoulder and poked a finger at the one hole that was off in the far upper left of the target, in the white area that meant I'd missed entirely. "Bet that would've scared the crap out of some low-flying birds," she said.

"It's generally considered bad form to poke people in the ribs while they're target shooting, Suze," I said between gritted teeth.

She snorted, loudly enough that I heard her even above the shots being fired on either side of us. "Yeah, the next time you're in a life-or-death situation, we'll all make sure not to break your concentration or surprise you while you're trying to make a shot. Besides" — she gestured to the rest of the shots — "you ended up doing fine. By the end of it I was seriously considering making things a challenge and giving you a wedgie."

"Don't even think about doing that on the next round," I warned her as I reached into my duffel bag and pulled out my most recent financial investment, an Ithaca 37 pump-action shotgun that I'd sawed down according to the instructions I'd found on a rather disturbing Web site.

"Oh yes," Suzume purred. "This is exactly what you should bring to a knife fight."

"Just hang a new target for me," I said as I checked it carefully, then loaded in four 20-gauge shells. I'd owned the Ithaca for just over a month, and it had taken suspending my Netflix, seriously scaling back my cable package, and then five straight weeks of eating nothing but ramen noodles and scraps from the restaurant to afford it.

Suzume put up my target, and I sent it out to fifty yards.

The main attraction of the Ithaca was its ability to blow an impressive hole in something at a price range that was not completely unattainable for me. Other than one very interesting day during a father-son gun-safety course where we'd received an excellent visual demonstration on exactly how much damage could be inflicted on a human stand-in (in that case, some very ill-fated cabbages), I'd never used a shotgun before my purchase of the Ithaca. I'd been taking a lot of time getting used to controlling the kickback from it, and also trying to increase my speed of reloading, given that it held only two shells.

I spent thirty minutes on it, working my way down to a 12-gauge shell, the largest type of ammunition that the shotgun would accommodate. When I was finished my arms and shoulder were aching, my target was demolished, and Suzume was looking profoundly bored.

"Paper targets will tremble in fear as you approach," she assured me as we drove home. Apparently I'd impressed her at some point in the day, however, either in my ability to be thrown around my living room or in my very masculine display of firearm prowess, because she not only chipped in for our delivery order of Chinese food that evening, but she even agreed to watch *Avatar* with me. She lasted halfway through the movie (admittedly only that long because of the presence of both Sigourney Weaver and the badass female helicopter pilot) before changing into her fox form and spending the remainder of the film playing with a balled-up piece of paper.

The next morning arrived without incident, despite Suzume again remaining on furry guard, and over breakfast we both agreed that whatever had killed Gage wasn't coming back, and that unfortunately neither of us had any more ideas for how to pick up its trail.

"I really appreciate your sticking around this weekend, Suze," I told her.

Chewing a mouthful of tofu bacon, Suzume gave me a very serious look. "What else are friends for?"

We looked at each other in silence for a moment, then she cleared her throat and we both occupied ourselves again with mastication.

The movers arrived just after ten to collect Gage's boxes, followed quickly by the cargo truck that would be taking Gage's car down to his parents in Florida. After it was done, I stood in what had been Gage's room and looked around. Once again it was just an empty room with a bed frame, bare mattress, and wood floors that were a decade overdue for sanding and refinishing. There was nothing left to hint about who had lived there and been my friend.

Suzume came up behind me and carefully placed one hand on my shoulder. "Are you okay?" she asked, and when I turned to look at her I was surprised to see something tentative in her eyes, rather than the usual brassy confidence that she seemed to bring to every situation.

"Yeah," I said, rubbing the back of my hand against my eyes and clearing my throat. I gave her hand an awkward pat, and received a brief squeeze in return. For a second we both froze, holding each other's hands. I registered how close she was, almost right up against me, her eyes just below the level of my shoulder. I could feel my pulse pick up and my breath catch.

Then we both let go and stepped apart at the same moment, resulting in a whole different kind of awkwardness. For a moment I almost thought that I could see a flush in Suzume's cheeks, which I immediately shrugged off as impossible. I looked back at Gage's room and sobered. "I just wish I didn't have to start looking for a roommate right now," I admitted. "It just feels really . . . disrespectful, you know? Like he didn't matter as much as he did."

Suzume walked over and brushed one hand lightly against the window. We'd replaced the trash bag with a sheet of plywood yesterday, but there was still a noticeable breeze. "Yeah," she agreed. "It just sucks."

I paused, then continued, voicing the nagging worry that had been rattling at the back of my mind for the past few days and that had made it hard to fall asleep the night before. "I know you and Chivalry keep telling me it was just a coincidence, and maybe you're right, but with me getting more involved with the family enforcement, how safe is any human who lives with me? I mean, really?" It hung in the air, and even though I'd been thinking about it, hearing myself say the words hurt. It was admitting that everything I was doing was getting me farther away from what I'd wanted to be for so long: just another guy.

"Would you like me to find you a roommate?" Suzume said suddenly.

"What?"

"Well, you're not wrong. Renting with a human isn't a great idea. You don't know that many supernaturals, and you can't exactly put up a Craigslist ad for what you need, so let me find you a roommate. I'll even filter out the douchewads for you." She looked uncomfortable again, and I realized that she was actually rambling.

I was honestly surprised and very touched. She had some very good points too; other than her, almost all the nonhumans I knew were those I'd met while doing ride-alongs as my brother enforced my mother's laws. I didn't think that any of them would welcome a social call from me—even if I'd actually met any who I would've been willing to live with, which I hadn't. "That's great, Suze. That would be a huge help."

"Good, then. I'll get on it." She knelt down and fiddled with the zipper on her bag.

"I really appreciate it. Thank you—I mean it."

The more I thanked her, the more uncomfortable she looked, so I dropped the subject and we headed out to my car so that I could drive her home before I had to get to work.

As I drove, doubts started seeping through my gratitude. Had I actually just given Suzume, prankster extraordinaire, carte blanche to find me a roommate?

I snuck a look at her out of the corner of my eye. She was looking back at me, and as I watched, she gave a wide, evil smile.

"Yes," she said, clearly reading my expression, "you did just agree to let me pick your roommate."

"Do not mess with me on this one, Suze," I said warningly. "I'm serious."

Her smile just widened, and I felt a distinct worry that I would end up regretting my impulsive agreement.

I dropped Suzume at her place and it was only by blatantly breaking the speed limit that I was able to get to work right before my shift started. As it was I had to run flat-out from where I'd parked my car to get into the restaurant, and I got several sideways looks when I arrived, sweaty and out of breath. But I lined up with the other waiters for the briefing, which was the part of the day where Chef Jerome explained each of the night's specials to us and had us sample the dishes so that we would be able to properly describe them to the diners. We were also given the day's set of allergy flash cards to memorize. Each card pertained to one of the major allergy groups, and it listed which dishes were safe to consume for someone with that allergy. Chef Jerome felt very strongly about people with allergies—namely that he didn't want any of them dying. For all of his other major faults (and there were several very notable ones), I had to also respect that Chef Jerome seemed to view people with allergies as a very personal challenge to his skills, and that it was his duty to make sure that everyone could come into Peláez and leave full and happy, regardless of their dietary challenges.

Of course, that was his viewpoint of people who *couldn't* eat something. For those of us who *chose not to* . . . well, that night Chef Jerome was clearly on a particular rampage, because I found myself being forcibly fed duck, turtle soup, and a sliver of foie gras. It was all amazing.

I had just seen Chef Jerome go thundering by me in the direction of poor Josh, holding a forkful of some kind of cheese, when someone shouted that there was a phone call for me. I frowned and hurried over to where Daria, the restaurant manager, stood at the door to the kitchen, holding the black cordless phone that usually lived at the reservation desk. Daria was usually pretty good about taking messages and then passing them to us during our shifts, but the policy about the phone being brought over was that it had to be a real emergency. The last time Daria had walked the phone over, it had been because the girlfriend of the guy who worked at the meat prep station had gone into labor a month early. So it was with a very real sense of trepidation that I took the phone.

"Hello?"

"Fort, it's me." Matt's gravelly voice rattled over the line. The sound of it made me freeze, inside and out, and a deep sense of foreboding rattled through me.

"Matt," I forced out between my numb lips. "What's wrong?"

"I found something," he said, and the bottom dropped out of my stomach. "We need to meet."

# Chapter 5

I finished out my shift in a haze and drove straight to Matt's office.

Matt's office was south of my own apartment, past Brown University and in the Fox Point part of town. Fox Point was an odd mix of older, gentrified houses and businesses and the remains of Providence's heavy industrialization from the turn of the century. For the most part it was a fairly pretty area, with relatively safe streets and an assortment of businesses that catered to an upscale clientele. Matt's office was actually a historic little house on Ives Street that a developer in the seventies had carved into four cramped offices, two on each floor. The second floor hosted a pair of perennially sparring realtors, and across the hall from Matt, a home decorator was ensconced in piles of fabric, tile, and floor samples.

At just past eleven I pulled into the back parking lot, which was empty except for Matt's familiar Buick. I'd had a key to the building for years, and I let myself in the back door and headed down the small and creaky hallway. At Matt's door I paused and knocked. I could hear his footsteps across the bare floorboards, and he unlocked his door and let me in.

From the looks of things, Matt was living in his office again. It was always easy to tell when that was happening, since his suitcases and a few open boxes were piled behind a small privacy screen that the home decorator had given him out of pity a few years ago during another of these periods. There were a few blankets and a battered pillow strewn across the old leather sofa that had come with the office, and some decades ago had probably belonged to an earlier owner's gentleman's library. Every surface in the office was covered in file folders, newspaper clippings, and yellow legal pads filled with notes and scribbles about various cases. Matt's mini fridge was barely visible below the clutter as it sat in the corner—it was actually my old mini fridge from college that I'd given him when I moved into my first apartment. Even though I knew that he probably couldn't afford to replace it, it made me feel better that he'd kept it even during our recent rift.

Matt was wearing jeans and a flannel shirt, with a somewhat incongruous set of bright red slippers on his feet. I would've made some joke about them, but Matt's expression was grim and the air was charged. He nodded at me.

"I'm glad you came, Fort."

"Of course I did, Matt. You said that you found something." I hid how worried that made me.

Matt didn't speak for a long moment, just stared at me with a shuttered look in his brown eyes. "They made an arrest, you know," he said finally.

I shifted uncomfortably under his piercing gaze. Once again I was reminded that it was a good thing that I'd never had dreams of being a covert operative. "I know."

He walked closer to me, stopping well inside my personal space. "Do you think that those were the ones who killed your roommate?" he asked in a deceptively pleasant voice.

I knew that he was testing me and that what he wanted was for me to admit that there had been a cover-up orchestrated by my family. "They were arrested, Matt," I said, refusing to go down that road. I couldn't see any way that it didn't end in his death.

"That's not what I'm asking." Standing in front of me, Matt should've looked tough, like a brick wall of muscle and intent. Instead, all I could see was his very human fragility and just how breakable he could be.

"I know." I looked around the apartment for a second, wishing I could think of a way to defuse this moment. I repeated, "You said you found something."

Matt ignored my comment. "The Scotts have leverage in this town, Fort. It took a lot of work to get copies of the investigation, to get people to talk to me. If you're not in on this, let me know and I'll follow it on my own."

He wasn't going to drop this, I realized, and I was going to have to work past this in a way that retained the ignorance that protected Matt while at the same time got the information he'd uncovered so that I could figure out if it was putting him in danger. "Matt, the thing is . . ." I paused, racking my brain for something to say that could somehow circumvent the worst of the truth while at the same time give him enough to let us move forward. Finally I said, "I know what my family is"—and *that* was certainly a whopper dressed up like honesty, but nowhere near what Matt clearly read it as—"but this isn't about them right now. My friend was killed, and now you're telling me that you've found something." I forced myself to look him straight in the eyes, and I reached deep inside myself, and when I asked it I meant it: "Can I trust you, Matt?"

I wished that I could really trust him. To tell him what I actually was and not have him look at me like a monster, assuming that he believed me and didn't just look at me like a crazy person. I spent a lot of time purposefully not thinking about it, but one of the things I valued most about Suzume's friendship was the fact that she knew what I was. There was no lying when I was with her, none of the deceit that was so treacherously and heavily entwined throughout every interaction I had with Matt.

But I'd told the truth to my foster parents, and they'd believed me. They'd died because they'd believed me, and I was determined that this wouldn't happen to Matt.

Matt's mouth gave a small, cynical twist. "Fortitude, I'm not the one who has secrets in this room."

"This one isn't a secret." I refused to look away from his eyes. "This is just about Gage."

Matt looked away first, letting out a gusty breath and shaking his head. Whatever decision he'd come to and whatever he'd seen in me in that long moment, some of the tension leaked out of the room. "Okay, Fort. Okay," he said, rubbing one hand hard against the back of his head. He pulled a folder off of the top of the pile littering his desk and passed me an oversized eight-by-ten-inch photo from it. I recognized the floor of my apartment first, then registered that I was looking at a picture of Gage's bare arm. There were his band tattoos, with their intricately repeated pattern of Celtic knots, and at the bottom of the picture was the grim sight of his bare, empty wrist. I swallowed hard and paid attention as Matt spoke. "Now, this is from one of the pictures that were taken at the crime scene. He had these bands tattooed around both wrists and biceps, right?" I nodded. When he'd first gotten them, I'd teased him for days about one set being just slightly higher than the other. "Take a look at this." Matt pulled a second picture out of the folder and laid it down on the first. This was a blowup of a guy around my age, standing in the middle of an apartment I'd never seen. He was smiling widely, a beer in one hand, wearing a sleeveless shirt. Immediately I realized that he had a set of tattoos that were identical to Gage's—Celtic bands at biceps and wrists, with the same interlocked black knots.

"Same tats, right?" Matt asked, clearly already knowing the answer.

"Yeah, that's the same. Who is this?"

"This is Rian Orbon. He went missing one night in February, but the police never found any evidence to call it a homicide, so it was labeled a missing person and eventually dropped. Orbon's parents hired me six months ago. I wasn't able to find anything, but when I saw your roommate's body the other night, something about it looked familiar." Matt tapped the photo. "I knew I'd seen the tats before. Could've just been a coincidence, though, right?"

"Yeah, maybe . . ." I said, my brain weighing the new information and not liking the potential result one bit.

"Exactly. So I called up a connection I've got with the Providence PD. Asked him if there was any chance he could poke around the missing person's sheets, see if there were any more with tats that match this description." Matt handed me another photo, and I looked at it almost reluctantly. This was a younger guy, Asian, awkward and gangly in the way that a lot of guys are in the first few years of college. "Brent Jung was a sophomore at the Roger Williams University metro campus. Went missing back in April. He'd had a fight with his girlfriend earlier in the week and things were tense with the parents, so the investigating officer figured that he just hauled off and would trickle back eventually when his money ran out. You can't see it in the picture here, but his RA mentioned that Jung had gotten tattooed just two weeks before he vanished—gave a pretty detailed description. I e-mailed him a copy of the Orbon photo last night, and he swears that Jung had an identical tat."

I frowned. "But these guys disappeared, and Gage was killed."

"Fort, I haven't been able to get a copy of the coroner's full report yet, but I talked with someone who works in the office. It wasn't just his hands that were cut off; it was also his tongue and his genitals." I could feel the color drain out of my face, and Matt nodded grimly. "My guy told me that there was also one long cut on his neck, but other than that there were no other injuries. To me, this suggests planning. I don't think Gage is the first person who has died this way—it might just be that his is the first body that was found."

"You think Rian Orbon and Brent Jung were both victims as well." As I spoke, my mind was racing. Suzume and I had been assuming that this was a random supernatural attack, that Gage had been in the wrong place at the wrong time, and that his killer had probably left the area. But this suggested that not only was Gage not the sole victim and his killer had been in the area a long time, but that there had been some substantial planning and premeditation. Matching tattoos? Whatever was going on was now much bigger than just Gage's death.

I hated that I even thought of it, but more bodies also meant that Gage's death probably *didn't* have anything to do with me, and I felt a small rush of relief. But that was quickly washed away when I looked back at the stack of photos. Something was very, very wrong here.

Matt began talking, interrupting my thoughts. "I think it's a stretch to imagine it's just a coincidence that we've got one body and two missing persons with the same tattoos. When did Gage get tattooed?"

"About a month ago."

Matt nodded. "Orbon and Jung's tats were both recent as well."

"So we need to find out where they got these tattoos, because that's the link." When had Gage become singled out, I wondered. When he got his tattoo, or was it even before that? I tried to remember what Gage had said about the tattoos or where he'd gotten them, but all I could come up with was a blank. There had been too many weeks of minimal sleep and excessive training. It seemed like I'd come home one day and there had been Gage, sitting on the sofa with medical gauze wrapped around his arms and surfing his iPhone for tattoo aftercare instructions.

"I already did," Matt said, and I snapped to attention, watching as he pulled another file off the desk. "I went to see Rian Orbon's father this morning, and we spent the whole day going through everything he had in his room. We found this at the bottom of a drawer." He pulled out a glossy advertisement card, the kind that usually arrived in my mailbox and went straight into the trash, and handed it to me.

*Iron Needle Tattoos,* it read. *20% discount.*

I stared at the card—there was a picture on it of a black Chinese dragon tattooed on an anonymous man's back. The longer I looked at it, somehow the more interesting it became. After a long minute I remembered that Matt was waiting for an answer. "Wow. This is just . . . I don't know." I shook my head, putting the card down on the pile of photos in front of me. It was hard to take my eyes off of it, and I wondered if all those hours of watching anime had finally ingrained some kind of Pavlovian response in me for Asian art. Good thing it hadn't been a *Sailor Moon* tattoo. "So we know where Orbon got his tattoo. We should figure out if Gage and Jung got theirs there as well," I finished lamely.

Matt eyed me. "Yeah, that's the place to start. But that's where you come in."

That finally distracted me fully from the card. I'd heard those words before—usually before I had to pose as Matt's accomplice. I didn't begrudge him the difficulties in being a one-man private investigative unit, and I'd gone on more than one stakeout, but I'd never quite heard those words without a frisson of suspicion after the time he made me pose as his boyfriend to infiltrate a gay swingers' club to catch a man's husband in the act of cheating. And cheating. And cheating again. "Me?" I asked with no small amount of trepidation.

"These guys were all in their twenties. I know a certain guy who matches that description, and unfortunately it is no longer me."

"You want to use me as bait?" I was having somewhat mixed feelings about this. On the one hand, this was a really good idea. On the other hand, I didn't want to encounter whatever creature had been killing people with Matt as my tagalong. It would be like trying to maintain a secret identity while dating a journalist. And I didn't care how good a show *Moonlight* had been or how much I liked Superman; it seemed like a terrible idea to me.

"Don't worry. I'll be backing you up," Matt said soothingly, clearly assuming that my reticence was more from a fear of ending up without tongue, gonads, and hands. "You just go into the tattoo parlor with that card and see what the reaction is. See who talks to you, and especially see if you get nudged toward the design that your friend got."

Now it was my turn to eye him suspiciously. "No tattoo, though," I clarified. No matter how cool that Chinese dragon had looked, I was no fan of needles.

Matt threw his hands up, exasperated. "Yeah, Fort. Why don't you go get a tattoo that will put you on the top of a serial killer's wish list? Christ, kiddo. We're just getting background here."

That was the closest he'd sounded to my old, nonsuspicious Matt all night, and I smiled a little. "Okay. Are you coming in with me?"

"No, I'll be staking the parlor out, though. I took a look at it today—it's across from a coffee shop, so I'll be parked in the front window, keeping an eye on you. Don't worry." And here he gave me one of those old, familiar, Uncle Mattie looks. "I'm not going to let anything happen to you."

"I know that, Matt." Knowing that he'd be across the street during my look around a potential monster den left me relieved, and I couldn't help but poke him a little. "Even though you said that before the swinger party, yet I still had my ass pinched so many times that I had bruises."

"Hazard of the job, Fort. It was important to stay in character." Matt smiled, his shoulders relaxing as he thought back to our old halcyon days. Then a shadow crossed his face and he stiffened again, turning away and making a show of taking the photos from me and tucking them back in the folders, leaving me the discount flier. "Anyway," he said gruffly. "Ten a.m. sharp, okay? When you're done come over and buy a cup of coffee. There's a booth in the back where we can talk and not be seen from the parlor."

The moment of détente over, we said an awkward goodbye, and I left.

Back in my Fiesta, I paused for a moment before turning the ignition, reviewing all the information I'd just learned.

"Shit," I muttered, and dug in my pocket for my phone, punching in Suzume's number by rote. As soon as I heard her sleepy "Hello" I was off and running. "Suze, I know it's after midnight, and I'm an asshole and I'm sorry, but I need you to come by my apartment tomorrow morning. Matt found something, and I don't think that whatever killed Gage was just roaming through."

There was a second while that clearly processed through her sleep-fogged brain. Then she made a small, frustrated sound.

"Forget tomorrow morning—I'll be right over."

The benefit of driving at that hour was that most of the traffic lights had been set to blinking yellow for the night, and I made great time back to my apartment, arriving before Suzume. Inside, I dumped my coat, toed off my work shoes, and put the glossy Iron Needle advertisement on the counter. A glance at the clock assured me that I had a few minutes before Suzume would arrive, and I took a quick shower to remove the worst of my work-related hair gel, having no desire to be subject to Suze's arsenal of speakeasy jokes this late at night.

I finished up and threw on a pair of sweatpants and a shirt just as I heard Suzume's familiar "Shave and a Haircut" knock at the door. As I went to let her in, the card on the counter caught my eye again, and for a second I wondered what kind of tattoo I'd get, assuming I ever got a tattoo. Not that I wanted a tattoo, of course, but I wondered how much it would cost to get a Tron ISO tattoo on my arm. Given how long my projected lifespan was, I would certainly get good use out of it.

Suzume had apparently saved time by not changing out of her pajamas, since I clearly remembered the pair of red argyle lounge pants that she was wearing when she walked in. Paired with an eye-searingly bright yellow hoodie, it should've looked bizarre. But as fiendishly clever as ever, Suze had put her hair into a set of pigtails, which somehow made the whole thing look intentional. I was starting to wonder if there was anything in the world she could wear that wouldn't add a kick to my heart rate.

I took my mind off of Suze's continued string of fashion triumphs by filling her in on what I'd learned. After I'd finished, she sat and absorbed it for a long second before delivering her thoughts, phrased with her usual grace and delicacy.

"Well, that certainly shits the bed on our working theory, doesn't it?"

"Yeah, I—"

She glanced sharply away from me. "Is that the card you were talking about?" she asked, pointing to the advertisement.

"Yeah." She got off her stool and went over to pick it up and studied it closely. When she didn't respond, my mouth suddenly took on a life of its own and started filling the silence. "It's something, right? Some graphic designer did a good job. I don't know if it's the font or the colors, but that is the best-designed circular I've ever seen in my life. I mean, I look at that thing and I actually start thinking that a tattoo is a good idea." I paused, but she continued to mutely examine the flier, so I continued. "It wouldn't necessarily be a bad idea, right? It would be like going really undercover. How do you think I'd look with a tattoo? Like, the crest of Hyrule on my right shoulder blade?" She finally stopped her examination and, with great deliberation, lifted her eyes to meet mine. Then, very slowly, she raised one terrible, feathery black eyebrow. I froze for a moment, then added, "If you don't know what that looks like, hold on: I have it on a T-shirt."

"I bet you do," Suzume said, with volumes of subtext. "But it's not the font. Or the tool with the dragon tattoo."

"What do you mean?" I stole a glance at the flier. No, the dragon still looked badass, even better than I'd remembered.

Suze held it up. "This card is glamoured."

It took a second for me to tear my mind away from visions of exactly how well I could pull off a tattoo to focus on what she'd just said, but once it started to penetrate the unusual fuzziness of my thoughts it cast a very harsh light on my recent monologue. "Glamour," I said slowly, practically tasting the word. "Like what the elves use to hide their ears and look human?"

Suze nodded. "Exactly. I don't know how many halfsies can do it, but I know that full elves can put glamours on objects to make them more attractive. Just like this." She wiggled the card, and when I looked at it again I could now just see the hint of the heat shimmer I remembered from when Lilah had broken the glamour on her ear for me.

I shared a grim look with Suze. "Elves running the speed-dating event that Gage disappeared at. Now elf glamour on the promotional card. Starting to look like a pattern."

"Sure looks that way, Fort. I'll ride along with you tomorrow to Iron Needle." That eyebrow went up again, and I knew with a sinking feeling that it would be a long time before I heard the last of my proposed crest of Hyrule tattoo. "With how you were reacting to that glamour, I'll have to keep an eye on you. Otherwise the next time I see you, you'll probably have a *Doctor Who* tramp stamp."

For one awkward second, I realized that the only way Suzume could possibly look hotter to me was if she had a tattoo of the TARDIS on the middle of her lower back. I was profoundly grateful in that moment that the kitsune were unable to read minds.

After far too few hours of sleep, I rolled out of bed and picked Suzume up at her house, and the two of us drove over to the Iron Needle.

A lot of legends revolved around iron being the one weakness to elves and similar fairy folk. I'd asked Chivalry about it over the summer at one point, when we were driving up to Boston to deal with a nest of kobolds that had taken Madeline's permission to eat stray dogs and cats and decided to apply it to people's pets. After Chivalry had read an article about a sudden rash of dogs being snatched out of gated yards, he had thrown me into the car for a quick lesson in diplomacy, and the topic had come up in conversation. He'd told me that there actually wasn't any true weakness to iron—the seriousness of the inbreeding and population crunch among the elves had become undeniable around the dawn of the Iron Age, and had reached truly critical mass just as the Industrial Revolution hit, resulting in a false correlation for the humans who came into contact with elven offspring so disease ridden and diminished compared to their parents that the humans had credited their sudden ability to overcome them with the availability of iron weapons. Which, in all fairness, probably helped a bit as well. I'd asked Chivalry why none of the humans who were telling the stories had picked up on that. With a rather exhausted sigh, he'd pointed out to me that these were the same kind of thoughtful scientific minds that had embraced bloodletting and treatments involving cow dung.

The neighborhood we ended up at was one that was in a slow state of deterioration. Two grocery stores were empty and boasted large For Lease signs. The small shopping plaza I pulled into had old and cracked asphalt, the kind where people's cars got stuck in the winter. Four businesses with grimy signs huddled together in one squat gray building that was crumbling at its edges. The Iron Needle was at the far right side, and its three neighbors made a perfect trifecta: a bail bondsman, a liquor store, and a check-cashing business.

"You take me to the nicest places," Suzume said.

"I can't believe Gage got his tattoo here." I mused, trying to picture Gage choosing this of all places to get inked. The front window of the tattoo parlor was blacked out, and the neon sign displaying its name was failing to light up two *n*'s and an *e*. "This place looks like an invitation for hepatitis."

"I'm feeling some begrudging admiration for whoever set that glamour." Suze was frowning. "For elf magic, that was packing some heat to get anyone through that door."

"You mean you weren't feeling respect last night, when it totally made me its bitch?" I felt moderately insulted.

"Fort," Suze gave me a very patient look. "Convincing you to get a dorky tattoo can't be that hard."

"What do you mean by that?" Trust Suze to refuse to leave me at *moderately* when she could take me all the way to *completely* insulted.

"Your ex-girlfriend convinced you to go vegetarian. And you're still vegetarian, even after you dumped her for cheating on you."

"I have plenty of other reasons," I defended. It was even true. While my decision to eschew eating meat had been primarily driven by my desire to date Beth, the choice to continue that had been because of what I'd discovered about the diet. It had helped quiet some of my less desirable, more predatory instincts. Since cutting out meat (other than the force-fed mouthfuls from Chef Jerome and some periodic backsliding, usually involving bacon), I'd found it far easier to ignore a few stimuli that had usually had my vampire side sitting up and taking notice. Feeding regularly from my mother had also helped, but I wasn't about to abandon any useful element.

Suzume rolled her eyes expressively, and I very pointedly turned away from her and looked across the street. The Starbucks looked like a lone outpost of the Roman Empire against Visigoths, and Matt was seated front and center beneath the green logo on the glass window. His favorite stakeout Red Sox hat was pulled low, and an open newspaper was providing cover for him, but I knew his methods from many years of exposure. I wondered briefly how the increasing shift to notepads and tablets would affect the private detective methods of camouflage, but shrugged it off as not my problem.

The inside of the Iron Needle showed the same highly questionable sanitary conditions as the outside, with a cheap vinyl floor that hadn't been mopped since the early years of the Clinton presidency, and a waiting area that looked furnished mainly with living room furniture rescued from the dump. There was a long counter that separated the front of the shop from the back, where the tattooing chair and equipment were set up. With the front window blacked out, the only illumination came from a set of rickety office ceiling lights, which were flickering ominously. A few half-full containers of rubbing alcohol and fat binders sat on a shelf behind the tattoo chair, beside an assortment of needles and many containers of inks. The walls were covered in layers of tattoo designs that ranged from the surprisingly delicate to the profoundly disturbing, with a distinct over-representation of the disturbing. In rare gaps between the pictures, knotty pine wall paneling was revealed. In the back was a half-closed door labeled EMPLOYEES ONLY.

There was a long silence after Suze and I walked in, as we both looked around and took in our surroundings. We were the only people in the shop.

"Okay," Suze said under her breath, finally looking impressed, "whoever made that card was *amazing*." Then, louder, she yelled, "Hello? Paying customers!"

The Employees Only door creaked open wider, revealing a man sitting in a wheeled office chair. From his ripped jeans, unraveling wool hat, and disturbingly soiled and frayed wife-beater undershirt that matched the general décor (which Matt's home-decorator office mate would probably have labeled Miasma of Despair), I deduced that this was probably the owner of the store. From the long and incredibly detailed arm-sleeve tattoos revealed by the undershirt, I assumed that this was also the tattoo artist.

From the hypodermic needle protruding from the inside of the man's arm and the glassiness of his stare, I could safely state that this man was a junkie of the first order.

"I hope we're not interrupting," I said automatically. Immediately after the words left my mouth I began mentally kicking myself. Years of Chivalry's pestering had ingrained social inanities that trotted out at the most insane moments.

"Nope," the man said, and pushed the plunger on the needle. I was relieved to see a look of profound disgust on Suzume's face that matched what I was sure was plastered over my own. "I'll be out in five. Look through the sample sheets if you want." With no visible change in his deadened expression, the man walked his wheeled chair backward again and closed the door.

There was a significant pause.

"He must have very reasonable pricing," I offered at last.

Suzume nodded. "And offer discounts."

Another large binder sat on the counter next to an aged and yellowed cash register, helpfully titled SAMPLES. I opened it up and started flipping through the plastic insert pages while Suze prowled behind me, conducting her own investigation with a few muffled sniffs. I'd turned only a few pages before I found what I was looking for, and I gestured Suze over. When she was at my shoulder, we both looked down.

Gage's Celtic band tattoo was in front of us, painstakingly rendered in ink on a small piece of paper. Beside it was a photo printout, obviously from someone's computer, of a shirtless guy with the bands tattooed at bicep and wrist, though the man's face had been cropped off. I'd flipped quickly and easily to this page, but I was physically incapable of going any further, even though I knew what I was feeling was obviously unnatural and another well-laid glamour. Just like with the advertisement, I could see the vague heat shimmer, but the knowledge of its false nature only barely chipped away at its allure. It was more compelling than any masterpiece I'd ever seen hanging in the RISD Museum, where I'd spent more than a few afternoons, courtesy of the reduced student-admission rate.

"Yup, that's Yahtzee," Suze said. "Same glamour, too."

I nodded toward the closed door. "So, I'm thinking elf?"

"Oh?" Suze gave me a look like a third-grade math teacher asking to see a student's work.

"Glamour on the card, glamour on the sample, and he's wearing a hat indoors that very conveniently covers his ears. Seems to point elf to me. Am I right?" I waited expectantly for her congratulations.

"Nope."

"Really?" I could feel my confidence deflating.

"Psych!" Suze laughed and held up one hand for a congratulatory high five. I glared at her, not wanting to reward her successful bait and switch, but finally had to give in. After all, congratulatory high fives didn't come along every day, and losing Gage had removed half my usual supply of them. "Yes, beneath the smell of BO and rampant pharmacological self-abuse, it's definitely the pine-fresh whiff of halfsie."

That was definitely a gross thought. I decided to try not envying Suzume's ability to identify supernatural species by smell if those were some of the potential downsides.

"Okay." I took a deep breath. We'd actually located a very real lead—the first one I'd ever dealt with without Chivalry's chaperonage. I concentrated, not wanting to screw this up. "Now, how are we going to get some information? Should we be sneaky, just pretend we're really here for the tattoo? Or good cop/bad cop? Or—"

I broke off as Suze walked behind the counter, pounded loudly on the knotty pine door, and yelled, "Hey, Legolas! Shoot it up and get out here—we've got questions."

"Or do that, I guess," I muttered, feeling distinctly miffed. "Suze, I think that's going beyond just the direct approach."

She ignored me completely as the door opened and one very wary-looking junkie stuck his head out.

"Who the fuck are you?" the half-blood, whole-junkie asked.

Suze pointed at me. "Vampire." Then at herself. "Kitsune." And then at him. "Worm food."

As the words managed to penetrate the owner's drug haze, he started looking extremely freaked out and raised his hands in a supplicating gesture. "Hey, hey, if this is about paying a percentage, I've got zip." He appealed directly to me. "Recession, man. Killing my business." We all looked around, and there was a very pregnant pause as we took in the filth of our surroundings, which clearly predated the housing collapse. He continued weakly. "And a slick place moved in two blocks away. All, like, fancy and shit."

In his world, *fancy* probably meant "hygienic." I cut in before he could continue his litany of woe. "This isn't about money."

He blinked. I was starkly reminded of the expressions cows made when faced with something new and unexpected—it was exactly this level of blunt-force stupidity. "It isn't?" he asked.

I picked up the binder and pointed to the drawing of Gage's tattoo. "Start talking."

Stupidity cleared away, leaving dawning comprehension and very real surprise. "Really? That?" He shrugged. "That's, you know, Neighbor shit." His lip curled derisively at the word, and he warmed to his topic, showing more energy than I'd seen yet from him. "You should be getting money out of them. Snobby pricks and star fuckers, all of them."

The thought of someone who had just so casually shot up in front of us passing judgment on anyone else blew my mind a bit, and I was also confused about the level of hostility he seemed to have. "But, um . . . aren't you . . ." I paused, feeling for the right words. "Kind of . . ." Suze shook her head, and the look in her eyes read *epic fail*. He kept looking at me blankly, and I gave up and finally just tapped the top of my own ear significantly.

"One of them?" he finally asked, then made an extremely rude noise when I nodded. "I'm one of their changelings, man," he said bitterly. "I spent the whole first fourteen years of my life thinking I was human. You know, suburbia, soccer practice, oboe lessons. Then one day I'm snatched by those fuckers and told I'm actually an *elf*"—he gave a shrill laugh—"and belong in their community. And it's not a choice, see, because they actually faked my goddamn death, and told me that the only way to keep my parents alive was to never contact them again."

"Jesus." I said, feeling a sudden rush of empathy. Yes, hard drugs weren't the best response, but it wasn't exactly like he could walk himself down to a therapist to work on that one. Maybe he was coping the best he could.

Though it still wouldn't have killed him to run a Swiffer over the floor.

"No, actually, we were Jewish," he corrected. "But, anyway, after all that shit it turns out that they just want me for the numbers, see? 'Cuz of their fucking 'population crisis.'" He actually made air quotes with his fingers. "But I'm just the dirt on their shoes, 'cuz I don't even have the juice to hide my own goddamn ears." He pulled off his wool hat, revealing a receding hairline and a set of distinctly nonhuman ears. The ears had the same point as Lilah's, with a soft dusting of dark brown fuzz along the backs that matched the few stubborn tufts of hair that still remained on his head, but there was a weird little sagging at the tips. They looked weak and almost unhealthy—which rather did match the rest of him. "I'm fine to knock up some changeling girl, but they don't want me near any of their own precious kiddies." He snorted and replaced the hat, patting and tugging it in place with the same nervous movements that I remembered from Lilah checking her braids. Though, admittedly, with Lilah there had been fewer noticeable needle track marks. "Not that I care, you know? They're all crazy."

"So, the glamour on that sample . . ." Suze prompted.

"No, that's not me. I've tried to, you know, put glamour on stuff before. Doesn't do anything. Man"—again that shrill laugh, and I had to work hard not to wince at the sound—"they were all so disappointed when they grabbed me. Told me I was practically human." He snorted again, not noticing when snot actually came out his nose. I glanced down at it, then forced myself to look away. "They consider that an insult, of course." There was a feverish brightness in his eyes now, and his words were getting faster, as if he couldn't get them out quickly enough. Clearly his drugs were kicking in.

"But you do a lot of favors for the Neighbors?" Suze asked, and I recognized the slyness in her voice.

Another wet snort. This time some of the snot that came out was bloody. Apparently he was not restricting himself to administering his drugs intravenously. "Shit, no. Got paid up front to put that sketch out."

"Who paid you?" I asked.

A ratlike look assessed me. "Hard to remember." He glanced over at Suze and said, with lots of emphasis, "Might need a little help."

Suze gave me a significant glance, which I was completely unable to decipher, and I shook my head helplessly. She rubbed two fingers together behind her back, nodding broadly. Again, I shrugged. Finally, exasperated, she snapped, "Bribe the man, Fort."

"*Oh*," I said, finally understanding. Embarrassment followed quickly. "Sorry. I mean . . ." I glanced from one to the other. "Never mind." I pulled my wallet out of my back pocket and offered the entire contents of my billfold.

My intended recipient looked at my offering and said, "Yeah . . . it's going to take more than eight dollars, man." At my expression he turned sullen, complaining, "Come one, everyone knows the vampires are loaded. Cough it up."

"Maybe I'd rather beat it out of you," I said, dropping my voice and stepping around the counter threateningly.

Unfortunately the guy looked completely unimpressed. "If you were going to do that, you would've already done it. Also, seriously, you really don't look like enough of a dick."

I wasn't sure how to respond to that one. Suze gave me a one-shouldered shrug and said, "Take compliments where you find them, Fort." Turning back to our junkie, she said, "Legolas — "

"Jacoby," he interrupted.

"What?" she asked.

"Enough with the gay little elf name. It's Jacoby. Jacoby Goldstein."

Unable to stop myself, I broke in. "Actually, I'm pretty sure that Legolas wasn't — " Suze gave me a *not now, dumbshit* look, and I stopped. "Okay, fine, never mind." Then, "Not that there would be anything *wrong* with being — " Now even Jacoby looked irritated. "Yeah, okay, shutting up."

After a quick check to make sure that this time I was staying quiet, Suze picked up again. "*Jacoby*, then. I bet you deal with a lot of impulse buys." She glanced around and shuddered. "And a lack of comparison shopping?"

"Sure, sure. Drunk girls walk out of here with lots of dolphins and flowers."

"I'm guessing you prefer cash transactions?"

"ATM is two doors down in the booze joint."

Suze turned to me. "You heard the man." She gave him a fast up-and-down look. "I'm thinking Ben Franklin?"

"If you bring along his twin brother, sure."

As the person paying the bribe, I broke in, saying, "God-damnit, I make minimum wage!"

Suzume ignored me. "Franklin with Ulysses S. Grant as his wingman."

"Suze! My rent is due in two weeks!" And there was no way on this earth that I was going to call Gage's grieving parents and try to get a partial payment out of them.

Jacoby looked flummoxed, then leaned in, dropped his voice, and asked Suze, "Are you sure he's a vampire? He sure doesn't sound loaded."

"It *is* a recession," she reminded him.

He gave a gusty sigh. "Fine, one fifty and I sing like frickin' Pavarotti."

Suze had the nerve to give me a thumbs-up.

One quick trip next door, where I was pleased to see that the owner of the alcohol store wasn't letting a little thing like two drunks sleeping in his aisles get between him and basic cleanliness, and I returned with much more of my weekly paycheck than I could actually afford to spend. As I handed it over I shot Suze a hard look and muttered, "Way to chip in, bestie."

"Just count your blessings I'm waiving my negotiating fee, Fort," she replied. She watched as Jacoby carefully counted the cash, then stuck it into the top of his underpants—clearly to prevent us from trying to take it back once he'd talked. Which was actually rather smart; even I was suddenly very willing to let the money go. "Now talk."

Looking significantly more chipper, he complied. "Beginning of January, one of the Neighbors came in. Told me he wanted me to do him a favor, so I said to screw himself."

"Who was it?" I asked.

"I don't remember, man. One of the older, really snotty fucks, always brownnosing it up, making like he was more important than he was. I remember him from the Neighbor gatherings, but he never wanted anything to do with the changelings. But now he wanted something from me, so he kept whining about how it was my responsibility to fucking serve our community and all that bullshit. I told him what he could do with that, but I was broke, so I said that I'd do whatever the hell he wanted for a little cash. So he took a stack of my business fliers and said that someone would come by with money and what I had to do." He shrugged. "Nothing happened for a few days, so I forgot about it. Then this chick swings in, has that sketch"—he pointed helpfully— "all jazzed up so that every young guy wants it. She gives me a few containers of ink too; says that if any guy comes in with one of my promotional cards that has a similar mark on it, I need to give him that tattoo with this ink."

"Do you know who the woman was?" Suze asked.

"Said her name was Soli. Girl was *hot* too—real sexy Latina." A happy look filled his eyes as he reminisced. Other parts of him were revisiting memory lane as well, judging from the front of his pants. Both Suzume and I took a few subtle steps backward.

"Another of the Neighbors?" I resolutely decided that I was not looking below eye level for the rest of the visit.

Jacoby shook off his mental IMAX moment. "No, but she definitely knew what I was, so I don't think she's human. I don't know what the fuck she was, but she paid enough that I didn't give a shit. And pretty soon after that a guy came in with one of my cards that had been glamoured like crazy, and I inked him up. That was good work I did too, because Soli went really nuts on me, saying that the tat had to be perfect. If there was just one flaw in it, I wouldn't get my bonus."

"Bonus?"

"Yeah, each time I did one of the guys with the cards I got a bonus."

"How many men did you tattoo with the ink?"

"Four of them."

"Do you remember any names?" I asked, hopeful but not with much expectation.

Shockingly, he responded with a nod. "Wrote all of them down. Mailing list, you know? Gotta use new technology to grow the business."

We both stared at him. It was as if a dog had just talked.

"I read," Jacoby said defensively. "Anyway, figured it couldn't hurt. Just in case Soli lost track of any of them or they didn't show up at the speed-dating thing."

"Speed dating?" I asked quickly. Suddenly a few things were starting to come together.

"Yeah. After I was done I had to give them another flier." Disappearing momentarily into his office, we could hear Jacoby rooting around in a stack of paperwork. He emerged a moment later with a small flier, the photocopied kind that usually rest in stacks on side tables in alternative coffee shops. He handed it to me, and I read through it fast. It was for a specific Providence-only speed-dating site, but what immediately captured my attention was the bottom of the flier, where the sponsor of the program had taken the chance to pimp themselves a little—the Dreamcatching logo was as predictable as I could've expected. "I've got glamoured ones," Jacoby continued, "but I just photocopied this one. You can have it."

"Thanks." I went as casual as possible. "How about that list of the guys you tattooed, while you're at it?"

"Sure," Jacoby said with equal casualness. "For another hundred bucks."

"Fuck," I gritted out. Another trip to the liquor store, where the cashier gave me an unnecessarily judgmental look while I cleaned out everything that was left of my most recent paycheck. I stomped back and shoved the money at Jacoby. "Here."

He gave a beatific smile, clearly already picturing exactly what he'd be spending this on. He went over to the counter, flipped open one of the thick binders, and carefully copied out a short list. When he handed it to me I scanned it—there was Gage, along with the two names that Matt had given me last night, but one name I didn't recognize: Franklin Litchfield.

While I was looking at the list, Suze took over. "How much for some of that special ink?" she asked. I winced. At this point she was either going to have to start chipping in for bribery costs or cover my utilities.

Jacoby didn't even glance up from his focus of shoving

his new wad of twenties down his pants to join the rest of his stash. "All out. Used it up on the last guy; haven't gotten any more yet." He sounded disappointed at the lost opportunity to sell out his employers further.

"How do you get more?"

"Soli drops it off. Not much—just enough to do the job. When I see her, I know some guy will be coming by in a week or so."

"Seen her lately?"

"Last month, right before I inked up this big blond guy." I felt a pang, recognizing the description of Gage. Jacoby shrugged. "Hey, that's it. Pleasure doing business with you."

I broke in. "Not so fast. What the hell is going on with this? This sounds pretty complicated—glamours, secretive women, advertising circulars. What are the Neighbors trying to do?"

Again that blank, bovine stare of complete incomprehension. "Dude, they're paying me. I don't give a crap what they're trying to do. Probably another fucking Neighbor pipe dream. That's all any of what they do is."

I looked at Suze, who shrugged one shoulder. With nothing left to ask, we turned to go.

We'd opened the door, and either the blast of fresh air or the unfamiliarity of natural light jogged something loose in Jacoby's brain, because he called to us, "Oh, hey, one last thing. On the house. That glamour they've been coating on stuff, that's nothing any of the Neighbors could've done. That was put on by one of Themselves. I don't know what the hell you're interested in this for, but smart people don't fuck with Themselves."

Jacoby's expression was as close to sobriety as he possibly got, and I asked with trepidation, "Who are Themselves?"

He smirked. "Never knew the vampires were so dumb. Themselves are the daddies, the motherfucking progenitors, the Ad-hene, the real deals."

"Muh?" Lost, I looked to Suzume.

She made a small tsk sound at my display of ignorance. "He means the elves, Fort. The full-bloods."

We didn't say anything to each other as we walked to my

car, both enjoying the escape from the stale air and questionable aromas of the Iron Needle. A few deep breaths each, though, as we leaned against the Fiesta. I needed to go across the street and somehow deal with Matt, but I paused to arrange my thoughts, trying to determine what and how much to tell him.

I looked over at Suzume. "*Four* victims now, not just three, and that's assuming that Jacoby sold us a full list. It's been going on for months now, it's super-complicated, and there are elves and some mystery woman at the center of it."

"What are you going to tell your PI guy?"

I winced a little, considered, then answered slowly. "I'll give him the list. He can run down the basics on the last guy, and while he's doing that you and I are going to get some better answers."

"Where from?"

"Dreamcatching." I handed her the flier and watched as she quickly assembled the pieces as well. "Any chance you'll wait in the car?"

She shrugged. "I can do that. One last thing about the tattoo parlor, though."

"Oh?"

"Whatever killed Gage has been there. More than once, judging by the smells."

I considered everything we'd just learned, then asked, "Maybe our mystery woman?"

A wide smile crept across Suzume's face as she looked up at me. "That's what I like about you, Fort," she said, real admiration in her voice. "You never underestimate the ability of women to commit homicide."

"Have you met my family? Kipling had it right about the female of the species."

Her laugh followed me as I hurried across the street and into the Starbucks.

Walking into the coffee shop, I inhaled the familiar, invigorating aromas. I'd spent months pouring coffee, but back at Busy Beans the primary aromas had been burned coffee, stale pastry, and despair. Given the money I'd just dropped on bribery, I should've resisted, but I decided that the lingering eight dollars in my wallet had just found their forever home.

I was careful not to look over at Matt as I got in line. He was always very specific about correct stakeout behavior, so I pretended to be unaware of the rustling as he put away his newspaper and got in line behind me.

"Get anything?" he asked quietly behind me, not bothering with a greeting.

Even with the tension between us, I couldn't help but feel a bit hurt. "Hey, Matt," I responded pointedly. He didn't respond, and it scraped at my temper, drawing something darker and colder to the surface, enough that the pimply teenager behind the counter actually took a sudden step back when I stepped up. Chagrin immediately filled me, and I dropped my eyes and muttered my order. I didn't want to know what I'd looked like in that moment, but something told me that it wasn't what I was used to, at least on my own face. Maybe I would've recognized it on my sister's.

I dumped all of my change into the employee tip jar as a silent amends as I walked over to the pickup counter and heard Matt step forward to place his own order. Working out so regularly with Chivalry had given me both a convenient outlet and a mask for some of the changes that transition was having on me, but this was the longest I'd been away from my brother since the transition began. Perhaps, I realized uneasily, training me hadn't been the only reason why Chivalry had kept me so close this summer.

I closed my eyes and mentally recited as many character names as I could remember from *Battlestar Galactica*, reaching for calm. I couldn't resist the impulse to run my tongue quickly along the edge of my upper teeth, testing my canines for unusual sharpness. When I found nothing, that was when I finally started relaxing.

Then Matt was next to me. We were out of sight of the front window, and now he was willing to look right at me, just when I wished that he wouldn't.

"Hell of an impression you made on that kid." His voice was too assessing.

Now I was the one who didn't want to talk. I pulled the list of victims out of my pocket and pressed it into his hand, not looking at him. Instead I focused on the barista prepping my order, which was apparently having a very negative effect, as steaming foam suddenly went everywhere.

"These are the guys who got the tattoo." I gave in and finally looked over at Matt, whose expression was completely blank as he looked at me.

He raised his eyebrows. "He had this info just lying around?"

I gritted my teeth, hearing the suspicion in his voice and unable to do what I knew I should've been doing, which was reassuring him of how innocent and helpless I was, not terrorizing Starbucks employees so badly that the manager was having to take over my order. "Good filing system. He's all about growing his business."

"Friendly." Matt's brown eyes were boring into me, and the ceiling lights suddenly seemed far too bright. "Handed it right over?"

"Bribed him," I said shortly. I knew that I needed to distract Matt, so I reached over and tapped the new name. "Can you look into that last guy? Franklin Litchfield?"

"Yeah." His coffee arrived before mine, and he took a long sip. "So, who's your girl?"

"Just a friend who tagged along," I said. As soon as Suze had insisted on coming I'd known that I'd be answering this question, so I wasn't surprised. I was only impressed that Matt had held it in so long. "Her name's Suze."

"I remember her from the other night. Pretty girl."

"Oh yeah." There was a pause while the cringing Starbucks guy brought over my order—a small black coffee for me and a double chocolate-chip Frappuccino blended crème for Suze, whose enthusiasm for sugar rivaled a hummingbird's. Matt and I both looked down at the very different drinks in front of me, and it suddenly occurred to me that this could be interpreted the wrong way. "We're not dating. Just friends. But she is pretty—I mean, not that that makes a difference—" I was starting to feel much more like my usual self when Matt broke in to my attempt to eat my own feet.

"Amy Grann mentioned a pretty lady."

"What?" The bottom dropped out of my stomach. The

police had dismissed everything she'd said as the fantasies of a severely traumatized child, but Matt had gotten close to her long enough to hear her story, and he'd believed enough parts of it to be very dangerous.

"When she talked about who saved her. It was a dark-haired guy and a pretty lady. A pretty Asian lady."

I tried to distract him, oddly enough, with the truth. "Yeah, but didn't you also say that she thought that the lady turned into a fox?" The thought of what would happen if Matt started trying to investigate Suzume made my stomach cramp. I trusted Suze to leave Matt alone right now, but the kitsune were just as careful as the vampires in policing their secrets. If Atsuko, the White Fox, discovered that a private detective had the wrong kind of interest in any member of her family, she'd send someone to take out a possible threat. In all likelihood, Suze would be the one ordered to kill Matt. I swallowed hard and decided to try to brazen it out. "I think Suze would tell me if she turned into a fox and saved little girls. Anyway"—I pointed at the paper again—"that's a real lead, so let me know where it goes."

Matt was completely inscrutable as he sipped his coffee, studying me like a bug. "Sure thing." I could feel his eyes burning into my back as I hurried out the door and across the street again. It was harder than it should've been to walk away from him. Instincts were pushing at me not to leave an enemy at my back.

But Matt wasn't my enemy, I reminded myself. Couldn't be my enemy. I just had to protect him from the truth. Which I was currently doing a fantastic job of fucking up at.

My face must've given Suzume a good idea of how the meeting had gone, because she took her drink and granted me her rarest of gifts: silence.

Halfway to Dreamcatching, I glanced into my rearview mirror and noticed a very familiar Buick two cars behind us. A shiver ran through me as I realized that Matt was tailing us. I refocused on the road ahead of me, careful not to alert Suze that anything was wrong, but unable to control the nervousness that made my hands shake until I squeezed the steering wheel harder.

I flicked a quick look in the mirror again. Matt had

pulled back and was now three cars behind me, the safer tailing distance that I knew he preferred. I didn't say anything, or even dare trying to lose him and bring him to Suze's attention. I didn't know how she'd react or if she'd try to discourage him herself. And now that he was connecting Suzume to the Grann incident . . . I couldn't risk him investigating the Hollis kitsune. But with the revelations at Iron Needle, I couldn't hold off on investigating the elf connection without Suze realizing that something was wrong. I was trapped, and I had no idea how I was going to keep Matt from joining the rising body count.

I kept my mouth shut and drove straight to Dreamcatching, praying that I wasn't leading Matt even further into danger.

# Chapter 6

Dreamcatching was just as eye-searingly precious and utterly deserted as on our first visit. Lilah was again at the front counter, this time sitting on a tall stool with a copy of *Middlemarch* open in front of her, halfway through, indicating that it had been another slow business day. Her hair was again braided into a fuzzy and shining crown around her head, and today she was dressed in a long yellow dress that was as sunny as the smile she gave us when we walked up to the counter. She'd either forgiven Suzume for last time, or, as a consummate professional, she was hoping that we'd come back to purchase a few pewter objets d'art.

She was polite when she greeted Suze, but there was a pleased look on her face when she turned to me, and her voice was playful and teasing when she asked, "Change your mind about the personal energy-bubble class?"

Even the knowledge that Matt was currently tracking my movements couldn't stop the infectiousness of her bright mood, and I felt my mouth tug into a reluctant answering smile. "Sorry, not quite. We've actually been looking into"—I glanced around, just in case I'd missed some hidden New Age shopper or the creepy, pregnant Allegra. Everything seemed empty, but I erred on the side of caution, dropping my voice and saying, as if I had a role in a sixties British spy thriller—"that other thing."

Lilah nodded reassuringly at me. "It's okay. I'm the only one in the front today. Tomas is working in the back office, and our part-time stock boy just took a new shipment." Her mouth quirked a little. "They're both Neighbors too, so you don't have to worry about dropping secrets." Then she wiped the smile away, and very seriously asked, "Were you able to find what killed your friend?"

I looked over at Suzume, expecting her to jump in and answer, but to my surprise she stayed quiet. She'd left a large gap between us, and was leaning against the far end of the counter, her fingers idly picking through a small bowl of glass beads. Despite her best attempts to remain innocuous, though, there was a sharp attention in her eyes as she watched Lilah closely. Feeling my look, she turned to me just long enough to give me a small, encouraging nod, as if to say, *You've got this.*

It was a bit surprising—I'd played a large role in our last questioning, but she'd definitely been in the lead. Passivity was a strange and unusual approach from Suze, and not one that I was in any way used to seeing. Assuming that she probably had some internal reasoning going on, I pulled my attention back to Lilah, who was waiting patiently for my answer. From the sympathetic expression on her face, it was clear that she was assuming that this was a difficult conversation for me to have. It was, just not for the reasons she was assuming.

"No," I finally answered carefully, "but we've found a trail, and were hoping that you could give us some answers."

She nodded, but she also looked a little surprised. "Of course, if I can help you, but I already told you—"

I pulled out the glamoured circular for Iron Needle and set it down on the glass counter in front of her. She broke off whatever she'd been about to say and gave a small sound of surprise. Her hands shot out to it as if pulled on a wire, and she immediately began running her fingers over it, her eyes narrowed in concentration, silently mouthing words to herself. It reminded me of watching a blind person reading braille, every part of them focused on the information their fingertips were sending.

"That was sent to someone who got the same tattoos as my friend," I said.

Her fingers never stopping in their restless movements over the paper, Lilah frowned. "Tattoos . . ." she muttered, shaking her head before she'd even finished the word. "No, I know who runs this store." She said it with utter confidence. "Jacoby wouldn't hurt anyone. He isn't well, but he wouldn't hurt anyone." As she talked, she lifted the card up and rubbed her cheek slowly against it. It was a strange movement to watch, because she seemed to have almost completely forgotten my presence. "Besides," she said, still focused on the card, "he could never have set this glamour himself."

I looked quickly over at Suze, but she remained fixated on Lilah, watching her in a way that very viscerally reminded me that she was a predator at heart. Without guidance, I pushed forward, saying to Lilah, "I know. He told us. One of your full-blood elves did. They hired him to give a certain tattoo with a certain ink to anyone who came in with one of those, and then hand them a flier that would lead them to one of *your* speed-dating events." I pulled out the flier that Jacoby had given us and showed it to her.

Lilah flinched at the sight of it and bit her lower lip hard enough for me to wince myself. She looked worried now, and the hands that were holding the card were shaking enough for me to notice. But she nodded at the flier, then very carefully began to run her mouth across the front of the Iron Needle card, letting her lower lip drag against the paper as she breathed in heavily, almost seeming to taste it. Her golden-brown eyes were noticeably more golden than before, gleaming more than they should've under the fluorescent store lights. I shifted uncomfortably, realizing in that moment that being a half-blood was much more than having a pair of pointed ears and a useful illusion trick. Lilah was as much a poser as I was—pretending to be human while hiding a nature that was very, very inhuman.

"Nokke didn't set this," she said, her voice low and much throatier than usual, different in a way that both set my own instincts on edge and at the same time rubbed down my spine like velvet. "Maybe Hobany," Lilah muttered. "Maybe Amadon." Moving as suddenly as a startled deer, Lilah dropped the circular back on the counter and pressed the heels of her hands hard against her mouth. Her eyes squeezed closed in a way that I recognized all too well, and when they opened again their brilliance was gone, faded back into the unusually pretty, yet passable for human, golden brown that I remembered. She looked straight at me and I could feel her fear in the back of my throat. "We need to talk," she said, quiet and intense, "but we can't do it here."

"What do you—"

She dropped her voice even further, low enough that I had to lean in to understand her. "Tomas is in the back today."

"Do you think we could ask him—"

She shook her head hard and interrupted me. "You don't understand. He's *loyal*, Fort. Human murders won't matter to him, not with this." She tapped the edge of the circular with one finger, suddenly looking unwilling to touch it again, like it was dangerous. Lilah whispered, "For some of the Neighbors, it goes beyond loyalty to the Ad-hene. It's beyond devotion." Her eyes bore into mine, begging me to understand.

There was a rustling behind her, the scrape of a shoe against cheap carpeting, and she jumped like a girl watching a slasher film. Her hand shot out, grabbing her thick copy of *Middlemarch* and yanking it quickly on top of the circular, blocking it from sight. Automatically following her example, I stuffed the advertisement in my hand back into my jeans pocket.

The beaded curtain behind her parted, and a tall guy with a weediness and awkwardness that screamed *high school student* leaned into the main store with an air of general apology for his very existence. From the straight dark hair that hung over his ears and his skin tone I would've guessed he was Hispanic, but his eyes were a brilliant, unnatural emerald green, indicating that wherever his mother had hailed from, his father was from somewhere very different. He was carrying a large brown box with an overflow of packing peanuts that scattered around him like a lazy snowfall.

"Hey, Lilah," he started, then caught sight of us and froze, a dark flush filling his cheeks. "Oh, sorry. Didn't realize you were with customers." I felt a distinct flash of empathy as his voice cracked painfully twice in that simple comment, his blush darkening each time.

Lilah turned partially to look at him, her face and voice immediately becoming warm and reassuring, reminding me of how she'd acted around Allegra. Her shaking hands, hidden from the boy by her body, were the only sign of her real emotions. "It's not a problem, Felix. What do you need?"

He coughed twice, and, apparently realizing that he now had no choice but to talk in front of strangers, muttered, "I was opening up today's shipment and I was wondering where you wanted me to set up about twenty crystal unicorns."

"I'm not sure. Give me a second and I'll come back and look them over."

Felix nodded, looking relieved, and hurried backward so fast that his box tilted dangerously and released a huge puff of packing material, but thankfully no crystal unicorns.

When he was completely out of sight, Lilah turned back to us. "He's just a little shy," she said apologetically. "He'll grow out of it." Her hands, still shaking, fluttered a little, and she cleared her throat hard before continuing, "and the teen years are always so hard for the changelings." I wondered if she was thinking of Jacoby, who had clearly not grown out of whatever exacerbated hard times the changelings suffered through in high school. Then she leaned over the counter and whispered, "Listen, I'll call you and we'll meet somewhere to talk." She pulled her book off of the circular and nodded at it, clearly wanting me to collect it without her having to touch it again. I stuffed it back in my pocket, her own revulsion translating to me. "I'll call you soon," she repeated forcefully, and I wondered if she was talking to me or to herself.

I mouthed a good-bye, and Suze and I headed out to the car. I glanced around automatically in the parking lot, but if Matt was still following us, he'd found a hiding spot that I couldn't locate.

We were both quiet during the three attempts it took for the Fiesta's engine to catch, but as we pulled out and into traffic I looked over at Suze.

"Well?" I asked expectantly.

"Hm?" She gave me her most innocent look, the kind she would probably give if found in the dead of night in the middle of a chicken coop with blood and feathers stuck to her mouth.

"Don't give me that. What do you think about what just went down?"

Suze dropped the act and looked back at Dreamcatching with suspicion written all over her face. "Lilah was being awfully helpful for someone answering questions that could implicate others of her own kind."

"Maybe," I agreed, then considered. "But it sounded like she was trying to protect and exonerate Jacoby when I first showed her the circular. She was worried about him. She didn't sound like she was trying to protect those full elves, though. I thought she actually sounded scared of them." I glanced over at the kitsune.

Suze spoke slowly, almost reluctantly. "Unless she's got a better poker face than I think she does, she was really shocked when she saw the card. And she wasn't faking being afraid. And I can't say for sure, but I don't think she lied to us."

I thought about it while we sat at a stoplight. "Jacoby was talking about the differences between the Neighbors and Themselves, and Lilah talked about some of the Neighbors being extra loyal. Do you think there are splits in the elf and half-elf community?"

"Makes sense with what I've heard." She mulled it over, stretching her legs out as far as the Fiesta's limited leg room would allow, then added, "Lilah doesn't strike me as someone drinking the elf Kool-Aid."

Part of me relaxed. My gut had been telling me that Lilah had been honest, but I'd wanted some independent confirmation. In the arts of detecting deception, I trusted Suze's gut more than mine—in the same way that people consulted art thieves when building museum security systems.

With that out of the way, I turned to my second-most-pressing question. "Who was Lilah talking about? Hobany? Is that actually a person's name?"

"Fort, doesn't your brother tell you anything? The elves

are in single digits on the real ones, the full-bloods. Those guys have life spans that are so damn long that the rest of us just call them immortal and leave it at that. No one except them and the Neighbors know exactly how many of them there actually are right now, but there are only five names that get thrown around."

"Amadon, Hobany, Nokke. Who are the others?"

My phone rang, my ringtone cutting through the conversation very effectively. At Suze's very expressive glance, I considered that if I was going to be tracking down a killer and unraveling secret plans much longer, I would probably need a more serious ringtone than the Tetris theme song.

Looking down at the number displayed, Suze raised her eyebrows. "How about you ask your new girlfriend? Guess she wasn't kidding about calling you soon."

I'd already answered the call, so there was nothing to do except make a face at Suze that promised retribution. She looked extremely unimpressed.

Lilah was talking fast and with a slight echoing sound in the background that made me wonder if she was calling me from a bathroom.

"Hey, can I meet up with you somewhere after the store closes at six?"

"Yeah," I said "I'm working a partial shift. Can you come to my apartment around eight?"

She immediately agreed, and I gave her the address.

I paused, then just went ahead and asked. "Lilah, why are you being this helpful?"

"I know about our treaty agreements that the Ad-hene made with Madeline Scott," she answered grimly. "And I've heard about what Prudence Scott does to people who break the rules. Whatever the hell the Ad-hene are cooking up here, I don't want innocent Neighbors to pay the price for it."

I certainly couldn't argue with that. "Okay," I said, talking through the awkward moment. "I'll see you at eight. Call me if you get lost." Thank God for inane social niceties, I thought as I hung up.

Suze was looking at me, assessing, clearly weighing something but not saying a word.

Irritated, I asked, "What, Suze? You're looking at me like I've got stuff on my face."

"No, just thinking." There were subtexts to her subtexts in that comment.

I sighed heavily. "Are you going to share it with me?"

"Just remembering that I still have my old boom box in a closet."

"What?" It was a good thing that I'd just stopped at a red light, because the completely left-field nature of that comment gave my brain whiplash.

"You can borrow it."

"I'm going to need more help on this non sequitur, Suze."

There was a gleam in her eyes that I didn't know how to interpret, but I was pretty sure that it boded poorly for me. "You know, to hold up outside Lilah's window."

"You're nuts," I said flatly.

"I can already see you composing your mix tape. Don't forget to put 'In Your Eyes' on it. Chicks dig that one," she said, with a little twist of viciousness on the last part.

I shook my head. "I have to go to work and earn back some of that money I just spent bribing a junkie, so I'll drop you off at your place so that you can keep yourself company with the crazy."

She made an affronted sniff, and we drove in silence for several long, uncomfortable minutes until finally she internally forgave me and made an innocuous and clearly peacemaking joke about a particularly obnoxious billboard ad, which started a normal conversation. It allowed both of us to ignore the suddenly tense undertone that had emerged, and when I dropped her off we said good-bye with an unusual level of politeness.

As she started to walk to her door, I abruptly leaned out my window and said, "Listen, Suze, about the roommate thing—"

"Oh, don't worry, Fort." And the expression on her face was definitely enough to make me concerned. "I am *all over* that."

I shuddered and went to work.

I brooded through my work shift, wishing that carrying

tiny plates of expensive food could occupy more of my thoughts and give me less time to try to puzzle through either why elves would want to kill Gage in such a confusingly convoluted manner or Suze's moodiness. I was able to come up with an equal number of theories for both.

As if in answer to my inner desire for distraction, it was a slow night on service and I had the misfortune to be tapped as the test server for Chef Jerome. Whenever he was working on new dishes, some unfortunate member of the waitstaff was picked to see how the dishes would work when introduced to the movement of a serving platter. Tonight that unfortunate person was me.

Most of the dishes that night were pretty usual. Delicate, ornate, yet surprisingly sturdy. Chef Jerome's experiment with halved coconut shells turned out to be not quite perfectly balanced yet, much to my dismay and Chef Jerome's invective-laden rage. And the final capper on the evening was working with Chef Jerome's newest creation, a strange variation on bombe Alaska that involved several pieces of fruit that had been exquisitely carved into flower shapes and then drenched in some mysterious combination of alcohol, and which Chef Jerome envisioned as being carried out while on fire. Unfortunately the mix on the alcohol was a little off, and sparks kept catching on my shirt and having to be beaten down by Chef Jerome's alert sous-chef, Melissa.

By the end of the ordeal Chef Jerome was busily working on adjusting the alcohol mix to retain flavor but burn slightly more manageably, and I was reflecting that my wish for distraction had come at the high price of my work shirt, which now had several burns.

I finished my shift at seven. Paying the fee at the parking garage made me wince and remember why I usually took the bus to work. There was a lot behind Peláez, but it was only for the customers to park in. Those of us who actually worked there and drove in had to fend for ourselves, which in this part of town generally meant dedicated parking lots. The Peláez managers were extremely ruthless in enforcing their parking preferences. One of the busboys earned extra money by going into the lot and cataloguing the parked cars every thirty minutes. If a car was parked in the lot for more than three hours, then steps were immediately taken to determine if it actually belonged to a customer. If it wasn't, then the tow truck was called.

I called Suzume while I worked on getting the Fiesta started. I waited impatiently while the phone rang, then was surprised to find myself in voice mail, which had somehow never happened before. Even more surprising was how professional Suze's voice mail message was.

"Hey, just wanted to remind you to head over to meet up with Lilah," I said. I paused, racking my brain for something to say, then heard the incoming call beep. "Oh, good, that's you," I said in relief. "Crap, I shouldn't have said that out loud. Shit, I— Okay, I'm just going to give up now. Delete this message."

I had a bad feeling that that message would come back to torment me in some way. Deciding to deal with that hurdle when it came, I picked up Suze's call and repeated the less idiotic portion of my voice-mail message.

"Can't make it, Fort. Sorry."

"What?" I was shocked, and felt a pang of hurt feelings. I had to ask, "Is this about before? In the car? Or later? I swear, I have at least seventy-eight percent faith that you are doing a good job trying to find me a nonhuman roommate."

"Keep your skirt down, Louise; your slip is showing." Her derisive snort and insult to my masculinity were so quintessentially Suze that I relaxed. "I'm not ditching you; I'm at work. My cousin Midori has been covering for me the past few days, but one guy asked for me by name, so I couldn't bail. I'll finish this as soon as I can and come over, but in the meantime I'm sure you can handle Lilah if she starts getting feisty."

"Feisty in what way?" I asked suspiciously. Suze responded with a combination of cat meows and cracking whip noises, and I hung up on her.

After I put the phone away and wrestled the Fiesta into gear (the clutch was slowly dying and needed to be replaced—which was unfortunately what I'd been saving up for before I'd had to bribe Jacoby), I froze, weighing Suze's words. Was this a date? I pondered that for a second, then relaxed. No, this was a strategic meet-up to discuss serious territorial business.

Besides, if it was a date, I still had a half hour after I got home to change clothes before she showed up.

As it turned out, I did not have that time. When I reached the top of the third set of stairs, I found Lilah sitting in the hallway next to my door. She was still wearing the yellow dress from this morning, with the addition of a bright blue coat that fell into that category of coats that seem to straddle the line between heavy button-up sweater and dedicated outerwear. Her coppery hair was loose for the first time, falling down her back in a wavy mass that suggested a much higher wind outside than I had personally experienced. A stretchy white headband with a cheery fake sunflower attached to it was doing double duty of both keeping her hair out of her eyes and providing backup cover for her ears.

Seeing me, Lilah scrambled to her feet. I noticed that her ability to blush extended not just to her cheeks, but down her neck and presumably to lower reaches as well.

"Sorry I'm early," she said, making a noble attempt to brush off her backside without being obvious about it. "It's a really bad habit of mine. Usually I bring a book and wait in my car until I'm only fifteen minutes early, but I took a cab tonight."

Despite the circumstances that had led to this meeting and my own brooding over it, I smiled at the image of Lilah waiting outside parties until some invisible social acceptability clock counted down. "No problem, as long as you don't mind that I'm still dressed for work." I gestured to my charred shirt and my pants, which had been on the receiving end of one overfilled serving of Chef Jerome's coconut soup. I'd tried some, and it was an extremely delicious dish, but balancing something that came served in a hollowed-out half of a coconut had been too much of a challenge for me.

Looking down, Lilah laughed. "Not at all," she assured me. Then: "It's not like it's a date."

From the look on her face, she knew her mistake the

moment it came out of her mouth. I gave a very strained, very fake laugh as I agreed, "No, not a date at all."

She faked an answering laugh. Then we both laughed together. It was horribly painful.

"Because it's not," she said, still fake chortling heartily.

"Nope," I answered.

There was a long pause as we stared at each other, caught in a social nightmare.

It was totally like a date.

"Would you like a drink?" I asked, desperate to do something to salvage the situation.

"Oh, sweet Jesus, yes."

The last time Chivalry had asked me if I wanted something to drink, the result had been Macallan 1926, which was part of the impressive collection of alcohol that he had built up during Newport's days as a port for the booze runners during Prohibition. I'd learned later that the bottle he'd brought out with absolutely no show or ceremony would've run upward of sixty thousand dollars on the open market.

In stocking my own personal liquor cabinet, I'd had to take a more restrained approach. For one thing, there wasn't a lot of cabinet space in my apartment, and my liquor cabinet actually doubled as my cleaning-agent cabinet. So when I needed the social-lubricating benefits of hard alcohol, I pulled out my trusty bottle of Banker's Club—a brand of rum so cheap that it actually came in a plastic bottle. The taste matched the price, and as I mixed us each a rum and coke, I hoped that the comparatively high quality of the Coca-Cola would cover up the worst of my cost-cutting sins. Or that it would be so horrible that she'd overlook the fact that, lacking clean glasses, I'd poured our drinks into matching coffee mugs.

Lilah did make a notable face at her first sip, which she immediately tried to cover up by complimenting the apartment décor, but the answer to the foul taste was the same as with most alcohol: drink more. By our second glasses we'd both managed to move past the initial social awkwardness enough to be making eye contact again, and I was able to give Lilah a more detailed description of the situation to date, from Gage's death to Matt's discovery of the tattoo link to the missing persons' reports, finishing with the morning's visit to Iron Needle and the subsequent discoveries there.

Finally, with no more background information left, I asked her what she knew.

Lilah pondered the contents of her mug for a long moment before answering, and when she spoke it was very slowly and reluctantly. "Nothing more than you're telling me, Fort, but I'm worried about which members of Neighbors Jacoby said were involved. I wouldn't use his phrasing—"

"You mean *older, really snotty fucks, always brownnosing it up* isn't accurate?" I asked dryly.

That made her laugh. "Okay, maybe it's a little accurate," she said with a hint of wry humor, but then she immediately sobered again. "We call ourselves the Neighbors because it was one of the politer terms used back in Ireland for the older race. We call the true ones who are left the Ad-hene, or Themselves if we're not being entirely polite, but there are a bunch of other names they'd respond to. Sidhe, the Gentry, Tuatha Dé Danann, elves—all are accurate terms, plus dozens of others." She tossed back the last of her drink, then looked at me seriously. "The vampires live a long time. How old is your mother?"

"She was born the year that Edward II of England was deposed by his wife. Fourteenth century."

Lilah nodded. "And your brother and sister?"

"Prudence was born during the American Revolution. Chivalry was born at the end of the Civil War."

"And there aren't many other races that live half as long as vampires, right?"

"As far as I know." I couldn't help feeling a small spasm of irritation. Lilah knew the answers to all of her questions, and the subject of exactly how many centuries of life I could reasonably expect to see always put me in a poor mood. "What's your point?"

"My grandfather was old when the Romans first stepped onto British soil. Old and in the middle of a war among the Ad-hene that had already lasted a thousand years and devastated the population, but they kept fighting and killing because that was what they *liked* to do. To them, having a child, raising it, training it—those were things that you did so that someday you'd have a worthy opponent to kill. They whittled themselves down from probably a million at their peak to less than a hundred before they actually started even trying to do something about it. When they finally stopped being able to kill each other, they turned to torture." Lilah's face paled under her freckles at some memory, and she swallowed hard, taking a long moment before she continued. "You don't want to see the inside of Underhill, Fort. There are captive Ad-hene in there who will never die of old age, and who every morning are tortured and flayed, and every night are healed so that it can happen all over again."

"I didn't know about that," I said quietly. "My brother didn't tell me." There were a lot of things Chivalry hadn't told me during the time we'd spent together during the summer, and I hadn't pushed him on any of them. In that moment I was shamefully aware that I hadn't pushed him because I hadn't really wanted to know—that, transition or not, I still desperately wished that I could've continued running away from who, and what, I was. And Chivalry had let me, and told me only about what I needed to know at the moment, or the things that wouldn't truly appall me, like goats for trolls or feral cat colonies for kobolds. Not a fifteen-percent surcharge squeezed from local supernatural businesses. Not the torturing practices of the elves.

Lilah continued. "Underhill's openings into Ireland were locked for a reason. The cost to do it was the potato famine, but they didn't catch all of the Ad-hene. My grandfather, Nokke, was the one who came to America, and he's the one who negotiated with your mother for a place in her territory where a gate to Underhill could be opened. One of the rules she made all of them swear to was that the only prey they could hunt or kill was themselves." She set down her glass on the floor beside the sofa and scooted closer to me. It wasn't a romantic scoot, but almost as if being closer to me was necessary to underscore how seriously she needed me to take what she was saying. Her voice dropped, intensified, and as she spoke about her people, I wondered if she'd ever said these things out loud to any outsider before. "This is why I'm telling you this, Fort. There are a few people among the Neighbors who know everything I've just told you, and probably even more than that, and they *idolize* Themselves. All they think about is how they can somehow breed their way back to a race that is closer to what the Ad-hene were—more longevity, more power, more"—she paused, fumbling for a moment, then her jaw tightened and she said what had stuck in her throat—"more of the bloodlust. My boss, Tomas, is one of them. Most of the parents of the three-quarter crosses are, to some degree."

"And you're not?" I didn't try to contain my curiosity. I was trusting her, and nothing so far had made me doubt that I was trusting her, but the fact remained that the people she was describing to me would consider her part in this conversation treachery.

Lilah shrugged and leaned back, the intensity of the earlier moment diffusing as we switched topics. "My parents are both Neighbors. Growing up, so were all the kids that I was allowed to play with. Everyone lived in the same area, and were really tight-knit. It's the secrecy, you know? It ties us together." She smiled a little. "I remember in elementary school a bunch of the teachers thought that we were a cult. Not really wrong, either."

"So, what happened?"

"A lot of things. I mean, the life itself is completely insane. My mom and dad are half siblings." She laughed cynically at my expression. "Yeah, you heard me. My younger sister? She's not just my half sister; she's my *aunt*. My god, it's like we're damn show dogs with this obsession with genealogical charts. I wouldn't be surprised if an AKC rep arrived to give me a pelvic exam. My prom date? I thought he was my second cousin. *He* thought he was my second cousin. Turns out, nope, he's actually my dad's son. Apparently Dad was getting put out for stud for a while. Would've been nice to know that *before* I got to third base with a biological brother."

"Wow," I said, not exactly sure how to respond to that. One thing was clear—a conversation with this much incest in it required a third glass. I pulled a bottle of Bankcr's Club over and poured us both three fingers' worth, not even bothering to add Coke. I took a long drink, then said, "That is beyond fucked up."

"Yeah," she agreed. "I don't know which was the biggest kicker—my baby sister or my prom date. But as soon as I graduated from high school, I was *gone*. Like, in-the-wind kind of gone. I moved out to Phoenix. Got a job, an apartment, a boyfriend I wasn't related to, did everything I could to pretend I wasn't what I was. I played human. Took a few philosophy courses at the community college, rethought a lot of the things I'd just accepted."

I recognized all of those things from my own life. My desire to escape my mother's mansion and every part of being a vampire that I could had begun far earlier, but college and its aftermath had been my pantomime as well. "I get that," I told her, and when we looked at each other it was with a deep sense of perfect understanding. There were large parts about ourselves that we each hated and would rather pretend didn't exist, yet at the same time couldn't escape. I knew what had pulled me back into my mother's close orbit, but I didn't know what had changed for Lilah, so I asked her. "Now you're back in Providence and working with other Neighbors. What changed?"

"It was really good. I lived like that for seven years." For a long second, clearly thinking about those years, she seemed lighter, happier. I wondered what she'd been like away from her family and Providence when she was playing human. Just like I'd been doing until recently. It occurred to me how similar we were—and the thought surfaced that if I was with someone like Lilah, I could go back to pretending most of the time. The thought was both enticing and disturbing, and I almost missed it when Lilah said, "I came back home last year, after my boyfriend wanted to move in together." She took a long sip of her drink.

"A three-thousand-mile relocation is definitely one way to say no," I noted.

"Yeah, not my smoothest moment. And I still hate Themselves and their shit. I mean, honestly, I hate it. My grandfather and the others ... all they care about is trying to inbreed us as much as possible to somehow get an end result that is more like them. And those seven years away from all of that were the best seven years of my life. But it was seven years of hiding. Not just my ears, but about how I grew up, what I thought about, what I was struggling with. And when he kept trying to get more serious, I imagined doing that for the rest of my life . . . and I came back. Because for all that shit, I didn't have to lie. They knew who I was, *what* I was, and they could understand. We might argue about everything else, but at least they understand."

Looking at her, I wondered how much it must have cost her to make that decision. Because I knew that it hadn't just been about leaving the boyfriend and Phoenix; it had also been about abandoning a dream. Once again, I knew how that felt.

"Were your parents happy?" I asked, knowing what the response would be. Madeline had been over the moon with delight when I'd (as she put it) "come to my senses."

"Oh, *thrilled*," Lilah said, and we shared rueful, knowing smiles. "Every time my dad visits my apartment he tries to toss my birth-control pills, my mom is frantic to set me up with a three-quarter Neighbor, and my baby sister has a few sociopathic personality quirks that we're all trying to iron out." I winced. At least Prudence left me alone. "But I can live some of my life around humans, and when I need to, there are Neighbors who are more like me to hang around. So, right now, it kind of works." Her golden-brown eyes were considering as she looked at me. "How does it work for you?"

"What do you mean?"

She rearranged herself on the sofa, giving the impression of digging in and getting comfortable. "You live away from your family, with humans. I asked around about you after the first time you came by the store. The rumor was that you were living human for years." She sounded honestly curious and slightly envious.

"Yeah, I guess I was." I thought about it. "It was easier to pretend to be one, and I thought I was happy." Looking at Lilah, though, I was struck again that she was someone who really had walked in my shoes. I'd never doubted the depths of Chivalry's love for me, but he'd made no secret of the fact that he couldn't understand why I struggled with what we were. And as much as I valued Suze's odd friendship, she walked through the world with utter confidence and comfort in who she was. So, looking at Lilah, I was honest. "But I think you're right—it's harder now, seeing my family more, being reminded of all the crap that comes with being a vampire, but it's also . . . better, in some ways. Like with Suzume—it's just easier to be friends with someone without having to self-edit every family anecdote or joke, or be afraid that someone is going to notice something that is physiologically inhuman and call the CDC or the *National Enquirer*."

It felt good to say it. And good to look at Lilah and know that she understood.

There was a pause. Then Lilah asked, with a playful grin, "Hey, is it true that your mom owns that?"

I laughed. "No, that one's just a rumor. Someone else started it to throw cover." Then, "But here's a good one: my mother's brother Edmund got *Dracula* published."

Lilah gaped. "No!"

Finally, family history that was actually amusing. "Yeah, he owned Archibald Constable and Co. and thought that all of the mistakes would make it easier for real vampires to lie low. He also owned the magazine that published Sheridan Le Fanu's *Carmilla*."

Lilah was now laughing so hard that she slipped sideways on the sofa. "Did he publish Anne Rice, too?" she managed.

"No, apparently that just happened."

That set both of us off, and it wasn't until we tapered off into small snickers and hiccuping giggles that we realized how close together we'd ended up. Her face was right next to mine now, close enough that I could feel the warmth of her breath on my face. Our shoulders were touching, and my hand, which a moment ago had been chastely sitting on my own leg, was now pressed between us. We froze, and a million possible outcomes flashed through my brain as we looked at each other, neither of us leaning in closer, but neither pulling away either.

I wasn't sure what would've happened, but the charged

silence between us was shattered when a sudden rapping noise, coming from my bedroom, echoed through the apartment. We jumped apart, Lilah giving a startled squeak while I made a noise that, while definitely not feminine in any way, was certainly not how Rambo would've responded.

Pulling together the shreds of my composure, I reached down for my inner spaghetti Western hero and said, "Stay here," to Lilah. As she remained on the sofa, leaving me to the hosting duties of investigating creepy noises, I rushed into my bedroom, cursing myself internally for not stashing some kind of weapon under the sofa at some point.

I flipped on the lights in my bedroom, but after a tense glance around, nothing looked out of place. I retrieved the Colt out from under my mattress, feeling deeply relieved once it was comfortably in my hand. The rapping noise repeated, coming from my window. I approached it cautiously, holding the Colt ready in a two-handed grip. With a deep breath, I stepped completely in front of the window, prepared to jump back or fire (or do both simultaneously) if Gage's killer had returned.

It was a distinct letdown to see Suze sitting casually in the tree outside my window.

She smiled at the sight of me and wiggled her feet, looking completely unconcerned about just how high up she was perched.

"Suze? What the hell's wrong with using my front door?" I yelled out at her as I pulled up the window and its screen, entertaining very dark thoughts about the gun still in my hand. Not that I'd ever shoot her. But a warning shot might someday be in order. Suzume had made window entrances into my apartment before, but she'd always done so in fox form, and usually only for legitimate pranking purposes.

"Just wanted to check out the lay of the land before I came in. Just in case exciting things were happening." I gave her a very dirty look, and she made a shooing gesture with her hand. "Scoot over, I'll hop in."

I watched in disgust as she climbed over the window ledge and inside. If she'd been parked outside for god only knew how long, then she'd certainly chosen her moment to knock loudly and scare the crap out of me and Lilah.

"My neighbors are going to call the cops, you know," I said, resenting how she somehow managed to climb inside the window with the grace of a prima ballerina.

Suze made a very rude noise that conveyed her opinion of my neighbors. "They don't expect to see me, so they didn't see me." She gave me a smug smile. "Yeah, I'm awesome. No JV-squad elf tricks here."

I'd seen Suzume's fox-illusion magic in action often enough to know that she had some room to brag there, but I wasn't sure that it was an entirely appropriate comment, given who she well knew was sitting in my living room.

As if thinking about her had summoned her, Lilah's head popped around my doorframe. "Oh, Suzume. I thought I heard your voice," she said, sounding relieved. Then, confused, she asked, "Why didn't you just come in the door?"

Suzume rolled her eyes dramatically. "Lord, now I have two people who need the CliffsNotes version." Then, with a thick layer of condescension, she said, "Fort can catch you up later, Keebler. But if what I overheard was correct, and you don't have a single new piece of information to add to what we already know . . . ?"

"Well, I might've added context and nuance . . ." Lilah started, but trailed off and gave up at the expression on Suze's face.

"Exactly." Suze clapped her hands loudly, making both of us jump again. "If you're both done whining about family pasts, then I have an *actual* plan that will help out."

"What?" I asked.

Suze gave me a brilliant smile. "We're going to break into the Iron Needle and see what Jacoby wasn't willing to tell us."

I stared at Suze in horror, and, glancing over, saw that Lilah was in a similar state of jaw-dropped surprise.

"It'll be fun!" Suze enthused.

An hour later Lilah and I were looking around nervously, still unclear how Suze had actually talked us into this scheme, while the architect of our discomfort occupied herself by picking the lock on the back door of the Iron Needle with a set of disturbingly professional implements. A security light from one of Jacoby's neighboring businesses was giving us just enough light to both let Suzume work and make me feel far too exposed.

"So . . . do you guys do this a lot?" Lilah asked awkwardly. Because of the need to be somewhat circumspect she'd had to exchange her blue jacket for my black hoodie, and it fit her about as well as a three-man tent, with the hem hitting just above her knees.

"Definitely not," I answered.

"Speak for yourself," Suze said. There was a soft clicking sound, and she smiled widely. Carefully removing her tools and tucking them back into her front pocket, she crouched down and motioned for me and Lilah to imitate her. Still hunkered down, she reached up, turned the knob, and pushed the door open just enough to poke her head into the building. It was pitch-black inside and after a tense moment, Suze dropped to her hands and knees and slunk her entire upper body through the doorway. A second later there was a loud crash, and I jumped a mile, feeling Lilah's hands grip my arm hard in surprise.

"Suze," I hissed loudly.

She pulled back and gave us both her best pityingly superior look. "Calm down for a second," she scolded. "I just pushed over his trash can." With that, she turned her attention back to the store, listening attentively.

While we waited, it slowly occurred to me that Suzume was deliberately testing to make sure that the building was unoccupied. We'd known from our earlier visit that the Iron Needle closed its doors at nine p.m., but whether Jacoby left the premises at that point was unclear. Lilah said that he'd been reduced to living in his store a few times that she knew of but wasn't sure if that was still the case, and glancing in all the windows (while doing our best to look completely surreptitious) had revealed nothing except that Jacoby had some aversion to sunlight and had blacked them all out, even the ones in the back. If someone was inside they would've come and investigated the noise that Suzume had just made, and we'd still be in a position to run away in a very Monty Python–esque manner.

I realized glumly that I was probably going to have to compliment Suze on her tactics later on. Nothing was more insufferable than Suzume accepting a compliment.

After a very long and stressful pause, with Lilah slowly cutting off the circulation of blood in my arm, Suze stood up and brushed off her pants. "Okay, all clear," she said, her voice pitched low. "If you find a light switch, hit it."

"No need," I said, taking my moment to prove that I was at least marginally prepared for this outing and pulling my extra big Maglite out of the small duffel bag I had grabbed on the way out of my apartment. Lilah finally noticed that she was clinging and disengaged herself with a muttered apology.

Suzume's expression as I switched on the flashlight was not quite as admiring as I'd expected. "What the hell, Fort?" she asked. "I thought that bulge was from your shotgun."

"Are you crazy?" I responded, shocked. "No!"

She frowned, then pointed at the misshapen pocket of my Windbreaker. "Did you stuff your .45 in there, then?"

"No."

"Then what did you bring?"

"Glow sticks," I said, pulling them out. "From my black-out emergency kit." She stared at me, appalled, and I said, "What? We're engaged in crime. That means flashlights and . . . you know." I waved the glow sticks, wishing that I hadn't chosen the multicolored pack.

"I'll take a glow stick," Lilah piped up helpfully.

"Quiet, you," Suzume said with a dangerous undertone before turning and laying into me. "Are you seriously telling me that you didn't bring a gun? Are you nuts?"

Her voice had gone up several octaves, and I had to fight to keep my own low when my natural impulse was just to snap back at her. "B and E my mother can cover up," I bit out. "That *plus* a firearm that I haven't actually registered and don't have a permit to carry? I'd rather *not* run up legal bills that exceed my college tuition, if you don't mind."

Suze shook her head in disgust, then shifted her dark gaze to Lilah. "And you? Tell me that you at least have a stun gun in that purse."

We all looked down at Lilah's purse, which was small and

made out of some nubby red fabric. My experience with my ex-girlfriend told me that it was the kind of purse that women referred to as adorable, and I strongly doubted that it contained a stun gun.

"Sorry, I really didn't expect the evening to go in a direction where weaponry was required," Lilah said dryly. "But I do have a spare tampon if you need one."

Suzume threw her hands up. I eyed her suspiciously, not liking what the conversation had suggested about her own assumptions for this trip. Wearing a long-sleeved jersey shirt and a pair of very close-fitting black pants (*very* close-fitting, and I'd been having trouble keeping my eyes in polite areas while she was picking the lock), and having mocked my earlier suggestion that she bring a coat given the early-October bite in the air, I couldn't imagine she had anything stashed beyond her usual switchblade. Knowing her too well, though, I asked anyway. "Suze, are *you* carrying?"

She rolled her eyes at me and suddenly produced a very long, very serious-looking fixed knife that was almost the length of her own forearm. There was no ornamentation to it at all—it was just very straight, slim, extremely sharp steel with a leather-wrapped black handle. There were no doubts that this was a knife made solely for the business of cutting things.

I jumped nearly out of my own skin at the suddenness and sheer implausibility of its appearance. "Holy crap!" I said, completely forgetting the importance of keeping my voice down. I lowered it immediately as my voice echoed through the empty back parking area, but couldn't help pointing out, "You brought a freaking sword!"

Suzume scoffed. "It's twelve inches. Still counts as a knife." She glanced at it, considering, then amended, "Maybe counts as a machete."

It was only through strong effort that I kept my voice low. "How the hell did I not see that?" I gestured generally to her clothing, which looked incapable of hiding that kind of weaponry unless she had taken off her shirt and rolled the knife up in it.

"'Cuz I'm awesome like that," Suzume said, her smirk

wide and shining in the light from my flashlight. She pointed at Lilah, then at herself. "Respect."

Lilah, who had been as surprised as I was when the sword emerged, hung behind me. "I didn't see a glamour," she said, sounding shaken.

Suzume snorted. "That's where elves always go wrong. I didn't try to hide the knife. I just used a little push that redirected where people looked so that they never noticed this was strapped to my leg."

"Redirected where?" I asked.

"My ass."

"Oh, thank god," Lilah said loudly, clearly relieved. We both looked over at her inquisitively, and she blushed brightly enough to be noticeable even in the poor lighting. "I'm just, you know . . . glad. That it was because of magic that I was noticing . . ." She trailed off, her mortification clearly only getting worse the more she talked. Then she gathered herself up and said, "And, hey, why don't we start looking for something incriminating instead of just standing around yapping." She grabbed one of my glow sticks, cracked it, and shook it decisively. It was bright pink. She frowned at it—apparently this wasn't quite the punctuation mark she'd had in mind—then pushed past both of us to walk in the back door of the building. There was a soft scuffle; then she snapped on a wall switch. The light in the room came on weakly, one of those cheap fluorescent overheads that needed time to warm up before they offered anything except an almost sullen glow. All the front windows were blacked out, so we didn't have to worry about anyone seeing anything suspicious from the street, even though this already looked like the kind of neighborhood where people minded their own business. We followed her inside, and I pushed the door closed behind us and relocked it before looking around.

We were inside Jacoby's office, which previously I'd only partially seen through a cracked door. A full view was even less prepossessing than the partial had been. Every surface was coated with paper—from old tattoo sketches to unopened mail with FINAL NOTICE stamped across the front. There appeared to be some furniture in the room, but it was observable only as vague shapes beneath the avalanche of junk. Bulging file folders sat stacked on the floors, topped off with partially eaten Hot Pockets and overflowing ash trays.

Lilah flipped her hair over her shoulder and resolutely started sifting through the top pile on Jacoby's desk, and I felt bad for not sticking up for her a moment ago. After all, I'd also found myself pondering Suzume's posterior assets with more than the usual intensity that evening and castigating myself for it. At least I hadn't been dealing with sudden internal sexuality concerns on top of it.

That brought my thoughts back to the root of the situation, and I eyed Suzume's monster knife, which she was still holding. "Isn't that a bit extreme?" I asked, in what I hoped was a withering tone of voice.

Suzume looked at me, surprisingly serious. "Fort, do you know what we're hunting?" she asked.

"No," I answered.

"Me neither."

I waited. Then, ". . . So?"

"So I'm keeping my options open here. I'd rather not be wishing at some point down the road that I'd brought my big-girl knife."

"Do you seriously call it that?" I asked.

The ghost of a smile played at her lips. "Well, I also call it Arlene."

I couldn't help it; I gave a brief, smothered laugh. Her point made, Suze slid the knife back in its sheath, which I now registered was indeed strapped to her right thigh and gave her a very Lara Croft kind of appeal. I forced myself to turn my attention to the piles of folders on the floor, but when I glanced back at Suzume a few minutes later, I couldn't see the knife again, even though I knew where to look. I did, however, notice again what a very nice backside Suzume had.

With three of us looking, we made good progress, but found nothing beyond useless papers, past-due bills, one disturbing discovery of at least twenty dirty needles sitting in an old soup take-out container filled with bleach, a few stashes of white powder that we all moved quickly past, and one comparatively innocent drawer filled with pot. We found the pile of glamoured Dreamcatching fliers that he'd described to us, and whole boxes full of apparently standard tattooing ink, but nothing that gave us any more clues than before. Lilah checked all of them, identifying each time that the glamours had been set by members of the Ad-hene. When we'd pulled her into the break-in party, it had been in the hope that she could identify the glamours of more participants in whatever the hell was going on, but our search was yielding no new leads.

We ended up in the part of the shop with the tattoo chair, with me poring through the thick binder of Jacoby's client list, looking for any names that he might not have given to us, while Suzume and Lilah made one last pass through his under-counter storage and broom closet, still finding nothing except more needles; more ink; a small stash of what may have been meth; and not a single mop, broom, or plunger (this also explained the state of his bathroom, which we had all agreed upon first sight could hold no clues whatsoever, and closed the door on firmly).

That was where we all were when the sound of a key being wiggled in an uncooperative lock suddenly emanated from the front door. There was no time for all of us to run for the back, and Suze shoved Lilah hard into the broom closet she was investigating and slammed it shut. I was relieved—Jacoby might not have been a big fan of the Neighbors, but with his willingness to exchange information for cash it was definitely not in our best interests for him to know that we were working with a mole.

But it wasn't Jacoby who walked in the door. Instead it was a tall woman with a figure that would politely be referred to as statuesque and impolitely referred to as slammin'. A great deal of it was on display in a short, fire-engine red dress liberally coated in sequins that was practically spray-painted onto her and definitely fit into the category of club wear. She held the keys to the store in her right hand, and in her left was an old-fashioned glass bottle, the kind usually seen in rows in antiques stores or old-timey seashore shops. The contents were distorted by the older style of thick glass, but it was filled barely a quarter of the way up with a black substance that, as it sloshed the sides, revealed a weird reddish undertone, as if oil and red paint had been poured into the same container but were failing to mix.

This, I realized, was undoubtedly Jacoby's "real sexy Latina," here to deliver some of the special ink for the band tattoos. We definitely weren't what she'd been expecting to find, but there was only a brief pause and a flicker of surprise on her perfect face, with its shockingly high cheekbones, and she strolled in, pushing the door closed behind her.

"Madeleine Scott's baby," she said, and gave a taunting, throaty laugh. "Stupid little vampire, poking your head out of the nest." She gave a nasty smile, showing a mouthful of teeth that were just slightly sharper than they should've been. "Poking your head where it doesn't belong. You'd better watch out, or someone will cut it off. Maybe me."

"Soli, I presume," I said, ripping off H. M. Stanley without a qualm, as I closed the binder I'd been looking at with a loud thump. Suze stayed behind me, in front of the closet where Lilah was stuffed. She wasn't hiding her sniffing, practically *whuff*ing as she sampled the air surrounding the new visitor. I glanced from Soli, who simply curled her lips into an approximation of a smile, back to Suzume. Suze caught my eyes and nodded once, and I knew from her face that the scents matched. This was the one who'd dumped Gage's body into his room like a sack of garbage.

I wasn't thinking of much when I started walking toward her other than the conviction that while I needed information from her, my first priority was going to be to hit her. That must've shown in my face, because she paused at the long counter that divided the front of the parlor from the back and set down the bottle of ink very carefully next to a pile of our belongings, which included the hoodie I'd lent Lilah and my heavy Maglite.

Her smile stretched across her face as she watched me come toward her. As I swung my first punch, she laughed.

I didn't connect. She was faster than I was, faster even than Suze had been when we'd sparred. Past my first punch I found myself suddenly busy blocking the blows she was directing at me. One fist slid right through my defenses,

slamming into my stomach with a power that didn't remotely match her size. I gulped air, but when she paused to
savor it I was able to grab her arm and shoulder and shove
her back against the counter, then nail her in the ribs with
a punch. It was like punching a brick wall, with none of the
slight give and flex that even a strike that landed directly on
bone should've yielded. Pain blossomed through my hand,
and I gave a sharp yell.

Distracted by my hand, I wasn't able to block in time,
and her return strike landed directly on my face, knocking
me down and onto my ass. She followed me down, her
hands wrapping around my throat in a way that should've
been reminiscent of all the fighting I'd done with Suze, but
instead suddenly showed me just how careful the kitsune
had been to hold back with me. Her hands went straight for
the vulnerable, pounding pulse in my throat and bore down
mercilessly. I wrapped my hands around her wrists, but
couldn't break her grip. All too quickly, red flared in my
vision and my lungs screamed for air.

One barely heard footfall was the only warning Soli had
before Suzume tackled her full-out, knocking Soli's hands
away and allowing me to gasp in a breath. For the first moment the two women were sprawled out on me, but Soli
rolled quickly, taking Suze with her, and the two were immediately scrabbling on the floor, wrestling for the top position. Height and weight were against Suzume, and as I
sucked in needed oxygen I saw Soli end up on top, and she
again went for the throat. Suzume knocked her hands away
and tried to throw her body far enough to one side to knock
the taller woman off, but Soli rode her down again and
punched her hard enough in the face to daze Suze.

I pushed off the floor, managing to get only as high as my
knees, but that was enough, and I threw one arm around
Soli's neck and the other around her torso and used my
weight to yank her bodily off of Suzume. As I pulled her
away Soli scratched violently at Suze, and I realized that
there was something very wrong with her hands—a long
black claw, curved like a heavy bird of prey's talon, was
punching through the tip of each of Soli's fingers, jutting out

beneath and sometimes even through the beds of her perfectly human-looking and French-manicured nails. There were long, deep slices in Suzume's shirt at her upper chest, with swiftly darkening edges that spoke of deep cuts in the skin beneath that were bleeding freely.

Soli's elbow slammed into the side of my head as I concentrated on trying to pull her farther away from Suze and I fell backward, losing my grip on her as she hopped up with eerie dexterity. On my back, I managed to kick her as hard as I could in the back of her right knee, making her wobble and struggle to keep her balance. She did, and the brief opening gave Suzume the chance she needed to get back up, and now that long, deadly knife was in the kitsune's hands. Suze struck, the long knife whipping so quickly that I would've had no chance to avoid it, but Soli was too fast, pulling to one side and letting Suze cut only air.

Suze had thrown too much weight into the strike, and for a second she was off-balance and unable to pull back, and Soli took the chance to rake a hand of those black claws across Suze's side, hard enough that Suze made a loud exclamation of pain and surprise. She pulled back sharply, barely getting out of the way before Soli's other hand swatted down on a similar path.

We were outclassed, I realized as I pulled myself up again. Getting close to Soli wasn't an option again with those claws, and I looked desperately for something heavy to throw, and finally spotted my heavy Maglite sitting on the counter. I yanked hard at the edge of my sweatshirt that it was resting on, pulling it into my reach but at the same time giving a hard knock to the glass bottle of ink that Soli had set down. It fell loudly to its side at my pull and then was swept off the counter completely as I grabbed the long flashlight, and hit the floor with an unmistakable shattering sound.

Soli's head whipped around at the sound, and her face finally lost its taunting expression, replaced by hot anger. I didn't pause, but took my opportunity and threw the Maglite straight at her head with as much force as I could put into it. She saw it coming and ducked a split second before it would've smashed into her, and it continued on its path, right into the large front window of the Iron Needle, creating a storm of flying glass.

Soli stayed in a duck, and I crouched automatically, throwing an arm over my head, but Suzume ignored the window completely and focused on taking advantage of her moment. The long knife sliced down—again, Soli was aware of the danger and moved with unnatural speed, but this time it wasn't quite fast enough. Cutting in a downward, right-to-left motion, Suzume had been aiming for Soli's neck, but instead caught her at the shoulder, digging in and slicing across her chest and arm.

The knife penetrated, but there was no blood at all. Instead her perfect skin tore like paper and a thick, white, viscous fluid welled out and dribbled slowly out of the wound site. The sliced skin suddenly slumped, handing open like an old, ripped shirt, revealing something beneath it that was hard, shiny, and black and looked like a beetle's carapace.

There was a momentary pause as we all stared at what had been revealed; then the room was abruptly filled with a dense reek of decay, forcing my brain to dig up a comparable sensory memory of when I was eight and on a Boy Scout hike that, due to the scout leader's misreading of a map, took us through a mile of boggy marshland. At one point I'd stepped on something more solid than the rest of the marsh, and when I'd foolishly kicked it, I discovered that it was the rotting, half-eaten corpse of a raccoon.

That had smelled almost as bad as this did.

Soli pressed one long finger into the cut, tracing the damage and scraping her talon across the black surface to produce a sound that was reminiscent of nails across a chalkboard. She looked up, not at Suze but at me, and I realized that she was now very well and truly pissed off.

"I liked this skin," she said, rage dripping from the words even as white glops of fluid hit the floor. "I wasn't ready to replace it." Her finger moved up, the claw dragging almost reflectively over what were, even at this juncture, some of the most spectacular breasts I'd ever seen. "You'll be paying for my new suit," she said, and even though I had no idea what she meant, I felt a deep chill of foreboding.

If that had meant nothing to me, it had meant a lot to Suze, because comprehension suddenly filled her face, followed almost immediately by horror.

"Skinwalker," Suzume growled, and Soli looked away from me to focus on her. "Your kind aren't allowed in this territory."

The word scraped against a memory of a half-listened-to lecture from Chivalry about the state of the territory, but before I could retrieve it, or Soli could respond to what Suze had said, the door of the shop slammed open and Matt stood solidly in the doorway, his old .38 service pistol in his hands and pointing at the room in general.

"None of you move a goddamn inch," he said, looking around, trying to figure out what was going on. His eyes went first to me, then, at the sight of Suze's extremely long knife, he refocused both his attention and the sighting of his pistol to her. Then he registered Soli, and the horrible moment where I saw his gun waver as his brain struggled against the incomprehensibility of what he was seeing seemed to stretch on forever.

Then Soli apparently decided that the situation had gone far enough, and went for the door. As she came toward him, Matt automatically swiveled the gun toward her but couldn't decide in time whether to squeeze the trigger. Thinking of those claws and just how vulnerable Matt was, I started for them as well, but Soli was already at him. Grabbing him with both hands, she threw him bodily across the room, and he slammed into me, knocking both of us backward and into the heavy counter. I lost sight of Soli and everything else as my head smacked against the floor, hard enough to disorient me.

Everything in my brain swam around for a moment, and from a long distance I could hear Suzume yell my name. I tried to push myself up and into a sitting position, but something heavy was lying across me. I blinked, trying to figure out what it was; then the smell of blood filled me, and everything that was me seemed to wink out like a blown candle, leaving just a raging hunger.

I sat up fast, and what had covered me fell to my lap. It was heavy, and as I panted in a breath I knew that it was a human that was bleeding. The smell wasn't just in my nose; it was in my mouth and covering my tongue and my throat, and I breathed it in, and all of the aches and pains that had been filling my body a moment ago were gone, and the only thing in my mind was that this was *so good*, but it could still be even *better*, and I wrapped my hands against the human and pulled it, unresisting, closer to me, even as I dropped my head down, down toward the blood that was dripping so beautifully.

It was less than an inch away when something grabbed my hair and pulled my head back sharply, and I snarled at the thing that had done it not just because of the pain that had erupted in my scalp but because it wanted the blood that was *mine*—

Then I was hit squarely across the face, right in the spot that even in my haze had still been throbbing dully from where something had hit me before, and something screamed, "Fortitude!" right in my face. When I blinked, that something was a woman with tilted, richly black eyes, and I blinked again and knew that it was Suzume, and that she was about to backhand me across the face again.

"It's okay—it's okay," I said, flinching backward as far as I could, given that she still had a death grip on my hair with her left hand. She eyed me, hard and suspicious.

"Is that you?" she asked.

"Yes."

"How do I know?" Her hand never wavered, and she seemed to be seriously contemplating backhanding me again for certainty.

"You could ask me my favorite color," I said weakly. "Or what the air-speed velocity of an unladen swallow is."

She didn't smile, but her grip on my hair relaxed, along with the look on her face. "Good," she said, shortly. "Now let me grab your buddy."

"What?" I looked down, and Matt was lying across my lap, unconscious. His head had hit the counter, and blood was still pumping merrily from a cut on his scalp. Horror bubbled up in me. "Oh, shit, Matt," I said. The memories hit me, and I rolled over and puked on the floor.

"*Timing*, Fort, timing!" Suze said, pulling Matt away from me as I continued to heave. My eyes were closed when I heard her yell, "Lilah! You can stop the courageous huddling you're doing and come give me a fucking hand!"

"Don't yell at her for doing the smart thing and what you told her to do," I muttered, keeping my head down. I felt a soft hand pressed against my forehead, and a handful of tissues stuffed into my hand. Cracking my eyes, my first impression was of just how frizzy Lilah's hair had gotten while she hid in the closet. It was like a copper chia pet—adorable.

"She's right, you know," Lilah said, guilt filling her too-bright eyes. "That's what I did. Even when you two were getting ripped up."

I wasn't sure what to tell her. I doubted her presence would've made any difference in the fight, but tactful phrasing was beyond me right now, and I focused on wiping saliva and the remnants of dinner off my face. As for the floor, it wasn't as if my puke made much of a difference in the sanitation level.

"We don't have time for this crap," Suze snapped. "With the noise we made, someone would've called the cops. Grab anything that's yours and let's get out." She jerked her chin at me. "Fort, Matt's yours. Get him."

"Suze, he's *sick*," Lilah broke in.

"And he's still the only one of us that can carry that much deadweight." She'd grabbed some paper towels and was winding them around Matt's head to stanch the blood. I wondered whether it was for Matt's benefit or to prevent a blood trail from forming. Probably both.

But she was right, as in many other things, and I pulled myself up and gritted my teeth. After what had just happened, I would've preferred to hide under my bed for a week before coming within ten feet of Matt, let alone having to not just touch him, but come so close to his bleeding head again. I reached for him, then flinched back, unable to do it.

Suzume jabbed me sharply in the side. "Suck it up, buttercup," she said. "We don't have time for you to have the vapors."

That pissed me off, and it was anger that let me pull Matt onto my shoulders in a fireman's carry and stand up. It was a good thing I'd been doing a lot of lifting lately — the beginning of my transition had made me stronger than I should've been, but Matt was solidly built with muscle, and as soon as his weight was on my shoulders I was immediately reminded of every bump and bruise from the fight.

I headed for the back door. Suzume was moving quickly around me, checking the floor and counters for anything that was ours. We were almost at the door when I remembered, and I turned to Suze and said, "Matt's gun—"

"Lilah, grab it. It fell by the door."

I looked back. Lilah hurried over to it, but when she reached down to take it she paused, eyeing it like a poisonous snake. The hesitation was brief; then she set her jaw and grabbed it firmly. With quick motions she swaddled the gun in my hoodie to conceal it from any curious eyes and stuffed the bundle under her arm.

It tugged at something inside me that wanted to protect her. But at the same time another part of me felt annoyed by it, by the understanding that Lilah would have to be protected, and there wasn't a choice to it.

For a horrible moment I wondered whether Suzume had felt those same conflicting feelings toward me when we'd first met, which had been while I was being mugged by Bruins fans.

We were halfway to the car when we heard the sirens. We'd been lucky that the area was mainly filled with businesses and it had taken that long. All of us stepped up our pace anyway, Lilah falling in beside me and doing her best to try to take some of Matt's weight by lifting his legs. It didn't exactly help, but I appreciated the thought. I also made a mental note to suggest that Matt cut back on his carbs.

In the interest of circumspection, my Fiesta had been parked three blocks down the street in the lot of an abandoned gas station. When we reached it we discovered that it had made a new friend — Matt's Buick was parked right beside it.

"Ever get the feeling we're being followed, Fort?" Suze asked. I didn't answer, instead focusing on doing my best to gently sit Matt on the ground. "We can't ignore this," she continued. "I know this isn't easy for you, but he was following you. He just came running into a fight and got a full look at something he definitely shouldn't have." She looked at me. "You know what your mother would tell you to do."

"He might've saved our lives by coming in when he did." Matt's face was far too pale, white even against his impromptu paper-towel turban. Blood was drying on his forehead and down his cheeks, making it uncomfortable for me to be so close to him because I could still smell it, and it still smelled good.

Lilah crouched down next to me, leaning in to look at him closely. "He should've been waking up by now," she said quietly. "If . . . we would need to take him to the hospital." I could hear what she was saying between the lines: if I wanted him to live, he needed medical attention. If I didn't, then I should probably do nothing.

The rules in my mother's territory were clear: if a human became a threat and endangered the secrecy that protected everyone, that threat needed to be neutralized. Sometimes it meant a bribe, sometimes intimidation, and other times it meant killing. Most felt that killing was the safest option. Lilah knew that as well as I did.

"Help me get him in the car. We'll drive him over to the—"

"Fort." Suze cut me off. Looking at her, I was struck by how torn she looked. Her voice gentled. "You know we can't do that."

"I won't let him die, Suze," I warned her, praying that she wouldn't push me. I didn't want to know what choices I might have to make.

We stared at each other, neither moving. Then she glanced away fast, took a deep breath, and said, "Put him in the backseat of his car. I'll take him over to my house and get someone to look at him."

"I'm not putting this on you," I argued. "If anyone is going to risk pissing off my mother, it's going to be me." After all, she wouldn't kill me.

"Oh, believe me, it's *going* to be you," she said darkly as she reached down and grabbed Matt's legs. "Keebler, make yourself useful for five seconds and pat him down for his keys. Fort, grab the torso." While Lilah checked his pockets, Suze leaned closer to me, her voice dropped, and I knew that this was as good an offer as she was going to make me. "I'll haul him home and get him checked out, but he's under lock and key until he wakes up and you talk with him. If we're lucky, that hit to the head rattled his brains enough that he won't start babbling about monsters and we won't have to go to our fallback position."

"And if we do?" I asked.

Suze started to answer, then stopped herself and took a deep breath. "We'll talk about it then."

I nodded slowly. "I'll follow you in the Fiesta."

"Better make a phone call while you're at it."

We lifted Matt together, both initially stumbling and barely holding him. "Fuck," I muttered, suddenly remembering our other crisis. "The skinwalker." There was a short list of creatures that my mother had banned from entering her territory. The skinwalkers were right at the top. I'd never seen one before tonight, but some of Chivalry's stories were trickling back to me. None of them were reassuring.

If I hadn't met Soli tonight and seen how easily she'd been mopping the floor with me and Suze, I would've risked hiding her presence from my family. With Matt's involvement, the thought of deliberately inviting the interest of the people who would be the first to try to eliminate the threat he posed was insane. But the fact was that Suze and I were completely outmatched. I needed my brother.

We maneuvered Matt into his backseat, with Lilah doing her best to sweep off an open area for him, then helped pull him in as gently as possible. He groaned once but didn't make any other sounds. There was a blanket crumpled up on the floor of the passenger's seat that I knew Matt kept stashed for long stakeouts, and Lilah pulled it out and tucked it over him. She tugged up the paper towels around his head to check on his cut, and I looked away quickly, shame choking me. Matt had gotten hurt, and my first instinct had been to capitalize on it, not help him.

Lilah climbed out of the car. "Looks like it stopped bleeding," she said. I felt her fumble around and pat my shoulder, then squeeze it quickly and drop her hand. I looked up. She was focused on me, and there was sympathy on her face. She hadn't seen what I'd tried to do, I realized, and she thought I was just unable to see Matt hurt.

Suze was frowning at Lilah, but when the half-blood looked away from me the expression wiped from her face. There was no hiding the annoyance in her voice, though, as she said to Lilah, "So, awesome night. We should do this again probably never. Gimme the keys. One of us can get you somewhere where you can wait for a cab."

The dismissal was clear, but Lilah shook her head with surprising firmness. "No, I'll help you get him to your house."

"What?" Suze was genuinely surprised. Frankly, I was as well—after the fiasco at the tattoo parlor, I wouldn't have blamed Lilah for taking the opportunity to bail.

Lilah pointed at Suzume's chest, where the long cuts Soli had inflicted were sluggishly oozing blood each time she moved, like a badly cut knee on a long walk home. "You've got to be hurting really badly. While I'm driving you can actually wrap those up or something. Unless you were really looking forward to passing out from blood loss at the first stop sign." She lifted her eyebrows, and even after everything that had happened that night, I felt the shadow of a smile play at my mouth. I knew from hard experience that this was the only way into Suze's good graces and away from the land of bad nicknames was by slinging sass and showing backbone.

"I'm fine," Suze grumped, but I noticed that she shifted slightly to make her cuts less visible. "Besides, like you can actually drive stick."

"Actually I can," Lilah said, then pointed. "Get in the car."

Suzume looked over at me, and I raised my hands and stepped back. "Don't involve me," I said. "I'll follow in the Fiesta."

We pulled out, with the Buick in front. Lilah might have been comfortable driving stick (as clearly evidenced by the fact that she managed to start it up without stalling), but my guess was that she wasn't a usual driver of older American cars that had been built along lines similar in size to humpback whales, and she drove very slowly.

I'd left my phone in the Fiesta's glove compartment before we'd headed to the Iron Needle, and I pulled it out now and dialed Chivalry's number.

It was ten thirty, and when Chivalry picked up he answered just above a whisper. Left to his own devices, Chivalry tended to keep the kind of hours that Ben Franklin would admire, getting up with the sun and consigning anything that aired on TV after nine p.m. to his DVR.

I cut straight to the chase. "Suzume and I found what dumped Gage's body."

"Oh?" he said. He was surprised, but then his voice warmed with pleasure and older-brother pride. "That's excellent, Fortitude. Do you need assistance?" Only Chivalry could find such a very polite way to ask if I needed help killing something.

Every spot where Soli's fists had connected felt tender to the point where a tub filled with ice had nearly erotic appeal, and, given its current special level of throbbing, I was seriously concerned that the spot on my cheekbone where Soli had punched and Suzume had backhanded me might've been at least fractured. As much as she'd done to hide it, I knew that Suze was in substantial pain from her cuts, though given how much better her healing ability was than mine, I knew why she'd downplayed them. And this was a situation where we'd outnumbered and startled Soli. The cavalry were definitely needed. I snorted and said, "I should say so. It's a skinwalker."

"Are you certain?" All of the relaxed congratulation was gone, and Chivalry's voice was tense.

"Really sure. We got a peek at the center of the Tootsie Pop."

"How badly are you hurt?" That Chivalry asked *how badly* rather than *are you* was a direct confirmation of the seriousness of the situation.

"Banged up, but we're both okay."

"Where is the skinwalker now?"

"Gone. Listen, Chivalry, there's some weird shit going on up here. The skinwalker is working with the elves on something."

Chivalry sucked in a breath. "You need to tell all of this to Mother. Get down here right now."

"No, Chivalry, I can't—"

"That's not a request, Fortitude," Chivalry snapped. "I want you to get in your car right now and come straight to the mansion. No detours, nothing. This supercedes everything. If you aren't in front of the mansion one hour from now, I'm coming and getting you." He hung up. Another sign that convinced me how serious this was—Chivalry wrote regular letters to the editor of the local newspaper complaining about the decline in phone etiquette.

"Oh, not good," I muttered as I immediately called Suze. When she picked up I explained the necessary change in plans, and she assured me that she and Lilah would be able to handle Matt. Hoping that was the case but unable to do anything about it, I made a quick, illegal U-turn and headed for the highway.

As I drove, most of my mind was on trying to sort through what had just happened. Skinwalkers were, unlike kitsune or the elves, native to North America, but my mother hadn't had any contact with them until western expansion had progressed well into areas like Texas and Arizona. They had been banned from my mother's territory more than sixty years ago, and the ones that didn't willingly relocate had been hunted down and killed by Prudence and Chivalry, and while my brother hadn't gone into the details, apparently they had made those executions grisly enough that no skinwalker had been sighted in the territory since, though Chivalry had once mentioned that the largest concentration of them was now in Miami, where they liked the heat, the city life, and the convenience of the everglades for dumping bodies.

That was the one thing Chivalry had emphasized: skinwalkers meant bodies. They were humanoid in shape but not in appearance. He hadn't gone into detail (and I had not pursued it), but I'd just gotten a small window into what a skinwalker looked like in its natural form. It was apparently a rare sight—true to their name, they stripped the skin from their victims and were able to wear it to blend in to the population. No one knew how long they could wear one skin for; Chivalry had known individuals who kept skins for months or even years, but like snails with shells, there was a large amount of "trading up," which occurred whenever a skinwalker caught sight of a face or body that it liked better than the one it was currently wearing. They were rapacious, violent, and deadly.

And I'd just pissed one off very personally. I pressed my foot harder onto the gas pedal. Suddenly seeing my family held an enticing appeal. Kind of like in the Three Billy Goats Gruff—Soli might've handed me my ass, but I was willing to bet that things would be very different with my big brother.

I tried not to think about what had happened with Matt. I didn't want to think about what I'd almost done to him, or its potential implications. There had been times in the past where blood had excited me and I'd felt cold, predatory instincts stir in me, but those had been only during the days when I'd been trying to avoid my vampire heritage as much as possible and had avoided coming home to feed from my mother. I'd never come so close to sampling human blood, and I'd never before lost all recognition of those around me. What frightened me was that I'd been drinking my mother's blood more regularly over the past few months than I had at any point since my late teens, and between that and my vegetarian diet what had happened shouldn't have been possible.

That I knew of. The information my family had provided me about what I could expect now that my transition had started had been about as helpful as Queen Victoria's pre-marital advice to her daughters. The idea that this might be my new normal made my hands shake on the wheel, and I forced the topic from my brain. Suddenly a skinwalker who seemed personally pissed at me seemed like a much better issue to ponder.

It was a weeknight and late, so roads were clear and I was able to make excellent time to Newport, pulling my car into the driveway at just past eleven. The house was completely lit up, twinkling like a jewel in the dark. I could feel the presence of my entire family in the house as I walked toward it. Prudence had avoided me for the past few months, pouting over my failure to get myself killed, and there was something intoxicating about feeling the certainty of all of them, a drumming knowledge in the back of my brain that tugged at the part of me that had come roaring out earlier that evening and was still crouched far too close to the surface.

No one was waiting for me, but I followed the pull of their presence unerringly to the small parlor to the left of the grand staircase that was reserved for family use and not quite as overwhelmingly decorated as the more public areas of the mansion.

Despite the season, a fire had been lit in the granite fireplace, and my mother sat on the rose-colored sofa tucked closest to it. She was wearing her typical set of innocuous camouflage, wide-legged light green grandma pants that accented her flowery pastel shirt, all topped off with her clunky eighties glasses and her best Barbara Bush hairdo. Chivalry sat to her left, much more dressed down than usual in a button down shirt and jeans, with a hollow and exhausted look around his eyes. Prudence wasn't sitting, but instead paced around the room. She must've been out on the town when she'd been called home, because she was dressed for the opera in a long black gown that sparkled when she moved, the full skirt swishing dangerously in her wake, contrasting the gleam of white shoulders and very generously displayed décolletage in the thinly strapped top. Her bright red hair was pinned up instead of hanging in its usual sleek bob, and the heads of the pins sparkled like the diamonds that I suspected they actually were.

Everyone was already looking at the doorway when I walked in, having undoubtedly felt my approach ever since I pulled into the driveway, if not even before that. Prudence gave me one sweeping look and continued her pacing, but Chivalry immediately got up and hurried over to me, concern filling his face when he reached out to touch my bruised cheek.

"What else, Fort?" he asked urgently, patting my arms to check for broken bones and eyeing the rest of me that was concealed by my clothing. Chivalry was able to hide his mother-hen streak most of the time, but when I was younger he'd always been the first to come running with a bottle of iodine whenever I came home after a bike ride with a freshly scraped knee.

I flinched away from his hand, as even his delicate probing had sent a blast of pain through my skull, but I gave him a pat on the shoulder. "Just bruises. I'm okay." He looked completely unconvinced, still scanning me anxiously for injuries, and I tried to make my voice more reassuring as I repeated, "Really, I'm fine. Suze actually looks worse than I do right now."

From her position on the sofa, Madeline frowned. "The kitsune was there? Atsuko was involved in your search?"

I shook my head. "No, Suzume was there as a favor to me. She's my friend." As much as that was the case, I'd met her extremely formidable grandmother, and had no doubt that the White Fox had at least tacitly given her approval for Suze's involvement.

"How interesting, Fortitude," Madeline said, seeming to savor the words. "I'm very pleased. The kitsune are a valuable alliance, and it's good that you are making a strong connection where other of my children"—she sent a quick, slashing look toward Prudence—"have not."

My sister continued stalking around the room but met Madeline's look with a glare of her own, clearly feeling and resenting our mother's dig. "The kitsune live in the territory under our sufferance. There is no need to beg for favors."

"No?" Madeline asked, then dropped her voice to a low hiss, surprising me with its level of anger. "Had Fortitude encountered the skinwalker on his own, without a strong ally, I doubt we'd be getting this report." Her blue eyes began to glow with the heat of her anger, reminding me of the Bunsen burners we'd used in high school chemistry. But as quickly as it had been revealed, Madeline pulled the anger inside again, banking and hiding it under her Betty White–

esque exterior. But it was still there, and the hair on the back of my neck stood up in response. I noticed that Prudence had slowed her pacing, moving slower, more cautiously, in the wake of our mother's temper.

Chivalry had also flinched at our mother's words, but he must've agreed with them because the pupils of his eyes were expanding, swallowing the benign hazel with gleaming black, and he snapped, "It should never have been an issue to begin with." He tugged at my elbow, leading me over to the sofa beside my mother. "Sit down and tell us what happened," he said, fussing until I sat to the left of Madeline. He immediately sat on my left, leaving me sandwiched between them. He gave our sister a sharp look. "Stop pacing, Prudence." She gave a small snarl at the order but obeyed, throwing herself into her favorite chair, a Louis XVI that creaked alarmingly at the sudden impact.

Everyone's eyes were on me now, waiting with varying levels of patience, and I took a deep breath and started talking. I began with the discovery of Gage's body and went from there—with one significant exception. I edited out Matt's presence entirely, instead claiming that Suze and I had found a glamoured Iron Needle promotional card while we'd been cleaning out Gage's bedroom and had simply investigated from there. Other than that I was honest about what had happened, including Lilah's involvement. Madeline and Chivalry both listened with frozen, intent expressions, but Prudence was clearly agitated by what I was saying. When I finished with the events of the evening, claiming that Soli had fled after Suzume had managed to cut her open enough to expose her nougaty center, Prudence couldn't restrain herself any longer. She exploded out of her chair and began stalking the room again, clearly enraged.

"This isn't the work of a moment," she growled. "Months went into this that we did nothing. Others will see this and act accordingly."

Madeline stayed focused on me and reached over to give me a small pat on my knee. "You've done very well, Fortitude," she complimented me, then glanced over at Prudence. "This will be dealt with swiftly."

Prudence ignored her. "Elves with some kind of plan, daring to bring the forbidden into our boundaries. The kitsune numbers are increasing. The witches are showing discontent. More movement among the lower creatures. Now a skinwalker at the heart of the territory." She smacked the edge of the fireplace temperamentally, cracking one of the granite stones, and said to Madeline, "They sense your weakness, Mother."

"This isn't the time for that, sister," Chivalry said. "We need to focus on what is at hand."

There was an intensity in the way that Madeline looked at Prudence, and the glitter of suppressed temper was back in her eyes, but she visibly restrained herself and, with deliberate blandness, said, "True enough." Then she turned to me and lifted one thin, liver-spotted hand to cup my chin. "This was fine work, showing good instincts. You will continue this fine, fine work for me, my son. You will be assisted," she glanced from Chivalry to Prudence, then back again, before hesitating a moment and then saying smoothly, "by your brother. But you, my darling, you will be in charge." She smiled, and her upper lip pulled back enough to display her long, thoroughly impressive fangs that, unlike Prudence's and Chivalry's, were fixed in place and too large to retract. "And when you find this skinwalker, as well as those responsible for her presence, it will be by your command that your brother shows the consequences of defiance."

There was a dreamy look in her eyes as she dwelled over the word *consequences*, and I knew that her thoughts were filled with blood and pain. I swallowed hard, but nodded like an obedient son. "Yes," I agreed, then looked at Chivalry. There was a hesitance in his face that surprised me, and I nudged him, saying, "Chivalry?"

He looked startled for a second, then collected himself and the mixed feelings vanished as if they'd never been there. "Of course, Fort," he said in his most reassuring voice. "You found something the rest of us had overlooked. It's right that you should continue to lead."

That was the brother I knew, and I relaxed.

Prudence snarled loudly, her delicate fangs sliding out

from their hiding places. She swept over in front of us and shoved Chivalry hard in the shoulder, knocking him back against the couch cushions. "Stop protecting him, brother. If Fortitude is to make adult decisions, then you can't keep wrapping him in wool." Her blue eyes, gleaming with temper, slid over to focus on me. "Bhumika is in complete renal failure, Fortitude," she said, and I flinched at the hard truth. "Her first dialysis is scheduled for tomorrow, along with a number of invasive and doubtless painful tests to determine candidacy for a transplant. The first time Chivalry left the hospital in three days was when you called him with the skinwalker information. And now he pretends to eagerly leave at your side."

I looked at my brother, but he didn't deny what Prudence was saying. He simply looked back at me, his face set in unreadable lines. "Chivalry, what—"

Madeline interrupted me, her voice an iron bell that filled the room and made even Prudence look cautious. "And your motives, daughter? Do you offer Fort a true choice between you and Chivalry as assistance, or a false one?" She studied Prudence intensely and asked, "Will you follow your brother's commands as if they were mine? Can you do this?"

Prudence didn't answer at first, looking at me instead. When I met her eyes, I was surprised to see that the restless anger and irritation that I was so used to was missing, and instead there was something else. It wasn't aggressive, but seemed almost . . . curious. I was shaken as much by the change as if the rising sun had been purple. Prudence gave a short nod to our mother. "Yes."

Madeline exhaled, long and thoughtful, those hard eyes examining my sister, weighing what she had just said. Then her attention shifted to me, and part of me shivered at her expression. I was being examined and considered as thoroughly as Prudence had been a moment ago, but I didn't have two centuries of starch in my spine to help me through it. It was a natural fear, I reminded myself, just like a bunny would feel when facing a saber-tooth tiger, and I did my best to hide it. After a moment Madeline gave a small nod and said, "Then there is a choice before you, my turtledove.

Which of your siblings will go back to Providence with you?"

Chivalry gripped my hand, and I tore myself from Madeline's absorbing gaze to look back at my brother. There was clear worry on his face now as he glanced at our sister; while our mother might've accepted Prudence's words, Chivalry was clearly not as trusting. "It's fine, Fort. I can go with you," he said, low and urgent. "Bhumika is getting the best care in the state right now, and she wouldn't be alone for a second."

I hesitated. Everything inside me wanted to take the protection that Chivalry was offering, knowing that he would do everything in his power to shield me not just from the physical threats, but also from hard decisions. If Chivalry discovered Matt's involvement, he would hesitate to kill him—not out of a belief that Matt shouldn't die, but because he knew that the death would hurt me. Prudence wouldn't do that.

I also wanted to take Chivalry so that he could continue to do what he had done for most of my life, which was to stand as a barrier between me and my sister. My foster parents' blood was on her hands, and she'd been the one to teach me the harsh lesson of what could happen to humans who found themselves entwined in our shadowy world of secrets.

But as much as I wanted those things, I also wondered how much it would cost Chivalry to leave Bhumika right now. She was dying, and nothing the doctors could do would stop that—she'd been dying from the moment that she'd married my brother five years ago, and he'd spent each day of those years cherishing the time they were together, knowing all too well that it would end like this.

I wished deeply that I could make the decision I would've made a year ago. But I'd changed since then, and that it was time to be adult enough to, for the first time, protect my brother. "No, it's okay," I told him, squeezing his hands with completely false reassurance. I looked over at our sister. "I'll take Prudence."

No one spoke at first, but everyone was looking at me, assessing the decision, weighing what this meant in the strange dynamics of the family. Finally Madeline nodded. "Very well," she said. She leaned forward, brushing a finger against my bruised cheek, and looked me over, her eyes seeming to catalog every injury, even those hidden by my clothes. She gave a small *tsk* of her tongue. "This is a deadly opponent, my son, and the elves have always had the loyalty of serpents. You will need to be a very wary little mongoose indeed, and a strong one." She pushed the cuff of her sleeve back and drew her thumbnail slowly across her wrist, making a short cut. Blood welled up sluggishly, thicker than a human's would've been, and much darker. She held the wrist up in front of my face. "Feed."

Craving rushed through me, but I hesitated, resting my hand against the middle of her forearm to keep her from pressing her wrist any closer. "I fed last week, Mother. It's too soon."

Chivalry put one hand on my shoulder, patting me soothingly. "She's right, Fort," he said. I still hesitated, but his hand moved to the back of my neck, not pushing but just gently guiding me forward. I gave in then, and I dropped my head willingly and drank. My mother's blood was thick, and I had to suck hard to get it into my mouth, where it seemed to sizzle on my tongue, and I shuddered as I felt the path of each drop down my throat and into my body. I was dimly aware of Chivalry removing his hand, but then the rush and excitement of my mother's blood, hinting at strength I couldn't even dream of, washed over me and the rest of the room dimmed, my world tightening around me until all that existed was my mother's wrist and my own mouth.

Feeding was always like this, but suddenly the memory of pulling Matt, unconscious and bleeding, toward me flashed in my mind, and fear lit my brain back up as I wondered whether that was the future that waited for me on the other side of transition—more than twenty years of a surrogate uncle's love disappearing in a wave of hunger that wiped away all identity and ties. I pulled my head back sharply, away from Madeline's wrist. She let me go, as she always had in times like this, but then another hand shot forward, grabbing my hair and forcing me back down to the blood.

It was Prudence's voice, hard and determined, that said, "None of that squeamishness, baby brother. This task does not call for weakness."

I pushed back, trying to get away, but she was older and stronger than I was, and neither Madeline nor Chivalry spoke or interfered with what she was doing. I was unable to resist the blood when it was right at my mouth and I continued to drink, long after I would normally have stopped, Prudence's hand remaining, inescapable, determined that I would drink to her satisfaction. I was completely full when Prudence's hand finally relaxed and let me up. It took me a few blinks to adjust to the room again, and I felt shaky, both from nerves and the rush of energy and excitement that bubbled up inside me.

The blood that remained at the surface of Madeline's wrist sank back inside her, and the cut tied itself together as I watched. But as she pushed her sleeve back down I noticed that she was shaking and somehow seemed smaller, weaker, diminished even, her face almost gray as she seemed to crumple up inside, looking suddenly as tiny and harmless as a truly human old woman. Chivalry reached past me, stretching out one hand to steady her, but in a sudden flash the old woman was gone and Madeline whipped her head around, those lips drawn back to reveal her fangs in a clear threat, her blue eyes bright enough to cast their own glow in the room. Chivalry's hand froze, then wrapped quickly around my shoulder instead, giving me one small tug toward him, away from my mother. Then she blinked and the glow was gone and her mouth relaxed, once again hiding what she was.

I was stunned and confused. "Mother? Are you . . . okay?" It felt strange asking the question or even letting it flicker my mind as a serious consideration. She was infinitely more powerful than I was, had spent centuries reigning as the dominant power on the entire Eastern seaboard, but I found myself asking it anyway.

Madeline pulled herself upright and waved one hand like a grumpy senior. "Go, Fortitude. Bring me back the true head of the skinwalker." Despite the tremors still running through her, she gave a very hard, extremely bloodthirsty smile that left no doubt in anyone's mind who we were dealing with. "I have a space on my wall that needs a change in décor."

I felt oddly reassured by that statement and got up with Chivalry, allowing him to herd me out of the room and back to the main foyer, Prudence close at our heels. When we stood at the front door, Chivalry cut a hard look at Prudence, even as he started talking to me. "Call me if you need anything, Fort."

Prudence smiled at him, her fangs still out. He met her gaze for a long minute, glancing away just before it would've been long enough to be considered a challenge. She was a century older than he was, a vampire just coming into her prime, far stronger than him. Chivalry backed up slowly, then headed up the stairs to his room, probably to change clothes before returning to the hospital. He glanced backward just once, to give me a significant glance, then turned the corner and was gone.

Prudence gave me a wholly nonreassuring smile and linked her arm companionably with mine, tugging me along until we were strolling together out into the parking area where the cars waited. I didn't like touching her, and I could feel my skin crawling at her proximity, but I forced myself not to comment. Too much was riding on my ability to control this potentially explosive situation and my sister's actions, with far too much at stake to pull my arm away like I desperately wanted to. We finally reached the cars, the Fiesta looking even scruffier than usual in its spot between Chivalry's Bentley and Prudence's gleaming new Lexus.

Having my sister as my backup, with me in charge, was not something I'd ever expected to happen, and it was already itching at me. "So, what are we going to do?" I asked her. "Storm Underhill?"

Prudence turned to face me, shaking her head slightly. "Underhill is older magic, brother. Not even our mother could enter and find her way out again without the permission of the elves. Its entrance may lie in our territory, but it is a hole no sane person would enter." She gave me a cool smile. "No, we don't go to the powerful ones. We'll hunt sideways, toward their mixed-blood scions. Find me one of those involved in this business and I'll shake out all the information you could desire." The gleam in her eyes left no doubt as to how she would "shake out" that information. Prudence took great pleasure in being the bogeyman Madeline used to keep the races that lived in the territory toeing her line.

Prudence continued. "I will need to gather some belongings and find suitable lodging in the city. You will need to rest." She reached out one long, perfectly manicured finger to touch my cheek. I flinched automatically, but the expected sharp pain failed to materialize, replaced instead with just the dull sensitivity of a week-old bruise. Her smile widened at my surprise. "You should never refuse Mother's gifts, brother. That will be gone by tomorrow, and you can renew your investigations." With her free hand she reached into her small clutch purse and removed a business card, which she handed to me. "Call me when you have determined your next step or if you need me to do something." Her voice turned serious. "Do not hesitate on this, Fortitude. You've done well so far, but a skinwalker is nothing to toy with. They were not exiled simply because of their poor table manners—they are dangerous. Even to us, if we are not on our guard. Especially for you, so vulnerable still in body and mind."

It was like talking to a body snatcher, and I couldn't hold it in anymore. "Why are you doing this, Prudence?" I asked suspiciously.

She lifted one carefully tweezed eyebrow and smiled coyly. "Doing what?"

"You know what." Her finger was still resting against my face, and I pushed her hand away, not hard, but firmly. "We don't like each other. Your birthday was ruined this year when Luca didn't kill me like you'd hoped. Now you're offering to help me out? What's in this for you?"

The coy smile widened, became as close to genuine as I'd ever seen on her face when my life wasn't in danger. "You've grown up since I last saw you, little brother." She pressed both hands against my face, holding them there with just enough firmness that I knew I wouldn't be able to dislodge them. "Things are changing. *You* are changing." She leaned in, her perfume swirling around me, and I couldn't suppress my shudder as she whispered, "I am curious." Then she let me go and walked over to her car, pausing just as she reached down to open the driver's-side door. She smiled again. "I'll be seeing you again soon."

I hesitated, then asked, "Prudence?"

"Yes, little brother?"

"What was wrong with Mother? Is she . . . sick?"

She gave me a long, considering look, the bright moonlight darkening her hair until she seemed constructed entirely of black and white. When she answered, Prudence's voice was gentler than I'd ever heard it before. "She's old, Fortitude. For all her power, all her strength, even for her there is only one path that age will lead to." She shook one admonishing finger. "Don't forget to call, or I'll have to track you down." Then she got into her car and drove away.

# Chapter 7

I pulled into Suzume's driveway at just before one in the morning. My phone battery had died while I was in the mansion, and I braced myself for what I might find inside. If Matt remembered, then I was going to have to convince him to keep his mouth shut. I had no idea how that could happen.

I knocked, and Suze let me in. Her eyes went immediately to my face, and she raised her eyebrows. "Looking a lot better, Fort," she said, and I could hear the speculation in her voice. I'd glanced in the vanity mirror a few times on my drive up, amazed at the way my injuries had healed almost fast enough to see.

I definitely didn't want to talk about it, though, and I said, "I could say the same about you," while looking significantly at her chest. She'd changed shirts, into a soft gray flannel men's button-up that I guessed she'd liberated at some point from a boyfriend. The top few buttons were undone, revealing part of the cuts she'd received in the fight with the skinwalker. She must've found a quiet moment to shift forms at some point because the cuts no longer looked fresh and angry, but were heavily scabbed over and almost faded. The kitsune were able to heal injuries quickly in their natural form—unlike the were-creatures, which were people who could take an animal form, the kitsune were foxes who could take a human form.

Suze apparently decided to shelve the rest of her questions about my fast healing, though from the glance she gave me I knew that line of inquiry was only postponed, not forgotten, and waved me inside. Keiko was sitting inside on the sofa, and she curled her lip in clear disgust as I walked in.

I kept my mind on priorities. "How's Matt?"

"He's okay," Suze said reassuringly. "He woke up on the drive here. Definitely wasn't feeling good, but apparently he's got a head like a cement brick. We tucked him into Keiko's bed."

Which explained Keiko's bad attitude. "Should he be sleeping?" I asked. "He was knocked out for a while. He might have a concussion."

"It's fine. The doctor checked him out. He's sitting in there with him now, giving him one last once-over."

"Doctor?"

"Oh yeah." Suzume shot a frosty glare at her twin. "Keiko's boyfriend. The one she said she broke up with two months ago."

Keiko's expression was equally chilly. "You were happy enough to use him to check out the human."

"It shouldn't have been an option," Suze said.

There was a lot of tension between the sisters, enough to make me regret that I couldn't just make an excuse and hide out in the bathroom while they snapped at each other passive-aggressively. This was far too reminiscent of Thanksgiving dinner with my family. But I needed answers about Matt, so I stepped closer to Suze, wincing as that placed me directly in the path of those very intense stares. "What does he remember?" I asked her.

Momentarily distracted from her familial gripe, Suze answered me. "We got lucky. He remembers seeing something weird about Soli, but he thinks that the head knock messed with his memory." And the topic having been raised again, she took a small step to the left to be able to give Keiko her undivided glare. "Keiko's doctor agreed."

"He has a name, Suze," Keiko said, shifting her weight as she sat in a way that reminded me uncomfortably of what Suze looked like in her fox form right before she sprang.

"I have no intention of learning it."

Frustrated, I cut in. "Seriously, ladies? Pretend I'm company." Now I was the focus for both of them, but their expressions were simmering with hot temper. I could deal with that better than an icy sibling battle. I asked Suze, "Where's Lilah?"

"She called a cab once Keiko got here. Said that she wanted to see what she could dig up at work tomorrow, and needed to make sure that no one suspected she'd had a long night." Suze turned to the fridge, pulling out a bottle of Moxie soda and pouring a glass for me without being asked. I winced a little at the sight of it, but took the glass without a fuss. Moxie was a New England concoction whose taste was like the distilled essence of old ladies, mothballs, and cats. But while I was glad that playing hostess gave Suze something to do other than bait Keiko, there was a weird undercurrent to her voice when she talked about Lilah, one I wasn't sure I could identify.

When in doubt, ask. "What's wrong? Did you change your mind about trusting Lilah?"

She pushed the glass into my hand and gave me a considering look. "No, she's being honest with us about her motives," Suze said slowly. "And if the elves are breaking Madeline's laws, then it's in her own best interest to help us figure out who the ringleaders are so that when the Scott retribution comes, which it certainly will, only the guilty get torn to shreds." She shifted the subject quickly and sounded much more normal. "And speaking of bloody carnage, tell me what happened when you filled your family in."

I nodded toward the closed door that led to Keiko's room. "Aren't you worried about them . . . ?"

Suze gave me a small, smug little smile, the kind she always seemed to wear when she was doing something particularly foxy. Something dangerous swam briefly through her dark eyes, reminding me again of what she was. "Keiko and I are taking care of it. Neither of them will hear anything other than what they'd expect—women's voices, the coffee grinder, things like that. If either gets the urge to leave the room, those voices will suddenly get into a very loud fight, enough to convince any sane man to sit tight a little longer."

Suzume had told me many times that fox magic was always as its strongest when it worked with someone's expectations—like a magical form of jujitsu, using an opponent's weight against them. Given the way the sisters were interacting, it was no great leap to expect a full-on screaming match to break out at any moment.

I summarized the trip for them. Hearing that Prudence was coming to the city to serve as my backup, both women paled visibly and glanced seriously at each other. When I'd finished, both were quiet for a moment, clearly weighing how the situation had just changed. Suzume spoke first. "I can call my grandmother, ask her to send over some of my cousins to help out." There was a grim satisfaction in her voice. "Let's see that bitch think she's so tough when she's facing us with a backup of four foxes."

Keiko cut in. "Four foxes?"

"Takara and Hoshi can handle themselves, and Rei is always up for a fight. I don't know what Mio's schedule is, but she could probably clear some space."

"You really think that's a good idea?" Keiko got off the sofa and walked around the kitchen island, which up until now had apparently been serving as some kind of demilitarized zone.

"A skinwalker is in the territory, something dire enough that Fort has been given Prudence's leash. This doesn't sound like we should be prepared for something big?"

Keiko looked straight at me, and I realized that her attitude toward me was more than just the general dislike that I'd assumed; she didn't trust me. "Now isn't the time to be reminding the vampires of our numbers. You're letting your"—and here her lip curled in disgust—"*friendship* blind you. Unless Madeline Scott makes a formal request to the White Fox, the kitsune have no part in this conflict." She addressed me. "You were just in your mother's company. Did she mention wanting our help?"

I paused, running through the conversation again in my head, then admitted, "No."

Keiko was watching me carefully, and there was a slyness in her voice when she asked, "But someone mentioned the kitsune, and not positively, didn't they? Who?"

I glanced at Suze, but she was focused on her sister. Looking back at Keiko, I said, reluctantly, "Prudence did. But it was just a side comment."

"About . . . ?" Keiko forced the issue.

"She said that . . . the kitsune numbers were increasing." Neither looked surprised, and I felt a moment of relief. "But that's no secret." Then I glanced again at Suze. I knew her well enough to read the look on her face, and I realized that something much more was at play. "Tell me what she meant."

She thought about not telling me. I could see from her eyes that a few months, weeks, maybe even days ago she would've made a joke and changed the subject. But then she made a decision, and it was clear that Keiko didn't like it.

"When the kitsune first came to the Scott territory," Suze said, "it was only Atsuko. A generation ago, it was Atsuko and her four daughters. Now those four daughters have produced twenty granddaughters, all in our prime, and my cousins are at an age to start having families. There are three great-granddaughters already, bringing the total to-day to twenty-seven foxes, and the floodgates are just opening. We're stronger than we were when Atsuko negotiated her treaty with Madeline. To a suspicious mind like Prudence's, I can see how that would be threatening." She paused, then said with emphasis, "Vampires might be the apex predator in this territory, Fort, but numbers matter as well."

Keiko elbowed past me to get close enough to talk directly at Suzume, cutting me out of the conversation. "Which is exactly why we need to be careful, Suze. A succession is coming, and we need to stay neutral to ride it out."

I felt a pang. This was what Madeline's weakness had meant, as well as Prudence's comment. The kitsune and everyone else knew that my mother was coming to the end of her life—everyone except me, that is. I wasn't sure how I felt about it. We disagreed over so many things. She had both protected me and sanctioned the deaths of my foster parents. But she was my mother—constantly watching me, caring for me, assessing me, killing for me. It was like loving an old, old crocodile that still occasionally ate people.

Suze was ignoring my existential crisis, more focused on her sister's comment. "I listen when Grandmother talks,

Keiko. I know that," she said, irritation clear in her voice. "How is it risky for us to make a show of force in *support* of the vampires?"

Keiko poked her finger into my chest, hard. "Everyone knows that Prudence and Fort are the most likely to clash. If they disagree about who to kill or how to punish someone"— and then she pointed to her closed bedroom door—"or if that human pokes his nose in the wrong place and has to be silenced, who would you support, Suze? Would you be smart and stay out of a sibling disagreement, or would you back Fort?"

Suze bristled with temper, but was silent.

Keiko nodded, her point made. "The cousins would follow you, and five foxes would be enough for a declaration of allegiance." She turned to me at last, her contempt clear. "And whatever your own ties to the kitsune are, vampire, we can't ally ourselves with weakness."

Keiko walked toward the phone mounted on the wall but was blocked when Suzume stepped in front of her. "What are you planning, Keiko?"

"I'm protecting all of us." Keiko shoved a shoulder against Suze, pushing her to one side, and grabbed the phone out of its cradle. "I'm going to call Grandmother and have her order you to stay out of this."

Too fast for me to follow, Suze whipped a hand out and pulled the phone away from her sister.

"Don't be childish," Keiko said witheringly.

Suzume was very serious. "Stay out of this, Keiko."

"How can I? You're confusing your loyalties."

Suze's voice dropped, becoming low and dangerous. "I'm confusing nothing, sister. I won't bring in our cousins. If I have to choose a side, it won't be for the entire kitsune, and Grandmother can just say that I'm a lone rogue. But you breathe one word of this, and I'll make a call of my own."

Keiko froze, then real rage spread across her face. "You'd betray me over *him*?"

"I never said that." There was nothing defensive in Suze's voice, just that rigid control that I remembered hearing from her only once before, when she'd abandoned me on a near-suicide mission. "But I'm keeping a lot of your secrets right now. You should be more careful to keep me happy."

The threat was clear, and as angry as Keiko was, she also apparently knew when her sister meant business. Her movements stiff and jerky from temper, she stepped away, leaving Suze holding the phone. "I won't be a part of this. I'm leaving."

"Until the situation is resolved, perhaps that's best. I suggest that you collect your human and go. I know you don't need to pack a bag. Most of your stuff is at his apartment anyway."

The sisters locked gazes in another of those subzero glares.

It was awkward, but at this point in a very long night I didn't think I could stand one more of those heavily weighted conversations where I had no idea what people were talking about. I said loudly to Keiko, "Thanks for bringing someone to check out Matt."

Both women turned those glares on me.

"What, we can't take a five-second break from the tension for basic manners?" I demanded. Suze managed a small grumble, and Keiko gave a very superior little sniff. That was enough to break me, and my temper flared. "Screw this subtext," I snapped at them, and walked over to the door to Keiko's bedroom and yanked it open.

Matt was lying on Keiko's hotel-perfect bedspread, looking much worse for wear, an ice pack balanced somewhat jauntily on his head. Keiko's boyfriend was sitting next to the bed, wearing blue medical scrub pants and a sweatshirt. He was a dead ringer for Rudolph Valentino in *The Sheik*, and the moment the thought crossed my mind, I congratulated myself on a worthwhile application of my film degree. I walked over to him and extended my hand, which he automatically shook. "Hi, I'm Fort. Thank you for looking after Matt."

"It wasn't a problem," he said, revealing a heavy South Boston accent that was a jarring contrast with his Prince of Arabia looks. "Keiko was just picking me up after my shift when her sister called us." He gave a small, happy wave, and I looked over my shoulder to see that Keiko was now standing in the doorway and was clearly far from happy about this introduction. But underneath the seething irritation that I'd come to accept as normal from her there was an interesting touch of anxiety.

I'd been punched a lot tonight, and I didn't have much sympathy to extend to her. Just to piss her off a little more, I gave her boyfriend my biggest smile and said, "I'm sorry. Everything has been such a rush and I didn't catch your name."

"Farid. Farid Amini." He smiled widely, and I noticed that Suzume had joined Keiko in the doorway, and their combined mood was dropping the temperature in the room to testicle-freezing levels. My new buddy Farid was picking up on the tension, but he was holding on to his bright smile with enough determination to turn his face slightly manic. "It was really great to meet you, Suzume. It's crazy that we've kept missing each other this long."

"Yeah. Crazy." Suzume was exuding all the invitation and charm of an enraged cobra.

Clearly seeing me as the one bright spot in the room, Farid redirected his desperate first-impression brightness my way again. "We should all go out some time. You know, double-date." There was the sound from the doorway of some partially suppressed noise, and it wasn't a reassuring sound, but Farid pushed forward. "My parents are just nuts about Keiko," he assured me.

I'd always thought of myself as fairly moral, the kind of person who wouldn't torment someone else, even if provoked. Therefore, I should've been much more disappointed in myself when I gave Farid a jocular smack on the shoulder and said heartily, "We *should* do that. Dinner, some bowling." I looked over my shoulder at Keiko and gave her just the kind of look I felt she'd earned after all the icy eye daggers she'd sent my way. "Just lots of time to get to know each other."

Keiko made a small, choked sound. Suzume had a face like a stone wall.

Farid nodded like a bobble head. "The girls will set something up." I ignored the muffled growl from behind us, but it was apparently finally enough to convince Farid that maybe he'd made enough of an effort to connect for this trip. "It's really late, and we should be going. But we'll definitely see each other soon." With that final burst of blind optimism, he turned to Matt and pulled together what was clearly his best doctor voice. "Now, Mr. McMahon, remember what I said. Lots of rest; change the bandage every evening. If you see signs of infection or if you're feeling dizzy, you have my card, and remember that the clinic is free."

Matt had been watching all of the interplay attentively, and now he nodded, careful not to dislodge his ice pack. "I really appreciate the house call."

Farid laughed. "No, you actually did *me* a favor. I'd actually never gotten a chance to see where Keiko lived." He looked at her, and my heart sank a little in my chest. The poor guy was absolutely in love with her. I'd gone vegetarian for a woman—I knew that look well. "I was starting to think you were married or something," he teased her.

Keiko stepped toward him, smiling through gritted teeth. "You're so silly, honey. See? No secrets at all." There was an almost collective wince from everyone else in the room at the size of that whopper.

"Not one bit," Suze said heavily. She looked over at me and Matt and said, "Let's give you guys some space."

I watched as everyone filed out, and wondered whether Farid was as oblivious as he seemed to be to the Shakespearian levels of star-crossed vibes that he and Keiko emitted. Or maybe Farid *was* picking up on their doomed aura, but he was one of those optimists who felt that good intentions and positivity could overcome all obstacles. Like people who sat up on their sofa one day and decided that they would climb Everest, even though they became winded walking up the stairs.

Or maybe it would all work out. After all, I clearly knew crap about relationships.

I looked down at Matt, who was pushing himself up into a sitting position. I leaned forward to help him, wincing at his level of wet-kitten helplessness. "Slow down, Matt."

Matt batted my hands away and steadied himself, letting the ice pack drop onto the bed. "It's fine, just a cut and a rattle to my brain box. No concussion; nothing wrong." He glanced at the door. "Some pretty impressive family tension there with that girl you're so sure isn't your girlfriend and her sister. That was a hell of a fight they were having."

From that I knew that at some point Matt had tried to leave the room and the kitsune illusion had stopped him. "They have fiery temperaments," I said blandly.

Small talk apparently over, Matt looked me straight in the eyes and said levelly, "So."

I'd known this was coming. I'd tried dealing with Matt by sidestepping his suspicions and hoping they would eventually recede, but it wasn't working. The events of this evening would have only solidified his concerns. So I switched tactics, drawing for inspiration on the lessons in New England winter driving that Matt himself had taught me; I steered into the skid. "Listen, Matt, let's go full cards on the table here. I was following up leads that I wasn't telling you about, and you were tailing me because you didn't trust me."

Matt was surprised, clearly having expected me to go denial again. He tilted his head, looking curious. "That's about the size of it," he said. Then he laid down his challenge: "So, why don't you tell me what I don't know?"

So I did. Not the truth, of course. But the lie I'd spent the entire drive back from Newport coming up with, one that was salted with just enough truth to be accepted. Drawing inspiration from Lilah's childhood story of her teachers, I told Matt that Suzume and I had bribed Jacoby to confess that Gage and the other men had been killed by a secretive cult, one that had deep ties to power brokers like my mother, and enough money that they could bribe confessions and cover their tracks. We were working with a fringe member of the cult who had been born into it and who didn't approve of their actions—Lilah—and we'd all broken into the tattoo parlor to try to find hard evidence that couldn't be dismissed. It was a story that offered an explanation for what was happening and also had the beauty of being verifiable—if Matt started looking into the ownership of Dreamcatching, he'd quickly find the links that many people had seen before of a secretive, wealthy, and very weird group that displayed very cultlike behavior. I watched as he absorbed what I was saying, and braced myself for the question that I knew was coming.

"Why didn't you tell me, Fort?" For the first time Matt pulled back the suspicion, and I could hear the hurt that it had been masking. After all, hadn't he known me since I was still hitting Wiffle balls? Hadn't he been the only one who'd never given up on finding Brian and Jill's killer? The suspicion had hidden the hurt, the betrayal. Now he was showing it, this vulnerability.

And to keep Matt alive, I had to be the bastard who would take advantage of it.

I looked at him carefully, hoping that I was judging him right, that I really knew him and his values as well as I thought I did. I was the closest thing Matt had to family, and I was about to gamble that Matt really loved me more than everything his old badge had stood for.

I took the chance. "Suzume and I were the ones who saved Amy Grann," I said, watching as shock and *I knew it* warred on Matt's face. "The guy who had grabbed her was in the house, we had a fight, and I shot him. A bottle of alcohol got smashed in the fight, and a candle was knocked over, so the fire was going, and we just ran. And we decided to keep it a secret." Close enough to the truth that I could commit to it and not radiate bad poker face. Close enough that I hoped he would believe me. Far enough from the truth that it could keep him ignorant—and alive.

There was a long pause as he looked at me, taking it all in. My gut clenched, but I forced myself to look right back at him. When he spoke, Matt's voice was unusually tentative. "So the files going missing? The evidence destroyed?"

I nodded. "I told my brother, and he made a call." I took a deep breath and added the last brushstroke to what I was hoping would be a masterpiece of bullshit. "That little girl is alive because of what we did, but I didn't want you to have to keep the secret. You were a cop, and what we did wasn't exactly legal."

Matt gave a loud snort and dropped his face into his hands, the snort turning into a semihysterical puff of sound that on any other man I would've called a titter. "Wasn't exactly smart either, Fort," he said. He rubbed his hands hard against his cheeks, then looked back up at me very seriously, and with a lot of fear in his usually unshakable brown eyes. "Fort, there's a reason why we have police instead of vigilantes. Vigilantes tend to get shot." He sighed heavily. "And now you're doing the same damn thing, with your not-girlfriend cheering you on. Playing goddamn Batman."

Funny, that was where I'd gotten the idea for the lie. After all, people kept Batman's secret.

There was probably a vampire-bat joke in there somewhere, but I refused to look for it.

I was committed to these lies now, so I pushed forward. "Gage's killers are in that cult. You saw one of them tonight."

Matt traced the edge of the bandage with a careful finger. "Yeah, that chick works out." I kept my mouth shut as Matt thought about it. "I saw your girl's knife, Fort, and I know that you have Brian's old gun, but what you're involved with is really dangerous. These people are killing guys in a very nasty way." He paused again, considered, and I saw him struggle with it. Really struggle. Then he decided. Reaching out, he grabbed my hands hard, squeezing with enough strength to impact the blood flow, and stared at me intensely. "You have to promise me, Fort," he said. "No more dumb shit like last night. We're looking for information, for evidence. Then we hand it to the police. There will be no dumb-ass heroics on this. Do you hear me?"

I looked at him, deeply humbled to think that he not only had believed what I'd said, but that he was offering this acceptance, this tacit blessing even, to my supposed career of vigilantism. I wished, suddenly and desperately, that I'd been able to tell him the truth about what I actually was and receive this open acceptance. It hurt that here was what I longed for most, and it was being offered for a lie.

I forced myself to nod, to look relieved and grateful. "Okay," I said.

Matt dropped one of my hands and reached up to squeeze my shoulder manfully. But apparently that was insufficient for what he was feeling, because with a sudden movement he pulled me in for a tight hug. "You little shit," he muttered, his voice tight with emotion. "You should've trusted me. I would never have turned you in." And, however falsely, I knew that I had my Matt back.

I choked, but hugged him back desperately. "I'm sorry," I said, and I was. So very, very sorry, for so many things.

The hug went on for a long time, then we both let go slowly. Matt coughed and rubbed a hand across his eyes. "Okay, enough of that," he said gruffly. "Let's see what that not-girlfriend of yours is up to."

Suzume was sitting at her table, flipping her way through a file that I recognized as Matt's. Matching folders were stacked around her. Apparently she'd taken the opportunity to look through Matt's car. She looked up with studied casualness when we approached, but flicked one careful look my way. I nodded slightly, and she relaxed.

"So, we're all on the same side?" she asked.

"Yes," Matt said, and emphasized, "the side that investigates but doesn't do dumb shit."

"Fine with me." Suze lifted one of the files. "So, when you weren't stalking us, you found some new information."

Matt ignored the jab and looked over at me. "Not too much. I got a hold of your friend's autopsy report, did some background on the new name you got from the tattoo artist."

I thought about it, weighing what we knew. "All of the guys were sent an ad for a reduced-price tattoo. They were killed after they got the same tat, but the ads were addressed to them specifically. So however the cult"—I sent a quick look to Suze, making sure that she understood that this was our cover story—"is picking their victims, it's happening before they get the tattoos." I pulled out one of the chairs and sat down, asking Matt, "What do these guys have in common?"

"Young, healthy guys. Three were from Rhode Island; one was from Massachusetts. Oldest was twenty-six; youngest was eighteen."

Suze flipped a page and said, "From your notes, there's an education link. Two were undergrads, Gage was a graduate student, one was entering a PhD program."

Matt shook his head. "Different colleges, and the age range and economic background could explain that."

"All Providence colleges?" I asked curiously.

"One was Boston," Suze said.

I considered, thinking back and trying to remember when I had come in contact with non-Brown students. "Maybe a club or a sports team?"

Matt still looked cautious but a little interested. "I wouldn't have expected to see mixing between so many colleges and different education levels."

Suze made a little *tsk*ing sound. "Maybe not with bigger, established clubs, but some of the little fringe ones have a lot more contact. Swing dancing, bocce." She shrugged. "LARPing."

"Really, Suze?" I asked, smiling. "You?"

She batted her lashed coquettishly at me. "I'm a woman of mystery, Fort. Don't think you know all of my layers." But when Matt pulled over the file to pore over and consider his notes again, she dropped the facade for a quick second, enough that I understood that she'd found something else, a real link, and that this direction was just to give Matt something to hunt to keep him out of our way.

Matt looked up from the file, and I recognized the look on his face. He was focused, considering, ready to chase down this possible lead, wherever it led him. "I'll make some calls tomorrow, maybe go to some of the campuses and ask around, see if there's anything." He eyed me, then Suze, then me again. "And you two will be . . . ?"

"Avoiding stupid actions," I assured him. "Lilah is going to poke around for us, see if she can learn anything. We'll keep you updated."

Matt nodded, then collected his folders, piling them up haphazardly. Suze reached into her pocket and withdrew his car keys, pushing them across the table.

"Are you good to drive?" I asked him, nervous.

"Doctor cleared me," he said, then dropped one hand to give my shoulder a light, reassuring squeeze. "I'll run home and get in a few hours of sleep. You should probably do the same." He eyed Suze wryly, and she gave him her very best lasciviously self-satisfied grin and rubbed her foot deliberately up my leg to make me jump. Matt shook his head and left, muttering under his breath about so-called non-girlfriends.

When the door shut behind him I did my best to grab Suze's foot, intending a tickling in retribution, but she jerked it out of my reach. "Having fun?" I asked her sarcastically.

"Loads," she said smugly.

"Funny." I dropped the game and asked her point-blank, "So, what's your problem with your sister's boyfriend?"

"I'm incredibly racist, Fort," she deadpanned.

I was irritated and didn't try to hide it. "Just say you don't want to tell me."

She lifted an eyebrow at my tone. "I'll talk about my sister if you want to have a chat with me about Matt." I looked away sharply and she nodded. "Whatever this cult story was that you told him, you know that all you did was stall him."

"No, this one could really work. He believes me," I insisted.

"And *when* that changes?"

"I'll keep him safe," I said, glaring at her, my voice a warning to drop the subject. She opened her mouth to respond, then reconsidered. Snapping her lips closed, she toyed with the edge of her placemat. When she didn't say anything, I relaxed a little, then asked, "So, what did you really find in Matt's files?"

She was still miffed and didn't bother to hide it, but she let me change the subject. "For one, he did get the autopsy." She pulled open a small notebook where she'd apparently been copying things from Matt's files and referred to a page. "Turns out that Gage's wrists, tongue, and genitals were all removed while he was still alive. Coroner was able to tell that the killer used a kind of surgical tool that cauterizes as it cuts, which is how Gage lived through it. What killed him was the cut on his throat. It wasn't a big cut, though; it probably took him at least twenty minutes to die. They also found ligature marks on Gage's ankles, and they think that Gage was tied upside down when he bled out."

I closed my eyes and shuddered. I'd known that Gage's death hadn't been easy, but I was cowardly enough that I hadn't wanted to know the details. "Christ."

"I also found a name." Suze flipped a page, then pushed the notebook in front of me. I looked down and recognized the list of the four victims that I'd bought from Jacoby.

"I got that this morning."

"Yeah, but I didn't look at it before you turned it over. Your buddy was a busy boy when he wasn't following us today. Franklin Litchfield died in a car wreck in June. It was a bad wreck, and there was a fire as well. Between the crash and the fire, no one really thought much of a few missing parts when they pulled out the corpse."

"So that's how they disposed of the body. But what about the name?"

Suze lifted up her placemat, which had been concealing a Hello Kitty file folder. "The kitsune keep an eye on our neighbors, probably a closer eye than the Scotts do right now." She opened the file, pulled out a stapled article, and handed it to me.

I skimmed the first paragraph, stopping when I recognized the name Dr. Lavinia Leamaro. Better known as Lulu, she'd been the first half-elf I'd ever met, introduced to me by Suzume when I'd gotten beaten up in a fight and needed to be patched up. "A Neighbor who is very familiar with medical instruments," I said slowly, remembering the autopsy findings. "That fits."

Suze's eyes glittered. "Keep reading."

The article was about Dr. Lulu's incredible success rate at treating infertility. Most women who walked into her office were pregnant within a year. That part was actually a hedge for the article to avoid humans looking closer. The truth was that, thanks to a witch on her staff, *every* woman was pregnant inside a year. She had established her practice as soon as she had finished her residency, and had almost thirty years of experience helping the unwillingly childless women of Rhode Island, and those who drove in from the neighboring states of Massachusetts and Connecticut. There were some snippets of interviews with various happy parents talking about the children they'd conceived against all odds, from parents of a newborn to one mother whose son, conceived through Dr. Lulu's intervention, had just been accepted into Harvard. A son named—

"Franklin Litchfield," I said, stunned.

Suzume nodded. "The ultimate success story. Miracle baby grows up, gets into Ivy League"—she tapped one finger on the list of victims—"dies seven months after that article is published."

I leaned back in my chair, trying to wrap my mind around the implications. "The guys are changelings? But Gage—"

"No, I would've smelled it. He was human." Suzume was certain.

I shook my own head, pulling myself back from my first response. "And the changelings are taken from their families around puberty. All these guys were with their families." I pushed my hands through my hair, trying to will my brain into making sense of this. "Were all of them from Lulu's practice?"

"I don't know, but I do know a certain doctor we should have a chat with."

I nodded grimly. "And I know a certain someone who will definitely know how to encourage Lulu to answer some questions." I held up my cell phone, and Suzume nodded in agreement.

Prudence answered her phone on the second ring. "Ah, baby brother," she said, sounding warmly pleased. "What is on your mind?"

"Suzume and I have a lead. Do you know Dr. Lavinia Leamaro?"

"Yes, she's a half-blood. Runs a very lucrative medical establishment." Trust my sister to remember people based on how much money we extorted out of them in the name of tithes.

"We're going to question her tomorrow. Can you meet us at her clinic?"

"Of course. Shall we say eight in the morning? I've always found it useful to pay calls before the start of business hours. And that's a comfortable time for me."

"That sounds fine," I agreed. After all, she knew more

about unfriendly investigation than I did, and she was old enough to avoid any exposure to the sun during its strongest hours. "See you tomorrow."

Before I could hang up, she cut in smoothly. "Good work, little brother. I'm very much looking forward to seeing what you do with this lead." Her statement was a conversational iceberg—superficially supportive, but with a lot going on under the surface. And with that, she hung up.

"Her being nice is creeping me the hell out," I said to Suze as I tucked my phone back into my pocket.

Suze gave me a warning look. "Just keep on her good side." I nodded.

There was a brief pause.

"So, a homicidal skinwalker knows my address," I said. "Mind if I crash here?"

Suze snorted. "At this rate I'm going to have to buy you a toothbrush."

Dr. Lulu's office of insta-preggo was in one of those medical plazas where an architect built one long gray rectangle and broke it up into a dozen different offices, distinguishable only by the different names written on the glass doors. Prudence was waiting for us when we arrived, and I saw her visibly wince as I pulled the Fiesta into the parking space beside her Lexus, like an automotive version of *Lady and the Tramp*.

"Your sister doesn't seem happy to see us," Suzume noted quietly.

"About sixty percent of that expression is for my car," I told her. At some point in my drive back from Newport the previous night, the already-present hole in the Fiesta's muffler had increased in size.

"So only forty is for you? That's so much better." We were getting out of the car, and I had a solid respect for my sister's sharp hearing, so I just glared at Suzume.

Prudence was dressed in her best Audrey Hepburn–avoiding-the-paparazzi imitation, with a large fawn-colored wool coat partially buttoned over a black Chanel dress. Oversized sun glasses and a wide-brimmed hat blocked out the morning sun, even though it was slightly overcast. Had it been a sunny morning, I knew that she probably would've broken out her trusty parasol.

She gave me a noticeable once-over, but for once managed to restrain any comments about my jeans and flannel button-up.

"Perhaps you should wait a moment while I gain entry," she said with a primness that indicated that my fashion choices for the day might be forgiven but would never be forgotten.

"You probably look a little closer to their usual clientele," I agreed, and watched as Prudence tip-tapped her four-inch Louboutin heels up to the door of Dr. Lulu's reproductive endocrinology practice, which, given that they didn't open for another half hour, was probably still locked.

While my sister knocked imperiously on the glass, I looked over at Suze.

"You're being quiet," I noted. I'd been amazed when Suzume had let that "usual clientele" comment pass without some kind of joke about Prudence's inclusion in the over-forty club that made the most use of fertility services.

"I'm being smart," she replied seriously. I looked down, surprised, and noticed just how carefully Suze was holding herself and the way that she was eyeing my sister, as if Prudence was an angry rattlesnake. "You should be doing the same."

Before I could respond, the little scheduling nurse I remembered from last time, a slightly anemic-looking blond woman in her thirties, had cracked open the door to talk with my sister, apparently lulled by her combination of femaleness and overt affluence. Even as she started explaining that the office wasn't open yet, Prudence was already pushing her way into the door. I scrambled quickly to catch up with her and slide in inside her wake before the startled nurse could close it, and Suze slithered in behind me.

"I have some very serious business to discuss with Dr. Leamaro," Prudence said in a tone of voice that promised dire retribution for anyone who crossed her.

"As I was trying to explain to you, there was an emergency, and she will not be in today," the nurse said. She probably wasn't even aware of how she was backing away from my sister like a nervous white rabbit, but some part of her had clearly recognized that she was facing a predator and latent survival instincts were clanging in her head. "I can reschedule your appointment, and you are welcome to leave a note for her, but I'm going to have to insist—"

"Insist?" Prudence asked, with enough *The Devil Wears Prada* malevolence that the nurse made a little frightened noise and stopped talking. My sister smiled slowly. "That's much better," she said. "Now be a love and call the doctor. Find out where she is. I know she left you a number."

"But—"

"We're old friends," Prudence said, dropping back into that voice that made the poor woman quake in her sensibly ergonomic footwear. "She won't mind."

"I'm sure you are her friend," the nurse said, her voice shaking. "But she said that her phone would be off all day. Everything will just be going to voicemail. Even if any of the women are going into labor, I'm supposed to refer them to one of the residents in the hospital. She's never done this before."

Prudence frowned and clicked her tongue. "I'm very disappointed in you. It's never good for someone to disappoint me."

I didn't like the expression forming on Prudence's face, and the nurse looked about ready to wet herself, so I broke in. "So Dr. Lu— Leamaro won't be in today. Is her assistant in?" Even if Dr. Lulu hadn't been a half-blood, elf magic didn't have any effect on fertility. When Suzume had investigated the practice's unnatural success rate earlier, she'd learned that the elves had hired a witch to ensure that every woman conceived. Of course, it was Lulu and her practice of semen switching that resulted in the women walking out of the office doors with the child of an Ad-hene inside them—and a whopping seven percent of those were born changelings.

The nurse looked intensely relieved to be able to answer something in the affirmative. "Oh yes, of course. Ambrose is in the back room, mixing prescriptions."

My brain stumbled a little. We'd never been formally introduced the last time we'd encountered each other, but my memory of Lulu's witch was of a man built along the same lines as a badger, but with a beer gut and a heavily salted vocabulary. Ambrose was not exactly a name that fit him, though it did suggest highly optimistic parents. I recovered myself and nodded. "Ambrose can answer our questions today. Thank you." I gave a small nod to Suzume. "Though my associate, Ms. Hollis, might have a few others that maybe you can help her with."

The nurse nodded enthusiastically, relieved that I would be taking my sister anywhere other than here, to talk with anyone other than her. Compared to Prudence, who was exuding homicidal intent like pheromones, Suze seemed downright cuddly.

Suze took the woman, who looked as emotionally battered as a sparrow that had just been chased with a leaf-blower, by the arm and led her back to her desk, chattering innocuous questions that the nurse answered by rote. Something in the gleam of her dark eyes made me wonder if Suzume was using a little fox magic on the woman, but I knew that I could trust her not to hurt the nurse, which was more than I could say for my sister, who was best avoided by the easily broken when her tantrums were thwarted.

Prudence and I headed silently down the peach-colored hallway decorated with framed photos of mothers and infants to the last door, the only one that was closed. There was a hand-written sign taped to it that read *Stay the fuck out*. Remembering who we were looking for, that seemed promising, and with a small nod to Prudence, I pulled open the door and we both walked in.

His back to the door, Ambrose stood at a long counter covered with various beakers filled with substances that reminded me strongly of the jar of rubber cement from my middle-school art classes, both in consistency and color.

At the sound of our footsteps, he spun around, yelling loudly, "May Vishnu ram each of his four damn hands up your ass, Maureen. When I said don't disturb me, I—" As soon as he caught sight of us, his voice ended on a gravelly choke, and the beaker he was mixing dropped from his suddenly slack hands. It crashed on the floor, and a soft pink haze rose from the puddle and hung in the air for a brief moment before disappearing. All color leached from his face as he just stared at my sister.

"Very good, witch. You know who I am," Prudence purred as she walked farther into the room, removing her hat and setting it down daintily on the counter.

Ambrose recovered enough to bob his head frantically and say, in a shaking voice, "Of course, Miss Scott, of course. I'd met your younger brother, but" — defying his barrel-like shape, his voice pitched almost into a squeak as my sister began tugging off her black silk gloves, one finger at a time — "of course we all know what you look like."

"I am pleased to hear that." Prudence dropped her gloves onto her hat and walked closer to the terrified witch. She ran one finger along the countertop as she went, looking over the assortment of tiny, stoppered earthenware bottles and one closed box that lined the area behind the beakers. "My brother has questions for you." She stood close to the witch, invading his personal space by a lot, and ran that one finger deliberately across Ambrose's stout stomach in a very clear threat. "I suggest that you answer them."

"Certainly, certainly." Sweat was dripping down his face. "Anything I know."

Prudence looked over at me, indicating that the floor was now mine. I cleared my throat and was surprised at how heartless my own voice sounded when I said, "Tell me why the elves are tattooing and killing young men."

"Uh . . ." The panic cleared from Ambrose's face, driven away by an expression of pure surprise. Whatever he'd been expecting or dreading me to ask, this hadn't even been on his radar, and for the moment he was caught too off guard to even remember to be scared. "Doing what, now?" he asked.

Prudence clearly didn't approve of the loss of the terror she'd worked very hard to establish, and she leaned well into his personal space. "My brother was quite clear." Her finger stopped stroking his belly and suddenly dug in slightly, and his breath caught in a sharp gasp as she dragged it across, leaving a small line of blood. "I suggest you consider which is more valuable to you — the loyalty you have to your employer or your attachment to your intestines."

Ambrose shook his head desperately, and words tumbled out of his mouth. "Tattooing, *killing*—listen, with no disrespect, I'm a dime-store potion witch. I've spent the last three decades mixing fertility potion after fertility potion for the elves because the money is good enough to put my kids through college and pay my mortgage. This isn't any of the great magic or anything that would require a death sacrifice."

"Death sacrifice?" I asked, picking up on the last term.

Ambrose nodded, looking relieved that there was something he could fill me in on. "Yeah, that's what you tattoo something for. You know, you're doing something that breaks a few of the big laws of nature, you need a little help to grease the wheels, you put a sacrifice tattoo on a chicken, kill it, and you have the whammy you need, plus dinner." He gave a weak smile, one that faltered and slipped away when his gaze darted over to Prudence's completely unimpressed expression.

This sounded useful, and I felt a tug of excitement, wondering if this was an actual lead at last. "And on a human? Like this?" There were a few pads of paper on the counter, and I pulled one toward me, along with a pencil, and sketched out a quick outline of a human form, then drew in my best effort at the tattoo bands, admittedly somewhat crudely. I pushed the sketch close enough for Ambrose to look at.

He gave it a long, considering examination, then looked up at me and said, in a carefully bland voice, "Not really an artist, are you?" He looked down again at my sketch, his large beetle brows pulling together in thought. He leaned forward cautiously, reaching for the pencil, watching Prudence out of the corner of his eye. After a moment she removed her finger from his stomach and shifted just a breath farther away from him, but it was enough to indicate permission, and he quickly ripped off my piece of paper and on a fresh sheet sketched out a series of designs, then pushed the pad back to me. "Did it look like any of those?"

I checked. They were all a series of interconnected knots,

but as I scanned through them, the last one jumped out at me. I'd seen it too many times over the past several days to mistake it, and I tapped it hard.

"That one? Bit old school, I guess," Ambrose said. Then, sounding almost reluctantly impressed, he continued, "The elves are pulling that shit? Well, I can tell you that no witch in the country did that for them."

"How do you know?"

Sounding more relaxed, Ambrose explained, "Firstly, death sacrifices are a work-around. You don't need to be a witch to make one work. Making the ink, sure, that's a witch, but you could buy that. Must be half a dozen witches in the Scott territory alone who would sell it to someone. But to actually off a human with it, karmically that is not" — he gave a sudden glance to Prudence and then rephrased whatever he'd been about to say, finishing lamely — "a good idea. No sane witch would do that for someone else. You do that if your town gets firebombed by Nazis, not because some dick elf hired you for it." I grimaced at what I was hearing. I'd been hoping that accidentally smashing the bottle of ink during the fight with Soli would've been more of a setback to their operation.

"Did your employer ever ask you to do that?" Prudence asked, and he flinched at the sound of her voice.

"Never," he said, sounding subdued and frightened again. "Ma'am, this is what I do all day." He gestured at the beakers on the table. "Fertility potions and more fertility potions." He paused, then looked uncomfortable, his tongue darting out to run nervously over his upper lip. "Though lately she has asked me to cook the occasional roofie."

That completely distracted me. "Um, roofies?" Worried, I asked, "What is Lulu *doing* to her patients?"

Ambrose frowned at me, looking annoyed rather than terrified. "Not her patients, dumbsh —" A subtle movement from Prudence reminded him of her presence, and he caught the word at the last minute, rephrasing it as, "Young man. No, those bakeless-oven gals are nice and desperate. They'll do anything already. Boss said it was Neighbor business. Anyway, my potion wouldn't hurt someone; just fogs the memory, makes the drinker nice and suggestible, gets them to do all sorts of things they would refuse to do under normal circumstances."

That sounded plenty hurtful to me. "You made that for her? That's horrible!"

Ambrose looked surprised, and shrugged. "Leamaro asked for it; I made it. What she does with it is her damn business."

"That is completely unethical," I said.

"Sir, do I look like I'm a pharmacist? Because I am not. I just cooked what she asked for."

"And didn't ask any questions." Disgust filled me and I didn't bother to hide it.

"Not my job to notice things," Ambrose said mutinously. Prudence made another small move, and he jumped a little, rushing to say, "But I may have noticed a few mornings in the past few months that the incinerator was used overnight. On something bigger than just some files." Prudence just stared at him, and he hedged. "Might've had some bones shards left, like a pig or something." She didn't blink, and he muttered, "Probably bigger than a pig." One last glare, and he admitted, "Could've been a person."

"Why would someone cut off a death sacrifice's hands? And the tongue? And genitals?" I asked.

Ambrose looked impressed at the list. "Every spell has more components and steps. The bigger the oomph, the farther you're trying to get from the natural workings, the more steps involved. But a death spell plus parts cut off? That's some serious shit."

Prudence leaned in and said, very quietly in his ear, "Tell me what the elves want, Ambrose."

"What they've always wanted, lady," Ambrose said respectfully. "More elves." He pointed again at the row of potions lining his table. "A human-elf cross occurs naturally. The potions just help it happen more frequently. The elves wanted more than just a half-blood, something that wouldn't happen normally, and my magic and potions were able to bend the rules a little to get them that—a cross between a half-blood and a full, with some extra help, gets you a three-quarter. But that's as far as it goes." He shook his head. "The true elves are going the way of the Neanderthal. Some genes left in a hybrid, and maybe the hybrids will eventually stabilize a full population, but the real elves will be long gone. And no great loss, if you ask me."

"And yet you serve," Prudence said.

"Ma'am, it's a living."

"Fortitude?" Prudence turned to look at me. "Mother placed this investigation in your hands, so I ask you, little brother." One fast move, and her hand was in what was left of Ambrose's hair, pulling his head far back, enough that he was yanked hard backward over her waiting leg, forcing his back into a steep arch. His whole body hovered off-balance, his feet pushed almost onto his toes. His shirt slid back, revealing a very pale stomach lightly dusted with wiry black hair, looking horribly exposed and vulnerable. The cut my sister had left before was a long, raw mark, and she reached past it and, very slowly and deliberately, raked all four fingers across his belly, leaving a trail of shallow cuts that sullenly oozed blood. She never looked away from me as she did it, and asked, in a perfectly polite and conversational voice, "Does he live? Or does he die?"

Ambrose made a high, helpless sound, too terrified to stay silent, but also too afraid to try to escape my sister's hold. I swallowed hard; the suddenness and the very controlled nature of my sister's violence had thrown me badly, but I fought to stay calm. I reminded myself of what Suze had said: I had to be smart about this, to act in a way that kept Prudence under control but also justified my actions to her in a way that she would respect and abide. I struggled to keep my face blank as I looked down at the frightened witch. I didn't like him. I didn't like how willing he was to cook something like a roofie potion with no concerns at all about how it was going to be used and on who, but I also wasn't sure that criminal indifference was enough to kill someone over—at least until I found out exactly how that potion had been administered.

Admittedly, I wasn't feeling too sorry about the man's bleeding stomach or the small, spreading stain in the crotch of his pants.

While I was figuring out what to say, my sister was looking substantially *less* polite. Her pupils were bleeding out, covering the blue of her eyes. Her fingers dug into his cuts, deepening them, and Ambrose cried out again.

"Sniveling rat," my sister muttered, her lip curling. "All you witches—scampering and gnawing at the edges. Would the other rats care if a cat ate one of you?" She dropped her tone almost to a whisper and spoke into his ear. "Of course not. More cheese for them."

Her fingers were flexing ominously, and I knew it was definitely time to derail this—if I could.

I made my voice as neutral as possible and said, "Witches are bought, Prudence. We should've been more aware of what Lulu was doing." I looked directly into my sister's sociopathic eyes and gave her a reason she would agree with. "And a witch can be a useful thing to have, especially one who knows who is in charge."

She paused, then nodded slowly, her pupils receding enough to show just a hint of blue. She let go of Ambrose, allowing him to fall into a boneless lump on the floor, staring up at us with the blink-free terror of a bunny facing predators. "True enough, brother," she said mildly. Looking down at the witch at her feet, she sneered. "Tell me where the half-elf is today."

Ambrose pressed his eyes closed and whispered, "I don't know—I swear by blood and bone that I don't know."

Prudence leaned down, examining him like a bug that she was still contemplating crushing. I cut in, reminding her, "If she didn't involve him in the planning, she wouldn't have told him where she was. After last night, they have to know that we're looking where they don't want us to."

Prudence clicked her tongue. "True enough," she acknowledged, and nudged Ambrose with the tip of her high heel. "Find new employment, witch. And if you learn something new about Leamaro, something that might be of interest to me, you'll contact us, won't you?"

"Of course," he slathered desperately.

"As it should be," Prudence said, satisfied.

I still didn't like the look in her eyes, and I said, "If there's nothing else, Prudence, we should probably go." I picked up her hat and gloves and held them out to her. After one last, almost longing look at the huddled wreck at her feet, she nodded slowly, but with an expression that was almost pouting.

We left the room. My heart was thumping wildly in my chest, but I was relieved that I'd managed to avert the maiming (if not outright murder) that I knew that Prudence would've preferred meting out in the interests of making an example of the costs of landing on her radar. Suzume was waiting for us in the hallway, her face very carefully arranged into an expression of emotionless obedience that was probably the best mask I'd ever seen her present. There was a set of folders tucked under her arm.

"Did you find something?" I asked her as she fell neatly into step beside me. Prudence's heels *tip-tap*ped behind us, an uncomfortable reminder of the very real danger she presented at my undefended back. We headed out the door, past the nurse who gave us a nervous look but added a professional smile as we went. Suzume had clearly taken the opportunity to work a little fox magic and smooth out our departure.

Suze tapped the folders. "I convinced my new buddy to check Lulu's records. All the victims were conceived here. Got the files, so we can look through to see what made them special."

Outside, the cloud cover had burned off, revealing a perfect blue-sky autumn day and a bright sun. Closing the office door behind her, Prudence winced and quickly replaced her hat and adjusted her sunglasses.

Noticing her discomfort, I started to ask, "Prudence, do you need to—"

She nodded, cutting me off. "Yes, it is time I returned to my hotel."

Relief filled me, but my mind was also working, trying to determine how best to utilize my sister's undeniable talent at eliciting honest answers from shady individuals. "Okay. We'll look into the files. If it's sunny all day, when will you be comfortable coming outside again?"

"Four, perhaps four thirty." She tilted her head forward, considering me briefly over the top of her sunglasses. "What would you like me to do, brother?"

"I want you to find Lulu. Soli knew who I was, so if Lulu's hiding, she's hiding from us. Can you find her?"

She gave me a small smile. "It will be a pleasure." She tugged her black silk gloves over her hands, protecting the exposed skin from the sun, and made another minute adjustment to her hat. "I will make inquiries while I rest in my room, and this evening I will start my pursuit."

The expression on her face made me deeply grateful that at this point the odds that Lulu was not neck-deep in this situation were minuscule. "Thank you," I said politely.

Prudence paused, then said, "That was good work back there, Fortitude." Then, with that staggeringly unusual statement still rattling in my head as I struggled to deal with the shock of being given yet another compliment from her in less than twenty-four hours, she turned quickly and was in her car and pulling out without waiting for a reply.

As we both watched Prudence's Lexus make a turn out of the complex and disappear into traffic, I said to Suze, "I assume you heard everything that happened in the back room."

She shrugged. "Might have."

"What do you—" the Tetris theme song erupted from my pants pocket, cutting off my question, and I reached down and pulled out my phone. I checked the screen, saw Lilah's name, and immediately flipped it open, raising my eyebrows at Suze. "Hello?"

Lilah was speaking quickly and excitedly. "Hey, Fort. I'm at Dreamcatching now. It's just me here, and I was looking around and I think I found something. Can you come over now?"

I glanced at the files under Suze's arm. "Yeah, Suze and I will be right over. We just found something too, and we can swap notes."

After an exchange of good-byes, we both hung up.

While we headed over to Dreamcatching, Suze paged through the files, reading with an intensity that would've left me with a distinct case of car sickness. As I stopped at a red light, I flipped my phone out and dialed Matt, checking in to see what he was doing. The call was a quick one—Matt was at the first college on his list, trying to run down any clubs and activities that could've brought the victims into contact with one another. I felt relief knowing that he was running down a fake lead that would keep him well out of danger for the day, and when he asked what I was up to, I assured him that Suze and I were just waiting to see if he could turn anything up, as both of us had to work that day and couldn't go anywhere ourselves.

I actually did have to go to work that afternoon, and I hoped that no one would notice that I had not had either the time or the inclination to wash my uniform in almost a week.

I said good-bye to Matt, and hung up.

Without looking up from the file in front of her, Suze began, "I—"

"If it's about Matt, don't say it," I said, cutting her off.

There was a long pause and then she glanced up at me, looking at me steadily. "If you want to keep that man alive, you need to separate from him. Soon."

My temper sparked and caught like dry grass in the summer. "You think I haven't considered that? You think I *like* having him in danger?"

Suze stared at me, her dark eyes narrowing. "I think that you and my sister have a lot in common."

The memory of Keiko watching her human boyfriend, and the almost visible subtext of their impending tragedy, filled my mind, and my anger guttered and died. Was my own attachment to Matt like that? But whenever I thought of giving him up, of dodging his calls or picking a fight and pretending that I didn't want to see him, or, worst of all, convincing him that the bond between us didn't matter and that I didn't care about him anymore, I just couldn't think about it. Matt was the last link back to my foster parents— he could tell me about anecdotes of Brian on the job, or reminisce about how he and Jill would argue politics over the table on the many nights he'd eaten dinner with us. I wasn't ready to lose that.

"Not now, Suze. Please not now." She started to say something, and I shook my head. "Let's just focus on the elves." I nodded at the file. "Anything useful?"

She didn't like it; it was clear, but she allowed me to

change the subject. That didn't mean she had to be happy about it, and her tone was lethal. "It's a medical file, and I am not a doctor. Right now I've got fuck-all except a detailed description of some woman's vagina."

"That's great. Keep on that," I said, and returned my attention to driving, grateful for the reprieve, while she muttered darkly under her breath.

# Chapter 8

At Dreamcatching, Lilah was watching for us, waiting anxiously just inside the door. She waved us in and closed the door behind us, flipping the little sign from OPEN to CLOSED.

"Aren't you worried about what your boss will think about your new definition of standard hours?" Suze asked, sounding almost unwillingly amused.

Lilah snorted. "I rang up a pack of incense as today's total sales. No one will notice, or if they do they'll celebrate our improving solvency." She led us through the beaded curtain and into the back rooms. I was entertained to note that in contrast to the soothing turquoise walls and careful ambiance of the front of the store, the areas where customers were not welcome looked like any other place I'd worked at—cement floors, piles of brown boxes, and the occasional ancient office chair that any OSHA agent worth his salt would wrap in hazardous-materials tape.

"Allegra went into labor early this morning," she said, leading us through the warren of boxes and into an old, dusty office with orange shag carpeting and a few motivational pictures framed on the walls—clearly the den of a manager. "Tomas is staying with her, and Felix works after he gets out of school, so I had a chance to search everything."

"What did you find?" I asked.

"Well, mostly that Tomas cheats on his taxes. And this." She slid open the bottom drawer of the desk, pulled out the folders that hung in it, and gestured for me to look.

I peered in. On the bottom of the drawer, where it must've slipped out of a file and worked its way down, was one page that was a partial view of an illustration that had been photocopied out of a book. Someone had clearly enlarged the image when they were copying it—there were a few squiggles of handwritten words around the image, but they were mostly cut off, and even the ones that I could decipher were in a foreign language. It was an ink drawing of a very familiar band of intricate knots, and beside it an anonymous male figure hung upside down from a tree, with those bands drawn on his skin at bicep and wrist.

Suze leaned in over my shoulder for a look and gave a low whistle. "That drawing of the band is the same one that Jacoby has in his design book. Someone trimmed the image from this page to give to him."

"It was the only thing in the whole office," Lilah explained. "I wouldn't have found it at all, except I was pulling out the files so that I could keep them in exact order."

"Tomas must've been originally keeping a file on this here but moved it later." I looked closer at the text. "Lilah, can you read what's written here?"

"Sorry, I took French in high school," she said apologetically.

I was surprised. "French? Not, you know . . . Gaelic?"

She gave me a very put-out look. "Not exactly an option in Providence high schools," Lilah said witheringly.

Suze pulled out her phone and waggled it. "Good thing we've got technology. Here." She'd brought in the files from Lulu's office and handed them to me in return for the photocopy.

While Suze started squinting at the page and tapping words into Google, Lilah pointed at the files. "What are those?"

"Actually, we were hoping you could help." I handed them to her. "These are files on each of the victims from Dr. Leamaro's office."

Lilah frowned. "What?" She flipped open the first in the stack and scanned through it quickly, flicking through most of the pages until she found what she was looking for. She nodded as she read it, but looked extremely confused. "He was a recessive," she told me, then checked each file in turn. "They were all recessives. That doesn't make sense."

"Why not? That means he was a changeling, just one without ears, right?"

Lilah corrected me. "No, a recessive is a human. The DNA that makes a changeling is completely dormant. Believe me, the Neighbors tried everything; there's nothing that can turn that DNA on. They gave up more than twenty years ago." Still frowning, she looked over at the illustration that Suze was examining and the drawing of the man hanging upside down. "Unless . . . Maybe this is something new, that they're trying to make active changelings."

"We talked to Lulu's witch. He said that that tattoo is for a blood sacrifice. That doesn't sound like something that leads to long-term health."

Lilah grimaced. "No, that doesn't sound good at all."

Suze snapped her fingers loudly at us, drawing our attention. "Hey, how does this help with the brainstorming?" She pointed to one of the few complete and legible words on the sheet, *sliochdmhorachd*, which I couldn't even imagine how to start trying to pronounce. "Apparently this is Scottish Gaelic for 'fertility.'" She gave me a wry look. "Sound like the elf theme song to anyone else?"

I thought back to what Ambrose had told us about his fertility potions' limitations. "Lilah, are the Ad-hene trying to breed something more than a three-quarter cross?" I asked.

She shrugged. "Sure, they've been trying for years. But it hasn't happened. The three-quarters, like Allegra and my sister, Iris, are as close as they've been able to get, and even that took magic."

"If a potion couldn't get them a cross between a full and a three-quarter, do you think that they'd be willing to try killing someone for it?"

Lilah gave me a pensive look. "Themselves never need much of a reason to kill humans. The only reason they don't do it more often is your mother set some pretty clear rules. If they thought it would get them the seven-eighths cross they wanted . . . yeah, they'd do that."

Suze broke in, impatient. "We can sit here and speculate on the why until the cows come home, but why not just concentrate on the who? Lulu is probably involved; that sheet proves that your boss is *definitely* involved. All we have to do is grab one of them. We get them to lead us to the rest of the group so that we can eliminate all of them, and not only do the murders stop, but we can even ask them definitively what the fuck they were up to."

I hesitated, but Suzume had a very good point there. "I guess." I looked over at Lilah, who was sitting cross-legged on the floor beside me, a few coppery curls escaping from her braid. I stumbled a moment, knowing what I had to ask her to do but hating it at the same time. There wasn't much of a choice, though, and I pushed ahead. "Listen, I know he's your boss and part of the community, and probably related to you in a few ways as well, but—"

She knew what I was asking and gave me the kindness of not having to spell it out. "I know, Fort. It's okay," she said, cutting me off. Her long skirt had pockets in it, and she pulled out a folded piece of paper and handed it to me. She'd known the moment she found the illustration in his desk drawer what I'd need from her. Her face was pale but resolute. "If he was doing this, then he has to be stopped. This is Tomas's address. With Allegra in labor, they won't be leaving the house today."

I opened the paper to check. There was the address, in a looping script that stopped just short of substituting hearts for *o*'s. "No hospital?"

"Not with Allegra. She'll want to drop her glamour to be more comfortable during the labor. Most of us were born at home because of that."

That gave another interesting explanation to the doctor's absence from her office this morning. "That's probably where Lulu is as well." Lilah nodded.

Suze put her phone away and tucked the photocopy in her back pocket. Standing up, she said grimly, "And since they know that the Scotts are looking into their business, there's probably a certain skinwalker present as well. And how and why that skinwalker got involved in this circle jerk is something to add to the list of interrogation questions."

I winced at the reminder of the skinwalker. That definitely cut out any plan of going over to the house ourselves. "I'll give the address to Prudence to track down this evening when she can go out again. She knows a lot more about skinwalkers than either of us do—she can just nab either Lulu or Tomas if they leave the house on their own." Given Prudence's tendency to create a body count, *grab a target* was a better direction than *eliminate*. That left hours today before Prudence would be able to leave her hotel comfortably, and I paused again, torn. "Do you think they could have anything planned for today? If all the people they're killing are recessive changelings, then that's a pretty substantial pool of potential victims."

"More specific, Fort," Suze noted. "Recessive changelings with the blood-sacrifice tattoo. We could always see if Jacoby tattooed anyone since we talked with him, or if he didn't give us all of the names in the first place."

"Or you could go one better," Lilah said suddenly, looking excited. "You said that everyone who was tattooed was sent to the speed-dating that the store hosted. Well, why not just go there and see if anyone has the tattoos?"

"There's another speed-dating?" I asked.

"Tonight!" She grabbed a stack of paper from on top of the desk, flipped through it, and withdrew a flier. "It's been scheduled for weeks."

"Don't you have to sign up for those things? In advance?" Suze asked.

Lilah smiled smugly. "Not if you know the coordinator who checks off the list and collects tickets. And with Tomas busy with Allegra, I'm going to be the only one there tonight. Since you're a guy and a girl, I don't even have to worry about the gender ratio being off—I'll just set up an extra table."

Suze looked over at me, her expression clearly demanding that I shoot down this plan. Apparently speed-dating was not her style. But the more I thought about it, the more I thought that this had potential. "This could actually really work," I said, picking up on Lilah's excitement. "What time does it start?"

"Six o'clock. You'll love it—it's at this really cute independent bookstore. Meet some new people, browse some books—this has everything!" Clearly Lilah had been giving people the hard sell for too long and just couldn't stop herself from talking it up.

I looked at the flier. "That's something else I'm not following here," I noted. "What the hell is up with these speed-dating things? Why didn't they just grab Gage when he got his tattoo in the first place? Or abduct him from the house?"

"House snatch involves the possibility of nosy neighbors or roommates," Suze said with a disturbing air of experience. "And given that they were faking deaths and disappearances, I can see why getting the victims to a controlled secondary location was done."

"Crap. I guess that explains the change," said Lilah, her coppery eyebrows arched almost up to her hairline.

"Change?" I asked her.

"Yeah, the speed-dating is something that Tomas has done here and here for a few years, but they used to be held in the store to increase foot-traffic. Then right after New Year's he started joining up with other businesses, and we were doing them a lot more often."

"More often?" I asked, worried at the implications. "How *much* more?"

Following my train of thought, Lilah looked at the flier and blanched. "It used to be once, maybe twice a year. Now, well, we're having two in as many weeks."

"Are there more coming up?"

Her golden-brown eyes were grim. "Four more next month."

"I hope you get paid extra for that shit," Suze put in.

Lilah shook her head. "I'm salary."

"Bummer." The women exchanged looks, for once perfectly in tune.

Reality suddenly closed in again, and I realized that even if going to a bookstore and having to fight purchase temptation when my expenses this month were already dooming me to a steady diet of ramen wasn't bad enough, I was scheduled to work through dinner shift tonight. "Oh, shit. I'm going to have to cut out early from work." I paused, reviewing it. "Crap, it's still a decent plan. Okay, I'll just tell them I've got to head out early." That was sure to go over like a lead balloon. No wonder most vigilante crime fighters were independently wealthy: the others were busy at work.

"Is your boss not very flexible?" Lilah asked.

"He kind of hates me very specifically," I said glumly. And as of the night before seemed to hold me personally responsible for the failure of the bombe fruit flowers.

Suze scoffed. "Don't make it harder than it is, Fort. Just lie your ass off and say you have to go to a wake. It's not like you bag out early all the time."

"I'm not going to lie about a wake," I said, hurt. "I'll just be honest and say it's a one-time thing."

She shook her head. "When you're whining about being unemployed again, remember who gave you the good advice about being deceptive that you ignored." Suze checked her phone. "Speaking of which, if you want to arrive on time to the job you're about to be fired from, maybe we should get going." She glanced from me to Lilah, then got that sneaky look on her face that I had come to distrust. "I'll just powder my nose and let you two say good-bye." As she headed over to the bathroom, I looked at Lilah uncomfortably, wondering whether Suze was trying to set us up or embarrass us, or actually liked me and was trying some kind of reverse-psychology thing. Knowing Suze, it could be any of those or none of those.

Lilah and I looked awkwardly at each other. Figuring out if a girl wanted to go out with me had never been my strong suit—though, in fairness, there also hadn't been a huge line of interested parties. Maybe Suze was trying to let me know that Lilah was into me, and that she herself was really not. I'd been the recipient of variations of that maneuver on a few scarring occasions in adolescence.

Clearing my throat, wishing that this entire situation could come with accompanying subtitles to explain undercurrents to me, I looked down at the file that Lilah still had open on her lap. This one was Gage's, and I noticed that the name Nokke was typed in the upper right-hand corner of the page. Desperately grateful for a distraction, I pointed to it. "Hey, isn't that your grandfather's name, Lilah? Why is he listed in Gage's file?"

Looking equally relieved at having a neutral topic, she shrugged. "Oh, that's just the spot where the Ad-hene paternity is listed. If Gage had been a changeling, they would've wanted to know."

"So Gage was actually your uncle. That's kind of weird to think about."

Lilah gave an amused smile—apparently my reaction to the crazy family trees she dealt with every day was borderline cute. "Yeah. But so are a lot of people. The changeling who is our stock boy, Felix, is also my uncle." She shrugged. "It kind of stops having much meaning to you. Your family is who was raised in the same house as you, not who happens to share a few extra strands of genome."

"Except for dating purposes." I noted, teasingly reminding her of the prom-date fiasco.

She laughed. "True. Then it starts mattering again." Then she looked over at me, and her smile had an extra layer of nuance. "Speaking of dating, remember to try to look the part tonight."

Well, that seemed almost certainly flirtatious, and I did my best to reciprocate. "I will launder my finest T-shirt for the occasion," I said grandly, and she gave a very ego-reinforcing laugh as a toilet flushed loudly nearby and Suze returned, giving us a very measuring expression.

Back in the car, I confronted her about it. "Suze, are you trying to set me up with Lilah?" I asked straight out, studying her face carefully.

She had on her best poker face. "She's nice. Cute if you like redheads who hail from West Virginia levels of inbreeding."

I pushed. "So, you think I should go out with her?"

With her keen instincts at driving me completely insane, Suze just gave a noncommittal shrug and smoothly changed the subject. "I think you should come up with better plans than undercover speed-dating. Bad cologne and desperation. You're lucky I have flexible hours, Fort. When I blow off work, it's for important shit. Like three-dollar martini night."

I let the topic change stand, returning us to more comfortable conversational waters. "I value your sacrifices, Suze. But if a guy shows up with those tattoos, we can keep him from becoming a blood sacrifice for crazy incest hounds. I'd call that a worthwhile evening."

"And while we're covering that end, who's going to be watching the tattoo parlor?"

"What do you mean?" I asked, surprised at how serious she'd suddenly become.

"If someone gets the tat of death, they're walking out of that shop. Someone needs to keep an eye on it, and I happen to know a person who is used to spending long hours watching front doors."

I knew who she was talking about, and felt my temper start boiling. "Are you nuts, Suze? Matt is chasing nice, safe, ivory-tower leads today. I'd rather not reinvolve him in the real shit."

"Your buddy isn't stupid, Fort. Eventually he's going to realize that there's nothing there and then he'll want back in. Instead of waiting for that to happen, why not give him a job now? Sitting in a coffee shop for hours at a time is pretty safe, and might actually be useful if he can spot a potential victim before we're able to shut down the whole operation." Suze's voice was cool. When she wanted to, she could play logic like an upright bass, and I ground my teeth together and tried to ignore it, focusing on the other cars in our lane as if our commute was the only thing worthy of my attention. Maybe she'd let it go.

"You know I'm right," she said, clearly having no intention of letting it go.

I hated it when she was right.

Suze and I had disagreements all the time, and about most subjects, but usually we let most conflicts die after a few sarcastic quips and a general agreement to disagree. This time it was different, and we sniped back and forth at each other for the entire drive back to my apartment and even up the stairs. I knew why she wasn't letting the subject go: everything about the plan made sense, and my only defense was that I wasn't comfortable with it. Calling Matt and pulling him back toward the real investigation scared the crap out of me.

Of course, once I'd admitted that that was my sole objection, I didn't have many options left. So after we'd cautiously made our way up the stairs and into my apartment (the caution being twofold—firstly that we'd been arguing for twenty minutes and were trying to give each other some space, but secondly that a skinwalker knew my address and we were keeping an eye out for a potential, if unlikely, ambush), I stood in my bedroom and called Matt.

It was a quick conversation, which, given how Judas-y I was feeling at the moment, was a relief. Just as Suze and I had known, there had been no activity or club link to be found at the colleges, and Matt welcomed the partial truths that I fed him and claimed were Lilah's discoveries from questioning fellow cult members, and agreed to stake out the Iron Needle and keep an eye on any customers who fit the profile.

I called my sister while I pulled on my work clothing, which was definitely overdue for a trip through the wash. I did my best with my handy bottle of Febreze while I filled Prudence in on everything we'd learned and passed along Tomas's home address, emphasizing that everyone except Soli was on a capture-alive-and-with-minimal-damage basis. She was happy to get a clear starting point, and promised that when she headed out she'd go straight there.

Once dressed, I also quickly packed up two duffel bags. The thought that Soli knew where I lived and had already climbed my fire escape once was enough to make my skin crawl, and I was planning on camping out at Suze's until everything was finally wrapped up. Into one bag went the basics of living—three days' worth of clothing, deodorant, and my *Firefly* DVDs—and into the other I packed the basics of staying alive: my Colt and the Ithaca 37, along with every round of ammo I'd accumulated.

For once, Suze had respected my privacy and stayed in the main room while I changed and packed. I'd been relieved by the decision, feeling that both of us needed a chance to decompress. As I walked out of my bedroom, carrying both duffel bags (one noticeably heavier than the other), I saw her sitting with very unusual meekness at the table. In front of her was a freshly made sandwich, and when I walked over to her, she nudged the plate forward, toward me, in an unmistakable gesture.

I paused, surprised. Suze didn't apologize often. Equally rare was her willingness to make food, and that she'd made food that was solely for me? This was blue-lobster levels of rare.

"I'm still right," she said, looking up at me. "But I'm sorry. I know you're trying to protect him because you care about him." I'd never seen Suze look that uncomfortable before—it was a foreign expression on someone who seemed to walk through life with the confidence and self-assurance of a small army. I felt both touched that she'd show me that face and also a little regretful that it was there.

"Thank you," I said, picking up the sandwich and biting in. Grilled cheese. So this was what apology tasted like. I swallowed. "Suze, I—"

She cut me off quickly. "Let's not get psychological about this. Just eat the sandwich and let's forget about it."

I looked at her until she met my eyes. "Okay," I said, and took another bite.

Her face brightened, her shoulders straightened, and I could almost feel the force of her confidence reasserting itself, like the gravity well of a gas giant. "Okay," she said, relaxing. "Now let's talk about this weasel-fuck speed-dating thing."

There wasn't enough time after I'd eaten to drive Suze back to her place and still get to work on time, so we worked out a plan that she would drop me off at Peláez and drive the Fiesta the rest of the day until she came back to get me for the speed-dating.

"Do not wreck my car," I warned her as the car idled behind the kitchen entrance of the restaurant.

"Of course not," she promised as she shimmied bone-lessly into the driver's seat.

"Or alter it in any way."

"Well, now you're just being unreasonable." She gave me

a wholly untrustworthy smile and pulled away before I could say anything else. I watched her merge into traffic, wondering bleakly if I'd ever see the Fiesta again.

Daria was extremely displeased when I told her that I'd have to leave early that night, and spent ten minutes emphasizing to me exactly how thin the ice was beneath the feet of my continued employment. But apparently never having missed a night of work before this was enough to prevent her from openly firing me, though the look in her eyes suggested that if someone had been standing beside me with a resume in hand at that moment I would've found myself out on my ass. I swore over and over that it would never happen again—and, with my current level of expenses, I was pretty sure that I couldn't afford for it to happen again.

I gave my best hustle that afternoon, assisted by the fact that Chef Jerome was still refining the bombe fruit flowers' alcohol mix in a corner and was less interested than usual in harassing me. When five thirty rolled around I ignored Daria's death glare and slipped out the back door, where, true to her word, Suze was waiting for me in the Fiesta, which, thankfully, looked to be in the same state of disrepair that it had been six hours ago, with no new additions.

Suze hopped out of the driver's seat and tossed me the keys, which I caught only because of my increasing vampire reflexes, as the vast majority of my brain was taking in her appearance. Apparently Suze had decided to embrace our activity that night, and had gone full shock and awe in her clothing choice. High heels and a short yet swishy gold dress were definitely a change from what I usually saw her in.

"Planning on breaking hearts and crushing dreams tonight?" I finally managed to force out of my dry throat.

"You know it," she said with a sassy smile. "If this wraps up early, we can go salsa dancing."

"Don't count on it," I said, watching as she strutted over to the other side of the car and poured herself into the passenger's seat. I shook my head and got in myself, slamming the door hard to make it stick. "I called Prudence half an hour ago from the bathroom. She went to the address Lilah gave us. It's definitely Tomas's house, but no one was there. Once we finish with this, we should probably swing around and help her hunt."

"No worries," Suze said, and flipped up the skirt of her dress, revealing not only a long, perfectly toned thigh, but also a very familiar knife strapped to that thigh. Apparently Arlene was along for the ride tonight.

"That is a textbook definition of a mixed message," I noted. Forcing my eyes away, I turned to start backing the car up, then froze again. "Suze," I said, impressed at how controlled my voice sounded. "Why is there a plushy Cthulhu doll staring at me from the back window?" From tentacles to wings to fuzzy green fur, never had the Elder God looked that cuddly.

She smiled at me, eyes glittering in the light from the setting sun. "I was going to give him to you for Christmas, but I didn't have much time to work with."

I shook my head and reached back to snag it, pulling it down from my back windshield and into the backseat. It was very soft, almost asking to be squeezed. I looked around the interior of the car but couldn't see anything else out of place. The wide grin on Suze's face gave me no hints—either I was missing whatever else she'd done to my poor Fiesta or it really had just been the Cthulhu, and now she was just seeing if she could trick me into thinking that she'd pulled another prank. Those were always her favorite types of jokes anyway—no work on her part, yet months of potential dividends.

I didn't have time to examine the entire car, so I just shook my head and concentrated on the drive to the bookstore, reminding myself sternly not to try to overanalyze Suze's wicked little snicker. I discovered halfway through the drive that she had also changed all of my radio presets to synth-pop stations, and apparently figured out a new way to save the settings so that I couldn't reprogram them.

A few of Providence's independent bookstores had survived the massive Barnes & Noble influx of the nineties, and the ones that had lasted were managing to hold on as the big-box Goliaths closed one by one, victims of their own business model. The site of tonight's speed-dating was in my own neighborhood of College Hill, holding on through that most reliable of clientele: college students, college professors, and intellectual hangers-on. As we walked into Books on the Hill, the intensely evocative aroma of brand-new books hit me, and I sighed deeply, my eyes immediately gravitating to at least three titles that I knew I had to own. On months like this I usually avoided Books on the Hill like the plague, because it could always be relied on to ravage my budget with the virulence of Ebola-Zaire.

"Suze, can I bum a twenty?" I whispered as we passed the new arrivals table.

"Neither a borrower nor a lender be," Suze said piously, speeding past me. We'd discussed the importance of not looking like we were together, but I glared at her back as she took complete advantage of the circumstances.

Books on the Hill had a small back room where author readings and signings usually took place, and tonight it had been stuffed with about two dozen small folding tables, each just large enough to accommodate a pair of chairs tucked under it. Lilah stood at a long side table covered with the tools of her trade—shiny geodes, scented candles, and the egg timer that would be dictating our romantic lives for the next two hours. Her hair was down and secured in place with another wide fabric headband that very conveniently covered the upper half of her ears. It matched her lilac-colored sweater and sensible khaki slacks—this was the most conservatively that I'd ever seen her dress, and I wondered if there was some unspoken rule about the speed-date moderator making sure not to outshine any of the participants.

"Your hair looks nice like that," I complimented her as she checked me off of the list and handed me a pen and a gridded sheet of paper that I would apparently be using to grade all of my five-minute dates.

Lilah blushed a little and smiled at me, unable to resist reaching up with one hand to self-consciously pat at her headband to make sure that her ears were tucked away. "You think so?" she asked.

"Yeah," I said. I was no expert on women, but I'd

learned enough from the dating world to know that hair-style changes should always be responded to with a com-pliment. "It's very fluffy." Not that I had a particularly deep reserve of compliments, of course, but Lilah's smile wid-ened appreciatively, and I gave myself a mental pat on the back.

Her smile dimmed for a second, and she nodded to where Suze had staked out a table already. Somehow she'd managed to get her hands on a copy of the *Kama Sutra*, which she'd plunked down right in front of her. Her arms were now crossed just behind it and there was a very defi-nite *Go on . . . ask me about it, chump* look on her face. I felt a distinct twinge of sympathy for every other guy in the room, most of whom were looking at her like weekend backpackers put down in the base camp of K2. They really, really wanted a summit, but were also slightly concerned that they might die in the attempt.

"Suzume looks very pretty," Lilah said. There was a dis-tinct undertone in her voice.

"She likes causing riots," I said. But seeing the way that Lilah's smile kept drooping like a wilting daisy, I noted brightly, "But you look really nice too. In an undercover CIA-agent kind of way." I wondered briefly if that was go-ing to read as well as it had sounded in my head. Thank God she was apparently willing to go with me on it, because she laughed.

I appreciated that she had politely avoided commenting on my own appearance. There hadn't been time to change, so I'd just taken off my bow tie, unbuttoned the top button on my white shirt, and done my best to turn my shellacked hair into something that looked effortless and spiky, but was more spray-glued clumpy. Suze had tried to remove a few of the worst stains on my shirt with a napkin and a bottle of water, but without much success, so I now looked like a stained and slightly dripped-on waiter on his smoke break.

I reminded myself that this was an undercover-surveillance mission to try to save lives, and that any rejec-tion I suffered during it therefore did not count toward my life total.

The event started. At its core it was pretty simple, based on the idea that you would know within five minutes whether you had any interest at all in the person sitting in front of you. We sat at the little tables and made five-minutes of polite chitchat; then the timer would go off, we would thank each other, and the guys would get up and have to move to the next table, during this process trying to mark up our little spreadsheets without being obvious about whether rejection was actually happening.

On top of everything else, I also had to do my best to check out my five-minute dates' wrists for any new tattoos. There hadn't been any female victims yet, but it seemed better to be thorough, though I was extremely glad that it was Suze's job to check the men. Whenever I was near her table, I was able to admire her technique of using very flirtatious hand-holding as a method of sliding cuffs up wrists.

The weather had been mild enough today that most of the women were in short sleeves or no sleeves, giving me an easy way to check them, but a few were wearing sensible cardigans, and those proved very difficult. Sleeve nudging within fifteen seconds of an introduction apparently came off as creepy and sleazy when I tried it, as opposed to sala-cious and irresistible like when Suze did it. Several times I just gave in and pretended that "So, do you have any tat-toos?" was an acceptable conversation starter.

What I had also failed to realize was just how exhausting it was to meet a new person every five minutes and attempt to sparkle as a potential mate. As the time ground along, I noticed that the women stopped being as polite to me— once they'd decided that they were not going to put a check next to my name, several dropped even the pretense of a conversation and began either scoping out the room for more likely prospects, eyeing guys that they'd liked better than me, or (in several cases) shooting looks of death over to the table where Suzume was holding court. I decided that I would never get desperate enough to do this for actual dating purposes.

Or if I did, I would choose a much better wingman than Suze. My wingman would definitely be a guy. And preferably with the kind of Quasimodo face and Hulk-like manners that would make me shine in comparison.

We were down to the last three dates, and I was desperately clinging to the light at the end of the tunnel when I sat at the next table and found myself face-to-face with my ex-girlfriend, Beth.

Or, at least, face-to-face with her skin.

That was Beth's face, with her olive skin and the one small chicken-pox scar under her left eye. Those were her rich black curls tumbling down to her shoulders. But Beth's dark brown eyes had never looked at me with that kind of icy malice and barely contained violence that froze me in place as I stared. *This isn't happening. This isn't happening*—my brain was stuck on repeat, like a trapped bee battering itself against glass. I couldn't be sitting here staring at that *thing* that was looking back at me from Beth's eyes.

"Soli," I managed to whisper between numb lips. I was carved out of ice, disbelieving, the shock rattling through me with the force of a storm.

A nasty smile spread across that familiar face, its features emphasized with more makeup than Beth had ever even owned. "I told you that you'd be paying for my new suit," she said, and even her voice was Beth's but with a different phrasing, a different accent. It was throbbingly familiar—the voice that used to whisper activist pillow-talk to me in the dark—but it was a stranger moving her mouth, forcing words up her throat, over her tongue and lips.

I'd only ever seen Beth in baggy peasant blouses, long beaded skirts, and the occasional maxi dress on more formal occasions. Now I saw what she would've looked like in a sleek black top and a pair of leather pants. I wanted to vomit—it was treating Beth's body, her flesh, as its own dress-up mannequin.

"What did you do?" I couldn't wrap my brain around it; I couldn't accept it. Beth, with her bright mind, her resolute idealism, her cheerfully cheating ways, *couldn't* be dead.

"Went shopping, dear." And that thing grinned so widely that I could see that there were teeth in the back of its mouth that were much too sharp to be molars. "You should be more careful with the privacy settings on your Facebook." She stretched out her hands, examining Beth's long artist's fingers with a connoisseur's eye.

This was worse than just Beth's death. This was a horror, a perversion, a *desecration* to see her move Beth's fingers.

Somewhere under that smooth surface was that hard black thing that I'd seen last night—crouching there and pulling the strings to Beth's body.

I wanted to tear it out with my bare hands.

My hands shook from the effort it took not to wrap themselves around the skinwalker's neck and squeeze. But she'd done this on purpose—we were surrounded by the banal chitchat of two dozen humans, none of them remotely aware that they were like blissful beachgoers in the opening scenes of a *Jaws* movie, completely unaware that death was gliding in their midst.

Soli continued smugly. "They might find the skin's meat. I wrapped it in a plastic bag and threw it down her building's garbage shaft." She giggled. "Those things are so convenient."

Somehow that horrible image of Beth's tortured remains cut through just enough of the urge to kill. My mind raced, trying to determine some foothold on the creature in front of me, some way to coax information out of it that would trip it up. Something that would expose enough of a vulnerability that I could slice it out of Beth like an excised tumor. I grasped the last thing she'd said. "So, convenience is important to you? Then why haul Gage's body up our fire escape and leave it in his own bedroom?"

She giggled again, and the sound was like a knife scraping down a chalkboard. "I figured that the vampires would have plenty of practice making bodies disappear, especially ones with no blood left in them." Then the pleasure leached out of her face and she pouted, Beth's full lower lip overly emphasized in dark red lipstick. "Staging an accident is boring, and the incinerator at the doctor's office is so slow that you have to wait half the night for it to finish. It's annoying. I wanted to have some fun. Hit a club." The pout was replaced by a frown, and in a mercurial change of mood, that malicious anger was back. "You weren't supposed to get that curious about a dead human. So this"—she tapped one long finger against the side of Beth's face—"is a warning. You and the fox can stay out of my business."

Part of me knew I should try to signal Suzume, or, hell, even try to text Prudence under the table, but I couldn't pull enough of my brain away from the rising bubble of rage that was keeping me fixated on the skinwalker, and suddenly I wasn't feeling like a frozen deer but like a rabid dog pulling against the end of its leash.

I leaned forward, across the table, and very deliberately said, "I'm going to kill you." My eyes felt strangely warm, but for once I didn't feel panic as I wondered whether the pupils were expanding past where a human's would. I didn't care if I looked like a vampire at this moment—in fact, I hoped that I did.

Whatever was happening, Soli didn't look impressed. Instead she gave a slow smile. "You're going to try," she corrected me.

The egg timer went off, indicating that our five-minute date was up. As soon as the sound registered through the room, Soli was out of her chair and moving fast for the back door of the store. I jumped up quickly enough that my chair fell backward and chased her. She was faster than me, and I had to dodge around all of the other men who had just gotten up to change tables, so she beat me out the door, but not by much.

The back door led to a small gravel customer parking lot that was lit only by a weak security light on the back of the building. As the door slammed behind me, I saw Soli running toward a car parked in the fire zone with its four-ways on. I raced after her and caught up enough that I was able to snag a handful of her dark, curling hair in my hand. It felt familiar—I'd run my hand a thousand times through Beth's hair. Now I wrapped my fist in it and yanked backward with all my weight, snapping her head back and arresting her forward movement. She stumbled hard but didn't go down, instead pivoting toward me, and then we were grappling tightly. I briefly got a hand around her throat, but she was still a lot stronger than me, and I was thrown hard to the ground, which knocked the wind out of me.

Instead of following up her strike, I heard the sound of running feet on the gravel and knew that she was heading for the car. I managed to roll to my side, but I knew I wouldn't be able to catch her in time. As I started to pull myself up, the sound of spinning tires on gravel filled the air, and I suddenly saw a set of headlights coming straight toward me. Then there was a hand at the back of my shirt and another on my arm, grabbing and yanking me out of the way just in time, and I could feel the rush of the displaced air as the car barely missed running me down.

I heard the panting breath in my ear, and I knew even without looking that it was Suze who had pulled me out of the way. We both watched as the car screeched out of the lot and disappeared.

"It was her, the skinwalker," I panted to Suze.

She nodded, then whispered to me, "There were too many people and smells in the room—I didn't know what was going on until I saw how you were looking at her."

"She has Beth's skin. Why didn't I notice her from the beginning?"

Suze's voice was grim. "I don't think she was there from the start." She yanked at me, tugging me back toward the store. When we reached the back door I could hear Lilah's voice, talking to people still in the shop, making up a story about a participant who had to leave early and how she'd forgotten her phone at the table, which her date had run off to try to return to her. I could hear the cooing murmur of the speed-daters as they accepted the story, talking helpfully about possible ways to locate the phone's owner.

The evening's events broke up soon after that, with the speed-daters all shooed back to the front of the store, where the bookstore workers clearly hoped that they'd top the night off with a book purchase. Suze ducked her horde of admirers and slipped out the back door again. I made a show of helping Lilah pack up her table as everyone else moved out. Not that I helped much. I couldn't get the image of Beth's marionette body out of my mind, and my hands shook uncontrollably. A polished geode slipped out of my grip and fell onto the table with a loud crack. I winced, and Lilah shot me a sympathetic look and started to open her mouth to say something, but I shook my head quickly, cutting her off, and took a deep breath and shoved down what had happened just far enough to fake functional for a little while longer. Ah, compartmentalization — my old friend.

Most of the daters had left when Suzume slid back in ten minutes later, shuffling up to where Lilah and I were putting candles into boxes.

"There's a dead woman behind the Dumpster in the back parking lot," she said quietly. "That's the person whose table Soli took over to talk with Fort."

A fat vanilla candle dropped out of Lilah's hand. "She killed someone? Just to do that?"

I thought back grimly to Chivalry's descriptions of the skinwalkers. "My brother told me that skinwalkers leave trails of bodies. I think we're getting a good idea of how they like to operate."

"What do we do about the body?" Lilah whispered, her eyes darting over to the front checkout desk, where blissfully ignorant literary commerce was taking place as everyone got in their last purchases before closing time, then back to us, pinballing between me and Suzume for a moment before locking onto the kitsune as the one most likely to have a plan. She was right — I was using everything I had right now to look passably normal even as Beth's death rattled through me. Constructing an actual response to this situation was far beyond me.

Fortunately, Suzume was more than willing to take command. "Soli grabbed her purse, might have taken her jewelry. Right now it looks like a mugging gone wrong — like it happened when she was walking to her car. I put a small illusion down to hide her for now, but I'll drop it when we leave. Someone will find her." I'd seen Suzume put a fox illusion on a dead body before, and knew how well she could hide something from unsuspecting minds. People walking to their cars could walk through the poor woman's blood and not even know it.

"Why did she do this? Just to taunt me?" I couldn't understand why Soli had taken the trouble to come tonight but then just run out.

Suze narrowed her eyes, considering. "She's working for the elves, and right now we're closing in on them. Maybe she was working on getting our attention focused on her and off her employers."

"Why? That won't help them in the long run," I noted.

Lilah suddenly lit up. "But it would in the short run," she said in a eureka tone of voice. She glanced around, confirming that we were still alone at the back of the store, and whispered, "Allegra's son was born this afternoon. A lot of people were excited. Even Themselves were excited."

I frowned, not following. "But Allegra's a three-quarter. That's still rare, right?"

Lilah nodded. "Yes, but it was more than that. There have been three-quarter-to-three-quarter babies born before—that generation is just coming of age, but it turned out that they're a lot like the half-bloods. They can have children with each other easily; they don't even need a witch potion. It's like the human part of our heritage stabilizes us, lets us breed. So they shouldn't have been that excited, but they *are*."

"Breakthrough-level excited?" Suze asked slowly, and Lilah nodded.

"I talked to a friend. His brother is a three-quarter and when he was talking about the baby, he was saying that this was important for the whole community."

The pieces were starting to come together for me. "Allegra had a baby today. So when would that baby have been conceived?"

Suzume shrugged. "Nine-month gestation. February-ish, right?" She looked at Lilah for confirmation, and Lilah paused to do a little mental arithmetic, then nodded in agreement.

I remembered standing in Matt's office, listening as he listed off the names and dates of the missing men. "Rian Orbon went missing in February. He was the first one with the tattoos."

Suze hissed slowly under her breath. "Death-sacrifice tattoos," she muttered, realizing what I was saying. She looked over at Lilah, whose eyes had popped wide at the implications. "February death, February conception. The speed-dates started being held away from Dreamcatching after New Year's—so January. And what have the elves been trying for that would make them excited?"

"A seven-eighths cross," she murmured despairingly. Then a thought clearly crossed her mind, and she looked almost physically ill. "There are more than forty women who are three-quarter crosses and are the right age to have a baby."

"And they'd apparently need to kill one guy for each," I agreed. "That's forty deaths."

Suze added on, "And who says that the women could only have one baby each? Lulu's practice has been producing recessive changelings for thirty years. That's a big pool of resources to draw from if your goal is to produce a whole breeding generation of seven-eighths crosses."

"All those speed-dates scheduled just for next month," Lilah said, still looking ready to puke at the scale of what was going one. "I think we can assume they're already working on that goal."

The implications were horrific, and I felt a surge of adrenaline as I realized how many people were at risk. "We need Tomas or Lulu—someone who can lead us right to the heart of this so that we can stop the whole thing." To Lilah, I said, "My sister checked the address you gave us; it's empty. If they knew my family was looking into this, where would they hide?"

She shook her head, her coppery hair glinting in the light. "I don't know. I've never been involved with them that far. They've never told me these things."

I rubbed the back of my hand hard against my forehead as some of the bookstore staff members came in to start cleaning up the tables and chairs from the speed-dating. "We need to head out of here. Lilah, can you talk to anyone who might know more about this?"

With clear effort, Lilah pulled herself together. "I'll try." She sounded exhausted. "A few of the Neighbors are having informal parties tonight—I'll hit a few and see if I can hear any gossip."

"Okay. Call me if you find anything out." Awkwardly I patted her shoulder, wishing there were a Hallmark card for

*I'm sorry you had to learn that people you are related to are murdering psychopaths, and that to prevent even more killings you have to betray even more people you've known since before you were potty trained.* And wouldn't that look cute in a kitten's thought bubble? Lilah gave me a small nod, and I knew that a little of that had translated.

Suze and I made our way to the car, both feeling very jumpy as we went. Once there, I called my sister—Prudence was still hunting for Lulu and not getting results, but after hearing about our encounter with Soli and that she was now wearing my ex-girlfriend, Prudence told me in no uncertain terms that unless I had special information or Suze had the ability to track a car by scent, the best thing we could do was find a safe place to set up for the night and to be ready to head out and join her if she was able to find someone involved in the murders.

"They have kept the details of their operation very close to the chest, apparently," my sister said, and in the background I heard a muffled scream that I decided not to think about very closely. "But I am confident my inquiries will eventually bear fruit."

"That's great, Prudence," I said. "Just remember that you need my permission to kill someone." There was another, less muffled scream, and I immediately amended that to, "Or maim."

"Very well, but you are limiting my options somewhat," she said, but there was amusement rather than irritation in her voice. Violence apparently put a little pep in her step.

Maybe it was knowing she was mellower than usual, or maybe I would've asked anyway. "Listen, Prudence, about the skinwalker—"

"Yes?"

I turned away from Suze, not wanting to look at her when I asked this. "The humans they kill to . . . use. It's just their body, right? There are no other . . . effects?"

"What do you mean, effects?"

"You know—mannerisms, memories. They don't *get* those things . . . do they?" I was dancing around it, not wanting to say the word *soul*. On one hand I felt almost silly and superstitious—nothing in my experience had ever suggested that we even had souls. But at the same time it felt deadly important, and saying it out loud would make my fear too real, too possible.

"Oh, that. No, none of that transfers." Prudence's voice was almost, well, on someone else I would've assumed that she was trying to reassure me. With it coming from my sister, I just felt confused. "No need to worry about the creature knowing phone numbers or whatever odd little pillow talk you might've shared with the meat. Don't let the creature try to fool you either — they are very accomplished manipulators and usually pick up plenty of information from the home of the skin."

Prudence's easy use of the words *meat* and *skin* ripped through me, but was no less than I could've expected. Her easy dismissal of Beth — I'd known better than to expect otherwise, but it didn't mean that it didn't hurt, and I wanted to end the phone call. "Thanks, that's — "

"Although . . ."

"Yes?" The skin on the back of my neck prickled.

"Well, I've never seen it happen to a vampire before, but just as a bit of trivia, the skinwalker *can* use the skin as a talisman for dreamwalking."

*"What?"* I didn't know what that was, but it sounded bad.

"Yes," Prudence practically chirped, as if she were sharing a delightful anecdote over coffee. "They can use it to torment the relatives and loved ones of the skin. No actual gain of information, just projection. Silly and useless, really." Her voice warmed and became that almost-reassuring tone again that set me on edge. "I've never even heard of a vampire succumbing — and a skinwalker once paraded around in my favorite bridge partner for weeks. I can't even *tell* you how enraged I was. Another one actually wore Chivalry's wife."

"That's horrible," I said.

"Well, she was quite tiresome — incredibly gauche and whiny thing; don't even get me started on her bad taste in clothing — but of course Chivalry was quite worked up. Not a single dream, though, and you know how much he utterly dotes on those wives of his, so I wouldn't be worried about any of that nonsense. Now, remember that this creature apparently likes to run Internet searches on you. Get a hotel room tonight."

I didn't like my sister or her methods, but in this situation it was hard to disagree with excellent advice. Forty minutes later Suze and I were carrying our bags into the cheapest room we could find that still offered two beds. We took turns in the bathroom, changing into jeans and long-sleeve shirts, the kind of clothing that could be napped in but would be appropriate if Prudence got a location and we had to run off into the night to god only knew where.

When it was my turn in the bathroom I took a quick shower, having learned from hard experience that sleeping with work levels of product in my hair resulted in very weird, almost sculpturally bad hair the next day. I rushed through the shower, not wanting to deal with my thoughts or the horrible ball of grief that I knew was waiting for me when I actually sat down and thought about Beth. What had happened to her and how her death was so utterly and inescapably *because* she'd known me. I was rubbing my hair dry with a towel when I came back into the room and found Suzume sitting cross-legged on her bed, a half-sausage/half-veggie-lover's pizza beside her, and a six-pack of beer on the floor.

I stared. My wallet was still in my pants pocket.

"Did you buy dinner?" I asked, shocked.

Suze gave me a measured look. "Don't get used to this," she warned.

We demolished the pizza. Afterward, sitting on the floor with my back leaning against my bed, carefully disassembling and checking each part of the Colt and the Ithaca before putting them back together while my phone remained frustratingly silent, I said into the comfortable silence that had fallen between us, "When this whole thing is over, I never want to talk about elf genealogy again. The last few days have been like some nightmare biology lesson. Like *Attack of Mendel's Beans* set in the Appalachian mountains, crossed with a PBS special on Egyptian pharaohs."

Lying on her belly, watching me from half-lidded eyes,

Suze agreed. "Amen to that. All this whinging and sacrifice magic fuckery is making me even gladder than usual that I'm a kitsune."

I tilted my head. "Why? How do you guys manage it?"

Suze shrugged lazily. "You meet a guy in a bar, you get laid, a few months later you have a litter of kits. Easy-peasy, and you even get a few free drinks in the deal."

I thought about it for a long minute. "So, you don't even tell the guy that he's a father?"

There was a very serious look in Suzume's eyes. "It's safer for everyone that way."

She hadn't said it to accuse me, I knew. She was stating a fact of life, a piece of the kitsune culture. But I swallowed hard, and the silence that fell wasn't comfortable at all. The guns were all checked, and I pushed them under my bed. Out of sight if someone glanced around the room, but right where I could get to them quickly. I climbed into the bed and rolled to face the wall, pulling the cheap hotel comforter over my shoulders. "I'm going to sleep," I said, my voice rough.

I was tired. Last night I'd gotten barely four hours of sleep, and the past few days had been brutal on many different levels. I felt battered—not physically, because the blood I'd drunk from my mother still crackled through my veins, healing my bruises and abrasions faster than they ever should've healed. But it was a mental exhaustion that made me feel like I wanted to just pull the comforter over my head and not get out of bed for a week. Too much had happened. Too many innocent people were dead because of grudges and agendas that they'd never even known existed.

It had been hoping too much that Suze wouldn't say anything, but when she did, her voice was very careful, and she picked her words as cautiously as a barefoot girl picked her way down a rocky beach. "Fort, do you want to talk about what happened to Beth?"

I shook my head, not looking away from the wall in front of me. "No, Suze, I can't. Not now. Not until Soli is dead and I never have to look at her again when she's . . ." I paused, not able to talk around the tightness in my chest, the confusion and the pain that I was pressing down as hard as I could to keep functioning for however longer I needed to finish this. I could start trying to deal with it then, but I knew that if I touched it now, I'd just be a shivering and rocking ball. And that's not what Beth or Gage or all those other people needed right now. "I just can't talk about it."

Suzume paused, then said gently, "Okay." And I heard the rustle of fabric as she reached over and clicked off the light.

The darkness felt comforting. I didn't have to try to control what was showing on my face anymore. I heard her shift around on her own bed; then everything was quiet except for the sound of both of us breathing and the distant *whoosh* of traffic on the street. A long time passed as I tried my best to think about nothing at all, but finally I couldn't stop it anymore, and I whispered, almost under my breath, "Suze?"

She heard me, of course. Even when she was human, her ears were sharper than mine. "Yes?"

I pushed the words out. "If, for whatever reason, I'm hurt or—"

She was moving before I could finish, and I heard the springs shifting in her bed as she rolled off and knelt on the floor next to my bed, wrapping one arm around me and pressing her forehead against the back of my neck. Neither of us said anything for a long minute, just breathing as she held me. For all the time we spent together, it was rare for her to touch my skin, but there wasn't anything sexual about this—despite the darkness, and tenderness of her touch, and the feel of her breath. It was comforting, as if she were wrapping me in all her wiry strength, both of body and will.

When she spoke, it was a whisper, but there was steel in it and a promise that I knew that she meant and would never break. "I'll rip the skin off that bitch's back," she said right against my ear. "Whatever happens, she won't get to keep what she stole."

It soothed me to hear that, relaxed the part of me that I didn't like and that needed blood and vengeance, but that I couldn't ignore tonight. I reached out with one hand, wrapping it around her elbow, letting my forearm rest against hers. Neither of us moved, and it was in that position that I was finally able to close my eyes and let sleep take me.

I knew I was dreaming, but it wasn't my dream. I was walking down a hallway, but at the same time it wasn't me who was walking.

It was like being at an art-house theater and watching a bad shaky-cam, low-budget movie. The perspective seemed off, and the color balance was somehow wrong in a way I couldn't quite define but that gave me a distant feeling of nausea. But I recognized the hallway I was walking down and apartment door I knocked on.

Beth opened the door—the Beth I'd known, with an open expression and a ready smile. What she saw erased her smile—she looked down at something on my chest and opened her mouth to scream. I was only able to see, not hear, but a hand that was mine but not mine slapped out to cover her mouth, and when I saw that hand, with its caramel skin and perfect manicure such a contrast to the long black talons that punched out through it, I knew whose dream this was.

But knowing didn't wake me up, and I was looking through Soli's eyes, feeling the movement of her limbs as if they were my own, as she shoved her way into the apartment, slammed the door shut behind her, and shoved Beth down to the ground. Those were her hands, yet my hands, that slapped a piece of duct tape across Beth's mouth to keep her quiet, then flipped her over and pressed one knee hard into the middle of her back to keep Beth exactly where she was. I could feel Beth struggling, trying to push up and get away, but Soli was too strong and held her down.

I felt an echo of irritation inside me. This wasn't my emotion; it was Soli's. She was irritated—irritated that she had to replace a skin she'd been fond of. Irritated that this skin wouldn't be as pretty. Irritated that this had to be done here, where the meat would have to be kept quiet.

And then all that irritation ebbed away, replaced by the

pleasure Soli felt, and I was forced to feel as she placed one long black talon at the back of Beth's neck, just at her hairline, and began to peel the skin off of her. I knew how much Soli enjoyed it as Beth writhed, because it wasn't just Soli feeling it; it was *me*—

I woke up when Suze slapped me across the face, and I knew from the blooming heat in both cheeks that she must've been hitting me for a while now. Someone was yelling, and it took me a second to register that my throat was sore because the person yelling was me.

The light wasn't on, but neither of us had closed the heavy drapes and moonlight poured through the window, illuminating Suze as she straddled my chest, one hand still drawn back to deliver another smack if it proved necessary. Her hair hung down around her face, obscuring it in a wave of black, but all of her attention was on me. I stopped yelling, and we both paused.

"Fort?" she said harshly. "That's the kind of night terror that needs a psychiatrist."

"It wasn't my dream," I said with surprising difficulty. For someone who looked so tiny and dainty, Suze was a little more weight than I liked on my chest. I nudged her leg with my hand, and she took the hint and dismounted me. Instead of returning to her own bed, however, she plopped herself next to me on the bed, her back resting against the headboard as she looked down at me intently.

"What do you mean by that?"

"I saw Soli kill Beth," I said. "Or start to, anyway. You woke me up before she finished."

There was a long pause. "I'm going to go on record that I hate this fucking skinwalker," Suze said. "And at the risk of sounding species-ist, I'm going to say that I don't ever want to meet another one."

"Noted and agreed." I struggled to keep my voice from reflecting the icy horror that was filling my chest. "So, apparently I don't have enough vampire-ness, and it can get into my head." Maybe it was because I wasn't through the transition. Or maybe it was something more. After all, my mother had made me differently than my siblings—she'd told me that but nothing else.

Suze's voice cut through my thoughts. "According to your sister, it's just the dreams."

My jaw dropped. "You're going to call this *just*? What the hell am I supposed to do now?"

There was a short pause; then Suze asked, "Have you ever studied the fine art of occlumency?"

I didn't hesitate, but smacked her as hard as I could with my pillow. It was one of those hotels that set up at least four half-size pillows on each bed, so Suze was immediately able to similarly arm herself, and for a few minutes the only sounds in the room were of pillows making contact and muffled curses as we engaged in a brief but very serious pillow fight. "This is not the time for a goddamn Harry Potter reference!" I finally yelled, and the pillow fight ended just as quickly as it had started. I dropped back onto the bed, breathing hard. "Seriously, Suze. What the hell am I going to do here?"

Suzume was also panting from the intensity of our pillow brawl, something that even under these circumstances made me feel a little better about myself. She wiggled back into her previous position of sitting up against the headboard, but now reached down and ran one cool hand over my forehead, wiping away the sweat that was only partially from our recent battle. Against my will, I felt myself relax at the soothing motion. "Go back to sleep," she said.

I pushed her hand away, deeply irritated. "Did you not just notice the crazy dream invasion?"

Suze resumed her stroking. "Yes," she said, finally sounding serious. "And this time I'll be watching for it. If it happens again, I'll wake you up even faster."

I paused, considering what she'd just said. But then I shook my head. "I'm never falling asleep again."

She *tsk*ed her tongue. "Of course you will. I'll even tell you a story." Her voice changed, no longer conversational, and took on the rhythm and cadence of repeating something she'd heard many, many times. "This is the story my mother told me, and her mother told her, and her mother told her, all the way back to when it happened, because this is a true story of our people."

"I don't think I'm included in that *our*," I noted sarcastically.

Suze's hand stopped stroking just long enough to smack me hard. "Shush," she scolded me. "This is the way the story is told." She cleared her throat and resumed the head petting, as if nothing had happened. And once she started talking again, I began to forget about being irritated with her and became absorbed in her story. "There was once a fox who went wandering far from her mother and her sisters and the den where she had been born. She traveled up and down the whole length of Japan, and she saw many strange things. One night, far from any dens she knew or caches of food she had left, she caught the smell of an *oni*. An *oni* is a vicious thing, strong and fast, and she had no sisters and cousins to help her, and most foxes would've hurried in the other direction. But this fox was a curious thing, and she followed the trail of the *oni* where it led her, being careful to move more silently than the wind. Eventually she found herself at a small house, where the *oni* was crouched beside the door, waiting to kill the man who lived there when he came outside in the morning. And this fox did an amazing thing, for not even knowing who lived inside that house, she crept all around, up onto the roof, and above where the *oni* was waiting. If she'd put one paw wrong and made a single sound, the *oni* would've heard and ripped her apart, but she didn't, and when she was above him, she jumped down and broke his neck with one bite. And the god Inari saw what she had done, and for her bravery he marked her as his own by making the tip of her red tail white. Well, the fox was very proud, but she was still a curious fox, and so she waited beside the door to see what kind of human she had saved. When the rooster crowed in the morning and the first light appeared, the man came outside. And when the fox saw him, she fell in love with him, which shows you what a foolish little fox she was."

That struck me as weird, and I interrupted her. "Wait. One second ago she was honored by gods. Now she's foolish?"

"No comments from the peanut gallery," Suze said in her normal voice. I grumbled under my breath but obeyed, and she resumed the story. "So she ran to the edge of the forest and changed into a beautiful woman, dressed in the finest garments. The man saw her when he went walking that night and he fell in love with her, and took her back to his house and made her his wife. She bore him a son soon after, and all seemed well, except that each morning the man's dog would bark at her, because the dog knew that she was a fox and not a woman. The fox begged her husband to kill the dog, but he refused, and one day the dog was able to get into the house and attack her. And the attack was so vicious that she had no choice but to turn back from a woman into a fox and run out the door and over the fence and across the fields, leaving her husband and baby behind." There was a long pause, and I wished that Suze hadn't let her long hair fall forward to shadow her face. I wondered what she was thinking about. Then she picked up the thread again. "And that is why foxes do not belong in the houses of men. But this is a true story. And the fox had loved and married an honorable man. Because when he saw his wife change into a fox and run away, he called after her and said, 'You may be a fox, but you are the mother of my son and I love you. Come back when you please, and you will always be welcome.' And so every night after that the fox would slip out from the forest, across the fields, under the fence, into the house, and sleep in the arms of her husband. But she understood then that they were different, and when she gave birth after that, it was to daughters who ran with her on four feet and lived in a den."

I waited, but Suze didn't say anything else, and clearly the story was over.

"So, the white in your tail?" I remembered when it had appeared. It has been after she'd risked her life to save mine.

"It's kind of spiritual. Supposedly it's a gift from Inari." Something in her tone told me that we weren't going to be talking about the circumstances that she'd gotten her white under—not now, maybe not ever.

"Who's Inari?" I asked, acknowledging the message and leading the conversation away.

"The god of rice."

"Um, rice?" It seemed like an odd fit. I would've expected a much more badass god for the kitsune.

"Yeah, *rice*," Suzume snapped. "It was a primary foodstuff, jackass. Every culture dependent on one item so heavily has a god like that. We had Inari, the Mayans had a corn god, and the Irish have their potato saint."

I paused. "Suze, there isn't an Irish potato saint."

"Are you sure?"

"Yes. Very."

"Fine, whiskey fairy. Whatever."

In the darkness I winced. "You are not exactly culturally sensitive, Suze."

"Fuck that noise," she snorted.

The conversation had definitely traveled a bit, but one element from her story was still bothering me. Very carefully, I asked, "I thought kitsune only had daughters?"

Suze shook her head. All of the playfulness from the potato conversation was gone now, and very quietly she answered, "No, that part is true, but only daughters are kitsune. A son would only be human. When a kitsune changes from fox to woman, and woman to fox when she is pregnant with daughters, the daughters change with her, because they are what she is. But a son is human, and if his mother becomes a fox when she carries him, the fetus will die."

I thought about what I'd learned and a connection formed in my mind that I hadn't considered before. "When you were arguing with your sister, it was about her boyfriend. And that she wasn't changing her form."

"Yes." I knew from her voice that Suze didn't want me to follow this any further, but I asked anyway.

"Keiko is pregnant, isn't she?"

I wondered at first if she'd just refuse to answer me, but after a tense moment Suze said, "She learned the wrong lesson from the story. Loving a human will only lead to grief." She stopped stroking and gave my head a little pat. I wasn't sure which of us was meant to be comforted by the gesture. "But she's only four months along. She has time to come to her senses. And in all the stories my grandmother has told me about the lives of kitsune in Japan, she only ever met one fox who gave birth to a son."

I had one last question. "Are you hiding all of this from your grandmother?"

But I'd reached the end of Suze's willingness to talk about her family, and she just patted my head again. "Go to sleep, Fort. I'll make sure that you don't dream."

I believed her. And when I closed my eyes again, I fell back into a dreamless sleep.

# Chapter 9

I woke up the next morning when someone began knocking on the door. For a second I was confused, mainly about why I had such a terrible crink in my neck. Then I realized that it was because a black fox was snuggled into a ball on my pillow and had nudged my head out of the way. Her tail was tickling my mouth, and as I pushed it away and rolled to my feet to head for the door, I ran a hand over my tongue to dislodge some of the hairs coating it.

I checked the peephole, then pulled the door open to reveal Lilah, looking scrubbed and fresh and carrying an armful of take-out bags that wafted smells of breakfast.

I'd texted her the hotel information the night before, but my surprise at seeing her must've shown on my face, because she immediately flushed. "Oh, sorry," she said. "I just figured I'd bring over—" and then the light pink of her cheeks suddenly flamed red, and I looked behind me, wondering what had set her off and figuring that it had to be Suze. Instead I realized what she'd noticed—there were two beds in the room but one was still perfectly made, with all the pillows still in order. The other, the one I'd had both a skinwalker-induced terror dream and a championship-level pillow fight in, was completely wrecked. It didn't take a rocket scientist to draw conclusions from those two pieces of data.

I knew that my own face was flaming as I began sputtering some attempt to explain the situation, and Lilah began backing up, both of us clearly wishing that the earth would just open up and swallow us whole so we could escape the conversation, when there was a sharp yip at our feet that made both of us shut up and look down.

Smelling a breakfast she hadn't had to pay for, Suze had scampered over, still on four fox feet. She was now balanced on her back paws and was stretching her muzzle as high as possible toward the bags of food in Lilah's arms. It was the kind of scenario that had viral YouTube video written all over it.

"Oh, that's Suze?" Lilah said, sounding startled, and I remembered that she'd never seen the kitsune in her true form.

"Yeah," I said, grateful that Suze's antics had apparently broken the cycle of awkward that Lilah and I had just been trapped in. Then suspicion kicked in. With Suze's almost pathological delight in pranking me, the very fact that she *hadn't* shifted to human form and let Lilah spot her lolling naked in hotel sheets was weird.

I eyed Suze, who was playing adorable fox and resolutely ignoring my attempt to catch her gaze. My mind began sorting through possible motives. Was this part of some elaborate long-con prank? Was she pranking me by *not* pranking me? Was she taking the situation seriously enough that— Wait, no. I dropped that one as unrealistic before I even finished it.

"So, the extra bed ... ?" Lilah asked, comfortable or curious enough now to walk inside the room. Eyes glued to the food, Suze tracked her.

"Apparently all she needs as a fox is a pillow. And she liked mine." I reached out and began helping Lilah set up the breakfast. As my hands fell back to years of ingrained wait-staffing, I wondered—between her painfully obvious "bathroom break" at Dreamcatching yesterday and the decision not to go full false-appearance romantic comedy just now, was Suze trying to set me up with Lilah?

Was Suze trying to find me a roommate *and* a girlfriend? The sane mind shuddered at the thought of such a situation.

I snuck a look at Lilah, who was lining up tiny containers of orange juice with a precision that hinted at either a past in the engineering sciences or a smattering of OCD. Did I *want* to date her? I certainly got along with her, God knows

I was attracted to her, and she had been sending off hints of possibly being into me (which I liked in a woman). I looked at Suze—who, still in fox form, had stuffed her entire head into one of the empty breakfast bags and was now attempting, skunk style, to back out of it. Not much guidance there.

This was not a thought process that could be conducted on an empty, uncaffeinated stomach, and I reached for the coffee (bless her soul, and true daughter of New England that she was, Lilah had hit up a Dunkin' Donuts) and mentally put a pin in the issue.

We talked as we ate—or, rather, the two of us talked. Suze stayed fox for the entire meal, comfortably curled in an armchair and simply pointing her dark muzzle at whatever food she wanted to sample next. If either of us didn't respond quickly enough to her demands, she also demonstrated that she was extremely willing to appropriate food we'd already put onto our own plates, so Lilah and I became very quick to respond whenever that imperious black nose pointed toward another egg muffin.

Between bites and feeding the kitsune, Lilah explained that she hadn't been able to pick up any new information the night before. Since Dreamcatching didn't open until eleven, she'd decided to swing by and see if we'd come up with any new theories ourselves, leading to the morning's perilously awkward encounter. I told her about the nightmare Soli had apparently sent me, and Lilah was suitably horrified.

"You need to talk to someone about that," she said. "Someone who has dealt with skinwalkers before. Have you called your sister?"

"Not since it happened," I admitted. "But she was pretty clear earlier that it's just dream projections." Though I would privately admit to a few qualms myself about the word *just* in that sentence.

Lilah apparently was in agreement. "That still sounds creepy. How long can she keep doing that? Can you even stop it?" She turned to Suzume. "Do you think Fort should talk to a witch? They might be able to cook him up some kind of magic Ambien."

We both looked over at the fox, currently licking egg off

of her whiskers. She paused, considered, then gave a small yip.

"Is that a yes or a no?" I demanded, and she moved her shoulders in what I assumed was an attempt at a shrug. "Suze, I'm trying to have a conversation with you here. Can you please change?" Suze's golden fox eyes narrowed, and she very deliberately turned around in her armchair and began grooming her tail.

"This is kind of awkward," Lilah noted, and I nodded. The sounds of Suze's licking filled the room. The subject of the skinwalker's ability to mess with my REM cycle apparently shelved, Lilah and I returned to the issue of how to track down either Lulu or Tomas. With no new information, the conversation very quickly just became a verbal chasing of tails.

This was different from a literal chasing of tails, which Suze decided to do under the table while we had our conversation. It was somewhat distracting.

When my phone rang I lunged for it, certain that Prudence had finally closed in on her quarry, but it was Matt instead.

"Fort, I'm at Iron Needle," Matt said, his voice low and tense, not bothering with any preamble. "There's a guy walking out the front door, and he has bandages on both wrists. He's got a shirt on and I can't see the shoulders, but this could be a possible victim—he's in the right age range."

Adrenaline immediately shot through my veins. "Is he alone?" I asked.

"No, he's with a woman. I just took a picture, let me send it to you."

When my cheap flip-phone had been destroyed a few months ago, Chivalry had taken the opportunity under the guise of a birthday present to upgrade me to the sleekest and smartest of phones that he could find, and had delivered it with every bell, whistle, and shiny new app that could be installed. So I was able to check Matt's photo without even hanging up on him, which turned out to not be a great thing because as soon as the photo filled my phone's screen, both Lilah and I responded with extremely loud and knee-jerk curses.

The photo was a distance shot, done as surreptitiously as possible with a small camera phone. But what we were looking at was unmistakable—that was Soli, walking in Beth's skin, and the young man beside her with bandages on his wrists and an almost sleepwalking expression was the changeling stock boy from Dreamcatching, Felix.

Suze bounced onto the table with agile grace, glanced down at the screen, and immediately jumped off and ran into the bathroom.

"Fort? What? What is it? Do you recognize them?" Matt's voice over the phone sounded very far away.

Lilah's eyes were huge, and she'd wrapped her hands over her mouth, clearly afraid to say anything that would be overheard. I cleared my throat awkwardly and stuttered, "Um, yeah, Lilah's with me, and she recognizes the kid. He's, um, one of the members of the cult." Matt was quiet, and I pushed forward quickly. "Matt, can you follow them?"

"Yeah," he said slowly. "I'll tail them."

"Don't lose them," I said, unable to keep the urgency out of my voice. "But don't . . . don't try to talk with them or anything. Don't let them see you."

"I know how to tail, Fort," he snapped, then, "Listen, I've got to get off the phone. I'll talk to you when I can."

He hung up. As soon as she saw me end the call, Lilah took her hands off her mouth and her words tumbled out. "That's Felix. Why would they be using Felix? He's a changeling, not a recessive. Why would that woman be with him?"

"They've just changed the pattern," I said grimly. "Or we were wrong about the pattern to start with. Maybe we missed a bunch of murders. Lilah, have changelings been going missing?"

"I don't know," she said. Her hands were shaking, and she shoved them through her hair. She closed her eyes, thought a moment, then shook her head. "I don't think anyone went missing, but I can't be sure. They're on the fringes of the community. I know only a few, and there are at least a hundred, probably more, that are under thirty and were taken from their parents."

The bathroom door slammed as Suze emerged. She was in human form again and had clearly dressed in a hurry. Pants and shirt were on but she was barefoot, and even though it was completely inappropriate under the circumstances, my brain couldn't help noting that she hadn't bothered with a bra. And that the room was a bit on the chilly side.

"Time to drop the speculation," she said, pulling her hair back into a quick ponytail. "Soli is with the sacrifice this time, and they know that we're looking for them. I don't think they'll be worrying about laying a false trail. Your sister hasn't found any of them yet. It's up to your detective now."

As if she'd summoned him, the phone rang. Matt was calling, and I immediately answered it. "Matt?"

"Lost them," he said, his voice clipped. "The girl was driving and they ran a red light. I was two cars behind—there was no way I could follow them."

"Shit." With that lead down the toilet, there wasn't anything left except to try to move Matt out of the line of fire. "Can you go back to the tattoo place? Just watch it."

"With a possible victim out there, you want me to get back on the stakeout?" Suspicion was heavy in Matt's voice. "What does your friend know?" Then, even more ominously, "Fort, I'm looking at this photo again and I've got to say, this girl is a dead damn ringer for that vegan ex of yours. What the fuck is going on here?"

My stomach dropped—Matt had met Beth only a few times in passing, but apparently it had been too much to hope for that he wouldn't recognize her if he stared at a picture of her skin long enough. I couldn't think of any way to smooth this over, and the fact was that we needed to put together some kind of plan quickly. I gave up and went for the most cliché way to escape this conversation. "What? Matt? I can't hear you! My reception sucks!" And I hit the End button.

Suzume gave me a slow shake of her head. "Really smooth, Fort. Not suspicious at all."

"I'll worry about that later," I told her. "Right now we need to figure out something to do. Lilah?"

Lilah was currently sitting on the edge of Suzume's bed, her face pressed into her hands, not exactly inspiring confidence. She didn't look up. "I don't know," she moaned. "Felix is one of us. I hired him. Tomas gives him rides home after work sometimes. We all chipped in to get him a birthday cake when he turned seventeen. How could they even think of using him?"

"You can have your crisis of faith later, Keebler," Suze said, derision glittering in her eyes when she looked at Lilah. "Right now your boss is planning on murdering the stock boy, and you going to pieces is *not* helping."

I tossed a glare at Suze and dropped down onto my knees in front of the shaken half-blood, putting my hands around hers and gently tugging them down to reveal her paper-pale face. Whatever she'd thought the Neighbors capable of, it clearly hadn't been the murder of one of their own. "Lilah," I said, as soothingly as I could, rubbing her cold hands. "If we can't stop it, Felix is going to die really horribly." She flinched visibly, and I squeezed her hands hard. "You need to help us, Lilah," I urged. "Is there any way you know to get either Tomas or Lulu's locations? Anything you haven't tried yet?"

She looked at me blankly; then understanding slowly filled her golden-brown eyes. There was something just a little harder about her gaze; one last illusion, one last, toughest belief she'd had about her extended family had just been stripped away. She nodded once. "I can get Dr. Leamaro," she said, her voice low and rough.

"Meaning?" Behind me, Suze crossed her arms, and looked distinctly disbelieving.

"I can get Dr. Leamaro to come to my apartment," Lilah said, her voice getting stronger, more grimly certain with each word.

I stared. "Why didn't you do that before?"

Lilah gently dropped my hands and stood up, pacing across the room. "Because I'll need to lie to a friend well enough that she believes me and calls Lavinia."

Suze shook her head. "You and Fort are so alike," she said in a tone that definitely was not implying a compliment, and reached down and pulled on a pair of socks. "This is definitely not the time to get panties in a twist over honesty. Do it now; apologize later."

I didn't like the tone of her voice, and I wouldn't have phrased it that way myself, but at this point I was in agreement with Suze. But I kept as much of that off my face as possible as I said to Lilah, "Let's head to your apartment, then."

"So, how are you going to flush out Lulu?" I asked as we drove to Lilah's apartment. She'd taken a cab to the hotel, and now we were all one rather awkward group in the Fiesta, with Suze choosing to stake out the backseat with the bags. I would've felt more confident in this plan if Prudence was on her way as well, but by the time the brainstorm had happened it was already ten a.m., and on a perfect blue-sky day like today my sister was already holed up in her hotel room.

"I'll tell her I might be miscarrying," Lilah said.

I nearly rear-ended the car in front of us, and the Fiesta's brakes squealed and threw all of us forward against our seat belts.

"Fort, when this is all over, we are playing some fucking poker," Suze griped behind me. "Recognize a goddamn lie."

"Yeah, definitely not pregnant." Lilah eyed me.

I could feel an impending question about her waistline, and I cut it off. "Why would Lulu care if you're pregnant?" I asked. "People are squirting out seven-eighths babies now—why worry about a halfsie's baby?"

Lilah shook her head. "You aren't understanding the mentality. This generation is what might make us a sustainable breeding population. Any of us who get pregnant, as long as it isn't with a human, is valuable to them. Besides, I'm going to bait the hook with something good, something I know she won't be able to resist."

"If she's hanging out with the Ad-hene, she probably won't buy a story about her favorite kind of incest," Suze noted dryly.

Lilah made a face. "Not that. But I've been getting the hard sell on one of the three-quarter boys lately. Cole's a jackass, but I went out with him a few months ago, just to shut everyone up for a while. He showed up wasted, ended up sleeping on my couch for the night. If I say now that I actually had sex with him, the person I'm calling will believe me."

"Who are you calling?" I asked. "You obviously don't have Lulu's direct number or you would've already handed that over."

"Peggie," she answered. "She's a half-blood like me, and we've been friends since we were toddlers. But when I left after high school, she stayed. She's not quite a true believer, but if I call her with this and say that I don't know whether I wanted to keep the baby or not, I know she'll act for the community and call Dr. Leamaro."

All these crosses and hybrids were sloshing together in my head. "What would a halfsie and a three-quarter produce again?"

"A five-eighths," she said readily, unintentionally highlighting exactly how creepy this whole situation was. "Not as good as a three-quarter but definitely better than a half-blood. Dr. Leamaro won't risk one being lost."

"Punch the gas, Fort," Suze said. "I have officially topped out on the amount of fractions and pregnancy talk that I can handle for the damn day. I'm really ready to start kicking ass instead."

"Fair enough," I muttered, inching the speedometer upward.

Lilah lived on her own in a cramped one-bedroom apartment, furnished with the best in space-saving Swedish interior design. She'd placed the call as soon as we'd arrived, and since then Suze and I had been crouched uncomfortably in Lilah's coat closet, waiting to spring into action.

"How long has it been?" Suze hissed loudly, managing to elbow me in the kidney as she shifted position.

"Two hours," I snapped, checking my watch in the sliver of light from the cracked door. "Shut up." I kept shifting my weight, trying to stave off pins and needles.

"This isn't going to work." Suze had gone very much on record as a doubter of this plan.

I had a lot of her doubts, but it had become clear that

this was our best shot at this point, and I poked her with my own elbow and made a shushing sound.

"Guys, a car just pulled up." Lilah had been positioned at her front window since she placed the call, and I could hear the jumble of fear and adrenaline in her voice. "Door is opening . . . Yeah, it's Lavinia, and she's alone. She's got her medical bag. She's coming up the walk."

My heart thudded in my chest, and I could feel Suze tense beside me. Both of us were positioned so that we could peer out of the partially opened door. Lilah had drawn back from the window—we'd all agreed that it would look less suspicious if she wasn't waiting right at the door, especially since she wasn't supposed to know that her friend had called in the doctor. When Lulu's loud, impatient knocking filled the small apartment and Lilah moved to answer it, I carefully thumbed off the safety on my Colt.

Lilah pulled open the door, revealing Dr. Lavinia Leamaro, and exclaimed loudly in fake surprise. I winced at the sound—the theater had not lost any true daughter in Lilah, and the lie was written clearly across her face. But Lulu wasn't looking at Lilah's face—those brilliant green eyes that were such a surprise against her dark skin were fixed on Lilah's stomach, and for the first time I truly understood what Lilah had told me so many times.

When I had met Lulu, she had seemed normal enough—professional, if a little light on medical ethics. But now I saw the raw avarice on her face when she looked at Lilah's belly, and whatever mask she'd worn had dropped, revealing a base fanaticism that was fundamentally repellent to me.

"You should've told me earlier, Lilah! It took that Peggie forever to get a message to me." Lulu stretched out her free hand toward Lilah, grasping and feeling at her flat stomach, not even aware of the way that Lilah flinched at her touch. Her voice was thick with satisfaction. "It's Cole's, she said. You good girl. Your mother always said that you'd come around eventually. Now I'll just check you out—" And, not releasing either her medical bag or her grip on Lilah, Lulu walked farther into the house and pushed the door closed with her foot.

That's what Suze and I had been waiting for—the final

confirmation that no one else was coming inside, and that Soli hadn't been lurking somewhere. Lilah threw herself backward at the same moment that Suze and I burst out of the closet, managing to avoid tripping over each other. I held the gun on Lulu, and she froze in the middle of the room.

"So glad you could make it," I told her. Would I find the tool that she'd used to slice Gage apart in that innocuous medical bag? Anger bubbled up in me, and my voice was as cold as any of my siblings could boast. "I have a lot to ask you," I promised her.

Comprehension dawned on Lulu's face, followed immediately by a contorting rage. Ignoring the fact that I was aiming a gun right at her head, she turned and made a lunge for Lilah, a wordless shriek of anger ripping out of her throat. Lilah barely pulled back enough to avoid Lulu's grasping hands, and Suzume tackled the older half-blood to the floor. Lulu was fighting hard, driven by an anger that seemed to have almost pushed her past the point of sanity, struggling not to escape but to get at Lilah, and doing it with so much energy that Suze was clearly hard-pressed to subdue her. I turned the safety back on and shoved the Colt into Lilah's hands, hoping that she wouldn't drop it, and waded in to help Suze. It took both of us to wrestle her onto the ground, and after several breathless minutes when Lulu still wouldn't stop fighting, Suze was eventually left with no other option than to throttle her into unconsciousness.

From her own overnight bag, Suze produced a bag of wire ties, bungee cords, and thin but strong cord. I did my best not to overthink her possession of that particular bag of tricks. Lilah had a nice wooden office chair in her bedroom, and the three of us (mostly Suze, with me attempting to reproduce her best knots and Lilah showing a complete Girl Scouts epic fail) tied Lulu to the chair. Clearly uncomfortable with her role as Judas, Lilah retreated from the bedroom, while Suze and I sat down to wait.

We didn't have to wait long. In a few minutes Lulu woke up and immediately began screaming at the top of her lungs.

"Try all you want," Suze said lazily. "Lilah's neighbors are only going to notice that her TV is on very loudly today." Once again, Suze's fox tricks had proven extremely useful. Lulu stopped screaming and stared at them, her whole body quivering with rage. I couldn't help but be amazed at her reaction, even as I kept my face stony—my reaction to waking up tied to a chair would definitely have been pants-wetting terror, not foaming anger.

"That little bitch," Lulu snapped. "Oh, she will pay for this. I always warned that her parents were too soft, too—"

I cut in. "That's not what we're talking about today." I ticked the items off on my fingers. "Fertility magic. Hiring a skinwalker. Murdering at least four men in the past year. Those are the topics I'm interested in. You can start wherever you'd like."

Focusing her green eyes on me, Lulu hissed. "We pay the tithes on our businesses. Nothing else is of concern to the Scotts."

"Everything in this territory is my mother's business. Now start talking. Start by telling me where the skinwalker is and who hired her."

Lulu snapped her mouth shut and glared at me, sullen and mute.

I waited, then tried again. "Felix Ortiz was tattooed this morning at the Iron Needle. Where is he now?"

Lulu said nothing.

"Where do you kill the men?"

"I have nothing to say to you," Lulu said, her voice low and stubborn.

I had one card left to play. "You can talk to me or you can talk with my sister." The first hint of real fear flickered through Lulu's eyes, gone almost as soon as it appeared, but I noted it and pushed hard. "I don't think you'd enjoy Prudence's"—and I paused, saying the word almost as if I savored it—"methods."

Defiance and fanaticism flared. "It doesn't matter what you do. I will *never* betray the Ad-hene." And looking at her face and the complete absence of concern for her own safety, I had to conclude that Lulu really meant it. I met Suze's eyes and jerked my head toward the other room. She slid off the bed where she'd been sitting and followed me out of the room.

I closed the bedroom door carefully behind us and looked around. Lilah apparently dealt with anxiety by cleaning, because she was busily attacking her already spotless furniture with a dusting cloth. I asked Suze quietly to sit with the prisoner; given the extent to which we'd tied her down, I couldn't imagine Lulu extricating herself, but I'd seen enough James Bond movies to be leery about leaving someone tied to a chair and unattended for long.

I bypassed Lilah's cleaning frenzy and walked to the far corner of the kitchen—it was too small of an apartment for real privacy, but I wanted at least the illusion of it for this conversation. After a deep breath, I called my sister.

She was ensconced in her hotel room and answered my call on the first ring. After a quick exchange of greetings, I filled her in on everything that had happened. She listened without interrupting.

When I had finished, she said, "Well *done*, little brother," in such an approving tone of voice that I seriously wondered for a moment whether I was speaking to an impersonator.

"Uh, thanks," I said, still uncertain how to respond to this new, more supportive Prudence. "Listen. When can you get over here and question her? Apparently zealots are kind of tough to interrogate."

"The worst; that is true," she said sympathetically. Then, with an odd brightness, "I will head out as soon as this accursed sun goes down enough. Given what I've seen of the hourly forecast, about three, perhaps three and a half hours."

"That long?" I asked, horrified. My sister's tolerance for sunlight was definitely going down.

"Patience, brother. It will be all right. Make sure that the half-blood is secured and then leave her alone to stew. The wait will soften her up." I began to protest, and she made soothing noises. "I will get the information as quickly as possible, brother, I assure you. Now, listen to me, because this is very important."

"Yes?" I asked, reaching for a nearby pad of paper just in case I needed to take notes.

"Don't be nice to her. No food, no drinks, and definitely no bathroom."

"Um . . . ?" That last part made me very nervous. Lilah's apartment was carpeted.

"Urinating oneself can be an important part of being broken down," Prudence assured me.

I gulped. This newer, friendlier Prudence was definitely still my sister. "You're the expert," I managed, reminding myself that with a life on the line, I was probably going to be making a few *24*-esque decisions.

My reply apparently delighted Prudence, because she burbled happily, "Ah, Fortitude. The things I can teach you."

Even as my mouth made the appropriate good-byes, an icy chill went up my spine and I wondered whether I was really prepared for my sister's version of sibling bonding exercises.

It was a long, tense afternoon while we waited for my sister to arrive and begin torturing Lulu. With nothing else to do, I joined Lilah in the distraction of cleaning. Suze remained impervious to the atmosphere, shifted to her fox form, and took a long nap on the sofa (all four furry paws in the air) while Lilah and I defrosted her freezer and cleaned out her fridge. I tried calling Matt three times, but he didn't pick up, and I ended up leaving voice mails. I winced at what that might mean, but comforted myself with the knowledge that I hadn't told him what hotel Suze and I had stayed at, so there wasn't any chance that he had tailed us again.

When my sister arrived at a quarter to five, the first hints of orange were gathering in the clouds, heralding the start of a spectacular sunset. Being relieved at Prudence's arrival was definitely a personal first for me, but the feeling flooded through me as I pulled open the front door at her imperious knock to reveal her, her lacy white parasol adding an almost steampunk accent to her usual Stepford-wifish attire. Her blue eyes were gleaming and there was an eager spring in her step as I directed her to the bedroom. Clearly Prudence enjoyed her work.

"Wait here, brother," she told me at the entrance, and then entered alone, closing the door behind her.

The next two hours inched horribly by, with Lulu's screams echoing through the apartment. I sat on the sofa, tensing at every sound that emerged from the closed bedroom until the muscles of my body actually felt sore. Lilah tried covering her ears at first, but eventually just gave up and pressed against my side, burying her face in my shoulder. I stroked her bright hair with one hand, but there was nothing to say. For all the crimes that Lulu had committed, it was impossible to hear the sounds of her agony and not cringe.

I'd made the decision and the call that had led to the torture, I reminded myself over and over—I needed to accept the consequences and not try to hide from Lulu's screams. But as the sun set and the shadows deepened, I finally couldn't take it anymore, and I turned to Suze and begged, "Can't you hide those sounds?" I loathed my own weakness as I asked, but I just didn't want to listen to the surround sound of Lulu's torture for another minute.

Suzume had returned to her human shape shortly after Prudence had arrived and had positioned herself at the window, about as far away from where Lilah and I were sitting as she could get, staring out into the darkness. She didn't look at me as she answered quietly. "I can hide the sounds from the neighbors by replacing them with sounds that they would normally expect to hear—that's no real effort. But to hide the sounds from you, when you know the truth of what is happening in that room, would be much more difficult. I don't know where this night is going to lead us, and I can't spare the energy, Fort." She looked over her shoulder at me very quickly, turning away again almost immediately, some undefined emotion flickering across her face. "Not even for your feelings."

And time crept forward.

The clock had just ticked past seven when Prudence reappeared at the bedroom door and beckoned me over. A lazy, contented smile was spread across her face, and she was wiping one hand fastidiously with a monogrammed linen handkerchief that was already streaked in dark red stains.

"Come, Fortitude. I'm ready for you now," she said.

Carefully extricating myself from Lilah, I took a deep breath and walked over to my sister, reminding myself again of why this had to be done. "What's taking so long? Why isn't she talking?" I asked.

Prudence gave a low, amused chuckle and wagged one newly clean finger at me. "Ah, brother. You think it's easy to break a fanatic? You watch too much television. It would take me months, with every piece of agony just making her cling harder to her devotion, or result in nothing but a string of lies. No, I've just softened her a bit." She dropped one deceptively delicate hand on my shoulder and squeezed lightly, ignoring my barely hidden flinch as she touched me. "Tell me, Fortitude, have you learned much about the Neighbors during your investigation?"

"A bit," I admitted cautiously.

She nodded, then urged me in a tone that was weirdly reminiscent of my teachers when they had been trying to lead the class to a concept. "Think hard on what this wretch values."

I considered it, then said slowly, "She doesn't value her own life."

Prudence nodded again, pleased. "Precisely. True fanatics do not. So come in, Fortitude, and force her to talk by threatening what she does hold dear."

I followed Prudence into the bedroom, unable to keep myself from looking back once over my shoulder. Suze had turned away from the window to watch the exchange, and she gave me one short nod. Lilah was still sitting on the sofa, her large eyes red from crying. She crossed her hands over her mouth and glanced away from me. From the depths of my soul I wished that I could do the same.

Inside the bedroom, Lulu was still tied to the chair, just as we'd left her. But there were small trails of dried blood at the corners of her mouth, and a towel from the bathroom was pressed against her stomach, blotted with bloodstains. Remembering the way Prudence had threatened Ambrose the witch at Lulu's office, I couldn't prevent myself from being grateful that Prudence had covered up her handi-work, even though it made me both hypocritical and cowardly, as I carried an equal stake in her actions. There was a weird smell in the room, almost a combination of a poorly maintained men's bathroom and the back room of a butcher shop (another of my worse, short-term bits of employment). Seeing me, Lulu tried to spit but couldn't put any force behind it, which just resulted in a pinkish liquid dribbling down her chin.

If I ran away or threw up, I'd lose this opportunity. I forced myself to remember what Gage's body had looked like on the floor of his bedroom: cold, ruined, and tossed aside like garbage. I reminded myself that this woman was also responsible, at least in part, for the presence of Soli, and therefore shared in the guilt of Beth's death. That stirred up enough anger in me to push back my guilt and regret for her pain, and I forced confidence in my voice as I said, "I think you're ready to answer my questions now, Doctor."

Lulu gave a high, shrill laugh that made her gasp as it jarred some broken place inside her. "And why would you say that, when your sister has had no luck at all?" she taunted, glaring at me with no hint of fear. "You can go ahead and kill me now. I'll never talk to you."

I glanced at my sister behind me, but Prudence just gave me an encouraging nod. "I'm surprised you'd say that," I began, feeling her out, trying to remember everything I'd learned or had heard about the way that she viewed the world. "After all, what will your community do without their own pet doctor to churn changelings out of desperate women?"

At that Lulu's expression wavered for a second and a shiver ran through her, but then she shook her head. "Others can continue that work. Maybe not on the same scale, but it will continue. And it doesn't truly matter, because the time of the changeling is coming to an end."

A thrill of excitement ran through me. Just like that, she'd handed me the key to force her confession. I would've liked myself better if I'd hesitated or if I'd said what I did with the fates of the living in mind, but it was the thought of Gage and Beth that pushed me immediately forward. "Perhaps you think that," I said, leaning in and placing a hand on her shoulder. The bone moved, and I realized that it was broken. My stomach clenched, but I didn't move my hand. "But if you don't start talking right now, my sister is going to start hunting. For every minute you stay silent, she'll kill one of your half-bloods." Lulu gaped, horror suffusing her face, but I pushed forward brutally. "For every lie you tell me, she'll slaughter one of those three-quarter hybrids you've worked so hard on." A high, frightened sound emerged from Lulu's throat, and now she was shaking visibly.

"No, you wouldn't, you couldn't—" Lulu's wide green eyes darted between me and my sister.

"Look at my sister, Doctor," I said heartlessly. "Do you think she'll hesitate if I tell her to go and kill someone?" I didn't look behind me, but there was a soft rustling of fabric, and whatever move Prudence made caused Lulu to flinch hard.

Weakness and despair made the wrinkles in Lulu's face deepen, suddenly making her look her age for the first time I'd known her. She was beaten and she knew it. "What do you want from me?" she asked, voice shaking.

"I know that some of the Neighbors have been using a ritual to enable the conception of a seven-eighths hybrid. You've been using recessive men, tattooing and killing them. You brought a skinwalker in to help." I leaned even closer to her. "Now tell me the rest."

She wet her lips with her tongue, and when she spoke it was very slow and halting, each word sounding ripped from her throat. "It was Tomas who found it. We were all looking, all of us who are trusted, who are the inner circle, but he found it. He found an old witch up in Maine, one who had a collection of potion books. But she wouldn't let him look at them, and that made us think that she was hiding something. We couldn't risk the witch naming the Neighbors or the Ad-hene in a complaint to Madeline Scott, so that's when we hired Soli, the skinwalker. She killed the witch, brought the books back."

"What is Soli getting out of all of this?" I asked.

Lulu's mouth twisted in brief, cynical amusement before quickly going slack again. "Money. She didn't care what we did, as long as she was paid. And in one of the books we found a ritual, one where the only thing we needed from the witches was the spelled ink to make the tattoo. The sacrifice had to be special, not just any man off the street, so we used ones whose fathers were Ad-hene, the ones who had never bloomed."

"The coroner's report says that there were medical tools used in the amputations."

She nodded, and these words came easier to her, as if she were talking about something of no great consequence or importance. "Yes, that was me. Hands, genitals, and tongue needed to be removed without killing the sacrifice. We'd hang him above the couple; then the seed had to be planted before the sacrifice's blood stopped pumping."

I stared at her for a second, my mind unable to wrap around what she'd just said. "What do you mean?"

"I'd make an incision in the sacrifice's neck, then intercourse needed to be completed before the sacrifice bled out completely." She spoke briskly, for the first time seeming to regain that air of medical superiority.

I couldn't reply, and Prudence strolled forward next to me, looking completely unruffled, nodding and smoothly picking up the questioning that I'd dropped. "The purpose of those roofie potions that your witch cooked up, I believe. Hard to get most girls, even Neighbor girls, to participate." She gave a small, fastidious sniff of disapproval. "I'm sure nothing was needed for the elves to perform."

My brain was numb from the information I was still struggling with, and I stared at Lulu, moved beyond horror. "All those men. You delivered them when they were babies. And you're just . . . so calm talking about what you did to them." I couldn't understand it.

Lulu stared at me, icy and unmoved. "They were useless to us. All that promise, all that effort, and all we got were mewling human babies. They should've been grateful that they could finally be of use to their fathers." The fanatical gleam returned to her eyes, and her voice became triumphant. "And they were. The first baby was born yesterday, and there are three others twitching in their mothers' wombs. This is the way back to what our kind was meant to be."

Lilah's voice cut in, and I looked behind me to see her

standing in the doorway. She must've been listening to everything. Her eyes were fixed on Lulu, there was a dark flush in her cheeks, and something about the way she was holding herself hinted at barely restrained violence, as if her heritage was barely contained beneath her skin. "But Felix isn't a recessive, Lavinia. He's one of us, one of the Neighbors. Why would the skinwalker have taken him to Jacoby? Why would he be wearing those tattoos now?" Her voice rose with each question.

Lulu's lip curled. "As if a changeling is truly one of us," she said.

Apparently undistracted by the exchange, Prudence was tapping one finger contemplatively against her lips. Something occurred to her and she asked Lulu, "You're wondering how much stronger a hybrid you can create, aren't you? Whether a finer sacrifice will bring you closer to a true elf?"

There was a weirdly desperate tone in Lulu's voice as she answered Prudence, something that bordered almost on gratitude that someone in the room apparently understood their way of thinking. "Yes. You see. This is about the survival of our race."

Lilah laughed, high and hysterical. "Have you ever considered, Lavinia, that maybe we shouldn't be trying quite so hard to be like Themselves? That maybe they've died out for a reason?"

Lulu's head snapped back, as if Lilah had just said the most untenable heresy—which I supposed she had. But I broke in before the conversation could be sidetracked again. "Felix was with Soli this morning. If you aren't trying to cover your tracks from us anymore, then nothing would be holding you back from making the sacrifice quickly. Has it already happened?" The half-blood woman chewed anxiously at her bottom lip and didn't respond, which was enough of an answer in itself. I nodded. "It hasn't happened, then. Tell me where and when."

Lulu turned her face away from all of us, clearly struggling between her aversion to giving us the information we needed to stop the sacrifice and her fear of the consequences if she didn't answer. My sister moved forward, easing down beside Lulu and stroking the sweaty curls back from the tortured woman's forehead. When she spoke her voice was soft and almost loving, a horrible counterpoint to the content of the words themselves. "I will rip apart every hybrid girl I can find, Lulu," Prudence promised. "And I will leave you alive to watch while I destroy every hope your race has left."

No one doubted the truth of Prudence's promise, and it was the last torture for Lulu, who broke fully at last. Her eyes were shattered when she whispered, "It's tonight, just at moonrise. In the fairy circle outside the entrance to Underhill. They'll all be there, waiting for me to arrive."

I looked at Lilah, still standing at the doorway. "Do you know the spot?"

She nodded. "Yes," but something was clearly on her mind, and she asked Lulu, "Who are they using?"

Those brilliant emerald eyes glittered with malice. "You should know."

Betrayal covered Lilah's face. "No, no, not Iris. My parents would never agree to that." And I remembered then that Lilah's nineteen-year-old sister was one of the three-quarter hybrid girls.

"They are loyal," Lulu sneered, her voice like a knife. "They didn't question us, just agreed to give the girl the brew and have her ready for Tomas to pick up."

Lilah moved forward then, her hands reaching for the older woman, but I grabbed and held her before she could get close. She struggled for a moment, then gave up. "What time is moonrise tonight?" I asked her, hoping that she would somehow know offhand or that her finding the answer would manage to focus her attention.

Suzume stepped into the room at my question and held up my own phone, which I'd left in the other room. Apparently while we'd been embroiled in personal drama she'd made good use of my data plan. "Moonrise is at eight-oh-nine. We've got forty minutes."

"We need to get moving," I said urgently.

Prudence was still kneeling beside Lulu, stroking her dark curls with their periodic glints of silver. She looked over at me and asked, "You're point, brother. What shall we do with the good doctor?"

After the past few minutes' revelations there couldn't be much doubt, but I still hesitated for a second, looking at the woman tied to the chair who had participated in so much misery and death. But when I said, "Kill her," I was surprised at how hard and sure my own voice sounded, like a stranger's.

Prudence's hands moved in a blur, a crack filled the room, and Lulu's head slumped on a broken neck. I felt inside myself but couldn't even find a flicker of remorse. My sister stood up, and there was a gleam of approval in her blue eyes when she looked at me. "Very good, Fortitude," she said.

I looked away from my sister, her praise bothering me exponentially more than the body did. "Everyone in the cars," I said roughly. "Grab what you need for a fight."

The Irish entrance to Underhill was closed in 1845, locking the elves inside to hopefully murder each other out of existence. The magic that closed the gate had a high cost—the Potato Famine was just one of them. But despite the best efforts of the ones who worked that magic, one elf and several half-bloods weren't caught in the trap. They fled to America, ending up in my mother's territory, where they negotiated the terms for their residency. It took sixty-three years for them to craft the Rhode Island opening to Underhill, and after they'd managed it, my mother used her political influence to push the creation of a state park around the gate to ensure its security. That was the start of the Lincoln Woods State Park—627 acres open year-round, including hills, a freshwater lake, and equestrian trails, and all lay only eight miles from the heart of Providence and didn't even include an entrance fee.

Every stoplight was torturous as we drove, but I didn't dare risk running any of them, not when we couldn't afford the delay of a traffic stop. With Prudence following in her own car, Lilah gave me directions from the passenger's seat. As I drove, I tossed my phone back to Suze and asked her to put one last call in to Matt, to figure out where he was and keep him somewhere safe. She tried, but passed it back to me a minute later. It had gone to voice mail again. I cursed, then focused on getting through a yellow light a minute before it went to red.

The park was officially open only from sunrise to sunset, but to avoid trapping lingering hikers the entrance gates were never closed. As Lilah directed us to a small parking area, I noticed that there were several cars already there. The clock ticked over to seven forty-eight p.m. just as I turned off the engine.

Suze had grabbed our duffels on the way out of the apartment, and I removed my Colt and the Ithaca 37, checking each quickly to make sure they were fully loaded. Because the Ithaca could carry only two shells at a time, I pushed more into the pockets of my shirt and jeans. The Colt went into its own holster that I strapped around my waist, but there was no way around carrying the Ithaca openly, and I hoped desperately that if we ran across any innocent night hikers, Suze could trick them into thinking that the Ithaca was just an oddly shaped hoagie.

Suze herself was carrying her long knife in her right hand. On the drive over, Lilah had been persuaded to carry the unregistered .38 that Suze routinely kept in her duffel bag, but from the way she was holding it, it seemed unlikely that she'd be able to hit the broad side of a barn. The plan we'd worked out on the way over was one where hopefully the combined authority of me and Prudence would be enough to stop the planned sacrifice, but if that failed, then Lilah's job would be to try to get her sister and Felix to safety while the rest of us cleared a path for her and kept most of the potential harm away. Lilah had a very fixed and determined expression on her face that made me think that she'd be willing to pull the trigger tonight. Whatever internal qualms she'd had about her part in Lulu's fate had evaporated once she'd learned that her sister was in danger, and as I looked at her under the fluorescence of the lone parking-lot light, I was struck by how very brave and yet how wholly unprepared she was for where this situation could end up heading.

My sister, meanwhile, had waited with barely concealed impatience while we'd done our best to arm ourselves. When I glanced at her with a question on my lips, it died as she flexed her bare hands in anticipation of the almost certain conflict ahead of us. Prudence clearly had no intention of using any weapons beyond the ones that nature had already endowed her with.

My phone read seven fifty-one when I tossed it onto the seat of my car for safekeeping (it was too new and shiny to risk getting crunched in a fight) and locked the doors, and we all fell into a line behind Lilah and followed her down a dirt path. As we passed the tree line and the leaves rustled eerily above us in the creepy way of the woods in the night, I noticed again that I was seeing better than I should've as all artificial lights disappeared behind us. It was another sign of my transition, but I couldn't regret it at that moment— with whatever lay before us, I knew that I would certainly need every advantage my heritage could offer.

# Chapter 10

Lilah ran flat-out down a small hiking path, and the rest of us followed. Abruptly the path ended in a clearing, one of those rare natural forest glens where the ancient trees formed a perfect circle, edged in a ring of clover and dandelions. On the far side was the edge of a small hill, cluttered with rõcks except for a small, dark opening, the kind that evoked an image of raccoon dens or slumbering copperhead snakes. It was the sort of place that would stir a naturalist's heart, but in truth this was the fairy circle that marked the gate into Underhill.

It was a perfectly clear night, and the open field was bathed in the light from the stars. The growing radiance from the moon had almost fully crested the horizon, giving us all an excellent view of what was happening. Lacking the right kind of tree to hang their sacrifice from, the Neighbors had set up a portable scaffold, the type that I'd seen contractors use to touch up the paint in my mother's grand foyer, where they had to safely deal with restoration at a height of eighteen feet. Hanging upside down from the middle of the scaffold was Felix. He was fully awake and struggling, but they'd gagged him and he couldn't make a sound.

Several feet beneath him was an inflatable kiddie pool, bright blue and incongruously decorated with cartoon dolphins and starfish, a sight that made me regret the unnatural sharpness of my eyesight. Inside the pool was a young woman who bore too close a resemblance to Lilah to be anything other than her nineteen-year-old sister, Iris—the hair was the same, as well as something in her face, despite the fact that she was a three-quarter cross and showed the signs of a heritage that had far fewer ties to humanity. She was completely naked, her pale skin almost phosphorescently pale in the starlight, and she sat with her legs folded and a look of blank and uncomprehending docility on her face.

Circled around their two victims were ten figures who were intently focused either on the scenario in front of them or the slow progress of the moon in the sky. At first I'd concentrated on looking for Soli, but my brain stuttered when I realized from their completely distinctive silhouettes that five of those figures were full elves—the first I'd ever seen. The presence of so many of what remained of that dwindling, doomed population spoke more for how invested they were in this than anything Lilah or Lulu could ever have said.

They didn't notice at first as we came to the end of the path and passed into the fairy circle. Prudence and I moved naturally into the lead, with Suze and Lilah falling just behind us. But three of the figures broke away from the circle, three older half-bloods around Lulu's age who would've looked completely at home organizing a church jumble sale had it not been for the butcher knives in their hands as they moved toward where Felix hung. We were getting nearer but were still halfway across the clearing, so I raised the Ithaca above my head and gave one warning shot. That stopped them, and all wheeled around to face us, and I saw the last of the elves full-on.

They were all tall, at least six feet each, but with almost delicate builds displayed by the loose fur wraps that each wore around his waist, with nothing on the upper body. Their hair was long, ranging in color from one whose black hair seemed even darker than the sky above us to a brilliant blond, but it was clear that this wasn't the same as the hair of any human or hybrid cross I'd seen, and looked more like spun metal. From just above the hairlines of each of the elves emerged a full set of horns, as smooth and black as polished marble, and as long and pronged as a deer in autumn. There was a distinctly reptilian cast to their faces, wholly inhuman, long and disturbing, and those large eyes

I'd admired so much in Lilah were much different when seen in their natural setting. And yet I was almost viscerally struck by how beautiful each of them was. It was a terrifying beauty, nature at its most vicious, but even as we advanced toward them I could feel the echo of their allure and compulsion, and I understood why the legends referred to them as the Fair Folk.

Beside them were their most loyal half-bloods—two men and a woman, all holding knives—and one younger man, bulky like a football player and with a face like a pale imitation of the elves, clearly a three-quarter hybrid. And at the far end, standing just apart and behind the others, was Soli, smiling with Beth's mouth but with a venom that she had never been capable of.

The sound of the Ithaca rolled through the clearing, and we were close enough now that when I yelled for them to stop, it wasn't because my voice had to cover a long distance. The elves were the ones who moved toward us, just a step, but Prudence made a low sound and they froze where they were, almost immediately shifting their weight to make it look as if they'd stopped because they'd wanted to—like scolded cats deliberately lifting one paw to lick. In the car, Lilah had described in enough detail the five elves who allowed themselves to be seen to me that, looking at each Ad-hene, I was able to match their names to their distinctive coloration. She'd also warned me that some might not back down willingly. As they looked at us, it was clear that there were divisions among them—two of them, Hobany and Beron, were cringing at the sight of us and shifting their feet nervously. The other three, though, Amadon, Shoney, and Nokke, were simply staring at us out of those gleaming eyes, and they looked angry instead of afraid.

"Stop all of this," I ordered, forcing as much authority as I could into my voice and reminding myself that I was my mother's representative. Over the past few months I'd heard Chivalry give orders to those who lived in my mother's territory dozens of times, and I tried to put some of that confidence into my own voice.

"Why?" asked the one with golden hair, Amadon. "Madeline Scott can have no argument with what we do here, out of sight of any humans and in the company of our own kind."

"Killing people from her territory?" I asked. "Snatching them away and then making a halfhearted effort at disposing of the bodies?" Arguing about the evils of the deaths themselves would've been a waste—I was being as careful as I could to argue in terms that my mother or Chivalry would've used, and that the elves were more likely to recognize and hopefully back down from. Out of the corner of my eye, I saw Prudence give me a subtle nod of approval, and I felt a little reassured. If my argument was resting well with one sociopath, perhaps it would work with others.

"We would never break the rules that have been laid down," said another, in a whining and nasal voice. This one was Beron, who Lilah had told me was more cautious. "None of Madeline's stock have been poached—all who died were ours, from our bloodlines."

Another, Hobany, joined in eagerly, with his head and dark horns dipping like a sycophant toward my sister and me. "If too little care has been taken with disposing of remains, then the fault lies with our offspring, and we will gladly put them forward for your mother's punishment." Behind him, the half-breeds who had just been offered up as fodder simply bobbed their heads in agreement, their faces as they looked at the Ad-hene never wavering from open adoration.

Needing to keep this completely on track, I pointed at Soli. "And that? A skinwalker stands right beside you, a creature my mother has banned for over sixty years. What is your explanation there?"

"Is that your concern in this?" asked Shoney, the one with the dark hair. He turned for a moment and drew one of the half-breeds forward, a lanky man with wispy gray hair and unglamoured ears that were the only signs of his heritage. "The fault for that lies in our dear Tomas, so I'm sure that he would gladly pay the price for his foolish actions. Wouldn't you, Tomas?" The older man nodded eagerly, never looking away from Shoney's face, even when the elf reached out and with one quick movement ripped out Tomas's throat, the blood spurting across the elf's chest as the body slumped and fell over. Even after a lifetime with my family, the sheer casualness of the killing shocked me profoundly, and behind me Lilah made a soft noise of protest, quickly stifled. No one else reacted at all, and Shoney gave a thin smile as he looked back at me. "Are we all in agreement?" he asked politely, lifting his hand to his mouth to delicately lick the blood that spattered across it with a tongue that was altogether too long and thin.

I stared at him. "Not even a little."

Then Nokke spoke, his voice harsh, and from the way that Amadon and Shoney immediately snapped to attention, it was clear which of them was in charge here. If I hadn't already known his connection to Lilah, it would've been obvious from his hair. Even in the dim light of the rising moon, that hair would've put a newly polished copper teakettle to shame. "Enough of this. We have brought in the tools we needed to complete our work, and those who were killed belong to us." He sent a sharp look Lilah's way, the first time that any of them had acknowledged her. "As does your apparent informant."

Lilah's voice was frightened but firm. "Grandfather, you have to stop what you're doing. You can't kill your own child to try to create a better one."

"Can't I, granddaughter? What life I create is my property and mine to destroy at my will." His eyes narrowed. "When this is over, I think you will need a lesson in where your loyalties lie." The threat was very clear.

I moved slightly to my left to block the look that Nokke was shooting toward Lilah. "Her loyalty is where it should've been, with the one who rules all of you." I looked across the line of elves facing me, making eye contact with each of them, and worried that only two looked away. The odds were not in our favor, but there was nothing to do except push forward and lay everything on the line, and hope that self-interest won out in the end. "I speak for my mother, and I say that your plans for tonight's activities are over. Leave Felix and Iris unharmed, hand the skinwalker over to us, and go back into your hole. Do that, and I'll ask my mother to be merciful in her punishment. Disobey, and you will learn your own lesson about the costs of betraying loyalty to the Scotts." Beside me my sister shifted, putting her weight forward like a wrestler waiting for a match to start. Relief pounded through me—at least she was on my side.

There was a long pause as the elves looked at each other, some hidden communication clearly shared among them. Then Beron slowly turned back to me and nodded once. "Very well," he said, then turned and began walking away, followed almost immediately by Hobany. They crossed the clearing to the pile of rocks, then disappeared inside Underhill.

For a second I thought that everything would be okay.

Then Nokke hissed, opening his mouth wide to reveal a gummy smile more suited to an octogenarian anticipating pudding, but then at least fifty serrated teeth slid easily out of the gums, and I knew without a doubt that the attempts at diplomacy had ended and that the only course now was to fight. "I've bent my neck to your mother for long enough when it suited me, little vampire, but I will not be dictated to in this matter," Nokke said. And then everyone was moving at once.

The three remaining elves came forward in one fast, horned mass, but before I could take aim with the Ithaca my sister was in front of me, cutting off the elves and engaging with them. They were faster than she was, but she was clearly stronger and tougher, and almost immediately they fell into a loose net around her, moving in quickly to swipe at her but moving back before she could return the hit, like a pack of wolves harrying a moose.

While Prudence kept the Ad-hene busy, Suze, Lilah, and I began running toward her sister and Felix. The half-bloods managed to turn their attention away from the situation of the Ad-hene and did their best to block us, but they were holding those butcher knives awkwardly, as if the closest they'd come before this to serious combat had been a particularly resistant cut of chicken. The man came toward me, and for a brief second I considered whether to shoot him, but he looked so awkward and vulnerable—a fanatic carried far past where he should've stopped—and so instead I bashed him in the face with the butt of the Ithaca, crunching his nose and sending him tumbling to the ground. In front of me the half-blood woman, the tips of her ears peeking up through her soccer-mom haircut, hesitated at the sight of her compatriot's fate, then edged back, frightened, when Suze very deliberately lifted her long knife and moved toward her. While all of this was happening, Lilah ran straight to her sister like a homing pigeon, unassaulted by anyone.

I didn't follow Lilah, because strolling toward me was Soli, Beth's face pulled into a malicious smile. I didn't hesitate this time, shooting the Ithaca's remaining shell at her, but again she moved with a speed that I couldn't match, dodging to the side. The bullet didn't miss her entirely, clipping her in the side and causing enough damage to immediately stain her shirt red, but even though she stumbled at the hit she kept coming toward me, and I didn't have time to reload the Ithaca before she was directly in front of me and swinging. I was able to dodge her first strike, and I swung the Ithaca itself at her like a club, but she knocked it out of my hand and I was immediately too engaged with blocking her strikes to even try to reach for the Colt where it was holstered at my back.

Suzume had shadowed Lilah further, making sure no one went for her, but when she saw what was happening between me and Soli she immediately spun around and ran flat-out toward us. But she was so focused on getting to me that she didn't pay attention to who was around her, and the three-quarter hybrid man was able to tackle her from behind, bringing her down to the ground. The sight of it happening distracted me for just a second, but that was more than enough for Soli to gain the upper hand, and her fist drove into my chest like a cement truck, knocking me over. She followed me down, those long black claws slicing out of the flesh of Beth's hands, and I was barely able to grab her wrists, using all my strength to keep those slashing claws away from my throat. I could feel them gouging at my forearms as Soli kept ripping at me, and my brain somehow registered the feeling of the blood running down my arms more than the pain itself.

The Colt was now completely pinned beneath me and the Ithaca lost somewhere in the grass, even if I'd had a free hand to reach for one of them, which I didn't, as both were more than engaged with keeping Soli's claws just a hairsbreadth away from my throat. I could actually feel the air movement each time she reached for me, and I was horribly aware of the vulnerability of every artery that pumped through that spot she was reaching for with single-minded ferocity. I glanced around desperately, but Prudence was still pinned down—Amadon was writhing on the ground, both hands trying to push his intestines back inside his belly, but Shoney and Nokke moved around him without even a glance. Suzume's eyes were fixed on me as she stumbled to her feet, her long knife now painted red from tip to handle, and the crumpled body of her assailant behind her, but I could feel my arms shaking with the effort of holding Soli back, and I knew that Suze wouldn't reach me in time.

The crack of a pistol cut through all the noises of the fighting, and Soli was suddenly thrown backward and off of me as a gout of blood exploded from her shoulder. I looked, and five feet behind me stood Matt, his face pale, his eyes fixed and wide, but his feet were planted solidly and his hands were steady on his .38.

My stunned wonder at how the hell he'd followed me was washed away at the realization that he'd seen it all—monsters fighting on the grass of Lincoln Woods State Park—and for just one heartbeat I was frozen and unable to move past the knowledge of what this meant. But then the world came rushing back to me and there was no time to pause. Soli was pushing herself back up when I rolled forward and pulled out my Colt, and the first bullet caught her just below her neck. For one horrible moment the eyes that stared at me with utter surprise were Beth's, but I gritted my teeth and sent a second bullet into her head, followed immediately by a third, and the skinwalker went down. Half the skin of Beth's face was gone, revealing the shiny black carapace beneath it, and just enough to realize that not only did the skinwalker actually have mandibles, but also they were still moving, because Soli was dropped but still alive, and now her limbs were actually pushing her upper body upright again.

I drew in a panting, ragged breath and I lifted the gun,

intending to empty the rest of the clip, but then Suzume reached me. With no hesitation at all, she brought that long knife down and began the systematic removal of Soli's head. That white fluid I remembered from before foamed out, but after one last spasm the skinwalker stilled and didn't move again.

I was wobbling to my feet, and I forced myself to look back at Matt, frightened about whether his gun would be aimed at me now, but when I did I shouted desperately to Suze. The Neighbor with the soccer-mom hair had skirted the edge of the fighting, and while Matt had been focused on me and the skinwalker, she had attacked him with that butcher knife. Now he was on the ground, one hand pressing against a large red stain on his arm, and she was coming toward him again. At my shout, Suze was moving for them. I would've followed, but I saw Prudence stumble, and Nokke and Shoney moved in like jackals for the kill.

Trusting Suzume to keep Matt safe, I tightened my grip on the Colt and ran toward my sister. But just before I could reach them enough to trust a shot, Shoney attacked Prudence. The wide smile that crossed her face was his only warning, and one of her manicured hands shot out, grabbed one of his antlers, and with a low grunt from my sister a bone-crunching sound echoed beside Shoney's hysterical scream of agony as she ripped his antler completely from his head, accompanied by an enormous rush of blood, chunks of his skull, and several pieces of things I didn't even want to try to identify. Shoney collapsed onto the ground, twitching spastically as the blood continued to flow, and I could see the horror spread across Nokke's face as he realized that all of my sister's attention was now solely fixated on him.

I took a deep breath. "That's enough, Prudence," I yelled, and she stopped to look at me, Shoney's antler still gripped in her hand. Nokke looked at me as well, and this time his gaze swept across the clearing, and I could see the moment when he realized that he was the only one still left standing. Glancing behind me, I saw that the soccer mom was down, and Suzume was crouched beside Matt, putting pressure on his arm. She gave me a quick nod, reassuring me that everything was fine. I looked over at Lilah and saw that she'd managed to lower Felix and was now standing in front of him and her sister, the borrowed gun shaking in her hands.

I focused again on Nokke. "Are you ready to hear what I have to say, or do I let my sister take you apart one piece at a time?"

"Talk," the elf gritted between his clenched serrated teeth.

"This is over," I said. "Your breeding experiments are over as well. Keep the seven-eighths crosses you created, but if one more of those is born than is already conceived, the Scotts will take the price out of your skin." A spasm of rage passed over Nokke's face, but after a pause he dipped his head in reluctant agreement. I continued. "Clean up your dead." Movement caught the corner of my eye, and I glanced over. Seeing that negotiations had begun, Lilah had put the gun away and was leading the two younger Neighbors toward us. I glanced at her grandfather and added another condition. "It's clear that we can no longer trust you to behave, so from this moment onward your representative will be making monthly reports about your activities to my family."

Nokke frowned. "What representative?" I pointed silently at Lilah. He fumed, "You cannot be—" But Prudence inched forward, clearly eager to inflict more damage, and he broke off his statement, sucking his anger down again. "Yes. My granddaughter will deliver the reports."

"In perfect health," I said coldly. "With no complaints about how she has been treated by her relatives." He nodded, clearly beyond speech. I looked over at my sister, who gave me a sign of approval. "Do you have anything else you think should be added, Prudence?" I asked.

My sister smiled slowly. "Only that our mother will doubtless have some ideas later on how the elves can . . . atone . . . for breaking her laws. I'm sure that I will be seeing more of them."

I nodded. "Sounds fair." I looked at Nokke again, seeing the rage and pride battling across his inhuman yet inhumanly beautiful face. There was no regret there. Not for the death he'd led his followers to, and certainly not for the deaths he'd caused. Without a word I quickly aimed the Colt and squeezed off a shot. Nokke fell to the ground, clutching his knee. I nodded, satisfied. "Now we're done," I told the Ad-hene. Crawling, his expression now pained, the elf reached a hand toward Amadon, still lying on the ground but his belly already knitting before our eyes, and hauled him backward. In a moment they were both gone, hidden back inside Underhill. Behind them were the bodies, including Shoney, who lay rigid in death.

My sister smiled at me, a grisly sight with her hands bloody up to the elbow. "Excellently done, Fortitude," she complimented me, and for a moment I relaxed. But she had turned her attention to Matt and was moving toward him, ignoring the hand I threw out to try to catch her, speaking as she moved toward the injured man. "Matthew McMahon," she said, pleasure dripping from her voice. "You really do seem to have quite a talent for making a nuisance of yourself. But this is the end, at last."

Suzume dropped Matt's arm and moved backward, and I could see the recognition fill Matt's face as my sister stalked toward him. His eyes darted from the body of Shoney to the ripped antler still lying on the ground to my sister's bloody hands, and back up to her face, and even as death incarnate came for him I could see him putting the pieces together. And the look on his face when he finally solved the case that had driven him for seventeen years was equal parts horror and euphoria.

"You," he breathed. "Whatever you are, it was you. You killed Brian and Jill Mason that night; then your family covered it up." As the truth that I'd spent so long hiding from him echoed from his mouth, I froze, my heart seeming to slow in my chest at the blow.

She laughed as she moved closer. "At least you can die a contented man, with no last secrets nagging at your mind."

Her arm was drawing back when I was able to move again, and I moved with the vampire speed that I'd only managed once before in my life, and I caught her hand in mine before she could strike.

She half turned to frown at me. "Brother, this is necessary. Even you can't deny that the detective has seen far more than we can allow."

I squeezed my hand tightly and shook my head, struggling for a reason, any reason, that would stop her. "This is a decision for Mother, not us," I stuttered, playing for any extra minute of time that would give me a chance to find a better plan.

Prudence's frown deepened, her eyes narrowing with that old suspicion that I hadn't seen in the past few days. She pulled her hand out of my grip, and she was strong enough that there was nothing I could do to hold it. "Don't play, Fortitude," she spit. "You know that there's nothing Mother would do except wonder why we bothered to ask her. This dog has yapped at our heels for years, and it was only for your sake that he wasn't taken care of long before now. Now he has seen truths that were not meant for him." Her lip curled. "If it's weakness that drives you, just turn your head. It will be done in a moment."

She turned back to Matt, and I knew that there was nothing I could do—I couldn't persuade her; I couldn't overpower her. Even Suze looked at me and slowly shook her head, knowing even better than I did that this had been a foregone conclusion the moment Matt had somehow found his way to the park and stepped foot in the clearing.

There was nothing I could do.

But that wasn't true.

I pressed the Colt against my sister's head, just at her temple. She froze at the feeling, and her brilliant blue eyes darted over to stare at me, and her jaw loosened in shock.

"What are you doing?" she asked, the shock already wearing off, replaced quickly by a brewing rage that promised to be far deadlier than what we had just faced from the elves. "You can't possibly be serious."

"Don't push me, Prudence," I warned her, and I knew in that long moment that I was capable of pulling that trigger, and looking into her eyes I knew that she knew as well. "Remember what happened to Luca."

Her upper lip curled and revealed her fully extended fangs. But I kept my arm steady, not even daring to breathe, and one slow step at a time, Prudence drew back from Matt.

I kept the Colt raised, lifting a second hand to steady my grip, and watched as she moved away.

"You are right in one small way, brother," she said, never glancing away from me. "All decisions truly rest with our mother. But who will be the first to present this one to her?" And with that my sister turned and ran up the path to where the cars were parked.

I glanced down frantically. Matt was staring at me, an expression on his face that I couldn't even bear to process, but Suze had dropped beside him and pressed her hands against his arm again. "Go!" she yelled at me. "I can handle this."

Behind me I felt a sharp push, and Lilah was behind me, nodding in agreement with Suze. "You need to get there first," she agreed.

I didn't need any more than that, and I was running up the path after Prudence, running faster than I knew I should've been able to, and I could feel the tendons in my legs shrieking with pain at the demands I was placing on them twice in one night. I reached the parking lot just as Prudence was backing up her Lexus in a cascade of gravel, and I was inside the Fiesta just as she pulled out.

As if sensing my need, the Fiesta started on the first attempt—something it hadn't managed at any point in the past two years. Without even pausing I threw it into reverse, and the tires squealed in protest as I set off in pursuit, beginning the long journey to Newport.

# Chapter 11

Despite all its efforts, the Fiesta's engine was no match for what was under the hood in my sister's Lexus, and every time we hit a straight patch of road she slid easily ahead of me. But I'd driven the route from Providence to Newport more times in the past few months than she probably had in the last decade, and I knew every passing zone, every banked turn, and every side road that I could slide down and make up a minute while she fumed at a light. She was also restricted by the apparent desire to not overly flout the speed limit and risk a ticket, which helped keep us close enough that fifty anxious, sweaty minutes later, she was less than a car length in front of me as we squealed down Ocean Drive and turned into our mother's driveway.

She was out of the Lexus first and running toward the front door, and I didn't even turn the Fiesta off as I stumbled out of the driver's seat and chased her, ignoring the steam that was rising from under its hood as I raced across the white gravel drive and took the pretty marble steps in one bone-jarring jump. I could feel the throb of my mother's presence upstairs, but Chivalry wasn't there—a frightening thought, and my heart pounded even harder at the knowledge that I'd be arguing for Matt's life without the help of my brother.

Inside the foyer, I caught sight of Prudence's disappearing figure as she darted down the hallway that led to the back of the house. I hesitated for a moment, unsure why she was going in the wrong direction when the pull of my mother's presence was clearly coming from upstairs. But I shook my head, thanking my own unusual good luck, and ran toward the marble staircase that swept elegantly to the second floor.

I'd just reached the landing halfway up the stairs when an enormous crash and a scream echoed from the direction that my sister had taken, and I turned around and was pounding down the steps and toward the sound before I even stopped to ponder what could possibly be happening. The truth was that I had no idea, so I simply let the instinctual knowledge that whatever side trip Prudence had chosen could not possibly bode well for me drive my decision-making process.

The sound led me to the small butler's pantry that Madeline had constructed around the basement door that led to my host father, Henry's, cell. A member of the staff was always on duty here, making a show of polishing my mother's incredible assortment of silver while actually standing guard over the most closely guarded secret of the house. Now the door to the basement was hanging open and the staff member on guard, Patricia, an older woman who'd been in my mother's employment since her teens, was rolling on the ground, her upper body hunched around her arm, which was bent at an unnatural angle. Her polishing rag and one of the largest soup tureens lay on the parquet floor beside her.

"Oh, Mr. Scott," she gasped when she saw me, even in extremis being unable to call me by my first name. "Your sister—" And then she looked at the yawning door. Whoever was posted in the butler's pantry had control of the key that unlocked the door to the basement—it was a position given to only the most trusted of Madeline's staff members, the ones who had been with her the longest. If she said that someone wasn't allowed downstairs—even one of her own children—then whoever was posted there would obey. The key was still sticking out of the lock—apparently Prudence had taken it from Patricia and let herself in.

I shouted loudly for help, and, already hearing the scattered footsteps of some of the other staff, hopped over Patricia's recumbent form and ran down the basement steps as quickly as I could. There were plenty of people on hand at any hour who could hold Patricia's hand and call an ambulance, but whatever was going on down there was something that could only be left to the family.

At the bottom of the steps was the kind of serious security door preferred by banks or secret military prisons on television. Normally it opened only after it had scanned an authorized thumbprint, but apparently my sister hadn't been on the short list, because now the heavy metal door had been ripped half off its hinges and hung drunkenly from the ones that remained. I pushed my way past the remains and hurried into the sitting room of my host father's caretaker, Mr. Albert.

Mr. Albert was built along the same lines as a Sherman tank, and in the years before he came to work for my mother he had earned a living as a professional wrestler. I'd known him since infancy, and even on my wiggliest days as a toddler, when he told me to be quiet, I'd obeyed. Now, like Patricia one floor above him, he was pulling himself off the ground. One full wall of his sitting room was made completely out of glass so that he could observe Henry's behavior at all times, and through the glass I could see my sister walking quickly toward the enclosure where my host father lived.

I yelled my sister's name, but she didn't respond. I watched as she walked across the red line painted across the floor that no one except Mr. Albert or my mother were allowed to cross—largely for our own safety.

In his cage, Henry prowled as Prudence approached him. With his patrician features and dark hair with dignified wings of gray at his temples, Henry could've passed for any of the Boston Brahman politicians that my mother regularly entertained over dinner, except for the white surgical scrubs that he wore and the complete lack of sanity in his eyes. While Henry had fathered me in the traditional sense, every drop of blood that flowed through his veins belonged to my mother in a very literal way; he had been bled out and had her blood pumped into him, a process that had altered him physiologically right down to the DNA, leaving him changed enough to breed with my similarly changed host mother, but it had shattered his mind, leaving him pathologically homicidal. Over the years that he'd been imprisoned in Madeline's basement, even as he lived in a plastic cube with every interaction monitored more closely than the moon landing, he had killed two people.

And he was my tie to humanity, his life the last barrier between me and the full transition. My host mother, Grace's, suicide had begun the process, and Henry's death would finish it.

A horrible suspicion filled me, and I ran past Mr. Albert, calling Prudence's name again, but she didn't even glance backward. Reaching out with both hands, she gripped the edges of the door that kept Henry contained, and with a visible effort ripped it open, peeling it back from its locks like the top of a sardine container.

Henry was loose the moment the door was wide enough for him to pass through. Prudence reached for him, her deadly intent clear, but the changes my mother's blood had wrought on Henry's body revealed themselves when he moved quickly out of the range of her hands, then drove one fist into her stomach with enough power to knock a vampire more than two centuries old back and against the wall. The sight of that froze me where I stood—I'd faced a host before and with Suze's help I'd killed him, but this was Henry. Respect for his strange twilight part of my existence had always been thoroughly twined with the danger he posed to me. I'd never touched either of my host parents— they'd always been strange, piteous, yet frightening presences behind separating walls. And when Henry raced toward me with a speed that was not quite a vampire's but all too close, I found myself unable to move.

But he wasn't coming for me. I felt the breeze as he moved past me, close enough that I could've touched him had I not been as useful as Lot's wife post-saltification, but his target was Mr. Albert. With the loyalty of twenty years, Mr. Albert had pulled himself off the floor where Prudence had thrown him, collected his stun gun, and come to do his duty and contain Henry.

There were medals on the walls of Mr. Albert's sitting room from a grateful nation that attested to his courage, but there was fear on his face as Henry came toward him. I finally moved, realizing the danger, but too late. Mr. Albert's stun gun did its job, administering a jolt of electricity that filled the room with the smell of burned ozone and singed hair, but even as Henry's shoulders spasmed, his hands never stopped moving, ripping at Mr. Albert's chest with unnatural strength, just as his mouth closed on Mr. Albert's throat, then opened again as he began his best attempt to eat his jailor alive. And then Mr. Albert's screams filled the room.

I wrapped my hands around Henry's broad shoulders and yanked backward as hard as I could, but he gave a low growl and held on with all the stubborn strength of a dog with a bone.

I couldn't move Henry, and the wet, masticating sounds he was making were a horrible complement to Mr. Albert's screams. I threw all my weight into pulling Henry, managing only to shift both of them a few inches, as Henry was not loosening his grip.

"Prudence," I screamed, desperate enough to appeal to her. "Help me!"

She was there then, her face unreadable as she responded to my plea, and somehow the two of us pulled Henry off, and with a grunt she flung him off Mr. Albert and a few feet away. Mr. Albert fell to the ground, and I dropped to my knees, desperately trying to decide where I should press my hands and administer pressure in the mass of blood that was now his throat and chest, even as his eyes rolled horribly and only small, strangled noises emerged from his throat.

"What are you doing?" I begged my sister, putting my hands over Mr. Albert's heart almost at random. "Why are you doing this?"

Then I was suddenly lifted by the collar of my shirt and shaken with enough force to feel my brain slosh in my skull. My sister's face thrust just an inch away from my own, and she glared into my eyes as I hung from her hand like a misbehaving puppy.

"This is for your own welfare, Fortitude," she ground out as she glared at me, "and I will not have you continue to *interfere*!" With that she threw me hard, and for a second I was completely airborne before I slammed against the wall, my head giving a sickening thud. I slid down, dazed and blinking, all the breath knocked out of my lungs and unable to do anything except watch as my sister stalked forward toward where Henry was crouched.

Henry fought and even landed a few more blows, but with no further distractions my sister quickly emerged on top. Long cuts on Henry's face and arms oozed unnaturally dark and viscous blood, and when my sister wrapped one hand around his throat and drew her other back for the killing blow, Henry actually seemed to relax in her grip and wait for the inevitable.

But the blow didn't fall—Prudence's hand was caught and held by Madeline, who had moved so quickly that in my rattled state I hadn't even registered her approach. Now my tiny, ancient mother stood holding Prudence's hand, and her rage was so deep that for the first time in my life I saw my mother's glowing blue eyes change to black pools.

"My will was clear," Madeline growled, and neither her Barbara Bush haircut nor her conservative pink housedress could conceal that this was an alpha predator. Those long, fixed fangs gleamed under the harsh fluorescent lights. "Why have you crossed me?"

Prudence didn't loosen her grip on Henry's neck, and her needlelike fangs were fully extended when she snarled back at my mother. "Whether it is sentimentality or ego that holds you back, it is enough. Fortitude's transition has been held back for two decades, and I am saying *enough*. Perhaps it is too late; maybe he's ruined—more human than vampire. But I am putting a stop to your games."

With her free hand Madeline swiped at her daughter, and Prudence dropped Henry to block it. Henry lay on his side, not moving as far as I could see, but that dark blood was staining even more of his formerly white scrubs, and I was unable to see from my vantage point whether he stayed still out of passivity or because of injury.

Madeline and Prudence had now locked hands, each pushing against the other with enough effort to outline every muscle in their arms. Both women were sweating heavily enough that their hair looked like they'd just emerged from the shower, their hands shaking wildly with their effort. For an endless moment neither could move the other and they were locked in place, but then there was movement and it was from my mother. It was so slow that at first I thought I was imagining it, but then I realized what I was seeing—Prudence was pushing our mother's arms backward. She was winning.

I saw the moment that Prudence realized it herself—the flare of triumph across her face. But then Madeline gave a low growl that seemed to emerge from the floor beneath her feet, and her black eyes began to glow. When she pushed again, it was with a strength that my sister couldn't match, and Prudence was forced back and then down. First into a small crouch, then down until her knees touched the cement floor and she was kneeling before my mother, gasping with the effort. Madeline continued pushing, hard resolve on her face, until an awful cracking filled the room and Prudence's hands flopped backward on identically broken wrists.

A howl of pain emerged from my sister's throat and she seemed to fold inside herself. My mother stood still for several heartbeats, her chest heaving as she wobbled on her feet. Those gleaming black eyes bled down again to her natural blue, but somehow her eyes seemed duller than usual, as if the conflict had exhausted her on more than a physical level.

Madeline stared down at Prudence as if nothing in the room existed, from me crumpled against the wall, just barely able to lift myself to my elbows, to Mr. Albert's mangled body, now horribly still, to Henry, still crouched where my sister had dropped him. Her rage was gone, and when she spoke to Prudence, our mother's voice was actually tender. "My darling, my dove, my daughter," she crooned, looking down at Prudence. "So strong, and almost ready to leave my nest. But not today, love." And one of her hands flashed out and another crack filled the room, followed immediately by my sister's agonized scream as Madeline broke her leg at the thigh, the bone protruding horribly from the wound. "And not tomorrow," Madeline continued, her voice still gentle even as she kicked out with one foot and Prudence's ribs snapped. "My will is still your law." She looked down at my sister and then leaned down to run the tips of her fingers so lovingly over Prudence's cheek. There was a strange, fierce pride written across my mother's face. "But soon, dearest, very soon now," she promised. Then she straightened up, or as straight as her age-slumped shoulders could achieve, and with a stern nod said, "Now go," in a tone that brooked no dissent.

And Prudence went. There was no walking on her horribly broken leg, so my sister crawled, pulling herself one painful inch at a time across the floor. My mother didn't say another word, simply watching my sister's agonizing progression. I pulled myself into a sitting position as she passed, my head finally ceasing its spinning, and Prudence looked at me just once as she crawled out of the room, leaving a long, red trail behind her.

My sister had once joyfully sent me to what she had hoped would be my death. Over the past few days she had been my strangely willing ally. And now I had stopped her from killing Matt and then Henry. In that one look there had been rage, plus a venomous dollop of bitterness and betrayal, but there had also been something else in the way that she had looked at me, something that my mind shuddered back from even naming. Because what she'd done tonight in defying our mother, she had done, somehow, in my name and for my sake. I shivered at the sight of what I'd seen in that look, because part of it had been the same kind of love that I was used to seeing from Chivalry, and it terrified me. I watched in silence as she left.

Madeline came over to me, pressing her wrinkled hands against my face and cataloging every injury, clucking as she saw the long slashes that the skinwalker had left in my forearms an hour and a half and a lifetime ago. But apparently finding me in no truly concerning condition, she gave me a small pat on my head and went to where Henry lay.

Irritation crossed her face as she looked down at him, and she poked at the open wounds that Prudence had given him with one finger, testing how deep and serious they were. Henry didn't blink even when her questing finger dipped to the second knuckle, instead just lying limply and staring at her. Madeline gave a grumpy huff when she finished assessing his injuries.

"Back to your cage, Henry," she ordered flatly. "You'll need my attention, but I'll put you back together later."

Like a puppet, he stood at her command and shuffled back into his cage, stepped around its ruined door, and crossed to its center, where he sat down heavily. His weird gaze found my mother again and watched her, unblinking. I'd never seen my mother interact with my host parents before, and it was disturbing, as if her presence had removed those last shreds of a personality that still clung like spiderwebs to the inside of his brain.

Ignoring her creature, Madeline finally crossed over to Mr. Albert's body, leaning down and pressing her palm briefly to his forehead. "Ah, Albert," she sighed, "faithful to the last." The regret in her voice was real. I only wished that the regret had been more than that of the lady of the manor memorializing the death of a loyal hound.

"Tell me why this happened." My voice sounded strange in my own ears. It was hoarse, as if I'd been screaming, but I knew that I hadn't been. And there was no entreaty or request—it was a demand. I'd never used that tone with my mother. I hadn't been aware that my voice was even capable of that tone in the same room as my mother.

Madeline swung her head toward me and slowly straightened up from Mr. Albert's body. Whatever she saw in me was enough that when she answered, she didn't bother to pretend to misunderstand me. "Your sister wished to complete your transition."

"Now tell me the rest," I said. "Tell me what she meant about my transition being held back. Tell me what she meant by it ruining me. Tell me how you *made me different*. Tell me everything."

"Everything, my darling sparrow?" Her eyes narrowed and became speculative. "Perhaps, my son. Perhaps." She held out one deceptively fragile hand, the skin pulled tight against the knuckles and age spots dotting it. "Give me your arm, Fortitude. Escort me back to my rooms, and we will have a conversation."

I hauled myself painfully to my feet and the room spun around me at first, but it quickly steadied. I touched one hand tentatively to the back of my skull and could feel the blood matting my hair, but after a moment I felt better. Not good by any stretch of the imagination—every part of my body felt battered and various levels of painful or sore. But I could walk, and I went to my mother and offered my arm in the best gentlemanly manner that my brother had drilled into me. We walked out together, and it quickly became apparent that there was more than etiquette at play here—in sharp contrast to how she had come down to the basement, now my mother was distinctly weak and wobbly, more and more of her weight resting on me as we continued. The walk to her rooms was slow, and as we arrived back into the main house we were surrounded by a horde of the staff members, all quietly and efficiently descending with mops and scrubbing rags to remove all signs of the conflict that had taken place. I saw one woman down on her hands and knees, carefully wiping up the blood trail that my sister had left as she passed this same way. It ended at the top of the stairs, so I could assume that some of the staff had carried Prudence the rest of the way to her old rooms. A pair of grim-faced men armed with tranquilizer guns brushed past us and headed down the stairs into the basement, followed at a distance by a small fleet of outdoor staff members carrying sheets of plywood to serve as temporary doors. But there was no running or yelling, and every staff member we passed nodded their heads and greeted us respectfully.

Eventually we reached Madeline's mother-of-pearl-gilded sitting room, and I gently assisted her into her favorite pink satin armchair. She relaxed into it with a grateful sigh, for once relaxing the excellent posture that had been drilled into her from centuries of corsets. There was a red light blinking from a small, innocuous device on her side table that I had never quite noticed before, and I realized that Mr. Albert must've hit the panic button in his room at some point, which was how she'd known to come downstairs and save the day.

I eased myself down onto the sofa, not worrying whether I might leave stains on it. People had died tonight. The sofa could be reupholstered. I watched my mother and waited.

For a moment Madeline paused, seeming to sink even farther into her armchair. She gestured to the table in front of us, where her favorite Sevres tea service was set up on a tray, the pot still steaming gently. Apparently this was the activity that she had interrupted to come downstairs. Without saying anything, I leaned over and poured a cup of tea, then passed it over to her. She nodded her thanks and took a long sip, then swallowed carefully and began speaking.

"Our kind has always been slow to mature, slow to reproduce." Her voice was slow and almost academic, and I hung on every word. "When my grandfather was young, it was not uncommon for a vampire to boast four offspring over the course of a lifetime, but by the time I was ready to leave my own nest and establish a territory, two offspring was something to strive for. I came to this new land, where no other vampires lived, and when I was ready I brooded— and was rewarded with Prudence. I followed all the old traditions with her—when she was born, I killed both of her host parents, and their blood was her first meal when she was less than an hour old. And she is everything that I as a parent could've wished for, everything that our kind hold ideal—she is intelligent and vicious and a survivor."

She paused and took another long drink from her teacup. I measured what she had told me and said, "But that's not how you made me."

Madeline set the teacup down carefully in its saucer. "No," she agreed. "Because Prudence is my pride and my joy, but she is not what our species needs." She put the saucer decisively down onto its tray and sat back in the chair, her posture perfect and elegant again, and steepled her fingers. "Humans have always vastly outnumbered our kind, but that is as natural and acceptable as deer outnumbering wolves. They were not a threat. This began to change when technology developed and the humans became more organized. Our kind slipped into the shadows, just as most other sentient or magical species did, and any who did not at once learned their lesson during the Inquisition or the witch burnings. To many we are a myth, and that is safe. But it has never been possible to hide our existence from all—some are useful, and when properly deployed can serve in their own way or maintain the secrets. But others know what we are, and seek to kill us. As technology passed from wooden clubs to steel swords, from swords to pistols, those who sought to kill our kind found success easier to attain, and there were those who died. When I was a child in my mother's castle, our kind did not find this a cause for concern—many who died were young or stupid or weak. The strong remained, and we fought among ourselves for territory or prizes, not fearing a decline in our kind at first, for too many assumed that stronger offspring would be brooded to replace the dead. And there were so many that were foolishly squandered and lost . . . my own first fledgling, my little girl, killed at barely half a century over a squabble. I left England then. . . ."

She went silent for a long moment, frowning. I didn't say anything. She almost never talked about Constance, my sister who had died in England before Rhode Island had even been granted the royal charter that brought it into existence. Then Madeline seemed to shake herself out of older thoughts, and continued. "I crossed an ocean, settled in a new land, had another daughter to replace what I'd lost, but I was paying attention. And even we who live as long as we do can stand to learn the lessons of a new age and join them with the lessons of history. There were wolves in the forests of England when I was a child—great wolves. But they were long gone at the dawn of the 1800s, hunted to extinction. Other extinctions were happening in this time, and I realized that our species was very precariously perched. We are long in maturing, longer in reproducing. As great as we are, we are vulnerable."

This made sense to me. "An apex predator," I suggested. "Like a great white shark."

Madeline nodded. "Precisely. The words for what we needed would not come until Darwin's studies, but I had already realized before the *Beagle* sailed that what we needed was to change. To adapt. So when your brother was born, I killed the host father at birth, but I left the host mother alive until he was twenty. I discovered that her life held his transition at bay—your sister, like me, transitioned naturally as she left childhood and passed through puberty. But for your brother it did not happen until the day his host mother died."

I stared. I'd known for months that something about me was different from the average vampire, but I'd had no idea that my brother was also different. "Chivalry . . . ?"

"Yes. And you can see the differences. His lack of fixated self-interest, his devotion to his wives, the real love he feels for them. This is different. The bonds between vampires are always strong from parent to child, but less within the sibling nest—more from socialization than instinct—and beyond that there is rarely anything."

I was confused. "So, by leaving both Henry and Grace alive . . . by having Jill and Brian raise me . . . you wanted me to be able to *love*?" The thought set my foundations, not to mention everything I'd ever thought of my mother, reeling.

Madeline chuckled softly, amused. "You make me sound like such a romantic, darling. No, love for your fellow man and the empathy that seems to hound you to the point of immobility were side effects that must be lived with." The smile disappeared from her face, and she was entirely serious again. "No, my darling. I wanted you to have self-control, and an understanding of humans and their behavior that your sister and I, and even your brother, lack."

"Did your experiment work?" I asked.

A slow smile that had nothing to do with humor and nothing particularly nice about it spread across my mother's face. "Who can say for sure, my darling? Transition, despite your sister's best efforts, has not been completed. Who can know what butterfly will emerge from your chrysalis?" I shuddered as the realization of how much I could lose, and how close I'd come to losing it tonight, filled me. Madeline's sharp eyes caught it, and her smile widened. In deceptively gentle tones, she asked, "Now, why don't you tell me what action you took that so enraged your sister that she would defy me in such a way? I find myself quite curious."

There was no point trying to lie to her or to sugarcoat the situation. I knew that Prudence would be only too eager to fill in any gaps that I left, and in the worst way possible, so I forced myself to tell my mother the unvarnished truth about what had happened with Matt, what he had seen, and how I had stopped Prudence from killing him. The smile was long gone from Madeline's face when I finished—she was grim, and her lip had curled back from those long fangs. Clearly she was very unhappy and the focus of that unhappiness was on me, not my sister. There was a long silence when I finished, broken only by the soft sound of my mother tapping a nail thoughtfully against one of those heavy fangs. It was a creepy sight and an even creepier sound. I waited, barely able to breathe, knowing that Matt's life hung in the balance.

When Madeline finally spoke, it was slow and almost reluctant. "You are close to an adult," she began, her blue eyes considering as she assessed me. "I will let you make this decision—but remember that he and his actions are your responsibility now. If Mr. McMahon is dangerous to us, you will have to kill him. Not me. Not your sister. Not even your brother. *You*."

I nodded as a surge of relief filled me, followed almost immediately by an equally strong rush of dread. Everything rested now on whether I could convince Matt to keep quiet and hide the explosive truth that he'd seen in the clearing. I wasn't sure if I could live with myself if I had to kill Matt—frankly, I wished I could be sure that I wouldn't be able to—but at least this was a chance. Such a slim one, but if Matt could be persuaded not to talk . . . if, if, if. But it was a chance, and I grabbed at it with both hands, even if its edges were as sharp as knives.

"Okay," I said simply.

All of the energy seemed to drain out of my mother, and she leaned completely back into the chair, almost sinking into the cushions. Her blue eyes were strangely drained, and the color looked almost gray. Exhaustion was suddenly clear in every part of her, as was her immense age. She waved one thin hand vaguely. "Off you go, then, my darling. Much to do. Your brother can handle everything else here." A moment later I could feel the thump inside of myself that indicated that Chivalry had just entered the mansion, and I wondered how long my mother had been aware of his approach.

I left quietly. Madeline's eyes were already drooping as I eased the door closed. I hurried down the hall, knowing that I needed to get back to Providence as soon as I could and see what was waiting for mc on that side. I passed Chivalry on the staircase. From the expression on his face my brother clearly knew that something was very wrong, and he gave a wordless shout at the sight of me, but I shook my head and moved past him.

"I'm sorry," I said, not slowing down. "I can't stop and talk. Mother will tell you everything."

The Fiesta was still running in the driveway where I'd left it. Thankfully, the engine had stopped steaming, but when I put the car in gear and headed out the driveway there was a very new and deeply unhappy rattling sound from the engine, a clear sign that there would be many consequences for what had happened tonight. I pulled out onto Ocean Drive slowly, babying the car, and praying that it would get me all the way home. I couldn't imagine what kind of figure I would present to a AAA tow driver.

I'd shoved the Colt under my seat for safekeeping, and now I retrieved it and dropped it on the passenger's seat after checking to see that the safety was engaged. Then I picked up my phone and called Suzume, wondering what had been happening in Providence during my own adventures in Newport.

I could hear the question in her voice the moment she answered on her end, but she didn't ask whether Matt was doomed or not. Instead she simply told me that they were both in my apartment, waiting for me. Lilah was gone, having had to take Felix and Iris home. I thanked her and let her know that I was on the road and that I'd be there as soon as I could.

"Oh, and one last thing," Suze said just as I'd been about to hang up. "Apparently your Fiesta is hot."

"What?" The Fiesta had been called many things, but never that.

"That's how Matt knew where to find us. At some point he stuck a GPS tracker on the Fiesta. When you talked with him this morning he realized that you were still holding out on him, and he spent the rest of the day tailing us. So that's how he was able to arrive like the cavalry."

"Shit," I said, but I was too tired to put any force behind

it. I'd wondered briefly how Matt had somehow found us, but had frankly had far too many other pressing topics on my mind (primarily how to keep him alive) to fully explore the topic. "Okay, I'm coming back." We exchanged good-byes, and I hung up.

The drive back was very slow, the Fiesta making progressively louder noises of protest as we went. I was exhausted, my head splitting from my trip against the wall, the slices on my arm throbbing, and a thousand other sore spots making themselves known in a general miasma of misery. And I would've gladly spent a year in this condition, with no hope of even a bottle of hydrogen peroxide to clean out my cuts, in exchange for not having to face Matt.

When I finally limped home, the Fiesta gave a sputtering rattle when I turned the key in the parking lot of my building. I gave the steering wheel a pat—it was very clear that the Fiesta would need a long visit with my mechanic before it drove me anywhere again. Matt's big Buick was in the parking spot next to mine, so it was clear how Suzume had gotten everyone away from the park.

I climbed the three flights of stairs to my apartment very slowly, but finally there was no putting the moment off any longer, and I let myself into the apartment.

Matt was tied to a chair in the middle of my living room. Suzume's creepy hostage kit was still riding in her duffel bag in the trunk of the Fiesta, but she had apparently been quite willing to MacGyver herself a solution, and Matt was tied up with several of my long tube socks and the two formal ties that usually lived in the back of my closet. It should've been funny, but the closed, hostile expression on Matt's face when he looked at me kept any part of it from being humorous. The left sleeve of his shirt had been cut off, and there was a clean white bandage wrapped around the spot where the half-blood elf had cut him with the butcher knife.

Suze was sitting on the sofa, within easy grabbing distance if Matt showed any signs of wiggling out of his bonds, but she got up immediately when I came into the room, her face very carefully set in neutral lines.

I paused for a long moment at the door. I'd spent the

entire drive over thinking about what I would do and what I could say, but all of my carefully prepared speeches flew out of my mind.

"Suze," I said quietly. "Can you give us some privacy?"

Those dark eyes bored into me, trying to figure out what I had planned, but I knew that she failed, because I didn't even know myself. Then she nodded and walked past me and out the door. I heard her footsteps going down the steps as I pushed the door closed behind her, and I realized that she was actually doing what I'd asked—going far enough away that she couldn't hear what we said.

I pulled another chair away from my battered table and sat in front of Matt. He still said nothing, just studying me with those opaque cop eyes of his.

I took a deep breath and started talking.

It wasn't what I'd planned, but at that moment I did what felt like the only right thing to do—I told the truth.

I told him the truth about the Grann murders. I told him the truth about how Jill and Brian had been killed. I told him the truth about what I was, and the things that lived in the world under a veneer of normalcy. I told him everything.

As I did it, I knew that it was probably the stupidest thing I could've done. I also knew that it was the only thing I could've done.

He didn't say a word, simply listening stone-faced as I upended everything he'd woken up knowing this morning. And when I was done I leaned forward and untied him, then sat back and waited for his response.

At first he just looked at me, as if he'd never seen me before in his life. Then he leaned forward, very slowly and deliberately, and put his hand on my jaw. I knew what he was looking for, and I opened my mouth, forcing myself into passivity as I felt his thumb push my upper lip aside to reveal my teeth. I waited while he examined me, and when he finally took his hand away from my face, I said quietly, "I don't have the fangs yet. But I will when I'm older."

"Did Brian know what you are?" It was Matt's first question, and it struck me hard. Unable to speak, I just shook my head.

"How many people know about ... about all of this?" Now Matt got up from the chair and began pacing the room, and I could see the first edges of anger rolling in, like dark clouds before a storm.

"A few," I said. Then, looking at him, I repeated urgently, "Matt, you can't tell *anyone.*"

"Or what?" His voice was cold as he glared across the room at me. "Your sister will kill me?"

"No." I swallowed, then said the words. "It would have to be me." Matt froze in his steps and stared. "That was the deal I made tonight to keep you safe. But you have to be careful."

His face was frozen. "Would you do that, Fort?" Matt asked slowly. "Would you kill me if I was a threat?"

The question hung in the air between us. I paused, then said, almost begging, "It's not just my safety, Matt—" And I broke off because suddenly Matt's cop mask broke and I saw what lay beneath—the hurt, the stricken betrayal—and I knew the mistake I'd just made. "Damnit, I can't just act for myself!" I yelled.

"But that's who I always acted for, Fort. For you." Matt's words fell between us like stones. His voice dropped, became very quiet, but I shivered at his expression. He meant every word. "Don't call me," he said. "I'm not a danger to you. But we're done. Right now, this second. We're done."

I started to say something, anything, trying to deny what had just happened, but he wasn't listening to me anymore. I reached for Matt when he crossed the room past me, but it was as if my hands didn't even exist, like I wasn't there anymore. Then he was out the door, closing it gently behind himself, and his footsteps echoed briefly from the hallway and were gone.

Matt was gone.

# Chapter 12

I was on the couch when Suze came back up into the apartment. I didn't know how much time had passed since Matt had walked out—all I knew was the numb, broken feeling that filled me.

Suzume didn't ask any questions. Since she would've seen Matt leave, maybe there weren't any questions to ask. Instead she silently took me by the hand and led me into the bathroom, where she sat me down on the side of the tub and began the meticulous job of locating, cleaning, and bandaging all of the various cuts and bruises I'd accumulated that evening.

I studied her as she used surgical tape to carefully attach long gauze pads in place over the long cuts that Soli had left along each of my arms. Bruises mottled her own face, and cuts ringed the knuckles of her hands.

"Haven't you shifted yet?" I asked quietly. Those visible signs of the damage she'd taken herself in the fight could've been long gone if she'd returned to her four-legged form.

She shook her head, splashing yet another cotton ball with a few drops of iodine. "I can do it later," she assured me, then leaned forward to dab the iodine against a cut on my forehead that I hadn't even been aware of.

When I was fully bandaged, she led me into my room. My Ithaca 37 was on the bed, and I looked over at Suze in surprise. I remembered it being knocked out of my hand during the fight with Soli, but I had assumed that it was lost. Suzume gave a casual shrug. "We had some downtime before we had to leave the clearing, and I found it in the grass where you'd dropped it."

"Thank you," I said, but she turned away and began to fuss over pulling down the sheets, and then pestered me until I got into the bed and allowed her to tuck me in like an infant.

"This isn't going to help," I said softly, when she'd finished.

"Just go to sleep," she urged. "Everything will be easier to deal with in the morning."

There was something in her face that made me reach out and catch her hand as she turned to go, some strange hint of withdrawal. "Are you leaving?" I asked.

"Yeah," she said, not quite looking at me. "You'll be okay. I got a call from Lilah when you were driving up from Newport. Your brother already called all the elves left, and just about everyone else in the community he could get a number for. Madeline laid down her punishment, and Lilah's sure that no one will be coming for you."

I stared at her, trying to decipher the look on her face. Certainty filled me. "That isn't it," I said. "Why are you leaving?"

She finally met my eyes, but she was in full poker face mode now. "Lilah said to tell you that she'll call you in a few days once she gets everything settled with the Neighbors."

"What does that have to do with anything?" I asked, but she just gave me one long look and left the room. I heard the front door close behind her.

Too much had happened tonight for my brain to process this last curveball. I got out of bed and padded to the front door, throwing the slide bar and checking the locks. Then I crossed back to my bedroom. Reaching under the bed, I grabbed the old pair of slippers that served as my spare ammo container, and pulled out a few bullets for the .45 and a set of shells for the Ithaca, and carefully loaded both guns. I checked the safety on my Colt and slid it under the extra pillow on my bed. The Ithaca I placed on the floor, within easy reach of a quick grab. Then I got back into the bed and listened to the silence of the apartment.

I would've thought that sleep would never come, but my

exhausted body had other ideas. I closed my eyes on a blink, and I was asleep.

I felt every bump, scrape, and pulled muscle the next morning, and I hobbled around the apartment like an old man, dry-swallowing aspirin and surrounding myself on the couch with a combination of soft quilts and bags of numbing ice cubes.

As it turned out, I had nowhere to go. When I called into work to ask if someone else could cover my shift, I discovered that I'd already been fired. Apparently I'd been scheduled to work the full dinner shift the previous night, but I'd been so focused on what had been happening that Peláez had never even crossed my mind. I was unemployed again, at the start of yet another dual job-and-roommate hunt.

I decided that I could take a few days before I started looking and worrying about my situation. I swallowed another aspirin, curled up on the couch, and put on my *Firefly* DVDs.

I napped a lot that first afternoon, letting my body heal. The only interruption to my quiet day occurred when my brother called me in the early evening, telling me that we would be taking a Sunday afternoon sail with Bhumika on the *Gay Belle*. I tried my best to get out of it, pointing out that the Fiesta was in no condition to be driven and I had no money to pay a mechanic. In a voice that brooked no dissention, Chivalry told me that he'd come and pick me up. With no escape, I finally gave in.

I left four messages on Suzume's phone, but she never picked up. I felt both annoyed and a little worried, but my feelings were allayed when I opened my door that night. Instead of the pizza I'd been expecting, a guy about five inches shorter than me but around my own age offered his hand and a polite smile. "Hi. I'm sorry that I was running a little late, but my study group ran long." He shook the hand that I'd automatically extended.

"Um . . ." I racked my brain but was still lost. Next to his rich brown skin tone, I felt as pasty as a fish's underbelly. Bad luck that I'd never been able to get even the slightest tan. "Are you sure you have the right apartment?"

He looked startled, glanced at my door number, then back at me. "Yeah, number three above the bra shop. I'm Dan Tabak." I stared at him blankly. He dropped my hand and the polite smile, now looking annoyed. "We've been e-mailing all week about the apartment."

Comprehension dawned—after all, Suze had said she'd find me a roommate. I looked at him closer—he was working a level of stubble that on me would look hungover, but on him looked like he probably had a special setting on an expensive razor. His short and curly black hair had an impressive level of coif, and I was trying not to feel self-conscious that I was in my pajamas with bandages up both arms and a black eye while he looked red-carpet ready in a pair of business slacks and an indigo blue dress shirt with just the collar button undone.

He was also distinctly irritated with me. "Listen, you said in the e-mail that you had a room for rent. If you reconsidered, then you could've let me know before I drove—" He pulled out a piece of paper from his pocket, which I snagged and glanced over. On the page were directions to the apartment, sent from my own e-mail account. Apparently Suzume *had* figured out my password, since I knew I'd never used *Laters* as a closing in my life. I smiled—Suze had found me a nonhuman roommate, just like she'd said she would. And delivered him to me, true to form, as a Hollis-special prank.

Dan was still good and pissed, but I cut him off. "My last roommate was murdered, but most of the people responsible got killed last night—a few of them by me. My best friend is a kitsune, so she set this whole thing up without telling me, which is why I don't know who or what the hell you are, but the room is move-in ready. We go fifty-fifty on rent and utilities, due first of the month. You get half of the storage space in the basement. Parking is in the back, and if you want to use it you have to talk with the landlord about renting a spot. I don't know if Suze told you, but I'm Fortitude Scott, so be sure that you're okay with that."

There was a long pause while he processed it. Then, "Of course I know who you are." He huffed an annoyed breath, like a bird settling ruffled feathers. "And I'm a smoker."

"That's fine as long as you only do it outside or on the fire escape."

"And a law student at Johnson and Wales U."

"The commute there is easy."

"And a ghoul."

I paused. Chivalry had told me about the ghouls, who required a regular diet of human flesh to survive, but I'd never actually met one before. He'd assured me that they were actually one of the lower-key species in the community, very rarely breaking rules or making waves, but I couldn't contain a small mental *ew* response. I eyed Dan again—he sure didn't look (or *smell*) like what my mental image of a ghoul had been, so I clarified, "So you eat . . . ?"

"Human organs, yes." He rolled his eyes at my ignorance. "But since I'm a *ghoul*, not a *Wendigo*, I get them from the morgue or a funeral home." He cut off my next question. "Yes, I keep them in regular butcher paper so you don't have to see them, and, *yes*, I label them so you don't have to worry about eating them by accident." Something in the way he rattled off that list made me wonder how many other supernatural creatures weren't exactly lining up to be a ghoul's roommate.

"Oh, that wouldn't happen," I assured him automatically. "I'm a vegetarian."

He looked taken aback for the first time in the conversation and eyed me suspiciously for a beat. "Let's try month-to-month to start with until we're sure it works out."

"Hold on," I interrupted. "I haven't said that you can rent from me." There was one last disclosure, and I knew that this one would probably be the deal breaker. "The window is broken in your room, and the landlord is really shitty about repairs."

Dan shrugged. "That's fine. My boyfriend is a contractor."

*Jackpot.* "When do you want to move in?"

"My old lease is up at the end of the month."

And just like that, I had a new roommate. I called Suze to thank her, but she didn't pick up, and I left another message.

I tried calling Matt's phone once, but he didn't pick up. I

tried to leave him a voice mail, but there was nothing to say, and after a minute of dead air I just hung up.

The next morning Lilah came to visit me. I ushered her inside and we ended up perched on my sofa in the same spots we'd occupied earlier in the week. But this time we were finally both comfortable enough with each other that it didn't take cheap alcohol to start the conversation. She sympathized with my injuries—the cuts on my arms were too deep to be scabbing over yet, and changing the bandages twice a day had reached the point where I was taking a lot of preemptive aspirin. She'd managed to get through the fight in the fairy circle with no visible wounds, but when I asked how things were going for her, she didn't pretend that it hadn't been hard. After all, she was now a traitor in the eyes of many of the Neighbors, and it was only fear of the Scotts that had prevented the Ad-hene and her grandfather from torturing or even killing her.

Like me, she was suddenly unemployed—Dreamcatching's owner had been one of the casualties of the fight, and she'd decided to quit before his daughter could fire her. We teased each other a little, bantering comfortably about the unemployed life, and talking about where each of us was thinking of looking for new work. At one point I asked her whether she would try to find work with another of the Neighbor businesses, and she shook her head.

"I'm going to be figuring out how to live outside the community again," she noted a little regretfully.

"Are you sure you want to do that?" I asked.

"I don't think I have a choice."

I tilted my head and considered her. "If the Ad-hene and their stooges were keeping the killings secret from so many people, then they must've thought that anyone outside of the most rabid fanatics would have objections. Was that not the case?"

"Definitely not. The whole community is reeling. Killing the recessives, what was done to the three-quarter girls who were drugged to participate, and finally the whole idea that they would've been willing to kill Felix . . . I'd say it's pretty much chaos right now."

I reached across and gently took one of her hands in

mine, and smiled at the surprise that spread across her face. "Chaos in a group can be an opportunity for new leadership," I told her.

Her coppery eyebrows arched up her forehead. "Me?" she squeaked. "Themselves would never allow it."

"Why not?" I asked, warming to the idea myself. "I told your grandfather that you are the new liaison to the vampires, and I meant it. Why not take that piece of authority and build some more? It was leaving all the control in the hands of fanatics that started the problem. And maybe this could be a chance for you to build the kind of community that you want—one that isn't as obsessed with reclaiming old glories as in making a safe life for the Neighbors."

She smiled at me. "You're very persuasive, Fort."

"Am I?" I asked. "Usually not. But it seems pretty obvious to me. You can't be the only hybrid who isn't chained to the altar of the elves, and maybe it's time that numbers made a difference. The Ad-hene rely on their descendents for whatever piece of the future they'll have, and maybe it's time for you guys to start making decisions for yourselves, not for them. After all, you outnumber the crap out of them."

Lilah nodded slowly. "Shoney's death really shook a lot of people up. None of Themselves have died since Underhill opened up again." She squeezed my hand and considered it for a second, finally nodding. "I'll think about it," she promised. "But even if I can't be the Napoleon you're hoping for, maybe I don't have to be all on my own." Then she leaned over suddenly and kissed me.

At first I was just surprised. It had been a long time since I'd been kissed, and Lilah was a very nice person to be kissed by. Her mouth was soft against mine, and something about her skin and her beautiful curly hair smelled like honeysuckle and springtime. When I lifted my hand up to cup her head, I could feel the tip of one pointed ear against my palm and the chinchilla softness of its fur and the way it twitched at the contact made me smile against her mouth. Everything about the kiss, and about Lilah herself, was as sweet as spun sugar.

And that was the problem. When I lifted my mouth from hers and leaned back, she looked up at me with those huge golden-brown eyes and I realized even as I brushed one thumb against the freckles that painted her cheek that those weren't the eyes I wanted to be looking into.

She read the truth on my face and scooted backward slightly. "Is it Suzume?" she asked. "I'm sorry. I thought the two of you weren't together."

I dropped my hands, pulling them back into my own lap. "We're not dating," I explained. "And I don't know if she even likes me like that, but, yeah, it's Suzume."

I'd been on the other end of this kind of conversation many times, so I was able to admire how gracefully Lilah nodded her understanding and carefully gathered up her purse and coat, as if she'd been ready to leave anyway.

We walked to the door together, and as I opened it for her, I reached out and caught her wrist. "Lilah," I said, "I know it's not . . . you know . . . but I really would like it if we could be friends."

She didn't quite smile at me, but the gold in her eyes brightened, and she nodded. "I'd like that too."

"And I meant what I said earlier," I added. "I think you'd make a great Napoleon."

Lilah laughed, half in disbelief, but also half in real amusement, and we said good-bye.

I left three messages on Suzume's phone that evening, but she didn't call me back.

Sunday was cool but sunny, a perfect day for the last sail of the season. Bhumika was ensconced in the most sheltered area of the deck that Chivalry could find, wrapped in several fleece blankets and tucked onto a mound of cushions that my brother had obtained for the occasion. Meanwhile Chivalry and I, dressed according to my brother's strict dress code of correct yachting apparel, which consisted of white slacks, polo shirts, and jaunty nautical sweaters and caps, worked with the sails as the *Gay Belle* darted merrily across the waves of Narragansett Bay.

We didn't talk much. Most of Chivalry's attention was focused on Bhumika, whose pleasant smile couldn't offset the tight, painful lines that were etched into her face, or the fact that a full oxygen mask was affixed across her face for the entire trip. But we all smiled and did our best to pretend that this was just another lovely afternoon, and not so clearly the last time that she would ever set foot on the deck of this boat until the day her husband would board with a box of her ashes to scatter.

Chivalry and I talked only once about the recent events. Bhumika had dropped off to sleep, and my brother and I had weighed anchor in a small sheltered spot of the bay to break open the picnic basket that Madeline's cook had prepared for us.

"You did well, little brother," Chivalry said, handing me a sandwich. I looked at it and sighed—typical as always, it was roast beef. I tucked it back into the basket and removed a small container of fresh deviled eggs.

"How do you figure that?" I asked. "Prudence hates me more than ever, and because of what I did she actually ended up challenging Mother directly. Matt learned everything that I've been trying to hide from him. And a lot of people were killed." People who should never have been in danger, and whose names felt branded across my soul— Gage, Beth, and poor Mr. Albert.

"All of those things are true," my brother acknowledged. "Though Prudence's feelings for you, as I've always said, are much more complicated than you're willing to admit. But do you know what I see? That you negotiated when you could, you were willing to fight when negotiation failed, you made allies who showed loyalty to you, and you were also willing to make hard decisions when you needed to." Chivalry patted my shoulder roughly.

"And Matt?" I pressed.

Chivalry looked away, across the waves of the bay and toward the graceful lines of the bridges in the distance. Above us seagulls massed and made their long, lonely caws, eyeing our sandwiches greedily and hoping for some handouts. "I would have killed him, Fortitude," he admitted finally. "It would've been as quick and painless as I could make it, but I would not have chosen to leave Mr. McMahon alive." He turned back to me. "But you made the decision that you did. Let us simply hope that it turns out well."

"Do you think it will?"

He paused. "I hope it does, brother. For your sake, I truly do." Chivalry glanced over to where Bhumika was sleeping, and a deep, old sadness filled his face. "I'll need some ... time over the next few months."

"To be with Bhumika," I said softly, and he nodded.

"Yes. But after seeing what you were able to accomplish on your own with the very difficult elf situation, I have no doubts that you'll be able to police the territory in my absence."

"Police the territory?" I asked, my jaw dropping. "On my own?"

"You can do it," he said encouragingly. "I even have your first assignment. We received a tip that a group of selkies in Maine are sinking local fishing boats that haven't paid protection."

"And you want me to—what?"

"Look into it. Locate the ringleaders and put a stop to it."

I stared at him, in his wide-brimmed Panama hat, looking so confidently at me in the early-afternoon sunshine. "You think I can do this?" I asked.

He rested a hand on my shoulder and squeezed, smiling. "I know you can."

"But ..." I floundered for a moment. "My car isn't even running. I can't get to Maine."

"Is that all you're worried about?" He smiled. "Your car was towed to our mechanic this morning, after I picked you up. He'll have it up and running again in no time."

"You towed ..." I stopped and looked hard at my brother, then asked suspiciously, "What else did you do?"

"Nothing!" he defended. Then, "I might have dropped a few months of rent off with your landlord."

"Chivalry!"

"It's nothing," he protested. "Just to help you find your feet with your new responsibilities." At my dirty look, he relented and said, "If it makes you feel better, look at it as payment for covering my responsibilities."

He had me there, and there was clearly no stopping what he'd already done, so I finally muttered, as gracelessly as possible, "Fine. But that's the end of it."

"Of course," he said. "Other than your salary."

"Chivalry!"

It was a long argument. Chivalry, of course, had wanted me on an exorbitant salary that would've left me feeling tied by the neck to my family. I argued him down to an hourly wage that was similar to what I'd been earning bussing tables—but still higher, since Chivalry pointed out that I would no longer be earning tips, and the work would probably amount in some weeks to barely part-time. And with that we were both left moderately satisfied, and mostly unhappy, just like any good compromise.

We hauled in the anchor and set the sails, turning the boat back toward the dock. The breeze filled the sails, and the seagulls soared above us.

"If you wanted to get some new clothes, I could always—" Chivalry began, and I threw a sandwich at his head.

When I got home that evening, I left another two messages on Suze's phone.

The next three days passed slowly. I'd started making calls to look into the selkie business, but I knew that I was making as many excuses as possible to hang around my apartment and wait for Suzume to show up. But no matter how long I waited or how many messages I left on her phone, there was no knock on my door, and no pitter-patter of fox paws on the tree outside my window.

The Fiesta arrived back from the mechanic on Thursday, its engine once again patched and coaxed into working order. It still couldn't start on the first try, and the mechanic muttered about how it would've made more sense to just buy a new car entirely given the level of rust eating away at the underbody, but I was glad to have the Fiesta back in its old spot, even if it had taken my brother's money to make it happen.

I left one last message on Suze's phone. Then I got into the Fiesta and drove over to her house.

Surprise filled her face when she opened her door and saw me standing on her stoop. We stood for a long minute just looking at each other.

"I want you to be my partner," I blurted out, completely ruining the script in my head that I'd been composing for the last few days and practicing periodically in the mirror.

She tilted her head in that familiar foxy way. "I'm going to need context for that one," Suze said.

I took a deep breath. "I want you to work with me, like when we were looking for who killed Gage. But this would be official. When I go out to do stuff or investigate things for my family, I want you to be with me on them. I'm heading up to Maine tomorrow to look into some selkies, and I'd like you to go with me."

She looked at me for a long moment, those dark eyes as deep and fathomless as the ocean at night.

"It'll probably only be part-time work, but you'd get to beat people up," I added to sweeten the deal, and a wide smile broke out across her face.

"Does this job offer come with a salary?" she asked.

"Send the bills to my mother," I said. "But if you're going to do it, do it because you want to, not for the money."

"I do want to. Screening clients for my grandmother is boring as crap, and I already got Midori to agree to take over," she said, and I grinned. But she looked serious again, and asked, "Did Lilah ever come talk with you?"

"She did." I paused. "But I'm not dating her."

Suze lifted one eyebrow in a very good Spock impression. "Why not?"

I took the plunge. "Because I want to date you."

Surprise covered Suze's face, but I could see the brief, intense flicker of emotion in her dark eyes before she hid it. Then she frowned and both caution and a warning were evident in her voice when she said, "Lilah is better for you. She's sweet and nice. I'll never be those things. The two of you could play human together but still understand each other—everything you want. I've never wanted to be anything except what I am."

I nodded. "I know all those things, but I want you."

Frustration covered her face at my refusal to get with the program. "I can't, and I wouldn't, change who I am."

"I know. And I like you just the way you are."

"You haven't really thought through it," she insisted. "When you do, you'll know that Lilah is better for you."

If this had been over the phone, I would've been slowly crumpling inside at her words, but this was why I had had to come over, because I could see the truth on her face. "You aren't saying that you don't like me," I said, and I could feel my pulse racing with excitement. "You aren't saying no."

The rare flummoxed look she gave me was enough to make me finally give in and smile so hard that my face ached. She stayed silent.

My grin widened even farther. "That's what I thought, Suze. I'll wait until you tell me what you *really* think."

Her eyes narrowed dangerously. "Do you really think you can outwait a fox?"

"I'm a vampire," I said. "I've got time."

I reached into my jacket pocket and pulled out the surprise that I'd brought her and pressed it into her hands.

She stared at the blank CD in her hands. "What's this?" she asked.

"It's a mix CD. But I'll have to borrow your old boom box if you want me to play it outside your window."

She laughed then, the sound clearly surprised out of her. She stared at me for a long moment, then stepped aside to let me in. After all, we were partners now, and we had a trip to Maine to plan.

Suze played the CD I'd made her later. It was one long loop of "The Imperial March."

## ABOUT THE AUTHOR

**M. L. Brennan** lives in Connecticut with her husband and three cats. Holding a master's degree in fiction, she teaches basic composition to college students. Her house is more than a hundred years old, and is insulated mainly by over-stuffed bookshelves. She is currently working on the third Fortitude Scott book.

CONNECT ONLINE

www.mlbrennan.com

ALSO AVAILABLE FROM

# M.L. BRENNAN

# GENERATION V

Fortitude Scott's life is a mess. He has a terrible
job, a terrible roommate, and he's a vampire…
sort of.

Fort is, actually, still mostly human. When a new
vampire arrives in town and young girls start
going missing, he decides to help. But without
having matured into full vampirehood, Fort's
rescue mission might just kill him…

**"Engrossing and endearingly quirky, with a
creative and original vampire mythos, it's a treat
for any urban fantasy lover!"**
—*New York Times* bestselling author Karen Chance

Available wherever books are sold or at
penguin.com

**facebook.com/acerocbooks**

# Penguin Group (USA) Online

*What will you be reading tomorrow?*

Tom Clancy, Patricia Cornwell, W.E.B. Griffin,
Nora Roberts, William Gibson, Catherine Coulter,
Stephen King, Dean Koontz, Ken Follett, Nick Hornby,
Khaled Hosseini, Kathryn Stockett, Clive Cussler,
John Sandford, Terry McMillan, Sue Monk Kidd,
Amy Tan, J. R. Ward, Laurell K. Hamilton,
Charlaine Harris, Christine Feehan...

You'll find them all at
**penguin.com**
**facebook.com/PenguinGroupUSA**
**twitter.com/PenguinUSA**

*Read excerpts and newsletters, find tour schedules*
*and reading group guides, and enter contests.*

Subscribe to Penguin Group (USA) newsletters
and get an exclusive inside look
at exciting new titles and the authors you love
long before everyone else does.

**PENGUIN GROUP (USA)**
us.penguingroup.com

S0151